THE DAUGHTERS OF IZDIHAR

THE DAUGHTERS
OF IZDIHAR

BOOK ONE OF THE ALAMAXA DUOLOGY

Hadeer Elsbai

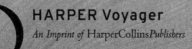

HARPER Voyager
An Imprint of HarperCollins Publishers

THE DAUGHTERS OF IZDIHAR. Copyright © 2023 by Hadeer Elsbai. All rights reserved. Printed in the United States of America. No part of this book may be used or reproduced in any manner whatsoever without written permission except in the case of brief quotations embodied in critical articles and reviews. For information, address HarperCollins Publishers, 195 Broadway, New York, NY 10007.

HarperCollins books may be purchased for educational, business, or sales promotional use. For information, please email the Special Markets Department at SPsales@harpercollins.com.

Harper Voyager and design are trademarks of HarperCollins Publishers LLC.

FIRST EDITION

Designed by Angela Boutin
Maps designed by Jeffrey L. Ward
Title page background © eigens/stock.adobe.com
Title page ornament © anuwat/stock.adobe.com
Chapter opener ornaments © inspiring/shutterstock.com

Library of Congress Cataloging-in-Publication Data has been applied for.

ISBN 978-0-06-311474-6

23 24 25 26 27 LBC 5 4 3 2 1

To my mother, who always knew this would happen

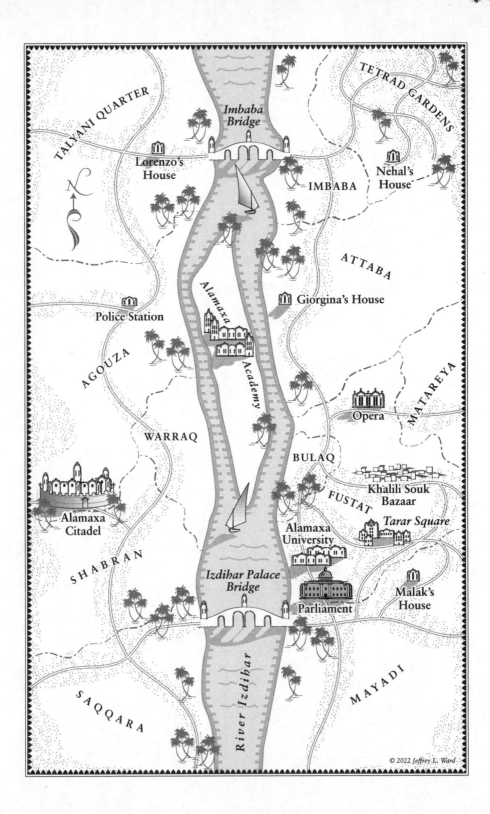

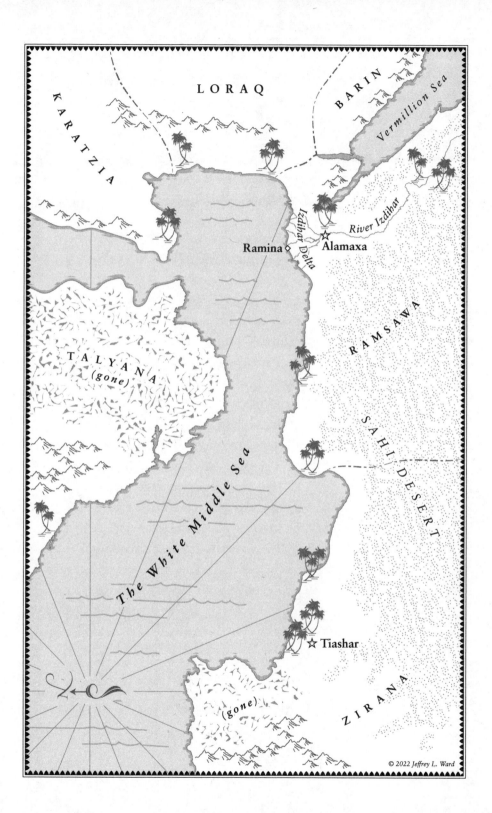

THE DAUGHTERS OF IZDIHAR

NEHAL

NEHAL DARWEESH WANTED TO SPIT FIRE, BUT UNFORTU-
nately she did not have that particular ability. Instead, she pulled out
the liquid contents of a glass of water and separated them into rather
large and ungainly droplets, much to the irritation of her mother,
Shaheera, who found herself the unfortunate target of the storm.

Shaheera was leaning against a vanity laden with various concoc-
tions of oils and perfumes. Her arms and legs were both tightly
crossed, her forehead slowly setting into an even tighter scowl. Her
corkscrew curls, which Nehal had inherited, were pulled back into
a neat bun and oiled to a perfect sheen. Slowly, she began to tap her
foot in warning.

Finally, when Nehal's rain began to pool at Shaheera's feet, Shaheera clapped her hands together and snapped, "Enough!"

Nehal did not look at her mother, nor did she spare a glance for
the seamstress at her feet, who was doing her best to write down
Nehal's measurements while politely ignoring the gathering storm in
the room. Instead, Nehal stared out her veranda, which led directly
to a white-sand beach and an expanse of glittering blue ocean. The
veranda doors were open, as they nearly always were, bringing forth
a warm salt-spray breeze and the humming melody of waves.

"*Nehal.*"

She could practically hear her mother's teeth grinding together. With a pointedly loud sigh, Nehal closed her eyes, and the fat droplets returned to their glass, though the puddle on the floor remained; Nehal was nowhere near skilled enough to extract water from a rug. Still, she continued to ignore her mother, who had now begun to pace back and forth around her, skirting the edge of the large four-poster bed behind them.

"You would think we were sending you off to be executed, not married to one of the wealthiest men in all of Ramsawa," muttered Shaheera. "And you've met him; you said he was nice, that you liked him—"

Nehal could keep quiet no longer. "That was before I knew I was being *sold off* to him!"

The seamstress, a tiny woman of about forty, shot up, sensing the fight's escalation. With a halting look between mother and daughter, the seamstress said, "I've finished, my lady. Once I've completed all the adjustments, the wedding attire will be ready in a fortnight."

"Excellent," said Shaheera icily. "Thank you. You may go." She did not even glance at the seamstress. Her gaze remained fixed on her daughter, who was now glaring back with equal fierceness. The two stared at each other silently, a battle of wills reminiscent of their many arguments, until the poor seamstress scurried away and closed the bedroom door behind her.

"This is unjust, Mama!" Nehal burst out. "You and Baba always promised I could choose my own husband, just as Nisreen did."

Shaheera pinched the bridge of her nose. "Your sister found herself an excellent match. You, on the other hand, want to run off and be a *soldier*—"

"It's an honorable profession," Nehal protested.

"Honor does not pay debts," snapped Shaheera. "And women don't become soldiers. I've had enough of this nonsense. We've had the same conversation every day for a month—"

"Because you refuse to listen!" Nehal fumed. She picked up the periodical lying on her bed; the words *The Vanguard* were emblazoned across the front in bold, black calligraphy. Smaller text below read *A Publication of the Daughters of Izdihar*, and beneath that was a black-and-white photographic print of a young woman holding up a sign that read VOTES FOR WOMEN!

"If you would just *read* it—"

"Why would I need to read it when you've already told me everything it says?" Shaheera affected a mocking tone in a poor imitation of her daughter. "'Ramsawa's newly minted Ladies Izdihar Division! The first all-female military division in history—'"

"Because you don't actually *listen* to me, clearly," said Nehal irritably. "It's the Academy that comes first; what's wrong with going to school?"

"It's not, as you so innocently phrase it, just *school*," said Shaheera. "It's a Weaving Academy—"

"What's wrong with learning to be a weaver—"

"What's wrong is that you are neither a soldier nor a street performer," Shaheera snapped. "You're a highborn lady, and you need to act like one. Not to mention this is skirting the bounds of the law *and* religion. An impressive feat."

"It's a government initiative," said Nehal, "so they're hardly skirting laws. And as for religion, I know for a fact you and Baba don't give a donkey's ass about the Order of the Tetrad—"

Shaheera clapped her hands thrice. "Language!" she snapped. "You are a Lady of House Darweesh, not a street urchin, and I'll not have you act like one in this house."

If I were a street urchin at least I'd be able to do whatever I want, Nehal thought. But that did not seem like something she ought to say out loud. "Mama . . ."

"All right, regale me then, Nehal. What's your grand plan?"

In an uncharacteristic show of foresight, Nehal paused to consider her words. "I attend the Alamaxa Academy of the Weaving Arts. As an accomplished weaver, I'm recruited to join the Ladies Izdihar Division. I fight to bring honor to family and country."

Shaheera rolled her eyes. "Ah, yes, my daughter, a foot soldier engaged in petty border skirmishes, in a *women's* division no less. How *honorable*."

Nehal groaned and turned away from her mother. She wanted nothing more than to march straight down to Alamaxa and enroll in the Academy herself, but as a woman, she could not join without a male guardian's consent, which her father patently refused to give. It was one of the many infuriating ways in which Ramsawa insisted on infantilizing women.

There was also the matter of tuition: the Academy, newly reopened two years ago, and allowing entry to women only just this year, was free for men to attend, but women were required to pay tuition, which was exorbitant. And the Darweesh family was, as Nehal had recently discovered, in dire financial straits. Khalil Darweesh, Nehal's father, had become embroiled in gambling debts over the years, leaving the family close to destitute.

Shaheera gently pulled Nehal back to face her. "You have a responsibility to this family, to your younger siblings, whether you like it or not. You were never entitled to choose your own husband." The lines around Shaheera's mouth softened slightly. "And you know we wouldn't do this if we didn't absolutely have to."

At her mother's pitying look, Nehal swallowed some of her rage, though her throat burned with it. Her mother was right; they had few other options. It was a quagmire that made Nehal want to scream and cry all at once, as loudly and as inconveniently as possible. But it was her father she should be raging at, not her mother. It was his affliction and mismanagement that had found them in this mess. Now his sins were to become Nehal's responsibility. She would be sacrificed to salvage the family name from scandal and shame with the money her bride-price would bring in, along with a newly minted business deal her father would conduct with the Baldinottis—her betrothed's family—after the marriage contract was signed.

And it could only be her. Nehal's older sister Nisreen was already married, and her younger siblings—the triplets Husayn, Nura, and Ameen—had years of schooling ahead of them still, and at nine years of age, they were much too young to marry off advantageously. So unless Nehal wanted to see them illiterate and her parents destitute, she had little choice but to walk into this marriage.

But should she really have to sacrifice *everything*?

She knew, for the first time in her life, what it must feel like to be drowning, and she loathed it with every fiber of her being.

Nehal made one last attempt. "You could give me a portion of my own bride-price at least. I could put that toward tuition—"

"It wouldn't be *near* enough," snapped Shaheera, and once again Nehal was reminded of the depths of the Darweesh's financial straits. "And it's not just about the money, Nehal . . . it would be unseemly. Married women belong at home, with their husbands. Certainly not soldiering. Besides, have you thought of what being a soldier truly means? What if Zirana actually declares war instead of skirting around the topic, hmm? What then? Shall I sit quietly while my daughter gets herself killed? You're a highborn lady, so leave the soldiering to the rabble."

"Tefuret help me," muttered Nehal. But invoking the Lady of Water had done little to help Nehal thus far, and she had invoked her often. The gods did not tend to respond to their supplicants, even those they had gifted with weaving.

"Don't be melodramatic," said Shaheera in exasperation. "Do you know how sought-after the Baldinottis are? How many girls would be desperate for this opportunity?"

"If war *does* come, wouldn't my abilities be more useful on the battlefield?" said Nehal. "I could make a difference to the outcome of—"

"You have a very overinflated opinion of yourself, Nehal," interrupted Shaheera. "You need only worry about making a difference to your husband's household."

Nehal scowled, turned her back on her mother, and began to undress. She thought back to her meeting with Niccolo Baldinotti, barely a month ago. His unusual coloring made him stand out in her memories. Most Talyanis were practically indistinguishable from

Ramsawis, if slightly paler, and the majority had intermarried into the Ramsawi population and taken on their traits, but Nico was blond and blue-eyed, unlike anyone Nehal had seen before. They had spoken only briefly, and he had seemed rather good-natured. Unlike most men, he had been amused rather than disapproving when she had swirled the sharbat in his glass into a miniature whirlpool.

But once Nehal was firmly in the grip of marriage, the law would make Niccolo her guardian, making it necessary to obtain his permission to attend the Academy, join the army, or, indeed, do much of anything at all. And why would any newlywed, even one who seemed moderately progressive, give his new wife permission to leave him?

What was Nehal to suffer, in the end? She would be denied her own personal happiness, of course, denied the chance to discover the fullest potential of her waterweaving abilities, but there were many who would envy her such a life. Her own happiness apparently meant very little when compared to her family's lofty reputation.

Nehal finally slipped out of her many layers of suffocating fabric. The ocean sparkled in the distance, the waves calling to her. In Alamaxa, a desert city, there would be no ocean. There was the River Izdihar, of course, the beating heart that bisected the entirety of Ramsawa, but it would not be the same as the endless expanse of blue sea Nehal was accustomed to swimming in nearly every day.

There was no point in bringing this up. Her mother wouldn't understand; no one in her family could. Nehal was the only weaver in her entire extended family, and when they weren't teasing her for her abilities, or her lack of control over them, they were simply indifferent. When the Alamaxa Academy had reopened after nearly two hundred years of being shuttered, Nehal had watched with envy as men flocked to its doors. Then came the announcement that women could finally attend, and Nehal *rejoiced,* only to have this marriage sprung on her. Her one opportunity to finally learn more about the abilities the gods had chosen to give her had slipped through her fingers like the water she desperately yearned to control.

She might have finally had a chance to live among others who *understood* what it meant to hold this strange, rare power that had been equally scorned and feared since the Talyani Disaster. Instead, she was to be sold off into marriage to a man she barely knew.

With a growl, Nehal kicked the foot of her bed, causing the entire thing to rattle.

Shaheera glared at her daughter. "Nehal—"

But Nehal no longer had any desire to listen to another word from her mother. She walked out through the veranda doors onto the sand, which was hot enough to sting the bare soles of her feet, and marched toward the ocean.

2

GIORGINA

GIORGINA SHUKRY WAS HAVING A PARTICULARLY UNPLEAS-
ant day.

It had begun with the weather. A brief but powerful dust storm
had overtaken Alamaxa, slamming into Giorgina as she walked to
work. She narrowed her eyes against the storm and blindly made
her way to the nearest establishment for shelter, finding herself in an
expensive teahouse that demanded she purchase a drink in order to
remain on the premises.

Giorgina pleaded with the owner. "But—" She gestured helplessly toward the window, against which gusts of sand-laden wind
were audibly slamming.

The owner only looked her up and down, taking in her cheap
galabiya and faded black shawl, and said tersely, "Either buy something or leave."

After purchasing an exorbitantly priced drink, Giorgina settled
onto a plump cushion by the window and waited for the storm to
pass. It raged loudly for some time, until the air turned a sickly
red-brown, and eventually the sheltered teahouse grew stuffy and
humid.

She was uncomfortably hot and had spent money she could not
afford to lose, but even worse, this unfortunate detour meant Gior-

gina was late to relieve Anas of his shift. Anas, her boss of two years now, owned a tiny but oft-frequented bookstore that made most of its revenue off school textbooks and newspapers. He was a skinny, middle-aged man with a pointed face and sharp eyes, which he turned on Giorgina the moment she walked through the door, dusty and sweaty.

She tried to explain about the dust storm, which Anas might not have seen through the windows that were entirely concealed by books, but before she could utter a single word, Anas snapped, "If you can't show up on time, what is the point of you?"

"There was a dust storm," Giorgina finally managed to say.

"I don't care if Setuket himself descended upon the city and tore it in half," Anas snapped. "I expect you here on time. Is that clear?"

Then, in a huff, Anas departed, leaving Giorgina with a rather large shipment of books that needed to be unpacked and cataloged. She thought this may have been his attempt at petty vengeance, but the shipment had arrived last night (though it would not have surprised Giorgina to learn that Anas prepared acts of petty vengeance in advance, just in case the need arose). She began the exhaustive process of unpacking and cataloging.

Giorgina did not particularly like Anas, and he did not seem to like her, but then, she didn't think he truly liked anyone. He hardly ever spent time in his own bookshop when it was likely to be frequented by customers. Giorgina suspected this was because his demeanor caused most customers to flee, and that the main reason he had hired her—and hadn't fired her—was to draw in more clientele that he would not need to interact with.

In fact, when Giorgina had responded to the advertisement posted in the newspaper, Anas had essentially told her so.

"A pretty face like yours would bring in customers," Anas had mused, looking her up and down in a decidedly analytical fashion. "But do you have the pretty manners to match?"

He had tested her out for a day, lurking uneasily behind her as she dealt with a steady flow of customers. That same day, Anas hired her, but he had grown no warmer toward her in the two years they had known one another.

So, no, it was not particularly pleasant, but it was nothing compared to what Giorgina's friends and sisters endured. They worked in dark factories, toiling beside hundreds of other women under the cacophonous grind of machinery, or mopped the floors in cheap coffeehouses, enduring the leers and unwanted advances of strange men. Compared to them, Giorgina worked in luxury. And she loved the books and the magazines and the newspapers, all freely available to her. She'd never be able to afford such things otherwise. She could endure Anas's unpleasantness in exchange for such good fortune.

Hours later, Giorgina was finally done cataloging the new arrivals. Relieved, she went to put the list of books in the cabinet they kept in the back, but on her way, she stumbled into a tower of books she had meticulously organized by subject yesterday morning, causing them to spill into another tower of books and crash to the floor in a chaotic heap. She heaved a sigh, then set to reorganizing the fallen towers.

By the time Anas returned for his second shift, Giorgina was exhausted, and her day was nowhere close to being finished. She rewrapped her shawl around her head and left the bookshop to meet Labiba and Etedal. She hitched a ride in a mule cart for a piastre, but this only took her three-quarters of the way to her destination; no one would permit a mule cart to drive anywhere down Wagdy Street, where the lanes were clean and newly paved. Tetrad Gardens was one of Alamaxa's wealthier districts, with its freshly painted buildings, cobbled streets, and modern boutiques and cafes. There was no way a mule cart would be tolerated among the richly embroidered palanquins making their way down the lanes.

Giorgina walked down one of these cobbled lanes, her eyes on her destination. King Lotfy Templehouse stood at the close of the dead-end lane: a massive edifice constructed entirely of yellow stone, heavily carved with complex geometric patterns. A large dome sat squarely in the center, surrounded by four minarets in each corner, one for each of the Tetrad. The entrance was a gigantic archway lined in latticework, flanked on either side by enormous statues of the gods: Rekumet and Setuket on the left, Nefudet and Tefuret on the right. All four sat upright on straight-backed thrones, their hands held palm up on their laps, their faces stern and commanding.

Giorgina had always found these facsimiles of the Tetrad intimidating. Even the small little statues people kept in their houses unsettled her somewhat, though she knew she had nothing to fear from entities that had withdrawn from the world. But according to the tales told by the Order of the Tetrad, when the gods had walked the earth, millennia ago, they'd possessed a capricious nature, and she wanted no part of that. With a shudder, Giorgina turned away from the statues and headed into King Lotfy Templehouse.

Named after the first Ramsawi king, who had pulled together Upper and Lower Ramsawa into one unified nation, King Lotfy Templehouse was the grandest house of worship in Alamaxa. Giorgina had seen it before, but could never bring herself to go inside, though there were of course no rules keeping anyone out. No written rules, anyway—Ramsawa's class stratification did its duty in keeping the likes of her out: King Lotfy Templehouse was known to be exclusively frequented by Alamaxa's upper crust, of which Giorgina was decidedly not part.

Trying to remain inconspicuous, Giorgina walked toward the entrance hall, where dozens of Alamaxans were milling about. Everywhere Giorgina looked, she saw colorful embroidered robes and veils held down with ornate headdresses that looked like they amounted to Giorgina's entire yearly salary. Ladies teetered delicately in pattens that kept their satin-clad feet off the ground as they sipped on sharbat that was offered to them by templehouse attendants.

To Giorgina this seemed more like a party than a religious observance; it was certainly much more festive here than the ramshackle templehouse her own family patronized. Her heart rattled at the prospect of having to walk among these people in her shabby galabiya, but most paid her no mind, and Giorgina walked purposefully

toward a nondescript wooden door that opened into a poorly lit hallway so damp it made her shiver. Her footsteps echoed on cracked,
uneven tiles as she made her way toward the annex, through which
she found her way to the inner courtyard.

It was a modestly sized yard for such a gargantuan building,
but no less pleasant for it: a star-shaped fountain sat in the center,
filled with fragrant jasmine petals. Neatly trimmed hedges studded
with pink flowers outlined the entire courtyard. In each of the four
corners of the courtyard stood a tall palm tree, each heavy with ripe
dates. Beneath the shade of one of these trees, sitting at a somewhat
shoddy wooden table, were Labiba and Etedal.

When Labiba caught sight of Giorgina she stood and waved eagerly, her shawl slipping off her velvet-smooth black hair. Labiba
threw her arms around Giorgina and kissed her cheeks in greeting;
they'd seen each other several times a week for the last year, but
Labiba was always enthusiastically affectionate. Labiba's cousin
Etedal, on the other hand, only glanced up, nodded, and resumed
shuffling the papers in front of her.

In the sunlight, Labiba's eyes were as bright as almond skins, a
striking contrast against her deep umber skin. "It'll be a lovely place
to fundraise, won't it?"

"I still can't believe this Sheikh is letting you do this," said
Giorgina. She turned to look back, as though he might materialize.
"Where is he, anyway?"

"He was just here." Labiba looked toward the annex. "He had
to step away for a moment—oh, there he is!"

The Sheikh striding toward them was handsome and young,
younger than Giorgina thought Sheikhs could be; all the ones she
had seen had been her father's age. This man could not have been
much older than Giorgina. He was also not alone: walking beside
him, and deep in conversation with him, was an older man in robes
richly embroidered. Giorgina blinked, momentarily disoriented.

"Isn't that . . . the Zirani ambassador?" she asked.

Labiba followed her gaze. "Is it?"

Giorgina had seen that face in the papers: a gaunt yet coldly regal visage with deep-set eyes. She would have recognized Naji Ouazzani anywhere.

He and the Sheikh paused at the threshold of the courtyard; Giorgina could not hear their conversation, but it appeared passionate and animated. After a moment, Naji Ouazzani nodded and walked away, leaving the Sheikh to approach them, his expression transformed into a smile.

"Peace be upon you, Miss Labiba," he said jovially.

Labiba bowed her head. "Peace be upon you, Sheikh Nasef." She turned to Giorgina. "This is my friend Giorgina. She'll be helping us today."

"May the Tetrad bestow peace upon you, Miss Giorgina."

Giorgina smiled haltingly; she did not think she had ever been addressed so formally in her life.

Labiba continued, "I've told her all about you, and how you're such an excellent friend to the Daughters of Izdihar!"

The Sheikh laughed, somewhat awkwardly. "I'm a friend to anyone who does good works, really . . ."

"It's difficult to find a man who supports women getting the vote," offered Giorgina.

Nasef nodded vigorously. "Of course! The Tetrad created all of us equally, after all—well, that is, except for weavers." His lips pursed as he shook his head in obvious disapproval.

Giorgina couldn't help glancing sidelong at Labiba, but Labiba's smile was fixed in place, as bright as always.

"So, I'll just go fetch my congregants, then, if you're ready . . . ?" asked Nasef.

"Wonderful," replied Labiba warmly. "Thank you so much, Sheikh Nasef."

With a nod and a smile, the Sheikh departed.

When he was gone, Giorgina turned to Labiba and spoke in a low voice, out of Etedal's hearing. "Does he have any idea you and I are weavers? Any at all?" Labiba knew about Giorgina's abilities, but Etedal did not, and Giorgina would rather maintain that discretion.

Labiba shrugged. "It hasn't come up."

"And Malak? He must know about her."

Labiba smiled somewhat guiltily. "I . . . may have implied that she tries very hard not to use her weaving. And that she runs the Daughters of Izdihar in part to atone for being cursed with weaving abilities. Or something like that. I'm fuzzy on the details."

Giorgina raised her eyebrows, while Etedal, who had come around the table to join them, scoffed loudly.

"Other than his unfortunate views on weaving, he's actually pretty enlightened," insisted Labiba. "He's been a great help organizing these drives. Do you think we'd get any money at all without him? He's very dedicated to our cause."

Etedal smirked. "That, and he likes you."

"Oh, stop!"

"I'm telling you," insisted Etedal. "If he doesn't ask for your hand in marriage before year's end, I'll eat my shawl."

Labiba winked. "I'll hold you to that."

Giorgina ignored the cousins' banter. "You don't think this is dangerous? Isn't this the same Sheikh said to be involved with that cult, the Khopeshes of the Tetrad?"

Labiba waved her hand. "Oh, Giorgina, calling it a cult is so serious. It's nothing like that."

But Giorgina wasn't sure the Khopeshes could be so easily dismissed. What Giorgina knew for certain about the Khopeshes of the Tetrad was that they were mostly clerics who lobbied Parliament to introduce anti-weaving laws. But it also was rumored some of their members were responsible for acts of anti-weaver violence that had made the papers in the previous months, not to mention a number of their members preached particularly extreme views on weavers.

"So he *is* involved?" asked Giorgina in disbelief.

Labiba shrugged, but she wouldn't meet Giorgina's eyes.

But something else was bothering Giorgina: it didn't bode well that someone known to be as vehemently anti-weaving as Sheikh Nasef was so friendly with the Zirani ambassador. Tensions between Ramsawa and Zirana were high, and they were rooted in Ramsawa's growing tolerance for weaving. The reopening of the Alamaxa Academy had clearly incensed the neighboring nation. Naji Ouazzani was supposed to be in Alamaxa to negotiate a peace treaty, so it was distressing to see him having such amiable conversations with a Sheikh known for his anti-weaving views.

But before she could consider asking Labiba and Etedal for their input, she heard the shuffle of footsteps; Nasef had returned. The three women hastily covered their faces with their veils so only their eyes were visible, then stood behind the table, where they had set up the donation box, the record books, and a sign-up sheet for their magazine, *The Vanguard*. Anonymity was the only way Giorgina could countenance being a part of the Daughters of Izdihar at all, so she made sure her face veil was held tightly in place.

Sheikh Nasef reentered the courtyard trailed by his wealthy congregants. It was only the third time the Daughters of Izdihar had attempted to fundraise in such a wealthy templehouse so openly; normally, Malak made sure they were relegated to only public streets. But Labiba had apparently made an impression on Sheikh Nasef, who had offered up the templehouse to her, and it was not an opportunity they could afford to turn down, no matter how nervous it made Giorgina.

There were more congregants than Giorgina had anticipated; about fifty of them hovered around Nasef. Most looked curious, some hesitant, and others still appeared hostile, their eyebrows drawn together in angry frowns. A throng of sneering teenage boys were pointing and snickering. Giorgina tensed, and felt a faint tremble below her feet, along with a slight pressure in the back of her head. She dug her nails into her palms.

Stay calm, she instructed herself.

Nasef led the group into the courtyard.

"Did you know the Daughters hold weekly literacy sessions for neighborhood girls?" asked Nasef loudly.

"What do street girls need to read for?" said one of the teenage boys, to a smattering of laughter from his peers.

Nasef frowned but chose to ignore the comment. "To those of you wondering what your donations would be funding, it is just that: literacy initiatives. Food drives. Soap drives. Support for single mothers—"

"And militaries made up of women," interrupted one man, frowning. "A waste of time and resources."

Giorgina peered at this mustachioed man, then widened her eyes in recognition. "Is that Wael Helmy? The owner of the Rabbani Club?"

Etedal sighed heavily. "Yes. We can't go more than *one month* without some nonsense."

Giorgina glanced at her uneasily, before turning back to Nasef, who was responding vigorously.

"The Izdihar Division is a single project belonging almost entirely to Malak Mamdouh, and the Daughters of Izdihar are more than just one woman—"

"I doubt that," said Wael Helmy flatly.

An elderly couple wandered over to their table, distracting Giorgina from Nasef and Wael's conversation. She listened as Labiba, with a beatific smile, took down their names and their rather sizable donations.

"You're doing good work, my dears," said the elderly woman. "It's about time things change. Don't listen to small minds."

Beside her, her husband was nodding vigorously. The couple wandered away, clearing Giorgina's view; Nasef was still engaged in conversation with Wael.

"I'm telling you, the Izdihar Division has nothing to do with the Daughters of Izdihar anymore," Nasef was insisting.

"And can you guarantee they didn't use any of these funds to spearhead that bill in particular?" demanded Wael. "Or to fund another one of Malak Mamdouh's crazy ideas?"

A broad woman came up to Wael and put a hand on his arm. "My husband is just concerned about Malak Mamdouh's influence, Sheikh. Of course we support your efforts to fight poverty, but what of Miss Mamdouh's less savory endeavors? Her often uncouth behavior?"

At this, Etedal rose in her seat, despite Labiba's whispered warnings. "What uncouth behavior?" demanded Etedal. "Say what you mean."

Heedless of Labiba tugging on her galabiya, Etedal walked around the table until she was face-to-face with Wael's wife. Giorgina gripped the edges of her chair, hard.

Wael's wife seemed to hesitate, then said, "For instance, her rudeness to Parliament—"

"You don't think you deserve to vote?" said Etedal. "To run for office?"

"My husband votes for me," replied the other woman stiffly.

"That's all well and good, Lady Rabab," said Nasef gently. "But what of women with no husbands? Or women who disagree with their husbands? Isn't it better that all women have a choice to exercise their vote, whether they do so or not, just as men are given the choice?" He gestured around him. "After all, do the Tetrad not equally share their duties? Nefudet and Tefuret are no lesser, for being women."

One of the teenage boys spoke up. "You said it was blasphemy to compare yourself to the gods. You said only weavers do that."

"It is blasphemy to claim we are created in their *image,* or to say that we deserve their abilities," said Nasef. "For they are greater than we can ever be. It is not blasphemy to aspire to their models of behavior."

The boy shrugged, then resumed whispering to his compatriots, who were all giving Giorgina and Labiba what looked to be conspiratorial looks. One of the boys even *winked* at Giorgina. She frowned and looked away. Tension kept her shoulders high and stiff. The table wobbled. Giorgina took a deep breath, meant to steady herself, but it only pulled her veil back into her throat, choking her.

"It's all right, Sheikh Nasef," said Labiba amiably. She smiled at Wael and his wife. "I understand your hesitation, my lady, my lord." She inclined her head. "But if you'll let me—"

But Labiba did not finish her sentence, for at that moment a stream of water came flying above their heads, dousing Labiba, soaking their papers, and splashing Giorgina, who pushed back into her chair in shock.

The teenage boys exploded in laughter as Labiba wiped water out of her eyes in confusion.

"How *dare* you!" shouted Nasef, his pale face shifting into a simmering red. "Weaving? In a templehouse? And for such a *vile* purpose—"

Etedal was already striding toward the group, her hands curled into fists. Giorgina ran out and pulled her back.

"You'll make things worse," said Giorgina.

"I don't care," snapped Etedal. But Giorgina held on to her firmly.

"I don't condone this sort of boorish behavior, boy," Wael said disapprovingly.

"Fine, fine." The boy raised his hands in defeat. "It was just a joke. I take it back. I *can* take it back, watch this—"

He held out his hands, fingers splayed in a circle, and slowly began to bring them all together toward the center. Giorgina watched, mesmerized, as water droplets began to retract from their table, out of their soaked papers, and then, off Labiba, who winced.

"No, stop!" shouted Labiba. "You're not doing it right!" She winced again. Etedal broke free of Giorgina and ran at the boy, who was ignoring Labiba, his focus totally on his task, his tongue poking into his cheek in concentration.

Labiba flinched. "Stop, *stop*!" Her shout was punctuated with a flinging hand gesture, seemingly instinctive. Out of the gesture was birthed a stream of flame, sizzling with heat, that shot forward and struck the teenage boy in the chest before he had recognized what had happened.

His shirt caught fire. He screamed, a throaty wail of terror, and stumbled back, arms flailing, his own waterweaving skills seemingly forgotten in his shock and pain.

Etedal tackled him; the pair fell to the ground in a heap. She rolled him back and forth, pulled off her shawl and used it to douse the flames, and then, for good measure, ripped off the gourd of water he had at his side and, straddling him, poured the remaining water all over his chest. Giorgina watched this with her heart hammering, and she could do nothing to control the matching tremble of the ground beneath her feet. She shut her eyes tight and grit her teeth, willing herself to *calm down,* to quiet her mind, before she made the quakes worse, before anyone noticed.

The boy sputtered and gasped, then sat up and shoved Etedal off him. He scrambled to his feet, kicking up sand as he stood.

In the silence, Labiba, pale and wide-eyed, said in a shaky voice, "I'm sorry. I didn't mean that."

"Crazy *bitch,*" shouted the boy, his eyes wild. He took a step forward, but Etedal shoved him back. His friends approached, scowls on their faces, fists raised, while other congregants attempted to hold some of their number back.

"*Enough!*" thundered Nasef.

Giorgina jumped. All eyes turned to Nasef, who stood tall in the center of the courtyard, atop the fountain. Every line on his face was contorted in fury.

"This is a *templehouse of the Tetrad,* not a back alley," he hissed furiously. "I will not allow foul language or *brawls* or *weaving.* You should be utterly ashamed of yourselves." His gaze, suddenly hawkish and harsh and years beyond his age, pinned the boys, who had the grace to look sheepish. "You will leave. *Now.*"

The boys shuffled away.

"And your parents *will* be hearing about this!" Nasef called after them. "As will the Academy!"

Wael was shaking his head. "Do you see? Always trouble, where these women are." He took his wife and led her away.

Nasef stepped off the fountain carefully, his robes held in his hand. He glanced at Labiba, who was wringing her galabiya out. Etedal stood by her side, rubbing her back. Giorgina took two steps back and fell back into a chair; she could feel adrenaline rushing out of her limbs, leaving her bones light as feathers. The ground had stopped shaking, thank Setuket.

Nasef approached Labiba, who looked up at him hesitantly.

"Are you all right?" he asked stiffly.

"I'm fine," said Labiba hurriedly. "Nasef, I—"

But he held up his hand. "You're a weaver. You intentionally deceived me."

Labiba half-shrugged. "It never came up," she said quietly.

"I see." Nasef glanced back at his congregants, who were gathered in groups, whispering. "You could have burned that boy alive."

"She said she didn't mean it," snapped Etedal. "It was an accident, not to mention he *started* it."

"I don't weave." Labiba raised her voice over her cousin's. "For this exact reason. It's dangerous. I *agree* with you, Nasef, but I can't help—"

"It's not your fault you were never properly taught," said Etedal furiously.

Nasef shook his head; he struggled to meet Labiba's eyes. "I think you should go," he said, so softly Giorgina barely heard him. "There's been enough excitement here today. I'll need to calm everyone." With that he turned and walked away, herding his congregants back into the templehouse.

Labiba sank into the chair beside Giorgina. "I'm so sorry," said Labiba, her voice a half-laugh. She rubbed at her forehead. "This was a disaster."

Etedal leaned over the table. "There's always a disaster. People throw things at us. They yell, they call us names. It's all part of the deal."

Etedal was right. From the day Giorgina had become a part of the Daughters of Izdihar, she had seen it all firsthand. She was used to the outmoded views, the prejudice, the patronizing, paternalistic attitudes, even the violence . . . but what never ceased to infuriate her was people like those teenage boys, treating them all like they were just a joke, a spectacle to be laughed at. It was one thing to be seen as dangerous, subversive—at least that meant they were being taken seriously. But how many in Alamaxa thought the Daughters of Izdihar only a cohort of silly, empty-headed girls who could do nothing, who were just wasting everyone's time with stupidity?

Despite Nasef's claims to the contrary, the Daughters of Izdihar followed Malak Mamdouh, and Malak was convinced that they had a chance to change Parliament's mind in time for the signing of the new constitution, but based on what she had endured this past year, Giorgina wasn't quite so certain of that.

3

NEHAL

NEHAL GLARED AT HER WEDDING ATTIRE WITH A MIXTURE of contempt and disbelief. It was beautiful, to be sure, particularly the long shawl that would cover the outfit. It was bright red, soft and silky, with lines of diamonds and emeralds sewn into a crown at the top.

Irritated, Nehal shook her head and turned to her mother, who was waiting on her approval. "How much did this cost? I thought we had no money?"

As expected, Shaheera scowled. "Never you mind how much it cost. Would you have us dressing you like a beggar on your wedding day?"

As though to prove her point, a loud "Wow!" came from the doorway. Both women turned to see a scrawny brown child with curly hair standing in the doorway. Ameen, Nehal's younger brother and the youngest of the triplets, grinned at both of them, displaying the prominent gap between his two front teeth.

"It's so bright!" He was much louder than necessary, which brought Nura and Husayn running. They barreled into Ameen and peered over his shoulders.

Nura wrinkled her nose. "It's too red."

Shaheera smiled. "Red is a bride's color. It's traditional."

"It's still too red," Nura insisted. Husayn nodded in agreement, as he was wont to do. Then Nura ran off, Husayn at her heels. Ameen wandered inside and plopped down on one of the poufs on the floor.

Nehal turned back to her mother, who was glaring at her rather pointedly. Nehal understood the meaning of the harsh look: say nothing in front of your brother.

"Are you excited?" asked Ameen.

"Of course," Nehal forced herself to say through gritted teeth. She plastered a weak smile on her face that anyone but Ameen would have seen right through. "Very excited."

Shaheera nodded in approval. Nehal wanted to scream. The pitcher of water on the table beside them began to shake. As Nehal turned to it she felt her mother's eyes on her, a warning. Nehal took a deep breath, then another, and the water eventually stilled. Though Nehal had technically been weaving for years, she occasionally lapsed and allowed her emotions to get the better of her, instinctively reaching out in search of her element. The Alamaxa Academy would have helped her gain control of her powers, but there was little chance of that now.

Anticipating a lecture from her mother on how she should better control her "unwanted tendencies," Nehal turned and left the small parlor. It was her least favorite room in the house anyway, small and dark and facing away from the ocean. She wished she could leave behind thoughts of her upcoming nuptials as easily as she had left behind her wedding attire, but her worries followed as she made her way through a dark corridor and to the main parlor.

The wedding was to take place in Alamaxa, in the courtyard of the Baldinotti estate. Nehal had only glimpsed it the last time she had been there, for the party had been held on the rooftop garden, but it was gigantic, large enough to fit two hundred people easily, and lined with fruit trees and pink flowers. Shaheera had informed Nehal that they were to arrive in Alamaxa a week before the actual wedding party was to take place, in order to make preparations for the Night of the Henna, the Writing of the Writ, and the Zaffa. Her parents also hinted that she may want to speak to her future husband.

Nehal had thought about Niccolo Baldinotti often this past week. Had he known about his parents' plans, when Nehal had spoken to him two weeks ago? He had seemed unusually easygoing if he had indeed been colluding with his parents. Or had they ambushed him with the news as Nehal's parents had ambushed her? Was he now mulling over the unknown woman he was to spend the rest of his life with? Did he resent her as much as she resented him?

Nehal's questions brought her to the ocean. Her family's home, which had been in the House of Darweesh for generations, was perched right on the Middle White Sea, most of its doors opening directly onto soft, white sand. It was a massive, white-bleached estate, with six parlors, fourteen bedrooms, a gigantic courtyard, and its own bathhouse addition where the Darweesh women often spent their nights together.

Barefoot, Nehal walked until cool waves kissed her feet. She squinted at the sun, which hung low like a ripe orange, then waded into the ocean. She planted both feet in the sand, steadying herself, and reached out to the waves. Slowly, she brought her arms up, curling her fingers into fists as she took control of the water and drew it around her hands, forming two wobbly, awkward towers. Her pulse thrummed, blood one with the water, as she maneuvered the towers toward herself. Slowly, biting her lip in concentration, she uncurled her cramping fingers and shaped her towers into thin, whiplike streams, which promptly collapsed the moment she attempted to alter their pressure and wrap them around her wrists.

Frustration at her lack of skill rose to the surface like frothing milk. She had been attempting this technique for months now, to absolutely no avail. Much of Nehal's waterweaving was learned instinctually, and it was only when she had been discreetly gifted a book of waterweaving techniques by Nisreen that Nehal had realized the extent of finesse one could attain. The book—a tome at least a hundred years old—spoke of iceweaving and steamweaving, of waterweavers walking on water, or diving into the ocean and creating pockets of air for themselves. Marvels within Nehal's grasp, yet out of her reach, like so much else.

A strong wave overwhelmed her before she was ready. Water hit the back of her throat and rushed up her nose; panic momentarily fluttered in her chest when she went under. Weakly, she rose, cresting the surface, coughing and spluttering. Properly trained waterweavers were meant to rule the ocean, not the other way around. Edua Badawi, the so-called architect of the Talyani Disaster, had called forth a tsunami so powerful it had sunk the entire Talyani peninsula, and yet Nehal could barely hold these waves. She dragged her feet through the sand and collapsed on the shore, arms spread on either side of her.

Nehal had no delusions about her mediocre waterweaving abilities, but it was still a shock to find herself so lacking. She felt like a child, playing with toys far too dangerous for her. Worse, these shortcomings seemed to validate every skepticism the Darweesh family ever had about Nehal's abilities. All her life, Nehal had fought against rolled eyes, scornful smirks, teasing laughter, jokes about joining the circus. She had done her best to prove them wrong, to show her family that she was not a child playing at power. But even Nehal had her limits, and there was only so much she could accomplish on her own, without proper instruction.

But for now, she would continue to do what she could. Somewhat grudgingly, she got back on her feet, and attempted something requiring less brute strength and more finesse: she took up about a liter of water at her feet and shaped it into a snakelike cord, then began maneuvering it around herself, making sure not to spill anything as she continued to move the whip faster and faster. Nehal wasn't quite certain doing this actually improved her control, but she had no one to tell her otherwise. Besides, it gave her a sense of purpose, made her feel as though she were actually accomplishing something, moving forward, rather than simply sitting still and waiting for something to happen.

Nehal stayed in the ocean until the sun fell, turning the churning turquoise waters the color of the night sky.

IN MERE DAYS, days that felt more like hours, the week of the wedding arrived. The Darweesh family made the trip down to Alamaxa by rail. They rode in first class, of course, where the triplets enjoyed their own table, and Nehal sat by her parents, sullen and quiet. Her father did not look at her the entire ride, instead staring out at the passing desert landscape that grew dotted with huts and mud homes the closer they approached the city.

The moment Nehal stepped off the rail she knew she was in Alamaxa. She was immediately assaulted by a thick wave of heat and dust, along with the overpowering musk of sweaty bodies. She coughed, feeling sand on her skin and in her throat, and immediately wanted to tear off her heavy outer robe. How did women in this city wear such heavy attire if it was so damn hot all the time?

Immediately beginning to sweat, Nehal started to peel the robe from her shoulders when her mother tugged it back on for her.

"Have you decided to turn into a streetwalker?" snapped Shaheera.

Nehal scowled, then opened the robe as far as it would go without falling off her shoulders. Her mother pursed her lips but said nothing.

From the station they were picked up by a sleek palanquin with a camel on either end of it, led by a skinny teenage boy. It was spacious and plush inside, with velvet seats and a lattice window that obstructed the view of curious passersby, but unfortunately obstructed Nehal's view as well. She had to lean very close and peer out of the window with one eye, over her little siblings' heads, to see. Now that the city was to become her home, she wished to subject it to closer inspection than she had on her previous visits.

Alamaxa's roads were a medley of different constructions. Though some of the main roads were newly paved, others were uneven, ground into hills and slopes by millions of footsteps, which caused the palanquin to bob up and down. Tucked between dusty buildings, many narrow alleys and lanes had old, worn cobblestones. Most of the buildings possessed mashrabiyas: oriel windows with a lattice design, popular in Alamaxa because they hid the inhabitants from view while still allowing plenty of air to circulate. Men in shabby cotton galabiyas sat at outdoor coffeehouses, smoking shisha and playing backgammon. Women walked in pairs, some in the plain galabiyas and wraparound black shawls that were all poor women could afford, and some in the annoyingly heavy layering of clothing that upper-class ladies like Nehal wore.

Nehal sat back in the palanquin. It was so different from home, from quaint little Ramina, hidden by the sea. Alamaxa was busy, bustling, and though its possibilities were enticing, Nehal felt its distance from the sea. She flexed her fingers and sent out her awareness, looking for water to manipulate. In the distance she could sense the River Izdihar, bisecting the city into its East and West quadrants, and though Nehal knew it was massive and powerful, it was nothing like the open ocean, and much too far for her to do anything with at the moment.

"Nearly there," said Shaheera, fanning herself with a jeweled hand. "Nehal, that scowl will permanently mar your face."

Nehal looked at her mother and deepened her scowl.

They were expected at the Baldinotti estate for dinner that night, but first they stopped at their own estates in the Tetrad Gardens district of Alamaxa. Rather smaller and narrower than their home in Ramina, their Alamaxa household was a three-story building a dusty shade of brown, with mashrabiyas adorning the front and a courtyard sitting within it. Inside, they were greeted by three servants who had clearly spent the previous day scrubbing the place spotless.

Nehal pursed her lips, fuming. Three servants, in a house where nobody lived! No wonder they were losing money so quickly if they continued to behave as though they had all the money in the world.

Shaheera hurried Nehal and the servants into the baths to prepare. Defeated and exhausted from the long trip, Nehal surrendered to their ministrations as they dressed and powdered her. She wanted to snarl at them when they combed her hair down into braids so tight they hurt, but she caught her mother's warning look and grit her teeth instead. The servants attached a heavy jeweled headpiece and a veil atop her head and hooked long, dangling earrings into her ears. Once they were done, it was back into the palanquin, without the triplets this time; they had fallen asleep and were to remain with the servants.

The Baldinotti estate was, quite literally, triple the size of the Darweesh Alamaxa holdings. They were a cluster of three-story buildings that took up half of a clean, cobbled street. The outer façade of the massive buildings was a shiny, freshly painted taupe. On either side of the arched entrance were elaborate sconces set into the wall.

They were shown inside by a servant, past a doorway with fringed and tasseled curtains, and into a brightly lit parlor. The walls were brightly painted with various colorful peacocks, a plush blue carpet covered the entire floor, and cushioned silk divans extended around nearly the whole room. Large windows looked upon the inner courtyard; the date trees were like statues in the still, heavy air.

The House of Darweesh may have been older and more respected, but there was no question that the House of Baldinotti was richer. Nehal knew very little about the particulars of their business, but she was aware that they had been a wealthy House even before Talyana was destroyed in the war. The Baldinottis had sailed to Ramsawa's shores with the rest of the refugee flood, and though they had lost much in the Talyani Disaster, they had somehow managed to maintain their exorbitant wealth, which had only increased over the years. Then, a few decades ago, House Baldinotti had been officially elevated to become one of Ramsawa's official noble Houses, which granted them a seat in Parliament.

Shaheera was right—most girls would have been thrilled to be in

Nehal's position. But wealth held little appeal to Nehal when compared to weaving, and the freedom to use it.

Behind the fountain stood two people: an older man with tawny
hair and a short woman in an elaborate purple headdress. The pale
man, Lorenzo Baldinotti, embraced Nehal's father as though they
were two old friends, while Lorenzo's wife, Hikmat, placed the req-
uisite four kisses on Shaheera's cheeks. Then Hikmat swept Nehal
into an embrace, planting light kisses on her cheeks as well. Lorenzo
did not even shake her hand, but gave her a polite nod and smile.

Nehal ignored the parents' chatter, her eyes wandering over the
stately parlor, uncertain whether to be impressed or annoyed with
how ostentatious the room was. She was, however, drawn to the large
fountain, which she longed to throw herself into. Before she could
discreetly wander over and dip her fingers in the water, Lorenzo said,
"There's my boy!" Nehal turned, following Lorenzo's gaze.

Niccolo Baldinotti was very tall and very broad, rather stout if
Nehal were honest—and unkind—about it, with large, pale hands
and tawny hair like his father. A growth of pale stubble on his cheeks
prophesied a thick beard a few shades darker than his hair. The stiff
smile he gave them did not reach the clear blue eyes behind his spectacles, and Nehal was not surprised she was bereft of the mixture
of nerves and excitement those insipid stories always talked about
when ladies met their husbands-to-be.

"Lovely to see you again, Niccolo," said Shaheera, her smile
warm.

"Just Nico, please," said Nehal's fiancé.

Hikmat materialized beside her son, placing her hands on his
shoulders and steering him in Nehal's direction. "And here's the
bride!"

Nehal watched Nico's eyes quickly take her in, his expression
unchanging. She knew she was not what most people would call
pretty. Her eyes were wide, too round, and very heavy-lidded. Her
lips were just a bit too plump, her nose too drooping. The severe
braids her curly hair was drawn into only served to emphasize the

sharpness of her narrow, pointed jaw, and her small stature was overpowered by her headdress and veil. Nisreen liked to say Nehal was "striking," but Nehal would not be surprised if Nico thought she looked like a small, ugly doll, and she could not bring herself to care one bit.

They shook hands briefly in greeting, but then stood silently. There was much Nehal wished to ask him, but it was not something she wanted overheard by their parents, and other than that, she couldn't think of much to say to this stranger.

"Doesn't Nehal look lovely, Nico?" Hikmat asked pointedly.

It took far too much effort for Nehal not to roll her eyes.

"Oh, um." Nico looked back at Nehal, pink patches blooming easily on his frightfully pale cheeks. "Yes. Yes, of course."

Nico's stammer wasn't exactly promising. For all that Nehal did not want this marriage, for all that she did not care about how others perceived her looks, it would have been nice for her future husband to seem just a tad more excited about the prospect of wedding her.

Shaheera laughed lightly. "Why don't you two take some time to talk before dinner? Would that be all right?" She looked to Lorenzo, who nodded, though it had not really been a request.

"Of course! Nico, why don't you show Nehal the courtyard?" Lorenzo waved them both off. Nico led Nehal back into the hall and toward the back, into the courtyard. The date palms towered over her, creating large patches of shade. Shrubberies studded with pink and red flowers lined the walkways. There was a crescent-shaped marble fountain in the center, toward which Nico led Nehal. He sat on the ledge, so Nehal did the same, instinctively dipping her fingers into the water, which she began to swirl.

Once she was sure they were alone, Nehal demanded, "Did you know about this marriage when we last spoke? Because I certainly didn't."

Nico blinked, obviously startled, but his response was firm. "No. My father only told me last week. I had no part in this, nor did I want it."

At least they had that in common. Nehal peered at him silently for a few moments, assessing the veracity of his words, then nodded. "Neither did I."

They sat in silence for a few moments before Nehal spoke again.

"What was *your* opposition to this marriage, exactly?" she asked.

Again he seemed taken aback by her question, though she could not see what was particularly surprising about this conversation. "Are you . . . always so forward with strangers?" he asked.

Nehal scoffed. "You're hardly a stranger at this point, are you? Answer the question."

Nico frowned and looked away. He was silent for so long Nehal was about to prompt him again, when he said, "There's . . . someone in my life. We've been together for over a year."

Nehal raised an eyebrow. Her thoughts began to swim like hungry minnows. There might be an opportunity here for her.

Nehal scooted closer to Nico and asked, "Does she know about our marriage?"

"Not . . . not yet."

"I expect she won't take it well?"

A soft sigh escaped Nico's lips. "No."

Nehal leaned back and crossed one leg over the other. "I suppose your father decided marrying into my family was more rewarding than marrying into hers. What House is she from? What's her name?"

Nico hesitated, and Nehal waved her hand in the air. "We're going to be married. At this point, I don't believe there's any way around that. So you can tell me. I should know, anyway," she said.

"You wouldn't know her," said Nico. "She doesn't belong to any of the major Houses."

Nehal leaned forward, suddenly much more interested. "Oooh, a commoner? How rebellious of you!"

But Nico's expression seemed to darken at this. He glared at his feet.

Nehal cocked her head. "Did I upset you?" Before Nico could

answer Nehal shrugged and said, "Sorry. But perhaps I could meet her some time."

At that Nico's eyes shot up. "I beg your pardon?"

Nehal tried not to smile, for she had latched on to an idea that was cheering her immensely. "Well, I *assume* you're going to keep her in your life in some way?"

Nico spoke slowly, as though certain he was being led into a trap. "Our marriage contract very clearly prohibits that."

Nehal shrugged, keeping her expression carefully neutral. "I might be persuaded to amend the marriage contract to allow you a concubine. If you give me something I want."

Nico gazed at her warily. "And what would that be?"

Nehal leaned forward. "Your signed permission for my attendance at the Alamaxa Academy of the Weaving Arts. And the necessary tuition, of course."

Nico's mouth opened, then closed silently. "Can't you just grant me a divorce after your father receives the bride-price?" he asked finally.

Nehal stared at him. Could he truly be this clueless? "Of course I can't just grant you a divorce. Then you wouldn't be my husband, and your signed permission would be null and void. Not to mention you're an idiot if you think your father won't contest the bride-price if I divorce you so soon." She shook her head. "No, I have to legally remain your wife, for a few years, at least. But you can do as you like otherwise, with no legal repercussions, and maybe we can both get something we want out of this sham. That's my offer." She sat back and waited.

For a moment Nico stared blankly at her, and then he laughed, a short huff of disbelief that may have been a scoff. "I don't think either of our parents would like this arrangement," he said.

Nehal grinned. "All the more reason to do it, wouldn't you say?"

4

GIORGINA

WHEN GIORGINA WOKE, SHE WAS UNSURPRISED TO FIND
her skin clammy with sweat. She flinched, attempting to shake off
the uncomfortable sensation of sticky skin. Quietly and stealthily, so
as not to disturb her still sleeping sisters, Giorgina tiptoed around
splayed legs and outstretched arms until her bare feet stepped off the
sleeping mat and onto the cold tile.

Giorgina had a habit of waking in the early hours of the morning, before her parents and sisters and often even before the sun
itself. She enjoyed these few quiet moments that belonged only to
her; in a house with two sisters and two parents Giorgina had little
for herself. When she woke this early, she could take her time to
simply . . . exist. While she plaited her hair she would sit on the sole
low stool in the household and look out the window as the sun rose
and the lane slowly awakened with it. These quiet morning moments
were Giorgina's most cherished.

By the time Giorgina finished dressing she had begun to hear
the telltale sounds of wakefulness in the house. In the next room,
Giorgina's mother, Hala, stumbled into the washroom and began
to scoop water out of their bucket. Giorgina's father, Ehab, shouted
something that sounded muffled; likely he was ordering Hala to heat
up water for him. With a sigh, Giorgina bid farewell to her morning

moments of solitude and walked to the kitchen to begin preparing breakfast.

As Giorgina lay out a round tray on their rickety low table, Hala walked in and wordlessly began to assist her daughter. Together the two women prepared their standard breakfast: a large bowl of fava beans, two flatbreads, and a pot of black tea. They set it out on the steel tray, then curled up on the floor beside it to wait. Soon enough, Ehab walked in, plopped down, and began to eat. Hala and Giorgina followed suit just as Giorgina's sister Sabah walked in.

"Is Nagwa still sleeping?" Ehab asked through a mouthful of bread.

"She's just washing up," replied Sabah.

"Good." Ehab pushed the bowl of fava beans across the table toward Hala. "This needs more lemon."

Hala quickly acquiesced. When she returned Nagwa had arrived to join them, and Ehab had disappeared behind his newspaper.

Giorgina was the only one of her sisters to bear a Talyani name. When she was born with a shock of red hair that neither Ehab nor his wife possessed, Ehab had insisted on naming her after the Talyani grandmother from whom Giorgina had acquired the rare trait. In all her other traits, however, Giorgina strongly resembled her parents and sisters, who were all olive-skinned and dark-eyed.

Ehab shook his newspaper aggressively. "Those women are at it again," he muttered. "At a templehouse, this time . . ."

Giorgina stiffened but did not glance up from her bowl of beans.

"Where are their fathers?" Ehab continued. "Their husbands? If they had anyone to keep them in line they'd be at home like proper women instead of roaming the streets and causing a ruckus at templehouses . . ."

There was silence around the table; this was a rant familiar to the women of the Shukry household. Ehab Shukry needed no encouragement or response when he began to malign the Daughters of Izdihar or any woman who did not fit his particularly conceived feminine ideal. Giorgina knew better than to argue with him about any of his views. When her sister Sabah had tried it all she earned was a verbal tirade of abuse. Now the Shukry women knew to let Ehab talk and talk, and all they had to do was sit quietly and nod occasionally.

At the first lull in conversation Giorgina wiped the breadcrumbs off her hands and got to her feet. "I'm off," she said.

Ehab said nothing, blithely ignoring the hypocrisy of maligning the Daughters of Izdihar when he needed all three of his daughters to work to provide for the household. Ehab maintained his superiority as the man of the house only when it suited him.

It was only when the door swung shut behind her that Giorgina allowed her shoulders to droop and the tension in her belly to release. With a deep breath of warm morning air, she began her walk.

Most days, Giorgina was practically thankful for her family's poverty; her employment granted her much needed time away from her father. It allowed her to have some semblance of a life.

As it was, Giorgina lived a life of constant lies, a precariously built house of cards that could easily collapse and destroy her. Her parents did not realize her work at the bookstore was broken up into shifts, nor did they have an inkling of how much free time Giorgina actually had. Anas, despite his sneering demeanor, had never betrayed her to her father; whether this was due to hidden kindness or profound apathy Giorgina did not know and was not sure she wanted to find out. This allowed her to participate alongside the Daughters of Izdihar—albeit anonymously—and it allowed her to have Nico, whom she was about to meet for tea before her shift at the bookstore. She couldn't wait to tell him all about the temple-house incident. He'd likely already read about it in the papers and had no idea Giorgina was one of the women involved.

She and Nico had been seeing each other for a little over a year now, and in the past few months he had several times hinted at marriage and even intimated that she should expect a proposal soon. Once they were engaged Giorgina could finally tell her family about him and stop all this hiding and sneaking around.

When Giorgina had first met Nico, she'd had no idea who he was. All she saw was a slightly bumbling young man who shared her interest in scholarship and obscure history. He was so different from most of the men Giorgina knew, or heard about from the women she knew—he treated her like an equal, a partner, and was genuinely interested in her ideals and beliefs. And where he may have lacked obvious charisma, there was a natural warmth to him. Giorgina always felt so comfortable, so safe, in his presence, like she could be entirely herself. It was no surprise how quickly she'd fallen in love with him.

Later, she discovered he was a Baldinotti, and she could not help but rejoice at her luck. She would have wanted to marry him regardless, but she was not so much of a romantic that she could refuse to openly acknowledge the benefits Nico's background would grant her.

Nico's money and status would raise her family from poverty; no longer would her sisters and her father have to work from sunrise to sundown. Giorgina would gain so much: freedom from her father, freedom to continue her work with the Daughters of Izdihar, a life with a man who shared her values, a man as unlike her father as was possible. A man she loved, and who loved her. Perhaps she could even go to university. Once married, she could finally obtain what her class and gender conspired to deny her.

Eager as she was to see Nico, Giorgina did not even mind the walk through Tetrad Gardens, where he liked to meet. Her attire drew some stares, but Giorgina was accustomed to it and looked straight ahead as she walked, pulling her shawl tighter over her distinctive copper hair. She slowed her pace only once, to watch a weaver sweep sand away from his shop front with a wave of his wrist. She smiled at the elegant display, wondering if the man was a windweaver or a sandweaver. It was difficult to tell when sand was involved.

Giorgina herself had no fine control over sand. She was an earthweaver with absolutely no control over her abilities. She had read what she could—books procured from Anas's bookshop—but understanding the principles behind weaving did not help her perform actual feats, or maintain control over her weaving, which seemed to reach out and shake the earth whenever Giorgina's emotions stirred. The abilities were nothing more than yet another added burden.

When Giorgina arrived at Farouk's Teahouse, she took a moment to appreciate the shiny storefront before stepping inside. Farouk's was one of the more modern establishments cropping up in the wealthier districts of Alamaxa, which meant they hired waitstaff and had their guests sit on chairs rather than cushions. Giorgina was rather fond of chairs, and she liked Farouk's Teahouse for its sparse, modern look. The walls were painted a plain pale periwinkle, but intricate geometric crown molding ran the length of the ceiling, lending the room an understated elegance. The tables were draped with white linen that was so clean it surely had to be laundered daily. All of this meant Farouk's was extremely expensive, which meant it was only frequented by the very wealthy, which, thankfully, meant it was usually quiet and private, leaving little chance for Giorgina to be seen by her parents or anyone else she knew. She shuddered to think what her father would do if he discovered her dining with a strange man.

She spotted Nico immediately, sitting at a table tucked into the back of the teahouse. Normally, he would have been reading a book or newspaper, but today he sat with his chin resting in his palm, his expression distracted. She approached and took the seat across from him with a smile, but the one he gave her in return was unlike him: forced and joyless. Giorgina tensed slightly, but before she could say anything, Nico flagged down the waiter, a smiling young man in a white turban. He quickly scribbled down their tea order and left them to one another.

"What's wrong?" asked Giorgina as soon as the waiter was out of earshot.

Nico did not respond immediately. He ran a hand through his fine hair, causing it to stick up on one side.

"I have . . . I have to tell you something," he said slowly.

That much was certainly clear. A bevy of possibilities swirled through Giorgina's mind, but she did her best to avert her focus from any of them. "What is it?"

"My father, he . . . he told me . . . he's found me a suitable wife."

Giorgina shaped her face into a calm veneer, though underneath the table and out of sight she clutched at her galabiya. She convinced herself she had misunderstood.

To be certain, she asked, "What do you mean?"

"Everything has been set in motion, all the paperwork filed," said Nico, his voice hollow. "The wedding is in two days."

Giorgina felt humiliation burning her cheeks. She could feel all her hopes and elaborate fantasies crumbling to sand.

"Giorgina?"

"Two days?" she whispered. She looked down at the table rather than at Nico, her eyes finding a flaw in the linen. "I don't understand," she said slowly, her feelings cycling through fury and despair, both of which she did her best to conceal. "I thought you and I—we—you always said you would refuse an arranged marriage if your father proposed it."

"Giorgina." Nico covered her hand, which she had left carelessly on the table, with his own. Startled, she pulled back, for they were in public, and a gesture like that could easily draw attention.

But she made herself look at him as he spoke, taking in his pained stare.

"I *did* refuse him at first," said Nico. "But then he said . . . he said he had information about you."

Giorgina stiffened. "What sort of information?" she asked, though she knew, of course. There was only one event in her past she could be threatened with.

Nico hesitated. "He said . . . he said something about a . . . a pregnancy?"

Giorgina looked down into her lap and closed her eyes, the chatter of the teahouse doing nothing to overtake the cacophony in her own head. There was a roaring in her ears, an iciness in her veins.

If Nico's father somehow had proof that Giorgina had obtained an abortion, she was ruined. She knew what happened to fallen women, women who could not abide by the guidelines set to them. Not only would her reputation be in tatters, but she would find herself at the mercy of the police for obtaining an abortion when she was unmarried, a wholly illegal act.

Even if Nico's father did not have tangible proof, the word of a Baldinotti was nearly sacrosanct, especially when held up against her own. And even the tiniest *hint* of such a rumor would destroy her; not just her, but her family, her sisters' hopes of finding advantageous marriages. She felt like a naïve child. She should have been more careful. She should have known it would come to this, that Nico would be drawn back to his roots.

She should have known someone like him could never marry someone like her.

How had she found herself in such a predicament yet again? When, two years ago, she had found herself pregnant and unwed, the Daughters of Izdihar had saved her. She had been only twenty, clueless and gullible and terrified enough to walk straight up to one of the demonstrators and ask, as discreetly as possible, if they helped women like her. Though Giorgina had kept her face smooth and unconcerned, her question vague, Labiba had gazed at her so mournfully Giorgina knew there was no hiding her secret. But the other woman had taken it in stride. Though they were strangers to one another, Labiba had stayed by her side through the entire process, and the money for the abortion came from the Daughters' discretionary funds.

Her own father had never known. But, somehow, Nico's father did.

Giorgina had shed tears both over the child, which she had not wanted to give up, and the child's father, who had forsaken her the moment he learned of her pregnancy. After the tears dried up, she promised that she would no longer give herself away so easily. And yet, one year later, she met Nico, and six months after that she had found herself in his bed. Now she was perched on the precipice of betrayal yet again.

"Is it true?" Nico's voice seemed to come from far, far away.

Giorgina opened her eyes. Nico was looking at her with a mixture of pity and remorse.

"And will you think less of me if it is?" She had meant the words to come out cold and aggressive, but instead she sounded weary and hopeless.

Nico's eyes widened. "Of course not. You know none of that matters to me."

Giorgina heard the clatter of teacups and realized the entire teahouse was shaking. Nico looked around at the startled guests and leaned forward. Aside from Labiba and Giorgina's family, he was the only other person who knew about Giorgina's weaving, and her dismal lack of control over it. In a low voice, he said, "Giorgina, please, calm down. I already have a solution."

Giorgina took a deep breath, then another, and another. Slowly, the shaking receded, and the denizens of Farouk's shook their heads and retreated into their conversations; in a city of untrained weavers, most were used to the occasional small quake.

"A solution?" she said, in a small voice.

"I've met my—future wife," he faltered. "She's not keen on the marriage either. She wants to attend the Alamaxa Weaving Academy, and she agreed to alter our marriage contract, to put in a clause that allows me to keep a legal mistress."

Giorgina stared at Nico's shining face. He clearly expected her to be pleased. What was it that made men so oblivious? Was it the inherent privilege granted to them in life that prevented them from understanding what women were forced to endure? Was it that no matter what they did their reputations would bounce back, shiny and resilient, to be embraced with open arms by the people who would shun the very same in a woman?

A *legal mistress*. A concubine, in plainer terms. *His whore*, she thought more bitterly. Giorgina had aspired to more than what she was, to be a wife, married into one of the wealthiest, most respected families in Ramsawa, but reality had intervened. It had severed her aspirations with a scimitar and shoved her back down, to remind her of what she really was, and all she could ever be. Forever scorned, forever shamed, forever lowly.

Giorgina sat back, shaking her head in disbelief. "A concubine? It would destroy my reputation."

Nico blinked, light glinting off his spectacles. "What does reputation matter? You would be safe, and happy, in your own house, and we would be together. Who cares what anyone thinks? What does any of that matter?"

"Of course it matters! My reputation is all I have, Nico! It *matters,* because my parents would never speak to me again. My friends and neighbors would shun me. They'd think me nothing more than . . . than . . ." Giorgina couldn't bring herself to say the word she had just thought. She shook her head. "Our children would be bastards; shunned and excluded their whole lives. We'd be outcasts, all of us. What kind of a life is that for anyone but you?"

"But—"

"Not to mention your father could still easily report me, out of spite!" interrupted Giorgina.

"I would protect you," Nico protested. "Deny his claims, hire a lawyer . . . anything."

The waiter drifted back with two cups of tea. Giorgina stared at the sugar cube on her saucer; it was shaped into a palm tree. There was obviously an earthweaver among the staff, one skilled enough to be able to manipulate sugar crystals into such delicate shapes. Giorgina swallowed a rising lump in her throat.

Nico had not even glanced at his tea, or the waiter, which was uncharacteristic; he had a habit of profusely thanking staff for the smallest of tasks.

"Giorgina."

"There's nothing more to be done," said Giorgina, her voice barely a whisper. She felt a strong, unfamiliar rush of resentment.

None of this was Nico's fault, but Giorgina resented him anyway: resented his wealth, his freedom, his life. She resented him for being a Baldinotti, a wealthy, privileged man with a cruel, arrogant father.

She stood abruptly; the ground began to shake again. Her head ached, racing thoughts growing into distant, disembodied shouts. Giorgina sank her nails into her palms and began to run, ignoring Nico calling after her.

How had the trajectory of her life veered so far off course in so short a time? What sort of life did she have now? Jumping from one scandal to another, one betrayal to another . . . when had everything fallen apart? Was it because she dared look above her means? Aspire to something more? Would she continue to be punished until she learned her place and remained there? Until she was finally beaten down?

Giorgina had finally felt safe. She had found stability and love, and now it had all been ripped away from her.

She turned a corner and shoved herself into a nook between two shops and just before a sharp turn. Nico swept past her hiding spot; she watched him spin in bewilderment as he tried to locate her. She yearned to go to him, to be comforted by him and to comfort him in turn, but she dug herself into the wall instead. Finally, Nico turned the corner and disappeared from her view.

Giorgina was shaking, the tremble in her limbs mirrored in the quaking of the ground around her. She unfurled her palms, placed them flat against the cool wall behind her, and took a single deep breath, held it, then exhaled slowly. She did this until the trembling in and around her subsided. It took a long time.

5

NEHAL

SINCE THEY DESPERATELY NEEDED NEHAL'S BRIDE-PRICE, Nehal's parents used all their connections to fast-track the necessary paperwork. The ceremonial wedding was to be the following night, but legally, Nehal and Nico were now married; Nehal had the stamped and signed paperwork (with the amended concubinage clause, carefully snuck past her parents) to prove it. Now all she needed to enroll in the Academy was Nico himself.

Nisreen had arrived last night, and now she and Shaheera were occupied with last-minute wedding preparations. Nehal could not bear to join them. She wanted to enroll in the Academy as soon as possible, so she concocted what turned out to be a believable tale: that she and Nico had agreed to spend a day together before the wedding to get to know one another.

"Since we're now legally married, there should be no problem, Mama," insisted Nehal.

Her mother narrowed her eyes. "But people don't *know* you're married. There's been no wedding—"

"But the announcement made the papers today," interrupted Nisreen, with a wink at Nehal. Nehal smiled at her older sister.

Shaheera shrugged and acquiesced, servants were sent to the

Baldinotti household, and within an hour a thoroughly confused Nico arrived to pick up Nehal in his private palanquin.

"We agreed to spend the day together?" asked Nico as Nehal settled into the cushions. "If you're going to concoct plans, don't you think I should be told about them? So I don't look like a fool in front of my servants, at least?"

Nehal frowned at him. "You're unusually peevish." Before Nico could respond, Nehal held up their marriage certificate. "It's ready, so we're going to the Ministry of Education. You need to sign your permission in person."

Nico's expression darkened further. He looked away.

"What?" demanded Nehal. "We're both getting what we want, so what's wrong?"

"She won't have it." Nico's voice was soft, his gaze distant as he stared out of the palanquin's lattice windows. "My— The woman I— She refused to become a mistress."

Nehal's first thought was for herself. "But you'll still—"

Nico turned to her. "I gave you my word and I'm keeping it," he said flatly.

She relaxed. "Well, I'm sorry you didn't get what you wanted." She paused. "Perhaps I could speak with her and reassure her if she has doubts about my—"

"No," interrupted Nico. "It has nothing to do with you, not really."

"Well . . . the contract's amended, in case she ever changes her mind."

Nico said nothing, and Nehal sensed he no longer wished to continue this particular conversation, so she quieted as well.

The palanquin moved slowly, maneuvering its way out of the lane that held the Darweesh house and into the busier street that led to the Ministry of Education. They merged onto a road crowded with mule carts carrying wooden crates of mangoes and figs and persimmons, with passengers crowded among the fruit. They slowed down so much that a woman walking past their palanquin, a lattice tray of fresh flatbread balanced on her head, sped past them.

It was an especially warm day, the air weighed down by the searing heat. The sun beat down on their palanquin, turning it into a hot box. Nehal was sweating inside her layers, but she tried not to let the heat bother her, even though all she wanted was to throw herself into the nearest body of water. Instead, she occupied herself with the possibilities that lay ahead of her. Rather than spending her days as a bored society wife, Nehal would learn to fight. She would finally, finally, gain full control of her waterweaving. She would be among like-minded women who would not scowl at her weaving or back away in fear if she lost control for a moment. They would not treat her like an outlier.

And then she would graduate. She would join the army—she hadn't quite figured out how that would work with Nico, but she was sure she could arrange it. She was determined to rise through the ranks and become somebody, somebody important, whose name was spoken with respect because of her abilities and accomplishments rather than her birth or marriage.

With all that, she would gain freedom. No longer would she be beholden to parents or aunts or grandparents or husband. She would leave behind all the traditions that suffocated her, all the nonsensical little rules and guidelines meant to govern her behavior as a respectable young woman: dress modestly, laugh demurely if you have to laugh at all, avert your gaze, be more pleasant, smile more, but not too often and never at strange men—it was a messy litany of laws. Nehal had no desire to abide by any of them. Now she would not have to. She would become the person she wanted to be, rather than the one everyone expected her to be.

After an interminable amount of time, the palanquin came to a stop at the doors of the Ministry of Education, a rather ramshackle three-story building in central Fustat, where most of Alamaxa's administrative offices were located. It went far more smoothly than

Nehal had hoped: they found the right department, where they sat down with a harried-looking secretary whose spectacles kept sliding down his nose. They showed him their identification papers, which had photographic prints of their faces, and then their marriage certificate.

The secretary handed Nehal an enrollment application, which she carefully filled out, then signed. Nico signed his name beside hers, then dipped the signet ring on his finger into a pot of ink and stamped his personal seal. Nico paid the tuition in full for the entire year with a bank note, and the secretary informed Nehal that the start of term was in precisely three weeks, and more information would be mailed to her shortly.

And that was all. Nehal was officially enrolled at the Alamaxa Academy of the Weaving Arts, and she was to start in less than a month. All she wanted to do was smile, but as Nico dejectedly followed her out of the ministry, she managed to maneuver her face into what she hoped was a neutral expression.

Nico paused to buy a newspaper from the old man selling them at the doors of the ministry. In the palanquin, he unfolded the paper and began to read.

Nehal, who was buzzing with energy, couldn't take the quiet. "Anything interesting?" she asked. "Besides the announcement of our marriage, that is?"

Nico looked up at her. "Very much."

"Such as?"

Nico set the paper down on his lap with what Nehal thought was a silent sigh. "Mostly the new constitution."

Nehal knew about this only because of her subscription to *The Vanguard*, which detailed the Daughters of Izdihar's efforts to convince Parliament to expand women's rights in the new constitution, chiefly by giving them the right to vote and run for office. If Nehal thought about it too carefully, she grew infuriated—having to ask permission from these men for something that they ought to be given anyway—so she did not think about it much.

She remembered the last time she'd given her unwanted opinion on women's suffrage, at the dinner table with her family. Her cousin Hamed, who held the Darweesh seat in Parliament and was insufferably arrogant even at the best of times, wasted no time in mocking her.

"Voting?" he'd sneered. "Do you even have any idea who's running for office? Do you know anything about the state of this country?"

"I would pay more attention if I had reason to," Nehal had retorted hotly. "And why shouldn't I? Are my opinions worth less than yours just because I'm a woman?"

Hamed shook his head with a smirk, as though Nehal wasn't even worth responding to. That was when Nehal's glass of sharbat, reacting to Nehal's agitation, tipped over into her lap, and Shaheera told her to go change.

"When is the new constitution going to be finished?" Nehal asked Nico now.

"It'll be signed by the end of year, so—seven months." He went back to his paper and was silent.

"You read a lot," Nehal observed. She had noticed his collection of books at the Baldinotti estates and noted too that he usually had a book on him at all times.

Nico looked up. "I like reading." He paused. "Do you read much?"

"I can't say that I do," Nehal said. She did not even read *The Vanguard* cover to cover. Reading in general she found to be dull, and rarely could Nehal sit still long enough to read at length. She'd tried to read books on weaving, in failed attempts to teach herself more advanced techniques. She didn't want to learn weaving from dusty papers, anyway; she wanted a proper instructor, someone who could assess her stances and her technique.

"You know the curriculum at the Academy will involve reading, yes?"

"I know *how* to read." Nehal raised an eyebrow. "I'm not an idiot."

Nico blushed. "I wasn't implying—" He cleared his throat. "And what is it you plan to do after you graduate? I can't imagine your family would be happy to see you join the circus."

Nehal scoffed. "I'm joining the army."

Nico blanched. "And your parents are all right with *that?*"

"It doesn't matter what they're all right with, anymore, does it? Given I'm a married woman and all." What did her parents expect her to do about her waterweaving, anyway? Pretend it didn't exist, when shocks of her emotions were liable to disturb any liquid in the vicinity? Was Nehal meant to ignore the immense power she held at her fingertips, when it was the only power that truly belonged to her? How could she pretend away her weaving when it set her apart and above so many others? How could she simply tuck it away when she could achieve so much power that she might literally turn the tide of battles?

"It's not just the border skirmishes with Loraq," said Nico seriously. "What if we end up at war with Zirana? Then you'd have to fight in actual battles."

"Then I'll fight in battles," said Nehal. "At least I'd be doing something useful."

"You wouldn't be afraid?"

Nehal smirked. "I'm not afraid of anything."

"You should be," said Nico grimly. "War isn't all glory and honor—it's messy and bloody."

"Again, I'd like to remind you that I'm not an idiot," said Nehal. "You don't need to patronize me."

"I'm not—" Nico began to protest, then sighed.

"Besides, isn't that ambassador here to prevent a war?" asked Nehal. "What's his name? Naji something?"

"Naji Ouazzani." Nico shrugged. "That's not a guarantee of anything, though. Zirana's king is . . . volatile. And he's furious about the reopening of the Academy. Reports say he's raised taxes twice in the past year, and the revenue's gone directly to the military. Why would he do that if he didn't intend on war?"

Nehal knew only vaguely of King Hali of Zirana; she recalled reading something in *The Vanguard* about his draconian policies on weaving. Weavers in Zirana were second-class citizens, and actual weaving was punishable by death.

"I don't know what he thinks he's going to achieve," said Nehal. "It's not as though weavers are going to just disappear."

"Well, he certainly wants to eradicate them," replied Nico. "On some level I understand his fear, but—"

"You *understand*?" interrupted Nehal.

Nico was quiet for a long moment. "Do you know much about the Talyani Disaster?"

"I know enough." Stories of Edua the Destroyer had followed Nehal around as a small child on school playgrounds, the cruel taunts of other children indistinguishable from their fear. Edua Badawi, a prodigy and strange anomaly: a weaver with control over all four elements, and immensely powerful. Somehow, she had sunk an entire peninsula, and nearly all of the people living on it, decisively ending a war between Ramsawa and Zirana that had dragged on for decades.

"I've read survivor's reports of what happened," said Nico quietly. "Weaving at that level, it's . . . terrifying. Volcanic eruptions, sinkholes, waves high enough to block out the sun . . ."

"What does that have to do with Zirana?" asked Nehal slowly.

He looked intently at her; a glare of sunlight glinted off his spectacles. "They lost landmass too. And people. Their coastline used to be much closer to the Talyani peninsula."

Nehal shrugged uncomfortably. "Edua Badawi was an exception. She's the only weaver in existence to hold that kind of power."

"That we know of."

"You can't punish all weavers because of the actions of a single deranged woman," argued Nehal.

"That's not what I'm saying," protested Nico. "Weavers *should* be trained, and they should be taught to control their abilities, especially when they're so tied to emotional states. If King Hali's goal were to prevent more death, he would see that, but he's only reacting to his fears. I'm merely saying I understand his motivation; I'm not justifying it.

"And Edua Badawi wasn't deranged. She was purposely turned into a weapon of mass destruction." He hesitated. "We don't know if she intended to destroy Talyana like she did."

Nehal whistled. "That's a controversial statement. Especially coming from a Talyani." Nehal could easily believe it, though. How often had she lost control over even a small argument? If the rumors about Edua Badawi were true, the magnitude of her powers was enormous, practically godlike—what might a temper tantrum of hers look like?

Nico quirked his lips. "I'm far more of a Ramsawi now. I've never even seen Talyana, or what's left of it. I can't speak the language. I know hardly anything about it except what I can glean from history books."

"Still, you don't hear anyone defending Edua Badawi."

Nico looked thoughtful. "I don't know if I'm defending her. But she's an interesting figure. So much about her is shrouded in mystery. I don't know that we'll ever truly know what she was thinking when she did what she did."

They fell into a silence that felt far more companionable than their earlier ones, and Nehal tried once again to broach the topic of Nico's mistress. She couldn't help it; she was desperately curious.

"So . . . what do you plan to do about your . . ." Nehal scowled. "Can you at least tell me her name?"

"No," said Nico shortly. "And if anything changes, I assure you that you, as my *wife*, will be the first to know."

With that Nico hid his face behind his newspaper, and the silence grew tense once more.

6

GIORGINA

THE WEDDING ANNOUNCEMENT WAS IN ALL THE PAPERS. Pictures of Nico and the girl he was marrying stared at Giorgina all day while she tried to focus on her work in the bookshop. Giorgina had tried to avoid looking at his—she hated even acknowledging it, but she couldn't avoid the word—*wife,* but she quickly lost that battle: Nehal Darweesh's picture was of a young girl with too-large eyes and full lips. Giorgina knew little about the House of Darweesh except that it was one of the oldest noble lines in Ramsawa and was among the ten major Houses automatically granted a seat in Parliament.

Of course this was the girl Nico's father forced him to marry.

When Anas came in to take over from Giorgina, he idly picked up one of the newspapers and read the entire wedding announcement out loud.

"Niccolo Baldinotti . . . isn't this that blond Talyani who was in here last month?" Anas glanced at Giorgina over the newspaper. She shrugged, then returned to her work. "Their wedding is later tonight, apparently . . . they've rented weavers for entertainment . . ." He tossed the newspaper aside and made a shooing gesture at Giorgina, who left without another word.

To Giorgina, it seemed that all of Alamaxa was abuzz with news of the grand wedding uniting two grand families. Giorgina wanted to avoid thinking about the wedding entirely, and so she was perversely grateful she had another event to occupy her . . . and to cause her anxiety.

Giorgina made her way swiftly through the city, navigating a path she had walked dozens of times before until she was at Labiba and Etedal's apartment, which was on the third floor of a dilapidated, exposed-brick building. The entrance housed a butcher shop, so Giorgina frequently had to lift her galabiya and tiptoe around pools of blood. The cousins had acquired the apartment through Malak Mamdouh's influence, as women generally were not allowed to rent apartments without a male guardian's signature.

Labiba greeted her with a bright, bracing smile. Etedal was already at the rally, helping Malak and the others prepare.

The Daughters of Izdihar had held rallies before, of course—Giorgina had even attended some of them. But this one was riskier: they were setting up near King Lotfy Templehouse, where last week's fundraising had been so disastrous. They were far likelier to encounter opposition here among Alamaxa's upper crust.

"You're nervous," Labiba observed.

"Aren't you?"

Labiba began to pin her veil in place. "Always. I try not to think about it too much, though."

If only Giorgina had that ability; for her, worry and anxiety were constant companions, always sending tendrils of fear crawling up her skin, and more often than not sending quakes through the earth beneath her feet, along with a dull drumming in the back of her head. Considering how Nico's wedding announcement had left her feeling, it was taking a far more considerable effort than usual to keep her weaving at bay. She looked at the face veil Labiba had given her. It was identical to the one she had worn the previous week at their disastrous fundraiser: long and thick and black, with a heavy cylindrical wood piece meant to lay against the nose, to hold the veil in place. Giorgina placed it over her face and pinned it tightly to the veil covering her hair. She then drew a long black shawl over her entire body.

It was not a uniform, exactly, but there was an unspoken agreement among the Daughters of Izdihar that anonymity was their safest option. Only Malak, already infamous, and a few others, mostly older women, went uncovered. Arrests were not frequent, as the Daughters of Izdihar were skilled at very quickly scattering (Malak's windweaving was often useful in this regard), so members stayed safe from police and overzealous family members by remaining anonymous. But the precautions didn't hurt.

When they finished getting ready, Labiba strode purposefully out of the apartment, with Giorgina trailing behind her, her steps leaden. She wanted to do this, of course she did, but that did not mean she could make her heartbeat stop skipping, or force her tongue not to go dry, or stop her thoughts from racing too fast for her to process. When a slight tremor went through the ground beneath their feet, Labiba turned to Giorgina and reached for her hand, squeezing gently. Labiba's grip was firm and warm and familiar. Giorgina saw her eyes crinkle in an unmistakable smile.

When they arrived, about an hour before sunset, the Daughters of Izdihar were nearly finished setting up. At least two dozen women were gathered directly down the street from King Lotfy Templehouse, all but three covered in thick black veils. Most were holding signs and flags; hung on the wall behind them was a giant white banner that read VOTES FOR WOMEN.

In the center of the group stood Malak Mamdouh, easily identifiable: not only were her hair and face uncovered, but her arms were bare up to the shoulder. She claimed this made weaving easier, but Giorgina suspected this was hardly the only reason Malak dressed so provocatively; despite her mild demeanor, there was a part of Malak Mamdouh that liked to shock people.

Already tension hung in the air like an unpleasant stench; passersby were giving the group unfriendly looks and scowls. One man spat as he walked by. The Daughters of Izdihar paid him no mind;

they were far too used to rude behavior by now. A group of on-lookers had gathered around, drawn in by the spectacle. Carefully, Giorgina sidled up to one of the Daughters: Etedal, whose milky pale skin was visible through the slit in her veil that showed her eyes.

Malak walked to the makeshift dais the Daughters had raised and quickly soared onto it, an impressive—and needless—display of weaving that set the onlookers muttering. Malak held up her hands for silence, and, surprisingly, the muttering quieted, and so she began to speak.

Giorgina had heard Malak's speeches many times, and she had never failed to be riveted by her. There was something about the quality of Malak's oration, and it had little to do with her words, though they were superb. It was something about Malak herself: the way she carried herself, the way she spoke so calmly but firmly, the way her voice carried even though she did not raise it. How Giorgina envied that confidence. She couldn't imagine herself unveiled, up on a platform in front of so many people, trying to convince them of her controversial viewpoint; she would open her mouth and nothing would emerge.

Instead, Giorgina delivered her words and thoughts through *The Vanguard,* to which she was a frequent contributor. When Malak told Giorgina she had a way with words, Giorgina had felt the praise fill her chest like warm honey. She published under a pseudonym, but for a girl who had only graduated primary school, merely seeing her own writing in print was enough, even if no one but a chosen few knew they were hers.

Someone began braying like a donkey. Malak paused, her eyes slightly narrowed, and waited. Giorgina tensed, but they had expected this; that was why so many of them were here. They had anticipated a rowdy crowd. Malak waited until the jeering quieted, and continued to speak, but she managed only two words before a shout rose up in the crowd: "Someone shut this shrew up!"

Angry cries rose among the Daughters as the crowd grew more frenzied, a chorus of voices rising to join the first agitator. Calmly,

Malak raised her hand, and a light breeze swept through the Daughters like a ripple, unfurling their flags, which they raised. Then, as one voice, they began to chant, their voices carrying over the jeering cacophony of the crowd, which had, in the short span of a few moments, doubled in size.

Giorgina raised her sign and her voice, joining along with the Daughters' chant, their energy buoying her and giving her courage. The crowd did not relent; they raised their voices over the Daughters', their insults and jeers finding their way above the women's slogans. But the Daughters did not back down; in fact, some of them walked right up to the detractors and shouted right back in their faces.

On the outskirts of their circle, Giorgina saw a group of men begin to gather. To her surprise, they were holding their own signs. More troubling, however, was that many gripped wooden batons. A spike of dread ran through her, and before the first sign was held up she had guessed who these men were: the Khopeshes of the Tetrad.

The Daughters had not had any run-ins with them before, at least not in person. As it was, these men certainly did not look like respectable clerics; they looked like they were ready to engage in a brawl. They raised their signs and batons and began to shout their crude rhetoric and stamped their feet, calling up clouds of dust. Some of them smacked their batons against their painted wooden signs, creating a cacophony that spiked Giorgina's anxiety. Many had rusty khopeshes—the obsolete sickle-swords they had named themselves after—hanging from their belts.

Uniformed men began to circle around them: policemen, muskets in their hands. Giorgina stopped walking, causing Labiba to bump into her. They'd seen police at their rallies before, but they'd never had muskets, only batons. For the moment the police seemed content just to watch, but they held their weapons at the ready.

And then— Giorgina did not see who threw it, but she saw it sail through the air: a stone the size of her fist. It struck a Daughter in the back, forcing her to her hands and knees. Malak knelt by the fallen woman to check on her, then stood up and glared at the crowd. She took a deep breath, held up her arms, then flung them outward. A gust of wind erupted from her open palms, flinging one reedy man into the line of police. Malak, it seemed, had seen who had thrown the stone.

But it had been a mistake to use weaving against an already incensed mob full of anti-weaving cultists. They rushed at the Daughters with a speed Giorgina had not thought possible for such a large crowd. She was jostled backward, struggling to stay on her feet, as the swarm heaved itself at her. Panic made her knees tremble. She tried to pull herself away, but it was all she could do to keep from collapsing and being trampled.

From the corner of her eye Giorgina saw Malak fending off one of the Khopeshes, who rushed at her, swinging his baton haphazardly. She held out her hands and swept him back, but his compatriots caught him and joined him, until five men were attacking Malak at once. She fought like sliding silk, her movements lithe and graceful and so *quick*. With one smooth twitch of her wrist, one man was flung backward by a gust of wind. Then Malak held up both her hands, palms flat out, and the wind that erupted from her was so powerful Giorgina could *see* it; it rippled out like folded cloth and struck the remaining four men in the chest. Giorgina didn't see what happened next; Malak was lost to the crowd.

Not that she had time to watch Malak. Chaos was king here; the crowd fed on its madness, their frenzied shouts filling the air. Giorgina struggled, her breath catching in her throat like a sob when a disembodied hand reached out and squeezed her breast. She wrenched herself away blindly, swinging the flagpole she was holding, but more hands were on her: two grabbed at her veil and ripped it painfully off her head, revealing her face and distinctive, blazing hair, which tumbled around her shoulders.

Giorgina turned and looked straight into the eyes of the man now holding her veil. Leering, he tossed her veil aside and grabbed

Giorgina's wrist. Giorgina *froze*. She was still processing the fact that her face and brilliant hair were exposed; her thoughts had not yet caught up to what was now happening around her, and so she let the man drag her forward.

Then someone threw themselves at the man, fist outstretched; a dark, delicate hand drove itself into the man's jaw. He loosed his grip on Giorgina and stumbled back. Labiba tossed her veil back off her face and turned to Giorgina, amber eyes wide.

"Are you—"

But she was interrupted by the man, who had returned to grab her around the waist, nearly lifting her off the ground. Labiba screamed, and fire flared from her fingertips, catching on the man's sleeves. With a startled shout he dropped Labiba, who crumpled to her knees on the ground, and began to frantically put out the flames threatening to consume the man who had accosted her.

"Damned weaver!" came a shout, and then a baton emerged out of nowhere to strike Labiba across the back.

Labiba fell forward with a cry. The man who held the baton was thin and lanky, but his face was twisted, his eyes glinting and greedy.

"The Tetrad demands punishment for your transgressions, *weaver*." He drew a rusty khopesh and made to raise it, but this time Giorgina reacted faster than she had thought was possible: she retrieved her fallen flagpole and swung it at him with all her might. The heavy metal pole caught him in the jaw; Giorgina heard an audible crack. The man stumbled back, clutching at his face and moaning.

Then came the unmistakable sound of a musket being fired. Fresh screams pierced Giorgina's ears. The frenzied crowd grew madder as they scattered in fear. Someone shoved Giorgina violently in their haste, and she fell face-forward, landing roughly on her belly beside Labiba. She scrambled to her feet, dragging Labiba up with her. They had to escape this frenzy, get somewhere safe—

She and Labiba held tightly to one another as they fought their way through the crowd. From what Giorgina could see, most of the Daughters had fled. She and Labiba elbowed their way through the crowd until they were nearly outside the throng. Giorgina was about to breathe a sigh of relief but gasped instead.

There was a police musket pointed at her chest.

7

NEHAL

THE WEDDING CREPT UP ON NEHAL WITH A SICKENING speed. She had barely a moment to consider anything but the preparations at hand, which were taking up most of her time and energy and irritating her spectacularly.

"Why does this have to be so rushed?" she grumbled.

Shaheera glared at Nehal whenever she said this, mostly because they both knew Nehal knew the answer to that question: the sooner her parents received her large dowry from Lorenzo, the better off they were. But Nehal kept grumbling anyway, though she was partly pacified by the agreement she had managed to wring from Nico. She was enrolled in the Academy. She was going to be a weaver. The wedding did not matter; it was just something she needed to see through.

The Night of the Henna, the night before the wedding, was a raucous affair. It took place in the largest parlor of the Darweesh household, which was full to bursting with Nehal's numerous aunts, female cousins, and various other female relatives. Nehal was close with several of her cousins, whom she had grown up with, but she had hardly a moment to speak to any of them. Instead, she was trussed up, her hands intricately painted with henna, then wrapped in linen to preserve them. Ordinarily, at a wedding Nehal would be dancing and ululating, but tonight she could barely muster the energy for a smile. So she simply sat amid all the chatter and ululations and loud music. She fell asleep that night with a massive headache.

The following afternoon, a cadre of servants came into Nehal's room, led by Shaheera, to prepare Nehal for the Zaffa: the long, musical procession that would take her to the Baldinotti courtyard, where she would meet Nico, and together they would make their way to their dais for the Writing of the Writ. Nehal, exhausted and unenthusiastic, let the servants do what they did best. She did not fight them when they washed and oiled her, when they pulled her hair into braids, or even when they plucked a stray hair near her left eyebrow.

"It's looking like a lovely night, isn't it?" Shaheera said.

"Mmm-hmm." Nehal's eyes were closed. The servants were applying cosmetics, which Nehal hated: powder that would lighten her dark brown skin and hide her freckles, kohl to outline her eyes and make them look even larger and nearly owlish, oil to elongate her lashes, and carmine to paint her lips bright. Nehal often felt like she was wearing a mask when her face was painted like this, and several times she had forgotten all about the cosmetics when she dove into the ocean, only to emerge with a smeared face, to her mother's dismay.

But there was no chance of leaping into the water today, so Nehal stayed silent as the maids painted her like a doll. Then she was stuffed into her attire. The red veil and headdress that were placed on top of her hair were heavier than they appeared, straining Nehal's head the moment they settled into place. Shaheera adjusted the veil herself with a small smile. "You look beautiful, Nehal," she said.

Nehal said nothing. She had no intention of making this day a happy one for either of her parents. She would not allow them to forget that she was not a willing participant.

Ultimately, it was a pointless rebellion, and it only made Nehal feel like a petulant child.

With the servants behind them, ululating one after the other,

Shaheera and Nehal walked down to the parlor, where Nehal's family was gathered. When Nehal appeared, more ululations erupted, and the musicians they had hired began to beat their drums and blow into their horns. Nehal grimaced at the sudden explosion of noise. Normally, she loved Zaffa processions, but she could not bring herself to enjoy her own.

She was led out into the street. Someone helped her onto a saddled mule, atop which was a canopy held together by four poles, which were carried by four men standing around her. She settled into her saddle, thankful that she at least was not expected to walk in this heat with all this fabric on her; she already felt sweat pooling between her breasts and running down her back. Her mother, older sister, and cousins clustered around her.

The Zaffa, always a riotous, colorful affair, was particularly spectacular tonight, considering Nehal was a daughter of House Darweesh. Nehal's parents had clearly done everything they could to dispel any potential doubts about their funds. Musicians played at the front and the back of the procession. Fireweavers and sandweavers had been hired to perform elaborate tricks as they walked among the guests, drawing gasps of awe and delight. At the head of the procession was the most elaborate display of all, and one accomplished without weaving: a conical hanging frame made up of four revolving metal circles, stacked one atop the other, each holding twenty or so small lamps, all borne on the shoulders of two old men who looked like they could hardly carry themselves. But the lamps, numerous as they were, illuminated the street for a long distance, announcing the Zaffa even better than the musicians.

Nehal, buried under heavy fabric and an even heavier headdress, felt a tightness in her skull and pressure behind her eyes. She tried to focus on the weavers, but they were so far away from her that it was difficult to keep them in sight. She leaned back into her saddle and considered closing her eyes to take a nap.

The Zaffa traditionally lasted as long as it possibly could, with the procession taking frequent stops, so it seemed like hours later to Nehal when they finally reached the archway of the Baldinotti household. Slightly dizzy, she was helped off her high saddle. She stumbled a bit when her feet touched the ground, but was steadied by several people; some of her aunts and married cousins gave her reassuring smiles and knowing looks, making it clear she wasn't the first—and wouldn't be the last—bride to experience this vertigo. She blinked to clear her head, then followed the procession inside.

In the grand parlor was Nico, standing beside his parents and a crowd of his family and guests. He was dressed in red like Nehal, with an embroidered gold waist wrap and matching turban.

Shaheera squeezed Nehal's arm. "Doesn't he look handsome?"

Nehal said nothing.

Nico smiled bracingly at Nehal as she walked up to him; she could not help but soften and return the gesture. They were to be allies now, after all. They linked arms, at which time the ululations increased, and stood together awkwardly as the musicians played their music and their family and friends danced and clapped. Slowly, they began to take incremental steps forward to move the Zaffa into the courtyard, where the ceremony would begin.

The Zaffa did not officially stop until bride and groom were seated on their so-called thrones, high-backed velvet chairs atop a dais lined with flowers. Standing between the thrones was an elderly man wearing a high-collared black galabiya and black turban that did not quite manage to hide all of his white curls. The Sheikh who was to marry Nico and Nehal smiled at them as they made their way to the dais. Once they were seated, he set his materials down on the small table between the two thrones.

"And who is your guardian, my girl?" the Sheikh asked Nehal kindly.

At this Nehal's father Khalil seemed to materialize out of thin air, smiling proudly as he approached, ready to give his daughter away.

But this was one final indignity Nehal would not endure. "I will do this myself," she snapped.

Khalil froze, the smile slipping off his face. The guests were still chattering loudly among themselves and had not heard Nehal's outburst, but Nico and the Sheikh shuffled awkwardly as Khalil stiffly replaced his smile and stood silently by Nehal's chair.

The Sheikh raised his hands, demanding silence for the Writing of the Writ. Khalil's fingers drummed nervously on the back of Nehal's chair, but she could not bring herself to pity him. It was not unheard of for women to say their own vows, but they generally did so only if their fathers were deceased. As Khalil was alive and well and *right there,* it was expected that he would utter the vows and give his daughter away, and that he was instead relegated to the background was a clear dismissal. But it was the only power Nehal had left, and she fully intended to utilize it. If Nico could speak his own vows, then so could Nehal.

Once the audience quieted, the Sheikh turned his attention to the bride and groom. He placed Nehal's small hand beneath Nico's much larger one and laid a white handkerchief above them both.

"Now, you shall repeat after me," said the Sheikh. He turned to Nehal. "You first."

So Nehal repeated the words that felt like poison in her mouth: "I, Nehal Khalil Darweesh, marry myself to you, Niccolo Lorenzo Baldinotti, and take you as my master, and bind myself to obey you, and you who are present bear witness of this."

To which Nico responded: "I accept from Nehal Khalil Darweesh her marriage to myself, Niccolo Lorenzo Baldinotti, and take her under my care, and bind myself to afford her my protection; and you who are present bear witness of this."

With that the Sheikh produced a small, decorative silver kettle, from which he poured rosewater onto their handkerchief. Then he removed it, dropping it into a silver bowl, before sprinkling dirt over it. He threw in a hunk of incense before finally lighting the whole concoction, which emitted a heady scent of frankincense and burning fabric.

"Blessings be on the Tetrad. Praise be to Rekumet, who gifts us fire. Praise be to Setuket, who gifts us earth. Praise be to Nefudet, who gifts us wind. Praise be to Tefuret, who gifts us water."

Nico and Nehal muttered the prayer along with their entire wedding party. When the handkerchief faded into a few sparkling embers, the Writing of the Writ was over, Nico and Nehal were married, and the party began in earnest.

The musicians who had led the procession were common street performers compared to the quartet of musicians Lorenzo had hired to play. The weavers from the procession had been paid to last through the night, so they each found themselves a corner and continued to entertain the guests. Nehal settled back into her chair and kept her eyes on the weavers. She had never felt less like dancing in her life. Neither, it seemed, did Nico, who looked as dejected as Nehal felt. Their parents did not nudge them into dancing either; it seemed nothing further was required of them—the business of the evening was already done. The only time Nehal mustered a true smile was when she glimpsed the triplets, who had held hands to form a circle and were twirling in time with the music.

The wedding ceremony lasted well into the night. At the crowd's prodding, Nico and Nehal did dance together, twice. Nobody seemed to notice or care that neither the bride nor the groom was in any mood for it.

Finally, after the few remaining revelers trickled out, Nico and Nehal were herded back inside the house, through the saloon. A large, ostentatious palanquin awaited them by the door. The camels at either end of it were draped in frilly shawls that made Nehal grimace. Shaheera materialized and threw her arms around her daughter, but Nehal kept her own arms stiffly at her sides. She did not even look at her father as she walked past Nico and made her way to the palanquin.

As she was climbing in, she heard Lorenzo clap Nico on the back and, in a booming voice, say, "Be sure to hurry and give us grandchildren!" He then laughed loudly at his own words. Nehal turned in time to see Nico wrench his shoulder from his father's grip.

The palanquin's interior was as gaudy as its exterior, sewn with red velvet drapery and large, frilly cushions. Nico sat opposite Nehal and stretched his legs, careful not to touch her. She tore off her headdress, the loss of its weight a relief to her head and neck, and began to unspool her hair. When she was done, she leaned her head back and sighed.

Neither of them had much to say to one another, so the ride to their new home was silent. It was not a lengthy trip: their lodgings were only a few kilometers away from the Baldinotti estate.

Their new home was not quite as large as either the Baldinotti or Darweesh holdings, but it was still a spacious three-story structure, with several rooms, a bathing chamber, and two parlors. It also came with five servants, including Ridda, Nehal's personal servant brought along from Ramina, who was of an age with Nehal, and whose mother had been Shaheera's personal servant.

Upon arrival Nehal and Nico both retreated silently to their respective quarters; Nehal was keen to avoid any awkward conversations about marriage consummation. She assumed there was an unspoken agreement between Nico and herself that their marriage was in name only. Though, if Nehal were honest, she was curious— she was almost entirely inexperienced, and had Nico broached the topic of consummation, she did not truly think she would have turned him down. After all, she didn't have to love him to bed him. At the very least, it would have been an exciting novelty.

But Nico said nothing at all. Once Nehal was ensconced in her room, Ridda undressed her and placed her into a new nightgown that surely had been meant for a new husband's eyes, given how revealing it was. Once Ridda was gone, Nehal was not quite certain what to do with herself. She felt too restless to sleep or even to lie down, though she was deeply exhausted.

She walked to the mashrabiya and leaned against it, closing her eyes to listen. In Ramina, her room had directly faced the sea; rather than these silly mashrabiyas, they had actual balconies. Often, Nehal would have Ridda set up a makeshift divan on the balcony, and

Nehal would sleep there amid a cool ocean breeze, slowly falling asleep to the lullaby of its waves.

Here she could hear almost nothing at all. Though Alamaxa was a busy and bustling city, this house was located along a quiet alley . . . much too far from the ocean or the River Izdihar.

She made her way back to her bed. Forcing herself to climb in, she threw the majority of the pillows to the floor and tossed off the covers. Her nightgown itched, so she removed it, and instead threw on loose cotton trousers and an undershirt. She lay down in the center of the bed, flat on her back, and stared up at the ceiling. She was preparing for a fitful night of sleep when a series of loud thuds startled her.

Nehal sat up in bed, frowning at the dark. The thuds came again and again, until Nehal realized they were the frenzied knocks of someone much too eager to be let in. She leapt out of bed and threw on a shawl. Below, she heard footsteps rushing to the door, then muffled conversation, followed by Ridda shouting. Nehal strode to the parlor, where she nearly ran into Nico, who looked bleary-eyed, his hair ruffled from sleep.

In the parlor, Ridda was clutching her galabiya in dismay. "I'm sorry; I tried to stop her, but she pushed right past me!"

That was when Nehal's eyes found the pale woman standing in the midst of the parlor. Her muddy shawl had fallen to her shoulders, revealing a head of cropped curls and sharply hooded eyes that looked venomous.

"Who are you?" Nehal demanded. "How dare you force your way into our home?"

Nico stepped forward and placed his hand on Nehal's shoulder. "It's all right," he said. "I know her. This is Etedal—"

"Your mistr—?"

"Giorgina needs your help," Etedal interrupted even as Nico shot his new bride a warning look. His hand on Nehal's shoulder tensed, twitched, then fell away.

"Who is Giorgina?" asked Nehal. But she already knew.

Etedal turned her gaze to Nehal. "Giorgina is the woman your husband promised to marry before *you* came along."

Nehal bristled at the other woman's tone, at her presumptions, but Nico spoke before she could say anything.

"What happened?" he asked. "What's wrong?"

"She's been arrested."

Nico blinked. "What? How—at a rally? I thought you were careful, that—"

Etedal waved his protests away as though they were gnats. "Yeah, well, things got out of hand. Police took Giorgina and Labiba. Malak can get Labiba out because she's her legal chaperone, but they're not gonna release Giorgina to her, no matter how persuasive Malak thinks she can be." Etedal's eyes never left Nico's face. "You know why Giorgina can't call in her father. You need to help her. Pull some strings. You owe her that at least."

Nehal clucked her tongue, making up her mind in an instant before Nico had the chance to say anything.

"Ridda, fetch me my robe, but first tell Medhat to bring the palanquin around. Quickly!" The authority in Nehal's voice had Ridda running without another word.

"What? You—you're not coming," Nico stuttered.

Nehal raised an arched brow. "Don't be ridiculous. The police aren't just going to release her into the custody of a strange man."

Ridda returned to the parlor, a richly embroidered dark blue robe draped across her arms. She began to wrap it around Nehal, who spoke as she slid her arms into the sleeves.

"Police Commander Shaaban is a family friend; I've known him since I was a little girl."

"Of course he is," muttered Etedal.

Nehal gave her a grim smile. "I'm sure I can persuade him to make an exception."

And without another word, she headed for the door.

8

GIORGINA

GIORGINA SHIVERED VIOLENTLY.

Though it had been unpleasantly warm earlier in the day, the temperature had now shifted considerably. The police had tossed her and Labiba into a damp, humid cellar and taken their shawls. These men claimed to be concerned with protecting women and their honor, until those women stepped out of line and broke out of the carefully constructed ideal they were meant to embody. After that they were fair game for humiliation and punishment, which seemed to be the police's intention in taking away their shawls and leaving them cold and exposed.

"Come here." Labiba, who was sitting cross-legged on the cold, hard concrete floor, patted the spot beside her. "I'll warm us up."

Giorgina looked at her warily. "Are you sure? How's your back?"

"I can control a tiny little flame," Labiba assured her. "My back will bruise horribly, but I can't do much about that now. I don't think anything's broken, though."

Hesitantly, Giorgina knelt beside her. Labiba took a deep, steadying breath and held out her palm. Flames flickered, and Giorgina couldn't help flinching away. Labiba's eyes were closed in concentration; a lick of flame appeared in her palm but vanished just as quickly.

Labiba's hand fell into her lip. She sighed. "Why does it only come when I don't want it?"

A deep voice spoke behind them. "That seems to happen to you pretty damn often."

Giorgina and Labiba twisted around toward the bars of their cell, where the officer who had arrested them was smirking. He was tall and lean, with the muscular physique of someone carefully attuned to his appearance. Though entirely bald, he sported a thick, full beard, neatly trimmed in an attempt to offset the roundness of his face. A bronze nametag on his uniform read ATTIA MARWAN.

Labiba slowly got to her feet, and Giorgina followed suit, hovering behind her. "You don't know anything about me," said Labiba firmly.

"Is that right?" Attia ran his pale hands casually along the bars of their cell as he walked past. "Because I've been to quite a few of your little rallies." He shrugged. "Seems to me you shouldn't be weaving at all. Bad enough that you're out there making a spectacle of yourselves, but to bring fire into it?" He tsked and shook his head admonishingly, as though he were scolding a child.

Giorgina found herself unsettled by Attia Marwan. He seemed to be deriving a strange kind of pleasure out of taunting them.

"Tell me," he continued, his tone pleasant, "why do you cover your faces if you're not ashamed of your actions?"

"It's not about being ashamed," Labiba retorted. "It's to keep us safe."

"Of course it is," said Attia patronizingly. "Well, I can see you now." Attia put his face right up to the bars. "Nice to put a face to the fireweaver. And quite a pretty face it is. A shame you're such a shrew."

"A shame you hate both women and weavers," said Labiba evenly.

Attia laughed so loudly Giorgina startled. "It's not about hate. It's about maintaining order and safety. It's about the rule of law, which you and yours keep flouting, strutting around like you own the damn city." He gave them a mocking bow. "I look forward to seeing all of you rot in prison where you belong."

With that, he turned on his heel and left.

Giorgina heaved a deep breath. She stepped out of Labiba's shadow and leaned her head against the wall.

"Well, he was unpleasant," said Labiba casually. But Giorgina could see Labiba was rattled; her fists were tightly clenched at her sides, like they were when she was trying to prevent her flames from emerging.

"He's a policeman," said Giorgina wearily. "Most of them are unpleasant."

Labiba turned to Giorgina, her amber eyes shining in the dim light of their cell.

"What's going to happen to us?" whispered Giorgina.

"Malak will come." Labiba looked upward, as though she could sense Malak's presence through the walls. "And when she does, she'll get us out."

Giorgina wrapped her arms around herself. "She'll get you out, maybe. She's your legally appointed chaperone. But I can only be released to my father." Giorgina shook her head wildly, panic already springing into her throat. "If he finds out about this—"

Labiba pulled Giorgina into her arms and squeezed her tight. "Don't worry," said Labiba into Giorgina's hair, her voice muffled. "Malak will figure something out. She always does."

They sat together on the cold floor, leaning their heads against each other, their hands held tight. It seemed hours had gone by when two policemen—thankfully neither of them Attia Marwan—showed up outside their cell with a ring of keys.

"We're taking you upstairs to Commander Shaaban's office," said one of the officers. "I do not expect you to give us any trouble."

Labiba gave him her sweetest, most disarming smile. "We won't."

The officer's frown softened slightly and unlocked their cell. He and the other officer flanked Labiba and Giorgina on either side, leading them up a set of concrete steps worn down in the middle. Giorgina lost her balance as she tripped over her galabiya, and fell backward into Labiba, who held her steady and patted her gently on the back. Giorgina whispered a murmur of thanks as she gathered her galabiya and continued her ascent.

Upstairs, the air was much warmer and brighter, lit by the gas lamps that lined the hall. They followed the policemen to a closed office. The one who had spoken earlier knocked on a door, then swung it open. Giorgina followed Labiba inside.

Behind a massive desk sat a sharp-faced man with close-cropped hair and a hooked nose. Like most policemen, he sported a thick mustache. He stared impassively at Giorgina and Labiba as they sidled up to his desk. On the shoulders of his uniform were three stars marking his rank as commander. But Giorgina's eyes slid from him, her attention drawn to the woman lounging in the chair in front of his desk.

Malak reclined in her chair, one leg crossed over the other, her bare arm resting on the commander's desk. She wore no veil, robe, or shawl. She glanced once at Giorgina and Labiba, then shot a close-lipped smile at the commander, who Giorgina noticed was frowning at Malak's bare arm on his desk. Leisurely, Malak reached into her satchel and removed a small booklet, then held it out to the commander.

Without a word he reached out and took it, his expression impassive as he examined its contents. He looked up and focused his gaze on Malak, his mouth twisted.

"And why, exactly, is this woman in your custody? Does she have no father or brother to claim her?"

Malak cocked her head but did not lose her smile. "I'm not sure how that's relevant, Commander. Do you dispute the legality of the document?"

Labiba, who was holding Giorgina's hand, tightened her grip for a moment. The commander stared at Malak for a long, uncomfortable minute, but Malak did not avert her gaze. In fact, her expression did not shift at all; she maintained a pleasant, stoic countenance. Finally, the commander sighed and returned the document to Malak, motioning to his policemen with a wave of his hand.

"These riots of yours are growing tedious, Miss Malak." The commander hunched over his desk, his eyes never leaving Malak's. "I don't appreciate having my city in constant uproar."

"You can blame Parliament for that," said Malak conversationally. "They're the ones refusing to grant us our due. Or the Khopeshes, who attacked us when all we were doing was talking. Odd how I don't see any of *them* in custody."

The commander shook his head, then raised his hand in command as his two officers began to hand Giorgina and Labiba their shawls and veils. "Not the one with the red hair," he said.

Giorgina felt her stomach sink to her ankles, the acrid taste of fear crawling up her throat. Her hand within Labiba's grasp trembled. She knew she should speak, but her tongue seemed frozen; she could say nothing.

Labiba spoke up, lying with ease. "Sir, this girl wasn't demonstrating with us. She was only walking past and accidentally got caught up in the chaos."

The commander's eyes skimmed Giorgina from head to toe. "Is that quite right, miss?"

Giorgina parted her lips. She suddenly realized she was very thirsty. "Yes," she said hoarsely.

"Nevertheless, I can only release you to a male guardian or . . . legal chaperone." He said these last two words with bitter distaste. "Tell my officers your name so we can locate your guardian."

Giorgina could not speak. If she gave them her name and address it would be an easy matter for them to locate her father, but she was certain spending the night in the cold cell below would be preferable to being dragged out of prison by him.

"Come, Commander," said Malak. "The poor woman is terrified. Surely you can make an exception and release her into my custody."

The commander's mouth was a thin line. "If the girl is indeed innocent, that's all the more reason not to hand her over to you."

Malak laughed, a soft, trilling sound. "If only I were as corrupt as you seem to think I am."

Giorgina found her voice. "Please, sir," she begged. "My father is quite strict, and if he has to retrieve me from jail . . . it won't matter that I'm innocent. Can you not release me into my own custody?"

Giorgina thought she saw a hint of sympathy in the twitch of the commander's mustache, but the next moment he turned away and spoke gruffly. "The law does not permit me to release a girl into her own custody."

"One of the many reasons why we were protesting, Commander. The girl is a grown woman." For the first time, a hint of sharpness entered Malak's voice, even as her expression remained mild. "Surely you can use your esteemed judgment to determine she's of no harm to herself or others?"

The commander's eyes narrowed. Giorgina felt sure he was about to harangue them all, but before he could speak there was a tentative knock on the door.

"Come in," said the commander.

An officer slowly pushed the door open, his eyes wide. "I apologize for interrupting, sir, but the lady insisted—"

A short young woman with dark brown skin and unusually large eyes pushed past him—Giorgina vaguely recognized her—followed by Etedal and someone who made Giorgina's stomach lurch.

Nico.

9

NEHAL

SHAABAN SHOT TO HIS FEET, HIS CHAIR SCRAPING BACK-ward. "Nehal! What in the Tetrad's name are *you* doing here? On your wedding night?"

Nehal inclined her head. "Hello, Uncle."

She quickly took in the scene at hand. Uncle Shaaban, looking bewildered and a little irritated, flanked by two mustachioed policemen who seemed to be trying their hardest to maintain composure. A pretty woman with dark braided hair seated in front of the commander, looking at Nehal with mild surprise and anticipation. Two women standing beside Shaaban's desk, one with deep umber skin, shiny black hair, and striking amber eyes, the other with long red hair who looked very, very pale. Her dark eyes widened as they fell on Nico.

So *this* was Nico's lover.

But Nehal did not have time to linger on her or anyone else. She turned back to Shaaban.

"I'll be quick," said Nehal. "I'm here to ask you to release my friend Giorgina into our custody."

Shaaban settled back into his chair with a heavy sigh and rubbed at the stubble on his chin roughly. "And how exactly do you know this girl?"

Nehal shrugged. "As I said, we're friends, and I can assure you she had absolutely nothing to do with this demonstration. I can take her home in my palanquin. Medhat is waiting just outside."

Nehal could see Shaaban's hesitation. She had known the man since she was a child; he often spent his vacations with them in Ramina. He and Nehal's father passed hours upon hours playing backgammon in the courtyard, their rowdy voices echoing through the house all night. He had just been at her wedding a few hours ago. She knew he was a man who valued the letter of the law, so she understood his hesitation, but she could not allow him to succumb to it.

Nehal fixed her lips into a mixture of a pout and an obsequious smile. "You do *trust* me, don't you, Uncle? You would grant me this one favor, wouldn't you? As you said, it *is* my wedding night, and I wouldn't have come out if it wasn't for something truly important."

Shaaban tipped his head back and sighed again, then sat forward with a wry smile on his face, shaking his head. "Fine, fine, I suppose there's no harm in it." He inclined his head. "Lord Niccolo. Are you in agreement?"

Nico looked startled at being asked for his opinion. "Y-yes," he stuttered.

Nehal rolled her eyes. Leave it to Uncle Shaaban to ask after her husband's permission.

"Thank you, Uncle. We'll take our leave, so as not to take up too much of your time." She reached out to Giorgina. "Well, come along, then."

Giorgina stumbled forward hesitantly, as though in a daze. Etedal caught her around the waist and steered her out.

Nehal looked at one of the mustachioed policemen expectantly, but when he only stared at her blankly, she snapped her fingers impatiently and demanded, "Her shawl, please."

"Oh—of course, my lady."

Nehal took the shawl from him and followed the other women out, trailed by Nico, who was keeping his distance. Nehal quietly handed Giorgina her shawl as they walked toward the palanquin, where Medhat waited. When he caught sight of them, he sat up and jumped down to help them inside.

"We've got it from here," said Etedal.

It was Nico who responded, though his words were directed at Giorgina and not Etedal. "It's late. You shouldn't be on the streets alone."

"I've hired a palanquin, Lord Niccolo," said the uncovered woman. Nehal had not gotten too long a look at her in the office, and here in the street, it was too dark to properly make out her features, but something about her rang familiar. "We'll be fine. Thank you both for your help."

They turned away.

"Giorgina, I—" Nico began.

The red-haired woman paused and half-turned. The dark-skinned woman with her placed a protective arm around her waist.

"We need to get her home," she said softly. "It's already very late."

Nehal watched Nico swallow his words, his eyes shining as they trailed Giorgina walking away.

Nehal could not help feeling somewhat disappointed herself; she'd thought she might have a chance to speak to Giorgina, learn a little bit about what she was like. With a sigh, she turned back toward the palanquin, where Medhat helped her in. She settled inside, then realized Nico was still standing where she had left him.

She knocked on the side of the palanquin. "Nico!" she called. "Let's go!"

He startled, as though he had forgotten Nehal was there at all.

THE FOLLOWING MORNING found Nehal both bored and curious, a combination that usually led her into trouble.

She had spent the better part of the ride home with Nico pestering him with questions about Giorgina, eventually leading him to reveal that he had met her at a bookshop, and had even managed to yank the bookshop's name out of him.

So after Nehal woke up and breakfasted, she called for Medhat and departed for Giorgina's bookshop.

Soon enough Nehal discovered that Giorgina's shop was in a part of Alamaxa unlikely to be frequented by palanquins. As she lounged among her cushions, she drew back the curtains of her window and peeked at the roads as they grew decidedly dirtier and far more crowded. When the palanquin wove its way through the crooked, uneven streets, the crowds gave the palanquin curious glances. Some stared openly, their jaws dangling. It did not bode well for what Nehal had intended to be an inconspicuous visit, but there was nothing she could do about it now.

The shop itself was tucked into a little corner at the end of a narrow lane. Nehal tried to peer through the windows, but they were filled with books, so she could barely glimpse the interior. With a resigned sigh, she pushed open the door. Before it had swung shut, Nehal locked eyes with Giorgina.

The shop was not as well-lit as it could have been, but Nehal was still able to get a fair look at Giorgina Shukry.

She was taller than Nehal, and slimmer as well; her curves were subtle. Her hair was her most striking feature, thick and heavy and waist-length, a shiny dark red that glimmered like copper under the lamplight. In spite of her traditional Talyani name and unusual hair color, her strong nose, milky olive skin, and full mouth betrayed Ramsawi ancestry. Her eyes were strikingly dark, despite being shrouded in red lashes. A beaten black shawl was draped loosely around her shoulders, wrapped around a faded navy blue galabiya with frayed sleeves.

The other woman could not conceal her shock. Her black eyes widened, and the tiny book she had been carefully thumbing through fell shut.

Nehal strolled into the shop, her fingers trailing along one of the bookshelves. "I've surprised you," she said.

Giorgina opened her mouth, then closed it again.

"I know I probably shouldn't be here," said Nehal. "But we didn't get a chance to speak last night."

Giorgina looked stiff with tension. "Of course. Thank you for helping me."

Nehal waved her thanks away. "I didn't come here for your gratitude." She paused. "But I know about you and Nico."

Giorgina stared at her, stricken.

"You don't have to worry," said Nehal. "He told me himself. You should know neither of us wanted this marriage."

Still Giorgina said nothing.

"We came to an agreement," continued Nehal. "I'm sure he told you. He gave me something I wanted, and I granted him the legal right to a concubine. But he said you refused?"

Giorgina seemed to stiffen all over again, her arms tightening around herself. "With respect, my lady, you must see how that position would afford me little dignity."

"None of this 'my lady' business, call me Nehal." Nehal paused. "Of course I understand the nature of the position. I just assumed that was what you strove for."

"And why would you make that assumption?" asked Giorgina.

Nehal had blundered into an offense, as she often did. She had made an assumption that since Nico was wealthy and distinguished, marriage to a commoner would be unlikely. But was it any more unlikely than a woman of House Darweesh who wanted to become a soldier? To most people that was an equally absurd notion.

Nehal sighed and shrugged, dropping her veil of formality. "My mother says I don't always take the time to think through what comes out of my mouth. I didn't mean to offend you."

But there was no anger on Giorgina's face, only a kind of weary resignation. "I know," she said.

"Well then, tell me, Giorgina, because Nico refuses to—" Nehal approached Giorgina's desk and leaned in close, causing Giorgina to frown and lean back. "Why did Nico not defy his father for you?"

Giorgina blinked twice, very slowly. "Does it matter?" she asked.

Nehal straightened. "Of course it matters! It's all that matters. If Nico had showed some backbone, I wouldn't be stuck in this marriage, and you wouldn't be so miserable! If he actually had a good reason—"

"There's nothing to be done about it now," said Giorgina wearily. "You're already married."

"Well, I suppose, but—"

"It's over." Though Giorgina spoke as softly as ever, there was a finality to her tone that gave Nehal pause. "Even if Nico hadn't married you, his father would never have let him marry *me*. I see that now, and I see that I have to move on. Please let me move on."

Nehal thought she heard Giorgina's voice wobble, and for a moment she felt terribly guilty, an emotion she was not especially familiar with, and did not much like.

Giorgina took up her book once more, and directed her gaze toward the door, signaling the end of the conversation.

"Sorry to have bothered you, then," said Nehal carefully. At the door, she paused, then half-turned. "If you change your mind, you know where to find me." She paused again. "Or if you ever need help with anything. You can send a letter addressed to me, and Nico wouldn't ever see it. Or know."

Giorgina's response was a stiff nod; she wouldn't even meet Nehal's gaze. With a sigh, Nehal walked out of the bookshop.

10

GIORGINA

GIORGINA'S GAZE TRAILED AFTER NEHAL DARWEESH EXIT-
ing the shop. She felt dazed; one week ago Nehal Darweesh had
been a larger-than-life figure, one Giorgina had never even imagined
meeting, let alone speaking with. Today, Giorgina could say that
Nehal Darweesh had sprung her out of prison *and* had a private
conversation with her.

She was nothing like Giorgina had expected; the few wealthy
ladies who frequented the Daughters of Izdihar meetings were prim
and proper and mostly kept to themselves. Nehal was brash and direct, far too much for Giorgina's liking, and she had forced Giorgina
to once again doubt her decision to reject Nico. Nehal's presence
in the bookshop reminded Giorgina that in the space of a week her
life trajectory had veered entirely off course, like a runaway train.
There was no more Nico to lift Giorgina out of drudgery, no more
guarantee of a happy, loving marriage. What was left to her now?

Giorgina's wrist ached. She flexed it gingerly, grimacing as she
did so. This was the wrist that had been seized at the rally last night,
and the very same one Giorgina's father had squeezed even tighter
when she had returned home well past her allotted curfew. Giorgina
rarely saw her father so furious.

"I will not have my eldest daughter strutting home at this hour like a common whore!" he had roared in her face, spittle flying. When Hala tried to calm him down, he pushed her away and strode forward to tightly clasp Giorgina's wrist. "Do you want to be raped, you daughter of a dog? Is that it?"

"No," cried Giorgina. Tears welled in her eyes.

"Then you come home at a proper hour, not when the dancers and prostitutes are walking the streets! What will people say when they see you coming home so late? What will they think?" He shook Giorgina once, his grip on her wrist tightening. "I gave my permission for you to work that job and I can just as easily take it away! Do you hear me?"

When he released Giorgina her wrist had immediately begun to throb. When she looked at it this morning, she saw an ugly purple bruise coiling around her flesh like a snake.

Giorgina was only thankful he hadn't demanded proof of her whereabouts or asked to speak with Anas. If her father discovered she had been jailed, or that she had any association with the Daughters of Izdihar he so despised . . . the thought was enough to make Giorgina shudder. She was exhausted, and sad, and then Nehal Darweesh had walked in to remind her of it all.

Still . . . Giorgina wished she'd had the courage to ask her about this agreement she'd entered into with Nico. What highborn woman—or any woman, really—would so eagerly grant her husband the right to a concubine? Most women were desperate to incorporate a clause into their marriage contract that prevented such behavior. It could only mean that Nehal had absolutely no interest in Nico at all.

But that didn't matter. Legally, she was still his wife, and clearly she had no intention of divorcing him; whatever agreement she had entered into with him, it seemed she still needed him as her legal husband. Which left Giorgina with nothing at all.

Leaning over the desk, she took a deep, heaving sigh that did nothing to steady her nerves; it felt like something in her chest was struggling to leap into her throat. When the door of the shop creaked open, Giorgina braced herself, plastered a fake smile onto her face, and looked up, but then relaxed, for it was only Labiba, followed by an unfamiliar woman—no, not unfamiliar—

It was Malak.

Only it was Malak as Giorgina had never seen her before, dressed in a modest galabiya and black shawl. Giorgina stared, her mouth hanging open, until Malak winked at her.

"I thought it best not to draw any attention," said Malak in her soft voice. "After last night . . ." She and Labiba approached the desk; Malak reached over and gently touched Giorgina's hand. "How are you?"

Giorgina blinked, somewhat stunned—though she had been part of the Daughters of Izdihar for over a year now, she had never quite been so close to Malak, or spoken with her privately. Though Giorgina wrote for the magazine, everything was filtered through Bahira, Malak's assistant, or Labiba, who was Malak's very distant cousin, and whom Malak had helped settle in Alamaxa when Labiba and Etedal had run away from their family down south in Upper Ramsawa.

"I'm . . . I'm all right," Giorgina stammered. "You didn't have to come all the way down here; you hardly know me . . ."

"I know you're my best writer. And I wanted to apologize. I'm sorry everything escalated so unpleasantly last night." Malak sighed. "Coming up against the Khopeshes, and then the police, and being arrested . . . it must have been very frightening for you."

Malak's tone was slow and soothing, like a mother rocking her child to sleep with a song. It was both similar to and completely different from how she delivered her speeches: the bedrock of firm confidence was there, but whereas Malak's public speeches were enveloped by a cold anger, now her words were cooled by a soft sympathy.

"I escaped in the end," said Giorgina awkwardly.

Malak nodded thoughtfully. "Yes, that was quick thinking on Etedal's part, though I wouldn't have expected Niccolo Baldinotti to bring his wife along." When she looked at Giorgina, Malak's gaze was far too knowing, and Giorgina blushed, looking between Labiba and Malak.

"Oh, you . . . you know, then?" Giorgina asked stiffly.

Labiba shifted uncomfortably. "Etedal told her. It kind of just came out last night, you know, when he showed up . . ."

Giorgina was desperate to change the subject. "The Khopeshes . . ." she began slowly. "I thought they were mostly clerics? None of those men seemed like sheikhs . . ."

"Not if your only experience with sheikhs is Nasef," said Malak wryly, her gaze sliding to Labiba. "I'm sure some of them were clerics, but the others . . . hired help would be my guess. Their numbers aren't that large."

"I don't think Nasef would condone something like that," protested Labiba.

"Oh, I doubt he's their leader," said Malak. "I don't know much about their hierarchy, but I would be surprised if someone as young as Nasef was solely in charge, even with his pedigree."

"His pedigree?" repeated Giorgina.

"The House of Shawkat," muttered Labiba.

Giorgina startled; Nasef was from one of Ramsawa's ten noble Houses? "So his family could be funding the Khopeshes?"

"Well, all the family money went to his sister when Nasef became a sheikh," said Labiba. "Nasef made sure it went to Nagat and not a male relative, and he said she's not very interested in politics."

"You seem to know quite a bit about Sheikh Nasef and his family," said Malak wryly.

Labiba ducked her head. Her skin was far too dark to show a blush, but Giorgina knew her well enough to see she was embarrassed.

"Have you spoken with him since the fundraising event?" asked Giorgina.

"No." Labiba sighed. "I didn't know if he'd want to see me . . ." As though sensing Malak and Giorgina's judgment, she continued hurriedly, "He doesn't really hate *weavers,* you know; he just doesn't think we should use our abilities. It's not like he thinks we should be rounded up and locked up like what some of the other Khopeshes say—"

"But if he continues to associate with them regardless, what does that say?" said Giorgina in exasperation. She and Labiba had had this conversation before. Nasef thought weavers were blighted, thieves who had stolen powers that belonged only to the Tetrad— never mind *how* they were supposed to have stolen anything—and that they should spend their time in penance, praying to the Tetrad for forgiveness and inner peace that would help them contain their weaving. Clerics like Nasef believed that eventually, through enough prayer and penance, weaving would simply . . . go away.

The Order of the Tetrad had not always believed weavers to be thieves; before Edua Badawi destroyed an entire peninsula, the Order had believed weavers to be demigods, honored and chosen by the Tetrad. Now, clerics who still believed this were denounced as fringe heretics, sidelined into early retirement.

There were some clerics who were far more militant than Nasef, who believed that weavers should have no say in the matter at all, that they should be gathered up and forced to spend all their time in ascetic prayer, forced to self-mutilate and punish themselves to the utmost extent, in order to seek the Tetrad's forgiveness. Some even thought weavers were abominations who should be executed, though this tended to be a viewpoint more common in Zirana than Ramsawa, and was often the crux of the two countries' quarrels.

Considering how friendly Nasef seemed to be with the Zirani ambassador, though . . .

Giorgina shook her head.

"But he supports the Daughters of Izdihar!" countered Labiba. "He wants women to have the vote; he wouldn't send the Khopeshes after us."

"Perhaps he's changed his mind," said Malak softly. "I've

known many a man to change his entire belief system to get back at a woman."

"Get back at— I didn't do anything!"

"You lied to him about being a weaver," Giorgina said softly.

Labiba's full lips formed a perfect circle in surprise. "He's not like that."

Malak sighed. "In any case, as I said, I doubt he has full control of this group. It would be helpful if we could find out more; I'd been thinking of running a piece on the Khopeshes in *The Vanguard* . . ."

"I'll speak to him," Labiba assured her. "Today if I can."

Malak nodded thoughtfully. "You'll have to be careful."

"He's not like that," Labiba said again.

Malak then turned to Giorgina. "We haven't scared you away, have we?" Her tone was laced with a playful thread.

"I—no," said Giorgina. "Not at all." She was somewhat surprised to find that she meant it wholeheartedly. Despite yesterday's violence, despite the arrest, despite the risks . . . the Daughters of Izdihar gave Giorgina a purpose she lacked in all other aspects of her life. It gave her like-minded friends, a community that would catch her if she fell. It gave her the ability to speak, even if it was anonymously.

"Good." Malak leaned forward. "We're holding another rally in a few days, at the opening of the new Alamaxa Opera House. I can promise you that absolutely nothing exciting will happen there."

Giorgina's heart sank at being forced to disappoint Malak. "I—I can't. After last night, I can't risk coming home so late again, or my father—" She stopped, unsure what to say.

For a moment Malak's expression was inscrutable, but then her mouth softened into a melancholy smile. "That's all right," she said quietly. "Fathers can be difficult; I understand completely. If Labiba manages to discover anything about the Khopeshes from Nasef, can I ask you to write the piece for the next issue, then?"

"Of—of course," said Giorgina, her chest swelling with pride.

With a small smile, Malak turned to leave. Labiba shot Giorgina a grin and squeezed her hand, then followed Malak. When they were gone and the shop was quiet again, Giorgina felt bereft and lonely, and she wished she could follow them both out, wherever they were headed.

11

NEHAL

LETTERS BEGAN TO ARRIVE THE MOMENT NICO AND NEHAL'S
marriage was legalized. These were ornate, elegant letters, carefully
scripted, some gilded, some perfumed, all waxed shut with elegant
House seals. The servants gathered them into neat piles and deposited them in Nico's study. Now three collimated piles sat on his desk,
awaiting responses.

Nehal raised an eyebrow when Nico gave a small, resigned sigh
and began to sort through the correspondence. She watched him for
a few moments, leaning back on her palms, bare feet stretched. She
herself would likely not be in attendance at most of these events,
for she was to begin her term at the Academy in mere days. *That*
letter had arrived only that morning, explaining that Nehal would
be boarding at the Academy weekdays but would be permitted to
return home for weekends if she desired.

Nico, on the other hand, likely had little else to occupy his calendar, but he did not seem especially eager about this. He looked at
every letter as though it were informing him of the death of a close
relative.

"I'm sure you don't have to go to *all* of them," said Nehal finally.

Nico looked up and gave her a thin smile. "What excuse could I give? I have no profession and no more university to occupy me; refusing would be seen as a snub."

Nehal had recently learned that Nico had graduated with honors from the University of Alamaxa only months ago, having studied history and philosophy, none of which was surprising, given . . . well, everything about him.

Nehal gave a loud, dramatic sigh, expecting Nico to share in it, but he had already returned to the letters. He was meticulous: he would peel open an invitation, scan it thoroughly, pen a response, stamp it with his signet ring, then pencil the date into a little booklet that served as his calendar.

Bored, Nehal stood, stretching and yawning loudly. She strolled around the study, running her hands alongside one of the many bookshelves that now filled the room since Nico had had his personal library delivered. She removed one book that looked interesting— its spine was bright red—but when she ruffled through its pages she discovered that it was a tome on the eating habits of southern Ramsawis. In other words, a dreadful bore. She shoved the book back into place, then turned to find Nico frowning at her.

"Please be careful with my books," he admonished.

Nehal rolled her eyes but stepped away from the bookshelves, wandering back over to Nico's desk.

Nico looked up again, removing his spectacles for a moment. His eyes, blue as a clear sky, were almost unsettlingly pale. "You don't have to stay here if you don't want to."

"I don't have anywhere else to go at the moment." Nehal sank back onto the floor, crossing her legs in the process. She reached out, lightly clutching one of the unopened envelopes, but Nico took it out of her grasp and put it back in its proper place with a sigh.

"Do you want to help?"

"Not particularly." She rested her elbows on the desk and peered at him. "Are you going to give up on Giorgina, then?"

Nico flinched and said nothing.

"Come on, Nico, you can tell me!" She smirked. "I am your *wife*, after all," she added, with flair.

"It's not your concern," said Nico wearily.

"You really won't tell me why you went along with your father?" Nehal said. "You're a man, after all; don't the lot of you tend to do whatever you like, and damn the consequences?"

Nico flushed, then muttered something unintelligible under his breath.

Nehal raised a single eyebrow. "Please tell me you don't expect me to take that as an answer."

"Do you really have nothing better to do than to keep pestering me?"

"Unfortunately for both of us, I don't." Nehal tilted her head back, her gaze falling on the ceiling, from which a heavy chandelier dangled.

"What would you be doing if you were in Ramina?"

"Oh, you know." Nehal leaned back and grinned. "Swimming, usually. Playing cards with my cousins. Going to a party. There was always something to do. What do *you* do with your time?"

"I read. I study."

She grimaced. "Why?"

He gave her a puzzled look. "To learn? Because I enjoy it?"

"Yes, but to what end? What do you do when you've learned?"

"You don't—you don't have to *do* anything," said Nico, looking as though she'd offended his very existence. "It's fulfilling. Enriching. Knowledge makes up the very social fabric of society—"

"If you say so." Nehal sighed, then held her hand out. "All right, fine, give me something to do."

Nico smiled somewhat grimly, then handed her a giant pile of envelopes. Nehal stared at them peevishly, already regretting her offer.

NEHAL'S FINAL OUTING before her start at the Academy was at the behest of Lady Nagat Shawkat and her husband Adil Rifaat. The

Lady of House Shawkat and her husband invited Nico and Nehal to join them in the private box they had purchased for the grand opening of the Alamaxa Opera House.

Nehal knew very little of the Opera House; before coming to Alamaxa she hadn't much concerned herself with the city's affairs. However, when she informed Nico of the invitation, he snatched it from her hands, reread it himself, and genuinely smiled for the first time that day. Apparently, his father had not allowed him to use his funds to purchase a private box, but Nico had desperately wanted to attend. By the time he'd become emancipated and in full control of his own inheritance, the boxes were sold out.

According to Nico, the Alamaxa Opera House was an "architectural marvel" and a "testament to Alamaxa's appreciation of the higher arts." Nehal knew nothing at all of opera or its higher arts, but she was eager for a night out nonetheless.

Dressing like a proper lady was an ordeal; unlike Ridda and Giorgina—who wore only one or two layers, a simple cotton galabiya and a shawl—Nehal was outfitted in tiers. First came the wide, loose trousers, cream-colored, tied at her knees but loose enough to fall to her feet. Then there was the cream-colored blouse, with its ruffled sleeves. Atop the blouse was a tight-fitting jade vest, long enough to skim the floor, buttoned from bosom to waist, with sleeves that fell to Nehal's ankles. After that, Ridda tied a thick sash around Nehal's waist, the knot so complicated Nehal could not even attempt it.

Atop all this (this was the point where Nehal normally began to complain) was the final piece: a silk outer robe. It was beautiful, Nehal grudgingly admitted: dyed mandarin orange, embroidered with jade-colored silk in complex geometric patterns, but heavy. With a sigh, Nehal allowed Ridda to drape it on her, and to pull the dangling sleeves of her vest through the shorter sleeves of the robe.

Then, of course, was the veil and headdress, often the bane of Nehal's existence. The headdress was a heavy, gaudy thing to which was attached a long muslin veil. It hid Nehal's hair, which Ridda earlier had pulled into a curly chignon with two curls framing her face, and dangled to the back of her knees.

Her wrists, though barely visible, were adorned with gold bracelets, and around her neck Ridda placed a sparkling gold kirdan. Heavy gold earrings dangled from Nehal's ears. And of course, Ridda painted her face: reddened lips, eyes lined in kohl, eyebrows oiled and darkened. By the end Nehal felt like the trussed-up dolls given to children on holidays.

Nico was waiting at the front door, attired in his own spectacular uniform: a heavy cotton galabiya, girdle, embroidered robe, and turban. They were all in different shades of blue and speckled with embroidered silver stars. When he saw Nehal he blinked as though he'd just been knocked over the head. Nehal glared at him, barely paying attention to Ridda, who was placing Nehal's slippered feet into low-heeled wooden pattens. But Nico said nothing at all.

Once they were settled in the palanquin, Nico began to ramble about the opera. Nehal learned more than she had ever wanted to about opera's history, traditions, and vocal requirements. Nehal was exasperated and so, *so* bored, but Nico was so enthusiastic she did not have the heart to stop him and only nodded along, pretending to be interested. It was a relief when the palanquin came to a halt.

Nehal had to admit the Alamaxa Opera House was indeed architecturally stunning. It was a massive tessellated dome, done up in various shades of blue and gold, with a sparkling circular archway ten times Nehal's height. A sea of people tugged Nico and Nehal through the arch and into the interior, which was, if anything, more extravagant than the outside: marble walls and floors gleamed in the light of the candelabras set against every corner. The vaulted ceiling was inscribed with geometric carvings so intricate and dense she could not discern where they began. A set of stairs at the back of the room was laid with a thick red carpet, which led to a pair of shut arched doors decorated in the same dizzyingly detailed style as the ceiling.

Servants dressed in fine white galabiyas, thick black scarves tied around their waists, carried trays of chilled orange sharbat, crispy patties of falafel, stuffed grape leaves, and honeyed dates. Nehal snatched a falafel patty off the tray of a passing waiter and popped it into her mouth, crunching into its soft and salty interior. Nico's gaze was still fixed on the ceiling vaults. He reached out to Nehal blindly, his hands landing on her wrist.

"Do you see that detail?" he asked wonderingly. "Look at the leaves on that crown molding! That style is clearly influenced by Amedeo Mokhtar, don't you think?"

Nehal gave him a disbelieving look but was saved from having to answer by the arrival of a petite young woman, followed by an older man.

Lady Nagat Shawkat was a deceptively pretty, cinnamon-skinned young woman with honey-brown hair and an unusually upturned nose. Adil, her much older husband, was quite the opposite; he was pale and white-haired.

Nagat took Nehal in an embrace and greeted her with a kiss on each cheek. Adil did the same with Nico. To each others' spouses they merely extended hands to be shaken.

"I'm so pleased you were able to join us!" Nagat clapped her hands together and turned to her husband, who smiled.

"Thank you so much for inviting us," replied Nico effusively. "It's truly astounding; I can't imagine what the theater itself looks like!"

Adil clapped Nico on the back. "Come, my friend, I just acquired something I think you'll be quite excited to see."

Nico glanced back at Nehal, who made to follow him, but found her arm gripped rather tightly by Nagat, who was already turning away from her husband.

"Come, Nehal," Nagat whispered conspiratorially. "Let's leave the men to their business and let me show you around!"

"What business?" asked Nehal, but Nagat either did not hear Nehal or chose to ignore her. Instead, she led Nehal around the room, introducing her to various other guests, most of whose names Nehal promptly forgot. Then Nagat took her to a man standing in the corner by himself, a full glass of bright red sharbat in his hands.

"Yusry!" Nagat exclaimed. "I would like to introduce Lady Nehal Darweesh! Nehal, Yusry Sarhan is my cousin."

The man—Yusry—smiled and held out his hand. Nehal stared for a moment, before coming to her senses and shaking his hand.

Her hesitation was a result of the fact that Yusry Sarhan had the distinction of being the most handsome man Nehal had ever seen. He was as tall and broad as Nico, but wiry and well-defined where Nico was stout, with an exceedingly sharp, clean-shaven jawline and high cheekbones. His large doe eyes were a warm shade of honey and heavily lashed, and his lips were astonishingly full for a man. Unlike most men, who wore some form of turban or cap on their hair, Yusry's hair was free, a dense thicket of curls that rose up around his head like a cloud.

"Lovely to meet you, Lady Nehal," said Yusry pointedly. She blinked, drawing her attention away from his lips and back to his eyes.

"Yusry is from Ramina as well." Nagat looked between the pair of them. "You two share a love of the sea!"

Nehal did not recall having told this woman anything about her feelings for the sea, but Yusry answered too quickly for Nehal to contemplate this.

"Oh, how wonderful!" exclaimed Yusry. "I haven't been to Ramina in months, though . . . business keeps me stranded in Alamaxa, I'm afraid, but I much prefer the sea air."

"I completely agree!" said Nehal eagerly. "I'm a waterweaver, so as you can imagine, I prefer to be close to the ocean."

"Oh!" Yusry's smile widened, showing perfect, pearly teeth. "How absolutely delightful! Would you believe I've never met a waterweaver in person before? What can you do?"

Nehal grinned, raised her hand slightly, and turned the contents of Yusry's glass into a small whirlpool.

Yusry and Nagat let out startled laughs. Yusry held the glass aloft, the water whirling in tandem with Nehal's finger. She couldn't help but smile happily at Yusry's delight; it was rare that her water-weaving was met with something other than disapproving glances or rolled eyes, or, occasionally, fear.

Unfortunately, it seemed Nehal was not to be bereft of disapproval: a young man was swiftly approaching them, his forehead crinkled into an intense frown. He was dressed distinctively in a loose but high-necked black galabiya made of heavy cloth. He had a thick, dark beard but his hair was tucked under a rounded black cap. Nehal scowled. She had no inclination to be scolded by a cleric, but there was no way for her to make a quick escape.

Nagat's smile had faded slightly, but her poise did not shirk. "Nehal, allow me to introduce my brother, Nasef."

"*Sheikh* Nasef," Nagat's brother corrected.

Nehal raised an eyebrow. "You don't look old enough to be anyone's sheikh."

The cleric frowned even more, though Nehal had not thought that possible. Unlike Nagat, he was milky pale, but they shared the same upturned nose. "My age is none of your concern. What you should be concerned with is your wanton display of weaving."

"Nasef, please, not here," Nagat whispered. Her brother spoke over her.

"Weaving is not something to be trifled with," said Nasef firmly.

Nehal smiled; she was far too used to this argument. "Well then, Tefuret shouldn't have created me in her image."

As expected, Sheikh Nasef hissed at her blasphemy. "Her Holiness Tefuret has nothing to do with this," snapped Nasef. "You are meant to resist the temptation, not perform party tricks—"

"I'm afraid I've never been especially good at resisting temptation," Nehal said. Beside her, Yusry laughed loudly, and continued to chuckle even as Nasef turned to glare at him.

"I'm sorry, Nasef, but this is a party, not a sermon!" protested Yusry. "You're not supposed to ambush the guests."

"Don't even get me started on *you*," snapped Nasef.

Yusry's expression darkened, and that was when Nagat took her brother by the arm and dragged him away, muttering furiously under her breath.

"You grew up with that?" said Nehal.

Yusry shot her a tight smile. "And Nagat is so lovely . . ." He sighed. "It never ceases to astonish me that they're siblings." He frowned. "My little sister is a weaver, actually, due to start at the Academy soon. I try to keep Nasef as far away from her as possible. He doesn't even know—"

"Oh!" Nehal swelled with excitement. "I start at the Academy soon too! I'll look out for her; what's her name?"

Yusry shifted toward her with an excited grin, the candelabra lights momentarily turning his brown curls golden. "Mahitab. She's a sandweaver."

Their excitement buoyed their conversation; Yusry was clearly delighted with his sister and couldn't stop talking about her. He and Nehal chatted easily for some time, until Nehal spotted Nico in the crowd. He looked a bit flushed, though that was not surprising considering the heat and the press of bodies in the room. Yet there was an undeniable glimmer of excitement in his eyes, a slight tremble to his hands when he raised a glass of sharbat to his lips.

She would have asked him about it, but she was too caught up in her discussion with Yusry, so much so that she hardly realized they had been rejoined by Adil, Nico, and Nagat, who had exchanged her brother for an older, mustachioed man she introduced as Wael Helmy, the owner of the exclusive Rabbani Club and head of the House of Helmy. Nehal thought she may have received an invitation from his wife to dine at their club.

"Have any of you ever been to an opera before?" asked Wael.

Nico shook his head. "I've only read about them. Talyana used to put on some truly exquisite operas, if I recall correctly."

"Oh yes, that's right, they did!" said Adil. "I believe Zirana carries on the tradition now. I saw a wonderfully grand performance there in my youth."

Wael turned to Adil, his thick eyebrows raised. "No! In Zirana?"

Adil laughed. "Oh, but this was long before Prince Hali ascended the throne."

"Speaking of—look who's here." Yusry motioned subtly with his chin; Nehal followed his gaze and found herself looking at Naji Ouazzani, the Zirani ambassador. She had only glimpsed his picture in the paper once, but there was no mistaking him: he was the only person dressed in full Zirani regalia.

"Have you heard Ouazzani's latest demand?" Nagat asked quietly.

Nico nodded. "Apparently King Hali is demanding not only the closure of the new Academy, but a complete ban on weaving, punishable by imprisonment."

"That's ridiculous," said Nehal, startled.

"Ridiculous and unrealistic," said Yusry. "Wael, did you know Nehal is a waterweaver? And so skilled too! Show him the little trick you do with sharbat!"

Nehal raised her hand and began to direct herself to Wael's sharbat glass, but the man took an abrupt step back and raised his free hand. "Don't, please," he said firmly. "I tolerate weaving if I have to, but I don't hold with such nonsense in respectable settings, particularly from a lady such as yourself."

The patronizing slight may as well have been a slap to the face. Heat gathered at Nehal's collar; she took a step forward without really knowing what she was doing. It was only when Nico took her hand in his own that she realized she had been raising it toward Wael, who was busy waving down a passing servant to give him his half-empty glass, completely unconcerned with his own rudeness.

"But it's an astonishing skill!" protested Yusry. "I had no idea you were so religious."

"It's not just about the Order," said Wael, stiffly adjusting his sleeves. "It's a matter of decorum. Were we at a circus, perhaps, or at open war with each other, then it would be understandable, but otherwise I find it quite tasteless." He gave Nehal a jerky bow, as though to coat his harsh words with decorum. As he straightened, he added, "I doubt your husband would appreciate such a display."

Nehal opened her mouth and was about to deliver a stream of well-chosen swear words when Nico smiled and said, "I'm fond of Nehal's weaving, actually. It's what drew me to her the first time we met."

Nehal turned to him in some surprise. She had not expected him to defend her, nor to say anything that would indicate their marriage had been a willing endeavor on either of their parts.

Wael's eyebrows pinched together, but his lips twisted into a thin smile. "Of course. Every man is king of his own household, after all."

The traditional words and their implication—that Nico both owned and controlled Nehal—were irritating, but before Nehal could deliver a retort, the doors at the top of the central staircase swung open. As heads turned in their direction, Nagat sidled closer to Nehal and whispered, "I do apologize for Wael's rudeness! He's not usually quite so boorish."

Nehal patted Nagat's arm. "You have nothing to apologize for. I'm rather accustomed to such behavior from men and am quite adept at handling it."

Nagat gave a charming little laugh at that, but then the two women quieted as a squat man with a full white beard appeared in the arched doorway.

"That's the minister of the arts!" Nico whispered in Nehal's ear. She was fascinated by how fascinated her husband was with such trivial details, but smiled benignly at his excitement.

"Welcome!" boomed the old man. "For those of you who may not know who I am, my name is Essam Elbeblawy, and I have the honor of holding the position of minister of the arts of our illustrious republic." There was a brief smattering of polite applause at these words. "I am sure you are all as eager as I am to witness Ramsawa's first ever opera, so I'll keep this little speech short." Elbeblawy proceeded to thank several patrons and donors who had financed the

Opera House's construction. Nehal lost her focus halfway through this speech—it wasn't nearly as short as Essam had implied—and afterward could hardly recall a single word.

She looked up just as a booming applause overtook the room; she belatedly joined her peers but only managed to clap twice before the crowd began to move forward. It was finally time for the opera. She had no idea what to expect, but at least Essam had finished with his grandiose speech.

The theater was like nothing Nehal had ever seen; her lips parted involuntarily when she gazed at the room before her. The ceiling stretched impossibly high, and from it dangled a three-tiered gold chandelier that twinkled with at least a hundred gas lights. The floor was taken up by rows of red-velvet chairs, with red carpets in the aisles in between, but the walls looked like a simulacrum of honeycombs. Nehal assumed these were the private boxes, three tiers of them, wrapped around the entire room, each box separated from the other by a carved gold column and a velvet screen. The stage, set under a massive archway, was covered by a red velvet curtain with gold trimmings, the Ramsawi seal stitched into its center.

Yusry handed his card to an usher. "If I'm not mistaken, I believe even the royal family is here tonight."

Nico turned to him in astonishment. "The royal family? Here?"

Yusry nodded and pointed to a pair of private boxes shielded by red velvet curtains. "I'm certain they're in one of these boxes. I'd say determine where the best view and acoustics in the room are, and that's where they'll be."

Nehal barely acknowledged this. Prince Hani, who was the royal family's representative in Parliament, was actually close friends with her cousin Hamed, the Darweesh representative. Nehal had crossed paths with the prince several times in the past few years, as he'd taken to summering at the Darweesh estates in Ramina with Hamed.

Nehal wasn't fond of him, nor did Hani particularly like her: he was one of Parliament's most vehement opponents of weaving, in line with the royal family's general views on the subject. Still, at least they were little more than a decorative element in Ramsawa's government, granted no more than a single representative in Parliament.

The usher led them to their box. Nehal squirmed uncomfortably in her chair; chairs were uncommon in most Ramsawi households and Nehal was not particularly fond of them. As the crowd settled, Nehal continued to take in the sights around her. The column directly to Nehal's left was studded with intricate decorations, as was the golden railing her hands lay on. The mural above her, which she could see much more clearly from this height, depicted a stylized working of the Tetrad coming together to create the world.

Nehal grew distracted as the lights dimmed—the crowd exclaimed at what surely had to be a display of skilled fireweaving—and the curtain began to rise. From the orchestra pit below the stage, a solitary oud trilled a long, high note as the stage revealed the actors: at least twenty men and women dressed in outlandish costumes, their faces heavily made-up. One of the men stepped forward, fell to his knees, and began to sing in a deep baritone.

The words meant nothing to Nehal. She was almost certain he was speaking Ramsawi, though some sort of archaic dialect to be sure, but the dramatic way he sang made it difficult to understand unless she devoted her entire concentration to him. That was not a simple feat in a crowded theater that was steadily growing hotter and hotter. The stage was alight with fireweaving as the actors twirled among the flames.

Nehal placed an elbow on the railing and rested her head in her palm. Her eyelids began to grow heavy. Her eyes trailed off the stage and fell on her companions. Nico was leaning forward with rapt attention, smiling brightly. Nagat's hands were clasped at her chest and her eyes were shining. Adil, who had his arm around Nagat, was swaying his head in time with the music. Yusry sat with one leg neatly crossed over the other, his hands resting in his lap, but on his face was an expression of such contentedness it was startling.

The intense heat of fireweaving caused sweat to pool under Nehal's arms and between her breasts and even behind her knees. Her throat was parched, and her head had begun to pound from the weight of her headdress. The unintelligible singing—which began to sound a little like screaming—did nothing to help. Instinctively Nehal reached for the gourd of water at her waist, only to remember that Nico had convinced her to leave it at home for the night, and she had—for reasons she could not recall now—obliged him. She extended her senses into the air looking for other sources of water, but could only sense sticky sweat that she was nowhere near skilled enough to grasp, nor would she have wanted to if she could.

In her stiff, high-backed chair, Nehal squirmed, until she managed to find a position somewhat comfortable, and leaned her head back. Slowly, she was lulled into a state of half-sleep, only to be startled what felt like moments later when a burst of thunderous applause nearly shattered her eardrums. She blinked several times, then hastily brought her hands together to join in.

"It's even more astounding than I thought it would be!" shouted Nico.

Resisting an urge to shake her head in disbelief, Nehal grasped his arm to draw his attention, but Yusry spoke before she could.

"Shall we go fetch some refreshments before the second half?" he said.

"Second half?" Nehal looked at Nico in horror. "Is the show not over?"

Nico looked at her as though she had lost her mind. "Over? It's just the intermission."

Nehal's hand slipped off Nico as he started forward after the others. Silently cursing under her breath, Nehal followed, desperate for fresh air.

The sight that greeted them in the lobby stopped them in their tracks; Nehal stumbled into Nico, who steadied her without shifting his gaze away from the group of women standing silently in the center of the lobby. Five of the women had their faces almost entirely covered, with only their eyes visible, and they were all holding large signs bearing slogans demanding votes for women. One of them held a drum, which she was beating softly in a somewhat ominous rhythm.

The sixth woman, who stood somewhat unobtrusively behind her sign-bearing compatriots, wore no veil or outer robe, but was dressed elegantly in burgundy trousers and a short, black vest that left her arms bare. Her hair was a simple braid that trailed across her shoulder. For a moment, Nehal could not place her, but when the woman shifted and the light illuminated her face, recognition hit like a wave.

Malak Mamdouh.

Her presence seemed to freeze the room. The waiters stood at the edges of the lobby, hovering nervously with trays of water and sharbat, while attendees whispered among themselves, but nobody seemed precisely certain how to react.

Behind Nehal, Wael cursed. "This is ridiculous," he said loudly, then pushed forward so that he faced the Daughters of Izdihar. "You're not welcome here, and this is extremely inappropriate. Leave now."

Malak glanced at Wael somewhat impassively, with only a hint of amusement in the quirk of her eyebrow. "My ladies and I have all purchased tickets to this event." Her melodic voice, though quiet, nonetheless managed to fill the room. "We're as welcome here as you are."

"Not if you're going to behave like this," countered Wael. "This is neither the time nor place to—"

At this, Malak smirked. "Apologies, Lord Helmy, are we disturbing your pleasant evening with our silly talk of equality?"

While Wael flushed, Nehal could not help but grin. Her chest swelled with emotions she could not precisely identify, but she realized suddenly that her lethargy had completely dissipated. Looking at the Daughters, the way they disrupted the pompous decorum that had shrouded the evening, filled Nehal with a thrill. She felt an incipient desire to walk over to the group and stand with them, to fight viciously for herself in ways that had been heretofore denied to her.

Naji Ouazzani stepped forward, and all eyes turned to him as he spoke, addressing Essam. "Minister, surely these women should be escorted out?"

Essam appeared somewhat startled to be asked for input. He blinked rapidly, then said, with a nervous laugh, "There's no harm in a few signs, surely! Come now, come now, everyone, intermission is only a few minutes! Drinks, drinks for all!" The minister clapped his hands.

Nehal saw Naji's mouth twist in disapproval. He walked toward the Daughters of Izdihar, making a beeline for Malak Mamdouh, who stood her ground even as Naji got uncomfortably close to her. Nehal could hear nothing of the conversation, but Naji's expression was one of utter distaste, while Malak's was entirely placid, as though Naji were nothing more than a vaguely interesting sea slug. After another moment, Naji walked away.

The tension had yet to dissipate. As attendees wandered the lobby in search of food and drink, the Daughters of Izdihar maintained their vigil in the center, never quite allowing anyone to ignore their presence, the beat of their drum drawing constant wary glances. The crowd flowed around them, always managing to maintain a careful distance from the protestors.

All except Nehal. As her companions sought out sharbat, Nehal broke away from them and made her way to Malak Mamdouh.

"You were at the police station," said Nehal, by way of introduction.

Malak Mamdouh smiled and extended a hand. "It's lovely to see you again, Lady Nehal."

Somewhat dazed, Nehal grasped her hand and took her in. It was utterly surreal to be shaking hands with the woman responsible not only for the creation of the Izdihar Division, but for the Alamaxa Weaving Academy's decision to admit women. At the police station, so concerned was Nehal with persuading Shaaban to release Giorgina, she had barely glanced at Malak. Now, however, she had the opportunity to recognize what she had not before: Malak Mamdouh was beautiful.

Her dark eyes were long, sharp, and downturned, giving her a somewhat sleepy look that was allayed by sharply arched eyebrows. Her nose was thin, long, and very straight, matching her sharp jawline. Her mouth was a small circle, the arches of her top lip like two crests of a wave. Her skin was golden brown, like wet sand, but her hair, pulled back into a glossy plait, was of the darkest black, with a soft blue sheen.

"Enjoying the show?" Malak's voice was husky and rough at the edges.

Nehal's nerves strained in an odd way that made her blurt out the first thought on her mind. "I feel as though I'd rather die than go back in there. What is that infernal dialect they're singing in, anyway?"

Malak laughed softly, and Nehal thought she would do anything to make her laugh again.

"I believe it's Classical Ramsawi," said Malak. "We usually learn a bit of it in school."

"I was never the most dutiful student," Nehal admitted.

Again Malak laughed, a smile playing on her lips as she spoke. "I'm afraid I was *overly* dutiful as a student."

"Thank you for your work with the Weaving Academy," Nehal continued eagerly. "I'm starting there in a few days."

"Are you?" Malak looked pleased. "That's wonderful! You're a . . . ?"

"Waterweaver!" said Nehal proudly. "And when I graduate I'll join the Izdihar Division, yet another of your achievements." Nehal paused, her cheeks warm, fearful she was being too eager.

But Malak didn't seem fazed. "I only apologize that both require a male guardian's permission." Her expression hardened somewhat. "It never ceases to be infuriating."

Nehal shrugged. "Men are idiots."

Malak's startled laugh was soft, like a whispered breath. "I am surprised your husband granted you permission. There's not many husbands who would do that." She paused. "You must be quite in love."

Nehal could not help laughing aloud. "More like utterly indifferent to one another."

Malak's response was interrupted by the approach of Yusry and Wael Helmy. Though Yusry had on a polite smile, Wael's expression was one of annoyance.

"Corrupting another young woman, Malak?" Wael grimaced unpleasantly at Malak.

Malak did not rise to the bait; she only glanced at Wael as though he were no more significant than a passing fly. But he did not allow her to ignore him, walking close enough to invade her space and forcing Nehal to take a step back.

"I knew your father," hissed Wael. "He didn't spend a fortune educating you so that you could embroil yourself in a scandal every other day. Do you think he would approve of this behavior?"

"I'll thank you not to speculate on what my father would or would not approve of," said Malak lightly.

"It's a shame," continued Wael, as though he had not heard her. "Your family was one of the most respected in Ramsawa, and now you've dragged the Mamdouh name through the mud." He turned to Nehal. "This woman is a terrible influence, Lady Nehal. I highly doubt your husband would approve of your associating with her—"

Nehal snapped sharply, "I don't give a damn what my husband approves of, and *you* should learn to keep your opinions to yourself." She had had just about enough of Wael Helmy.

In the shocked silence that followed, Yusry cleared his throat. "Perhaps we ought to start making our way back inside?" With a spiteful glance at Wael, Nehal turned pointedly to Malak and extended her hand. "It was wonderful to meet you at last. I hope we can find time to speak again soon."

Wael bristled, then turned and marched off.

Malak's dark eyes sparkled. She smiled at Nehal like they were sharing a private joke. "Oh, no doubt we will." She leaned in closer to kiss Nehal on both cheeks, bringing with her a whiff of orange blossom. In a low voice, Malak whispered, "I hope you survive the rest of the show." Her warm breath tickled Nehal's earlobe, making her shiver. Nehal watched her walk away.

Yusry guided Nehal back into the Opera House with a gentle hand on the small of her back. "Wael is set in his ways. Older people often are."

Nehal scoffed. "So he doesn't like weavers *or* women?"

Yusry grimaced. "I suppose not."

"Is the second half as long as the first?" asked Nehal abruptly.

Yusry laughed. "You're not enjoying it, are you?"

Nehal paused; Yusry had been nothing but kind and she had no wish to hurt his feelings, but he seemed to catch on to her meaning despite her silence. He waved her discomfort away. "It's quite all right; it's certainly not a universal taste. Your husband seems to be enjoying himself at least."

"Oh yes, this is just to *his* taste."

"Well," said Yusry. "Think of this: all those feats of weaving we're witnessing on the stage? You'll soon surpass them at the Academy."

And, amazingly, that single thought helped her survive the rest of the show.

That, and the memory of Malak's breath on her ear.

12

NEHAL

THE ALAMAXA ACADEMY OF THE WEAVING ARTS WAS BUILT on an island in the middle of the River Izdihar. Nehal had known this, yet she was still astonished at the sight of it.

It was a collection of old, crumbling buildings, made of dusty limestone that looked like it needed a good shine. It was massive but nondescript, generally rectangular in shape; what distinguished it was how *tall* some of the buildings rose, so that they were visible even before Nehal reached the river.

Nehal's palanquin deposited her on the banks of the River Iz-dihar with very little; she had brought few personal belongings, as the Academy required and provided a uniform, to Nehal's delight. It consisted of simple cotton trousers and a short tunic, along with an optional veil for those who wanted to cover their hair. As far as Nehal could tell, it was identical to the male students' uniform, even down to the veil, which some of the male students used to wrap their hair up into a turban.

A felucca bobbed peacefully on the river, waiting to sail students to the Academy. Back before the war, there had been a bridge con-necting the island to the rest of the city, but it had long since fallen apart, and since the school was not in operation, no one had seen fit to rebuild it. Nehal presented her papers and stepped onto the swaying boat. The River Izdihar still didn't compare to the ocean, in Nehal's opinion—particularly here in central Alamaxa, where it was turbid and somewhat pungent—but it was still an open expanse of water, and Nehal delighted in it.

There was only one other passenger on the boat: a woman about Nehal's age, with the very dark skin of Ramsawis from farther south. A veil was draped so loosely on her head she may as well not have been wearing it at all; her dark hair was woven into multiple braids that grazed her shoulders and were threaded with golden beads. She nodded politely at Nehal, who sat directly across from her.

Nehal held out her palm. "Nehal Darweesh."

The other woman's wrist was laden with a column of golden bracelets that jangled when she took Nehal's hand in her own. "Shaimaa Basyouni."

A scion of House Basyouni. Nehal shouldn't have been surprised; with tuition what it was, most of her female classmates would probably be women from noble Houses or wealthy merchant families.

"So neither of us are natives of Alamaxa." Shaimaa cocked her head. "Have you lived in the city long?"

"Only about a fortnight. And you?"

Shaimaa looked toward the city around them. "It's my first time. It's quite . . . hectic. And lacking an ocean."

House Basyouni's holdings sat on the Vermillion Sea, just as the Darweesh estates faced the White Middle Sea. "I completely understand— Oh!" She was hit by a sudden realization. "You're a waterweaver, then, right? So am I!"

Shaimaa's polite expression fell into a wide smile, showing off a gap between her two front teeth. "That's right!" she said.

Before Nehal could excitedly tell her that she'd never met a fellow waterweaver before, the felucca swayed, and two more passengers came aboard.

They were both men, though the first was more of a boy, likely in his teens, short and skinny, with a full round face, protruding ears, and golden-pale skin. But his most distinctive feature was that he was

entirely bald. The second was older and broad-shouldered, with a clas-
sically handsome face and tight black curls. His pale forehead crinkled
in a disapproving frown when he looked at Nehal and Shaimaa.

"You should wear your veils more properly" was the first thing
he said.

"You should fuck off," replied Nehal easily.

Shaimaa covered her mouth but could not quite hide her snort
of laughter.

The man's eyes widened so much his expression was comical.
His mouth flopped uselessly, like a fish on land, until the bald boy
next to him clapped him on the back with a huge smile, causing him
to nearly stumble.

"Ha, that's hilarious!" He turned his wide grin onto Nehal. "Hi!
I'm Fikry! My friend here is Waseem. What's your name?"

Nehal smiled wryly. "Nehal. This is Shaimaa." Since the boy
hadn't bothered with surnames, neither did she. "New weaving students too?"

"Windweaver here!" said Fikry eagerly. "Waseem is a waterweaver. We rode down together from Tranta."

Tranta was a small farming town sitting squarely in the center of
the Izdihar Delta. So none of them were native Alamaxans.

"You shouldn't speak so rudely," said Waseem, having finally
recovered enough to speak.

"It's rude to order people around, and yet you keep doing it,"
Nehal retorted.

"Ha! Classic!" Fikry's grin never left his face. "Look at you two,
bantering already."

Shaimaa looked at Fikry with a mixture of bewilderment and
consternation, like he was a bizarre species she'd never seen before.
Nehal only laughed; she decided she liked Fikry very much.

THE ENTRANCE TO the Academy was a massive limestone wall,
embedded with giant statues of the Tetrad, their fists crossed over

their chests, standing vigil on either side of the relatively small square archway that led into a courtyard filled with sand. Nehal and the others followed Ihsan, a man well into his late years, whom Nehal was surprised to learn was not an instructor, but a fellow student. She supposed most of the students would be older; the Academy had opened itself up to adults only and hadn't put a cap on age. Nehal understood; even if she'd been as old as her grandmother, she would still have wanted to attend.

On all sides of the courtyard, tightly enclosing it, were square limestone buildings with tiny square windows. On the other side of the courtyard was another arched gate; Ihsan led them through this to reveal another sanded courtyard, this one much larger, stretching the length of the island. Though it was surrounded by tall buildings on three sides, its fourth side was open to the River Izdihar. With the three high walls and the rushing of the river, the school felt entirely shielded from Alamaxa, like it was removed from the city entirely, even though the city lay on either side of them if they stepped outside the walls.

They didn't linger in the courtyard; Ihsan took them into one of the buildings, which was surprisingly chilly compared to the stifling heat outside. Soon enough Nehal was grateful for the drop in temperature; the room Ihsan took them to was full of people, all chattering away. Nehal swept her gaze across the room; there were about fifty others. The youngest students looked to be around Fikry's age—older teens—and most were around Nehal's age, in their early or mid-twenties, but there was a surprising number of much older students, like Ihsan, as well. Thus far, Nehal and Shaimaa were the only women in the room. Nehal wondered how large the first female cohort would be. Everyone was due to arrive before sunset, so she wouldn't have long to wait before she found out.

She sat with Shaimaa and Fikry, with Waseem lingering on the outskirts of their little group. Shaimaa was studiously ignoring the occasional leers and winks from some of the male students, but Nehal scowled at several who had the temerity to make lewd gestures.

Her hand drifted toward the gourd of water she kept at her waist, and she cast out her awareness for the River Izdihar to reassure herself of its presence.

As sunset approached, more students arrived, until their number totaled only a little less than one hundred. Nehal counted the arrival of four more women, all of whom sat within close proximity to Shaimaa and Nehal, and one of these women, a young girl, rushed toward Nehal the moment she saw her. She was dressed somewhat old-fashioned, most of her hair wrapped in a veil tied at the base of her neck, except for a cloud of shorn curls floating above her thick eyebrows.

"Lady Nehal, yes? I recognize you from the papers!" The girl smiled excitedly, displaying two prominent front teeth that made her look even more youthful. "I was so excited when my brother said you'd be here; he told me to introduce myself so here I am!"

Nehal blinked, taking a moment to absorb all this, for the girl spoke very fast. Now that she had a moment to look at her, she could see the resemblance to Yusry: the sharp jawline, the high cheekbones, the sharp, regal nose. But where Yusry's features made him handsome, on his younger sister they were merely striking. Looks aside, Nehal felt a kinship with her immediately, and smiled back.

"It's lovely to meet you, Yusry's sister," said Nehal. "Do you want to give me your name?" She recalled vaguely that Yusry had told her, but she'd completely forgotten.

"Oh!" the girl giggled sheepishly. "Of course, yes, I'm Mahitab. Did my brother tell you I'm a sandweaver?"

"He did."

When Mahitab took a seat beside Nehal, Fikry waved with a grin. "I'm Fikry. So what's the difference between a sandweaver and an earthweaver, anyhow? I never understood that."

"There's different elemental iterations," Shaimaa intoned solemnly. "Earthweaving encompasses sandweaving, as well as things like crystalweaving, just like waterweaving includes iceweaving or even steamweaving."

Waseem looked confused. "Wouldn't steam fall under wind-weaving? It's air, isn't it?"

Shaimaa looked thoughtful. "I think it has to do with the composition of the substance. Technically, steam is made of water droplets, whereas air isn't. Though I wonder if the humidity content would make a difference . . ." She trailed off, staring into space, while Waseem blinked at her.

"Well, I've only ever been able to manipulate sand!" Mahitab piped up. "Though maybe that'll change here. I'm so excited to see what they have in store for us!"

As though Mahitab had been overheard, a line of people marched into the room, shutting the doors behind them and plunging the students into momentary silence. The seven of them marched to the dais at the head of the room and took their seats on the rickety wooden chairs that had been procured for them, so they sat looking down on the attendees, who stared intently at them. It was clear they weren't all Ramsawi.

They conferred with one another for a moment, murmuring silently among themselves, until one man stood and held up his hands for complete silence. Though he was dressed in a traditional Ramsawi galabiya and turban, his features were markedly foreign, and his words slightly accented.

"Welcome, new students, and to those of you returning, welcome back." He let his hands come together to sit on his belly. "My name is Yuri Saroukan. You may call me Mister Yuri. I am the acting headmaster of the Academy. I am a weaver of wind, and I will be teaching you the fundamentals of weaving.

"Beside me are my fellow teachers, who will be instructing you not only on the principles of your specific elements, but in combat and the history of our particular . . . talents." The others beside him nodded to the crowd as he introduced them one by one.

Yuri continued, "Of course, this year also marks our first class of female students." Though Yuri studiously avoided looking at Nehal and the other women, the other students' gazes wandered over to them. Mister Yuri, however, kept his gaze directed toward the center of the room, where the male students clustered.

"I am only going to say this once," said Yuri sternly. "You are all adults. I expect behavior befitting of adults, not adolescents. I will not tolerate juvenile antics. We are all of us weavers. Now—" He raised a hand toward the back of the room, where a line of servants was setting up platters of food. "In a moment, you'll be free to enjoy dinner, and then will be taken to your rooms to settle in. Classes begin tomorrow at sunrise. You should all have received your schedules."

Nods around the room confirmed this.

"Excellent. Finally, I would like to remind you—almost all of you are here at the expense of the Ramsawi government, who could only sponsor a limited number of you. Therefore, slacking will not be tolerated. You are working to become soldiers, with soldiers' discipline. You will behave appropriately, both in and outside the Academy, or your spot will be given to someone more worthy. That goes for you who *did* pay your own tuition, as well," he noted, finally looking at the clustered group of women.

Nehal couldn't imagine wasting even a moment of this opportunity.

After a dinner of flatbread and lentil soup—much simpler fare than Nehal was accustomed to—Nehal and the other five female students were led to their sleeping quarters by the only female teacher at the Academy. She was a stout Ramsawi woman of late years, named Sariyya Magdy, and she was the earthweaving instructor. According to the whispers of the other girls, Sariyya had been raised abroad in her youth.

They were in a building entirely separate from the men, and each woman received her own room, which Nehal suspected was part of what their exorbitant tuition paid for, though her room was very sparsely furnished for the amount of money she had handed over: a padded mat to sleep on, a low table, and a small dresser for clothing. A small square window looked out onto the courtyard.

And that was it.

With a sigh, Nehal stripped out of her outer robe, tossed her veil aside, and made her way to the bath chamber all the women would be sharing.

It seemed the others were all of the same mind, for Nehal found them all gathering in the bath chamber in various states of undress. One of them, a fireweaver, was lighting the braziers in the corners of the room.

Nehal spotted Shaimaa, who was peering at the bath basins with distinct distaste. When Nehal walked up to her, she sighed heavily. "You'd think with the money we've given them, they'd have at least updated the bath chambers."

Nehal had to agree; the room was a dismal sight, and a far cry from the opulence she was used to.

"They *have* updated it," said one of the other women blandly. "There's running water." A slightly older woman with wispy straight brown hair trimmed at her chin, she introduced herself as Dawlat Morsi, a windweaver.

From across the room, Mahitab, dressed only in a loincloth wrapped around her middle, waved and came over to join them. Free of its veil, her hair revealed itself to be a dense thicket of curls that fell nearly to her waist. "I'm not really sure how to start." She laughed nervously. "Usually a servant prepares my bath for me . . ."

"Yes, how have they not provided us with *any* servants?" Another woman with large barrel curls sauntered over, followed by the fireweaver who had taken it upon herself to light the braziers. "Do they really expect us to do all this ourselves? With what we're paying them?"

The fireweaver shrugged. "They probably want to treat us the same as the men."

"The *men* have paid nothing," said the first woman hotly. "Of course we get all the disadvantages and none of the advantages! How equitable! Besides, we have no way of knowing what *their* accommodations look like!"

Despite the truth of those statements, servants didn't magically appear. So the six of them, working together, were soon able to properly heat the chamber and get the basin faucets working. They even managed to fill the central bathing pool, though they only dipped their feet in the water as they chatted.

The pale, barrel-curled girl introduced herself as Carolinna Farino; her family owned half the Talyani Quarter in Alamaxa, and she was another fireweaver. Carolinna, Nehal thought wryly, must surely have been one of Lorenzo's contenders as a bride for Nico. She wondered if Carolinna and Nico knew one another; the Talyani population in Alamaxa was not large, especially as most refugees had intermingled with the Ramsawi population and become, for all intents and purposes, Ramsawi themselves.

The other fireweaver's name was Zanuba Gaafar, of Gaafar Holdings, the foremost tailoring company in Alamaxa; the very clothes Nehal was wearing were probably produced by this girl's family. As it was, Nehal and Shaimaa were the only ones belonging to Houses; Mahitab, though cousins with Nagat Shawkat, was technically a Sarhan, and so was not considered part of House Shawkat. Dawlat, who was rather reserved, revealed herself to be the wealthy widow of a date merchant who had circumvented the law to leave all of his wealth to Dawlat instead of his brothers, to whom much of the fortune would have otherwise gone.

"And are you all intent on joining the Izdihar Division?" Nehal asked.

Zanuba shook her head vigorously. "All I want is to learn not to burn things down."

"I'm too old for the army," said Dawlat.

"I have no interest in war," said Carolinna distastefully.

Shaimaa shrugged. "Realistically, I don't know if any of us are suited for army life. We could barely bathe ourselves, after all."

"We can learn," countered Nehal. "That's what we're here to do, after all."

"I don't know if my brother would let me join," said Mahitab, her eyes wide.

"You should do what you want," said Nehal, feeling only a small twinge of guilt at the thought of encouraging Yusry's little sister to join the army. "It's your life."

Mahitab smiled sheepishly. "Yes, but it's Yusry who has to sign the papers to let me join. Or my future husband, I suppose."

At this all the other women muttered under their breaths.

"Ridiculous," said Carolinna. "Malak has the right of it, you know."

"Do you know her?" asked Nehal, startled, but eager to hear more of Malak.

"I've been part of the Daughters of Izdihar since it began," replied Carolinna proudly. "And Zanuba too. I know it's suffrage all the papers talk about, but Malak is pushing for other reforms too, chief of which is allowing women to be our own guardians, so we can sign our own damn papers."

"Did you know the men here don't have a choice in the matter?" said Shaimaa suddenly. "They attend the Academy for free, yes, but then in exchange they *have* to enroll in the army, whether they want to or not. So they're constrained too, in a way."

"Our situations are not even remotely similar," said Nehal, just as Carolinna said, "Don't even try to compare our situations."

Shaimaa shrugged, unfazed. "Oh, I'm not saying our situations are the same, just that we share one particular aspect of one particular situation."

Carolinna rolled her eyes but said nothing.

"That's very pedantic, Shaimaa," said Nehal, but she grinned widely to show she was only teasing.

Shaimaa, Mahitab, Carolinna, Zanuba, and Dawlat: here were five other women, five other weavers just like her, with the same grievances and ambitions. For the first time in her life, Nehal felt an acute sense of belonging, like a puzzle piece finally fitted into its rightful place. She wondered if it was like this among the Daughters of Izdihar, when they held their clandestine meetings and their very public rallies—if part of why they fought so hard was not just to win their freedoms, but because they valued the camaraderie that came from shared goals.

Nehal had not thought of suffrage often, but she'd thought of her unequal station in Ramsawa, the ugly leers she got just walking down a street, her inability to make any significant decision without the approval of her father or husband. If the Daughters of Izdihar were working to upend all that, shouldn't Nehal do her best to help them?

"Carolinna," said Nehal. "How *does* one join the Daughters of Izdihar?"

13

GIORGINA

GIORGINA LEANED AGAINST THE BOOKSHOP COUNTER, PEN in hand, the ink drying on a newly completed sentence. She was nearly done now. Just another few sentences to close up the piece, and she would be ready to hand it over to Labiba, who would deliver it to Malak, where it would be printed in *The Vanguard,* the Daughters of Izdihar magazine, under the initials G.S.

The anonymity irked Giorgina only a little. In fact, she often reveled in the safety of it; any complaints about her writing were directed at Malak, who was surely far better equipped to handle them. In any case, she, Giorgina, knew that her words were being read by the public, affecting opinions and prompting conversations, and for now, that was enough.

She was pondering how to begin her final paragraph when the door to the bookshop creaked open. Giorgina set down her pen and looked up with a smile, ready to greet a customer, but stiffened when she saw it was Nico who had walked in.

He paused at the threshold uncertainly, and Giorgina was instantly transported to the first time she had met him, the first time he had wandered into the bookshop to ask if they had any biographies of Ratib Galal, the last true king of Ramsawa. Giorgina had directed him to their selection of biographies, which he perused for nearly an hour before coming up to the counter with three books that had nothing at all to do with Ratib Galal, but one of which Giorgina had herself recently read, which she told Nico. Two days later he was back in the shop, having read the book, and he invited her to tea.

It was difficult to believe it had been a year since that day. All that had happened between her and Nico, and now? Now he was married, and lost to her in every way that mattered, yet here he was, still.

Still.

"What are you doing here?" Giorgina was proud of her steady and neutral tone.

Nico approached the desk. Behind his spectacles his clear blue eyes were a little glassy, as though he hadn't slept. Giorgina was struck with a memory from a few months ago, of Nico excitedly telling her how he had stayed up all night to finish a particular book. The memory was a blow to her chest; she clenched her fists and maintained her resolve when Nico looked at her intently, sending shivers up her spine.

"Please," Nico begged. "Just give me a few minutes to talk."

Giorgina wanted to lean into him, to have him wrap her in his arms, to kiss him and run her hands through his soft hair. Instead, she kept her gaze firmly averted, blinking rapidly to avoid tears.

"There's nothing left to discuss," said Giorgina stiffly.

"I brought something to show you." He dug into his satchel and pulled out a wrapped parcel. Carefully, he placed it on the desk that served as a buffer between them and unrolled the wrapping to reveal a thin stack of papers that looked to be decades old. It was brittle and brown at the corners, the writing faded, but still legible. Nico gently pushed the papers toward Giorgina. It was a letter, dated about two hundred years ago, and addressed to, "My dear Rahma."

"Look at the sender," said Nico.

Giorgina's eyes trailed to the bottom of the letter. She read the name, then did a double take. She looked up at Nico, her eyes wide;

his lips were curved into an expectant smile. She looked down again at the letter. In the corner, a neat scrawl had signed "Edua."

Giorgina's fingers hovered over the paper, wanting to touch it, to read it, to absorb everything it had to offer her, but afraid of damaging it. She looked back up at Nico.

"Is this real?" she asked, voice nearly a whisper.

Nico nodded, smiling. "An acquaintance of mine discovered it in an abandoned trunk of belongings in Banha, when they were clearing old homes for a new development project."

"R. Amir," said Giorgina, the realization coming to her suddenly.

Nico let out a delighted laugh. "That was my first thought!"

Giorgina felt dazed, like a historian who had just made a life-altering discovery. The only known portrait that existed of Edua Badawi, which Nico had taken her to see at the National Museum, was signed by an R. Amir. No one had ever been able to discern the artist's identity, but the first initial matched the name on these letters.

"Have you read them?" asked Giorgina.

Nico nodded. "Not yet . . . I thought maybe we could read them together."

Giorgina looked away. She wanted nothing more than to read every sentence of every letter and to sit with Nico to discuss all the particularities. So many of their afternoons together had been spent like this; poring over the pages of a book, attacking some obscure research project no one else would have found even slightly interesting, debating the merits of different philosophies. His studiousness was one of the reasons she had fallen in love with him.

Now he was a married man, and to be with him in any way was a risk Giorgina could not take.

He had brought the letters to cajole her, knowing she would not be able to resist such a discovery. Somehow, that hurt even more. She curled her outstretched fingers into tight fists.

"I hope you give these to the National Archives," she said, in what she hoped was a neutral tone. "They belong there, where anyone can access them."

She avoided looking at Nico, and the disappointment sure to be on his face.

"Don't you want to read them?" The defeat in his voice nearly cracked Giorgina's armor, but she forced herself to meet his eyes with a blank expression. She could feel the tension coiled in him, could see the shape of unspoken words in his eyes.

"Of course I do. But that's not the point, is it?"

"What do you mean?"

Giorgina looked at him pointedly. "What is it you really came here to say?"

"That . . . that we can go back to the way things were before." Nico spoke in a rush, as though he feared Giorgina would not let him finish. "You don't have to come live with me, or be a concubine if you don't want to, but—we can keep meeting, can't we? I—I miss you."

Giorgina sighed at his willful naïveté. "You're married. The whole city *knows* you're married. You know what people would say."

"We've been careful before—"

"It's different now," interrupted Giorgina. "How can you not see that? Before, you were a bachelor, and nobody cared enough to pay attention to the girls on your arm. Now you're married, and to one of the most famous women in the country." She felt a curl of irritation at having to explain this to Nico, but wasn't his idealism part of why she loved him?

"Perhaps . . . perhaps you could come to my home. Not to live," he amended hurriedly. "But for . . . social visits. If people ask you could say you're visiting Nehal, that you're friends. She wouldn't mind, I know she wouldn't."

Giorgina very much doubted that. Perhaps Nehal Darweesh had truly not wanted this marriage, but once she realized there was no escape from it, it was unlikely she would be content to share her husband, not when she too had a reputation to uphold. And where would Giorgina be then, cast off and ruined?

"To what end?" Giorgina asked. "I'd still be nothing more than a concubine, in everything but name. I want a family, Nico. Children."

"I want that too," Nico whispered. "With *you*."

"How are we to have that?" Desperation clawed at Giorgina's voice as she fought to make him understand. "Shall I have illegitimate children? Be disowned by my family? Shunned by everyone I know?"

"I'll take care of you." Nico reached for her hand again. "You wouldn't have to worry. I would find you somewhere to live, and make sure you have money—"

Giorgina wrenched her hand out of his grasp. "You are defining a *concubine*, Nico. We're going in circles." She forced herself to look at him as tears burned her eyes. "And even if you were free to marry me, your father would still have the power to ruin me. There's no solution here. Stop trying to find one." She brushed her tears aside. "You're making this so much harder than it already is. Please leave. *Please*."

Then Giorgina turned her back to him. Slowly, she heard him gather up the letters he had been so excited to show her. She heard him shuffle toward the doorway, felt him pause as he pulled the door open. She wanted to turn around and tell him she had changed her mind, to come back, to stay with her for as long as possible, but of course she did nothing of the sort. She remained still until she heard the unmistakable click of the door swinging shut.

GIORGINA WALKED HOME in a daze, her nerves frayed from her brief conversation with Nico. Her stomach hurt terribly. She longed for a warm cup of anise tea and the quiet of solitude. But when she entered her home, solitude was nowhere to be found.

In the parlor, her parents were sitting with a strange man. Giorgina examined him, wondering if he was a friend of her father's with whom she was unfamiliar. He looked to be about Ehab's age, though he carried his years far better than Giorgina's father. He was admittedly a handsome man, eyes heavy-lidded and thickly lashed, dark beard neatly trimmed. When Giorgina entered, he stood; he was a head taller than her, just like Nico, but lanky where Nico was stout. He was as well-dressed as Nico too, his galabiya of high-quality cotton that matched his green eyes, his waist-scarf pale ivory silk. There was something vaguely familiar about him, but Giorgina could not quite place him.

"There she is!" said Ehab, smiling. "Come here, habibti."

Warily, Giorgina approached. She never knew what to expect when her father was in such a pleasant mood. Giorgina sat on a cushion beside her mother, who said nothing, but smiled in Giorgina's direction.

"She's always working so hard," Ehab was saying.

"I wouldn't expect her to work, of course," said the stranger.

Giorgina maintained a polite expression, but her skin prickled with fear. Though her heart raced, Giorgina's voice was calm when she said, "Baba, I'm sorry, I don't understand." And though it was the last thing she felt like doing, Giorgina smiled demurely.

The stranger leaned forward, one hand on his chest. "Forgive me, Miss Giorgina. Allow me to introduce myself. My name is Zakariyya Amin. We met at your bookshop some time ago? You helped me find a very readable book about steel production?"

The memory struck Giorgina like a sandstorm. Weeks ago, Zakariyya Amin had wandered into the bookshop looking for a particularly dense tome on the emerging steel industry in Ramsawa. After chatting with him for a few moments, Giorgina had recommended an alternate book more suitable to his needs. He had been pleasant enough and Giorgina had thought nothing of the encounter at the time.

And now he was in her home.

"I—of course, Mister Zakariyya, I remember." Giorgina forced a smile. She had a terrible feeling she knew exactly where this conversation was leading.

Zakariyya smiled kindly. "Your recommendation was spot-on."

"I'm glad."

He operated some kind of steel factory, Giorgina recalled. Something to do with selling railway tracks.

"Well." Zakariyya slapped his knees. "I should be off, then, and we'll be in touch?"

"Of course!" her father said.

The men got to their feet, so Giorgina and her mother followed suit, hanging back a respectful distance and nodding politely at Zakariyya. Giorgina stood immobile while her father chatted for another few moments with Zakariyya at the door. She could hardly make out the words. Once the door had shut behind him, she sank to the floor.

"Who would have thought?" said Ehab.

Hala placed a hand over her mouth and ululated, the piercing cry of joy filling Giorgina with a leaden weight.

"Hush, woman, he'll hear!" Ehab admonished, but he was still smiling. "Giorgina, love of my heart! I never dreamed you would find someone so suitable, but I'm not surprised. You're the prettiest *and* smartest of your sisters."

Giorgina cleared her throat. "I don't—I don't understand."

Hala put an arm around her daughter's shoulders. "What don't you understand about a handsome man showing up at our home?"

"No, I understand that. Just how did he—why—why does he want to marry me?"

Ehab sat down in front of his wife and daughter. He took Giorgina's hand in both of his own. "Well, he saw you in that bookshop! He said you caught his eye, that you seemed like a decent young girl, so he asked about you, and well, your reputation spoke for itself, of course."

It took all of Giorgina's willpower not to laugh hysterically at that.

"He's . . . he's much older," said Giorgina slowly. "Why hasn't he married yet?"

"Well, he's a businessman, habibti," Hala replied softly. "He's been focused on building himself up from scratch."

"That's the best part," interrupted Ehab. "He owns a steel company. He has his own house! You're going to be our saving grace!"

Giorgina swallowed again, the lump in her throat refusing to subside. "Baba, can I . . . can I have some time to think about this?"

Ehab's grip on Giorgina's hand tightened. "What is there to think about? He's a decent man, and rich, and he wants to marry you. There's *nothing* to think about."

Certainly not for you, Giorgina thought.

Exhaustion tugged on Giorgina's limbs, turning her bones into lead. Ehab left without another word. Hala kissed Giorgina on the cheek and followed to prepare dinner. Giorgina sat alone in the parlor, staring at her clenched hands, which had gone white.

Was this not why Giorgina worked so hard to maintain a sparkling reputation? To be deemed faultless and respectable? Wouldn't a man like Zakariyya, with his wealth, grant Giorgina a simulacrum of what she might have had with Nico?

But he was so much older than she was, as old as her father. And he did not want her to work—he had been careful in his phrasing, allowing his demand to be parsed as a generous gift. It was clear from his firm tone, though, that he would not *allow* Giorgina to be employed. He was handsome and rich, yes. But he would not have Nico's wit, or his progressiveness of thought. He would not read Giorgina poetry in Classical Ramsawi, or stay up all night parsing through historical tomes.

He might desire her, but he wouldn't love her. And she didn't love him, couldn't love him, the way she loved Nico.

With Zakariyya, Giorgina would not be a partner or a companion; she would simply be a wife. Perhaps she would not be miserable, but she would not be happy, satisfied, fulfilled. What would Zakirayya think of her involvement with the Daughters of Izdihar?

Would she have to hide that part of her life from him? Or would he want to be aware of her every move, so that she might be forced to give up this community of women that gave her some semblance of purpose?

Which would be worse? To live as a fallen woman, as Nico's concubine, shunned by all polite society? Or to be trapped in an unhappy marriage with a man she did not love, stripped of all she held dear?

It was suffocating that those were her only two options.

Giorgina's heart thudded painfully. Her tongue felt like an enlarged cotton ball. She knew her thoughts were racing beyond her control, that she needed to reach inside herself and *stop them,* but as she shut her eyes all she could detect was a tremble. Was it Giorgina who was shaking? Or, dear holy Tetrad, was she causing the building to shake?

Desperately, Giorgina knelt and clawed aside the threadbare rug so she could place her forehead against the cold stone floor. She took deep, slow breaths, counted each inhale, each exhale. She made her palms flat, laid them against the cold, hard floor and let the chill soak into her palms, into her pores.

Slowly, the shaking subsided.

Giorgina heard no screams or shouts, no footsteps running back and forth, so it must have been her own body shaking, not the building. Grateful for that small mercy, Giorgina sat up, her breathing far steadier now. She pushed all thoughts of Zakariyya into a small, dark corner of her mind. She could not think of him. She could think of hardly anything at all.

14

NEHAL

NEHAL'S FIRST WEEK AT THE ACADEMY WAS A GRUELING exercise in humility.

They began their days—every single damn day—at sunrise with combat and strength training. Their instructor, a formidable, mustachioed Ramsawi man by the name of Murtada, started them off running laps around the courtyard. Nehal had never run in her life, since she'd never been *chased,* and so after a single lap around the small courtyard she was bent over her knees, wheezing. She wasn't the only one, though: all the other women struggled, and most of the men as well. Fikry was the only one cheerfully running, as though he weighed nothing at all. At least Murtada had made it very clear, in a tone that bespoke no argument, that the men were to keep their eyes on the ground and not on their female classmates.

After running came strength training.

"What is the point of being a weaver if we still have to do the same grunt work as everyone else?" Waseem muttered loudly.

Murtada, hearing this, emphasized the importance of building muscle.

"Weaving may be magic, but there is a science to it." He marched with his hands clasped behind his back, impassively observing them struggling with push-ups. "The weight you can manipulate is directly proportional to your strength. If you have no muscle mass, not only will you be unable to manipulate weightier amounts of your element, but you'll tire easily."

"Fire has no weight," protested Waseem. "Neither does air."

"It's not about *literal* weight, dolt," Murtada shot back. "You're still manipulating mass, aren't you?"

Waseem blushed and looked away.

"The stronger you are, the stronger your weaving will be," continued Murtada.

Nehal, whose biceps ached and whose palms smarted from the hot sand, gritted her teeth and continued her exercises.

They were allowed a chance to rest their bodies after combat; their next class was Fundamentals of Weaving, taught by Mister Yuri, the Karatzian. This class was all about the science of weaving that Murtada had touched upon, and so Yuri started them off by re-iterating what Murtada had said about their weaving being reflected by their own physical strength.

"We are not gods, incapable of tiring," said Yuri in his smooth, accented voice. "We are gifted by the Tetrad, but we are not they. We are human and have mortal bodies. Weaving takes energy. You have noticed that when you weave for long periods, your muscles tire? This is why you must train with Murtada and grow strong, build your strength and stamina. Weaving is a muscle you must strengthen. And yet, this is not a perfect metaphor." Here he took a pause and looked imperiously at them to ensure they were paying close attention. "A neglected muscle atrophies, leaving it powerless. Neglected weaving means your power will run rampant at random, prey to your emotions. In other words, it is your *control* over your weaving that is the muscle, not your weaving ability itself."

With that, he dove into the complex relationship between weaving and the musculoskeletal system, technicalities that left Nehal struggling to concentrate.

Their next class separated Nehal from all but Shaimaa and Waseem, as they were to attend their first Principles of Waterweaving session, the class for which Nehal was most excited. Their instructor was a man with sleek dark hair who looked vaguely foreign but held the very Ramsawi name of Nagi; he might have been of mixed ancestry, which made sense: most of their instructors were either foreign or foreign-born, to have received weaving training sufficient enough to be instructors.

Nehal and Shaimaa were the only women in their class of twenty waterweavers, most of whom were students in their second or third year. Unlike Murtada, Nagi had not given them any particular warning as he led them to the larger courtyard and toward the banks of the River Izdihar, so some of the male students wasted no time in antagonizing Nehal and Shaimaa.

One sallow-faced man about Nehal's age made lewd kissing noises at her back. She grit her teeth and ignored him, but when his hand brushed her backside, she turned and punched him in the face.

It wasn't a particularly powerful punch. Nehal, for all her temper, had never truly punched anyone before, scrambling fights with her cousins notwithstanding. She seemed to have made the man angry more than anything else; he snarled and made to rush at her. Nehal planted her feet, prepared to stand her ground, when suddenly a rushing wave of water surged between them and almost as quickly solidified into an icy wall.

Nehal gaped at this feat; she had never in her life been able to manipulate a single shard of ice, let alone transform an entire wall of water into a sheaf of shiny, glittering ice.

Nagi approached them, his dark eyes glittering dangerously. "What is going on here?" he said with a scowl.

"He—" Nehal paused, suddenly unsure what to say.

"Talaat was being improper and disrespectful, sir," Waseem spoke up. "He was making lewd noises and inappropriate physical advances toward Nehal."

Nagi peered down at Talaat, who was doing his best to look unperturbed, and then at Nehal. "Is this true?"

Nehal nodded.

Nagi sighed. "Do you remember being told to behave like the adults you are? I understand some of you may be . . . flustered by the presence of women among us, but I still expect you to behave like gentlemen, or I'll have you scrubbing the school's bath chambers all night, *without weaving*. I will not have you waste my time. Am I understood?"

Talaat nodded tightly. When Nagi turned his back, Talaat gave Nehal a scowl, like she was something on the bottom of his shoe. She turned her back on him. Waseem jogged to catch up with her and Shaimaa.

"Are you all right?" he asked. "That must have been shocking—"

Nehal waved him off. "Nothing I haven't seen before."

"Oh—oh?" Waseem blinked. "This . . . happens often?"

Nehal and Shaimaa stared at him like he was a complete idiot, which he likely was, if he had just asked something like that. He had the grace to blush and look away. Nehal shook her head. He really was very pretty; this close, she noticed he had eyes the turbulent gray of storm clouds, and his general mien was quite delicate. Either he was a fool, or he was the most naïve person she had ever met. She hoped it was the latter. At the very least, he seemed well-intentioned.

Nagi split them up into two groups; the second- and third-year students were to spar against one another. Nehal struggled to keep her eyes off these dueling pairs as Nagi corralled her and the five other first-year students farther away. He lined them up along the banks of the river and gestured to the current.

"We'll start small," said Nagi. "Pull up some water and hold it."

This was second nature. This was simple enough. Nehal planted her feet and raised both arms. She extended her consciousness until she was as aware of the Izdihar as she was of the blood pounding through her veins. She caught hold of it, and then, with a grunt of effort, she began to lift. The water rose at her command, trembling slightly as Nehal pulled it close to her.

The others did the same, though one boy at the end of the line stumbled a bit and dropped his hold, having to start over again.

"Good," said Nagi. "But how much control do you have over your element? I want you to circle it carefully around me, without ever touching me. One by one. Shaimaa, you first."

Shaimaa obliged, guiding the water into a slow dance around Nagi, who nodded approvingly.

"Nehal."

Nehal mimicked Shaimaa; the others followed suit.

"Good, good." Nagi rubbed his smooth chin. "We'll try something different, then. Turn around. See that target?" He pointed to a round target stuck in the ground some fifty steps away. "I want you to try and hit that. It's malleable, so it'll swing backward if you manage it. Nehal, you first."

Nehal turned toward the pole, drew her water back, and shot it forward as fast as she could. The water lost momentum, however, and by the time it reached the pole it only drenched it harmlessly.

She heard a snicker she was sure came from Talaat, and she clenched her fists.

"Any idea what Nehal's mistake was? Talaat, since you seemed so amused?"

Talaat said nothing, and Nehal smirked.

"Nehal tossed the water and let it act on its own, relying on its own momentum." Nagi moved his arms and pulled up a column of water, then aimed it at the target. "That can be useful sometimes, but it's best not to let go of your element. Hold on to it at all times. Maintain your connection. Maintain control, and you'll be stronger for it." With that, he stretched his hands forward, and kept them held up and taut as the water hit the target and swung it back.

"Try again, Nehal," said Nagi. "Remember, do not let go of the water."

Nehal tried once more, pulling up another column of water from the river. She took a deep breath to steady herself, then pushed, but she found that the farther she sent the water away, the weaker the connection was. She had always needed to be very near the sea to manipulate it and had usually practiced her weaving while in the ocean. Though she maintained her hold on the water she couldn't push it with the same force Nagi had used, and the water hit the target very gently, barely causing it to move at all.

But to her surprise, Nagi smiled approvingly. "Better." He addressed them all. "You work to build not only your physical strength, but your connection to your element. The more you practice, the more natural it will feel." He clapped his hands. "All right! Waseem, you next!"

Once they had all managed to hit the target with some amount of force, Nagi instructed them to continue doing this for the rest of the class, while he went to observe the other students. And so they practiced and practiced; by the end of the hour Nehal's arms were burning, but she had managed to strike the target so hard it swung halfway back, which was more than anyone else had been able to do. She was also very pleased that Talaat—who for all his arrogance was also a first-year—was struggling.

Nehal's final class of the day found her reunited with all of the other first-years. History and Geopolitics of Weaving seemed like the sort of course that would entice Nico, but Nehal didn't see the point of it. It was taught by the youngest member of the staff, a Ramsawi man named Akram, who was not himself a weaver, and was likely of an age with most of his students.

He smiled at them all as they took their seats, most of them dragging themselves forward weakly, exhausted from the day's efforts. Every part of Nehal ached; she was so tired her limbs felt like they were made of iron and she was being forced to drag them around. She collapsed on a cushion with Shaimaa on one side and Carolinna on the other. Both looked as exhausted as Nehal felt.

"I know most of you are probably thinking this class is pointless," said Akram, his smile still wide. "But don't think of it as an academic class, think of it as . . . storytelling. A casual chat to wind down an exhausting day." They all started to smile hesitantly, and then Akram said, "With the occasional assignment," and groans abounded.

"Well, this is still a school, isn't it? All right!" He rubbed his hands together and bounced on the balls of his feet, his bright green galabiya swinging back and forth. "Let's start big. What is the single most infamous weaving event in history?"

There was a moment of hesitation and exchanged glances, and then mutters of "the Talyani Disaster" and "Edua Badawi" filled the room.

"Yes, excellent! Edua Badawi, the engineer of the Talyani Disaster!" He spun as he talked. "And just who was Edua Badawi? What do we know of her?"

"She was a madwoman," said Carolinna.

"She was a soldier," said Shaimaa.

Akram cocked his head. "Yes, and yes. What else?"

"She controlled all four elements," said Nehal. "How could she have done that?"

"How indeed? Thoughts?"

"How is it even possible to weave so many elements?" asked Waseem, his brow furrowed. "Nobody can weave more than one, right?"

Akram nodded thoughtfully. "And why is that?"

Shaimaa said, "Weaving is thought to come from a connection with the Tetrad. The Order used to believe that weavers were blessed by the gods, and the idea was that a weaver could only be blessed by a single god."

"That's one school of thought, yes." Akram perched against the wall. "Any others?" When he was met with silence, he continued, "Well! In ancient times, some believed that weavers were something like godly reincarnations."

"That makes no sense," said Carolinna scornfully. "There are four gods and far more weavers."

"But the gods don't exist on the same plane we do," said Akram. "Nor in the same capacity. Would one single human be able to contain the entire essence of a god? Perhaps the Tetrad can spread themselves across vessels."

"But . . . but why?" asked a bewildered Waseem.

Akram shrugged. "Oh, who knows? This is all theory, after all. Nobody *really* knows where weavers come from. Interesting, though, huh?"

Nehal had to admit it *was* interesting. She had often wondered about this herself. Why was she alone in her family gifted with weaving? Was it random? Had Tefuret chosen to bless her? *Could* she be carrying a bit of the goddess's essence within her? It was a thrilling thought. And Edua . . . was she simply an anomaly, or was there a way for weavers to access other elements? For Nehal her connection to water had come naturally, but was there perhaps a way to force a connection to other elements?

She was about to ask when Akram abruptly switched topics. "Did you all know Mister Nagi is half-Karatzian? And that Miss Sariyya grew up in Loraq? Tell me, why did Karatzia and Loraq maintain their weaving academies when we didn't until very recently? Who has the answer?"

"Karatzia was untouched by the Talyani Disaster," intoned Shaimaa, as though reading from a textbook. "They were unaffected by the trauma and political repercussions of the war and so felt no pressure to shutter their academies and sideline weavers."

"Very good!" Akram nodded. "Whereas Ramsawa, Edua's birthplace, was horrified by her actions, as was our rather volatile neighbor Zirana, who lost a good chunk of their country to her destruction. Zirana was always iffy about weavers and was ready to declare its own war on Ramsawa, but they came to an agreement: weaving was too dangerous to be allowed to persist, and thus peace reigned. Ramsawa shuttered its academies and purged its armies of weavers—until now." He paused. "I don't see any of you taking notes. There *will* be exams, you know."

And he continued on in the same fashion, jumping from one topic to the next with seemingly very little organization. Nehal struggled to follow along, taking notes randomly and haphazardly, until her wrist ached. After dinner, she and the other women had barely enough energy to crawl into bed.

It went on like that for the rest of the week.

At the close of their fifth day at the Academy, Nehal was ready for the weekend and the three days of rest it would offer her. They were all given the choice to remain at the Academy during the weekend or to venture into the city, and Nehal opted for the latter, along with Carolinna and Zanuba, who had agreed to escort her to a meeting of the Daughters of Izdihar. Mahitab was going home as well, to see her brother, and invited Nehal to join them both for dinner, which Nehal heartily accepted. Shaimaa and Dawlat insisted it was too much work to travel all the way to Alamaxa and back for only a few days and decided to stay and rest.

Many of the other students were not from Alamaxa and had no choice but to stay, and many simply chose to stay with their fellow weavers, to practice or socialize free of scorn (or worse). So Nehal found herself returning to the city in a felucca with Carolinna, Zanuba, Mahitab, and four male students she'd never met, who studiously ignored the women.

Nehal, who had instructed Medhat meticulously on her schedule, found him and their palanquin waiting by the banks of the river. He waved vigorously once he saw her and eagerly helped her into the palanquin. She sat back as they moved forward, luxuriating in the quiet opulence of her cushioned palanquin, and mentally mapped the next three days: tomorrow, dinner with Mahitab and Yusry; the day after, joining the Daughters of Izdihar; and the day after that, preparing once again to return to the Academy.

For tonight, Nehal intended to do only two things: eat far too much good food and sleep well past sunrise.

15

NEHAL

WHEN NEHAL HAD ARRIVED HOME THE PREVIOUS NIGHT, Nico was not there to greet her. Not particularly fussed, she had Ridda prepare a decadent dinner, which she enjoyed in the courtyard, and then she luxuriated in her private baths. She ran into Nico the following morning, though he barely acknowledged her. He looked as though he'd been up for days: his eyes were red and his hair was disheveled, and he seemed to be nursing a headache. When Nehal informed him of their dinner arrangements at Yusry's that night, he frowned at her.

"You have to tell me these things beforehand," he protested.

"I *am* telling you beforehand," replied Nehal blandly. "You've got hours to prepare."

Yusry and Mahitab lived on the outskirts of Nico and Nehal's neighborhood, in one of the newer developments: a stately, two-story home bordered on either side by mimosa trees. Nehal and Nico exited the palanquin onto a neatly cobbled lane leading to the front door.

"You came!" Mahitab swung open the door, her cheeks bright with enthusiasm. "Do you know we've not had visitors over in nearly six months? I've had the servants prepare seafood; I figured you must love seafood, being from Ramina!"

Yusry emerged from behind Mahitab, grinning, and placed a hand on her shoulder. "Hush, Mahi, and let them get their bearings for a moment."

"Oh, oh, of course!" A slight blush sprung into Mahitab's cheeks. "Come in, then!"

"Shall we?" Nehal quirked an eyebrow and offered her arm to Nico. He hesitated, then took it and led her inside.

The main parlor was dominated by a blue-tiled fountain; the gently trilling water smelled faintly of jasmine, likely due to the numerous petals of said flower floating on its surface. Yusry and Mahitab led them to the interior parlor, which was warm and heavy with the smell of food.

A large tray balanced on a low table had been set out; the four of them gathered around it. Nico bent his legs and stretched them under the table, while Nehal settled onto her knees and slid her feet out to the side. Yusry and Mahitab sat across from them, smiling at their servants as they brought out dish after dish.

There was grilled fish, charred and crispy, decorated with slices of lemon. Grilled shrimp followed, along with a tower of fried squid, and steaming bowls of orange rice flavored with onions and paprika. An ice-laden pitcher of hibiscus tea was set in the center of the table, along with a stack of warm flatbread. Beside the hibiscus was a far darker bottle.

Nehal sat forward. "Is that sweet wine?" Wines and spirits, though not necessarily banned in Ramsawa, were heavily regulated and a chore to obtain. No one wanted drunk weavers.

"Would you care for some, Nehal?" asked Yusry.

"No, thank you." Nehal didn't particularly enjoy the dulling effect of alcohol or its rotten taste. Nico, on the other hand, held out his cup.

Yusry and Mahitab were connoisseurs of traditional Ramsawi hospitality. They piled Nico and Nehal's plates with food before touching their own and swore thrice on their father's soul not to eat a bite until Nico and Nehal had tasted their food. They obliged heartily. For a few moments the only sounds were the clatter of utensils against bowls and the gurgling of the enormous fountain. A pleasant breeze drifted in through the open shutters behind them, cooling the room from the hot fumes of the food.

After they finished their meal servants hovered with ewers of water and empty bowls for them to wash their hands in. Then there was tea and treats: semolina cake drenched in sweet syrup, baklava stuffed with walnuts, and zalabia, little fried balls of dough soaked in honey. By the end of the night Nehal was certain her stomach had expanded three sizes; she did not normally indulge so much, but there was something about the air of this place that encouraged her appetite.

"Was the opera quite lovely?" asked Mahitab. "I was supposed to go, but I fell ill. I was so upset!"

Here it was Nico who could not resist answering. "Incredible. It was the most majestic spectacle I've ever witnessed."

Nehal rolled her eyes, and Yusry laughed at her. "Not for Nehal it wasn't. But then, you were more taken by Malak Mamdouh, were you not?"

"I was not *taken* by her," countered Nehal. "I just admire what she's doing."

"She's such a fascinating woman," said Mahitab eagerly. "I've read all about her. Did you know she broke off her engagement to her cousin when she was only seventeen?"

Nehal leaned toward Mahitab, fascinated. "Is that so?"

Mahitab nodded, clearly pleased with Nehal's undivided attention. "Oh, yes. Her family had made the agreement even before she was born, and her cousin courted her and everything. Then she just called it off and went to university instead! The family was well known even then; it was such an enormous scandal!

"And she had the second highest state exam scores in the country, can you believe it? She was one of only three women in her cohort in Alamaxa University. She got engaged at university but called it off *again*."

"No wonder her name's dragged through the mud so often," commented Yusry. "Calling off two engagements? Unheard of."

"Her family disowned her, I think," said Mahitab, nodding.

"*How* do you know all this?" asked Nehal, laughing.

"It's all in the papers!" exclaimed Mahitab. "They talk about her so often. Did you know one time she called men *insects*?"

"I'm sure that endeared her to members of Parliament," said Nico dryly.

Mahitab shrugged. "It got their attention, if nothing else. But Nehal, you must tell me, what was she like in person?"

"She was lovely." Nehal sighed dramatically. "We didn't have a chance to talk much at the Opera House; unfortunately, we were rudely interrupted by Wael Helmy."

Yusry laughed. "A boor, that man."

Nehal wrinkled her nose. "That's exactly what Nagat said."

"Unfortunately he's one of the richest businessmen in Alamaxa, if not the entire country, so he thinks he's entitled to his boorishness. And his dislike of Malak Mamdouh."

"Hmm." Nehal cocked her head. "Perhaps he should attend one of her meetings and get to know her better, like I will."

She felt Nico's eyes slide to her. Yusry raised his eyebrows. Mahitab, who had listened eagerly when Carolinna and Nehal made arrangements, only smiled knowingly, then turned to her brother.

"Yusry, can I go with Nehal?" asked Mahitab. "Please?" She turned back to Nehal. "I've been trying to convince him to let me go for months, but he says it's too dangerous."

"Really, Yusry?" Nehal quirked an eyebrow. "A soiree, too dangerous? I thought you supported the Daughters of Izdihar."

Yusry shifted uncomfortably. "I support what they stand for. But these things escalate with Malak Mamdouh at their head. Did you hear how they clashed with the Khopeshes last week? Three of them were arrested, and who knows how many got hurt?"

Nico twitched, his knee knocking into Nehal's. She gave him a sidelong glance; his forehead was set into a determined frown.

Nehal swirled the dregs of hibiscus tea in her glass. "I've seen Mahitab weave; she's far from defenseless. Perhaps you should let her judge the danger for herself."

The challenge in the statement was evident; Nehal felt Nico's eyes on her in warning.

But Yusry only grinned good-naturedly, his teeth bright in the candlelight. "When she's older than sixteen, I'll be sure to let her make all her own decisions."

Mahitab pouted, but her expression softened when Yusry jokingly ruffled her curls.

The servants brought out another round of tea, and then shisha. Yusry, Mahitab, and Nehal all partook in the water pipe, the tobacco sweet and thick with molasses, but Nico kept his distance. He was quite occupied with the wine; neither Mahitab nor Nehal had touched it, Yusry had only taken a single glass, and yet the bottle was nearly empty. When Nehal looked at Nico's bright red cheeks, it was obvious where the wine had gone. Yusry, ever the accommodating host, had the servants bring another bottle of wine before the first was finished, and Nico reached for that too.

They chatted well into the night; talk soon turned to politics.

"If you ask me, I think Parliament is going to enshrine weaving into this new constitution," said Yusry. "Disbanding all the Weaving Academies after Edua Badawi was always an overreaction. Enough time has passed that they're starting to see that now."

"Enshrining weaving?" said Nico in a slightly slurred voice. "When Zirana wants us to ban it entirely? Wouldn't be very smart. Especially not when Zirana already thinks we're training weavers to invade them."

"Surely not!" exclaimed Mahitab.

Nico shrugged. "They don't see any purpose to weaving besides military. And when they think of the military, they think of Edua Badawi."

"Weaving isn't just for fighting," protested Mahitab.

"Yes, there's always the stage," said Yusry. "Nehal, have you considered joining the Tetrad Troupe?"

Nehal barked out a laugh. "Ha! And give my mother a heart attack? Not that that isn't an appealing option some days . . ."

They fell to laughing, except for Nico, who Nehal felt staring at her. She thought he was going to say something disapproving, and she was ready with a snappy retort, but in the end all he did was reach for more sweet wine.

"Weaving can be practical too," said Mahitab earnestly. "The bridges across the River Izdihar were built by earthweavers, you know, and they've stood for hundreds of years."

"Yes, well, I hear King Hali's not the most logical fellow," said Yusry.

"The Zirani envoy is, though," said Nico. "Hopefully Ouazzani can be more reasonable than his king, though he still has to defer to him."

Yusry shuddered. "Ugh, a *monarchy*. Imagine having absolutely no say in your own country's affairs."

"Yes, imagine that," said Nehal dryly.

Yusry grimaced sheepishly.

"We're only marginally better, really," muttered Nico. "Ten of Parliament's fifty-two seats go to noble Houses. And the royal family still gets a seat. And who gets elected? Wealthy, educated men."

"I'd say we're more than *marginally* better," protested Yusry. "King Hali runs a dictatorship. His prisons are filled with dissidents."

"Don't mind my husband, Yusry," said Nehal. "I think perhaps he's had a little too much to drink." With that, she plucked the half-full wineglass from Nico's hands. He tried to swipe it back but missed entirely. Nehal set the glass down with a smirk. "I think it's time for us to go."

Yusry and Mahitab protested profusely, but Nehal insisted, and thanked them both for the wonderful dinner, while Nico silently glowered. When he finally got to his feet he swayed slightly. Nehal made sure to give him a wide berth; she was getting stronger, yes, but there was no way she could support Nico if he fell over, and she had no interest in being knocked to the ground.

During the short palanquin ride home, Nico was quiet, though his expression was troubled.

"What's eating at you?" asked Nehal finally, to break the silence.

Nico turned to her in surprise. "What?"

"You've been in a foul mood all night, and the wine hasn't seemed to help. It's fairly noticeable."

Nico looked out the window and was quiet for so long Nehal was about to prompt him again, when, without looking at her, he said very quietly, "I went to see Giorgina."

"Today?"

"A few days ago."

"I presume it didn't go well?"

"No. I—I think it may be well and truly over between us." His voice cracked slightly, and Nehal could think of nothing to say in response, so they endured the rest of the ride in silence.

At home, they went their separate ways, as they always did. Once Nehal was out of her fancy clothes and in a simple cotton nightdress, her curls loose and strewn past her waist, she trailed over to the mashrabiya in the corner of her room and glanced at the peaceful lane before settling among the cushions, a vat of water in front of her.

Nehal held out both hands, fingers splayed as though she were clutching a ball, and she pulled the water out of the bowl. Smiling, she shaped it into a sphere and held it there, swirling the water around itself endlessly. It was not an especially practical trick, but it was very pretty, and it certainly demonstrated a profound control.

"That's impressive."

Startled, Nehal nearly lost her grip on her trick, but she only stumbled, the water pausing in its flow as she turned to see Nico leaning on the doorframe. He was in his own nightclothes, his hair free of his turban and strewn in loose waves. Even his spectacles were gone, and he looked entirely different without them.

He walked hesitantly into the room until he was standing beside Nehal. He nodded at her swirling sphere. "Is that what they're teaching you at the Academy?"

"Some of it," said Nehal, a little defensively, for there was a hint of derision in Nico's tone that she did not like.

He sat beside her with a small groan. "Relax. I like it." He paused. "Did you know Giorgina is an earthweaver?"

At this Nehal let the water splash back into the bowl and turned to Nico, who looked somewhat horrified at what he had just said.

"Please don't— I shouldn't have said that," he muttered. "She doesn't like talking about it. Please don't tell anyone."

"I don't have anyone to tell," said Nehal carefully. "Did she . . . did she also want to go to the Academy?"

Again Nico took his time answering. "She never mentioned it. She did have trouble with control, but . . . I don't know. I think mostly weaving frightens her."

"That's sad," said Nehal decidedly. "She should have a chance to fall in love with her abilities. She should never be frightened of her own powers."

Nico was giving her a strange look; a mix of surprise and something close to tenderness. It was an expression Nehal had never seen directed at herself, not from Nico, not from anyone. Her stomach tightened, but she refused to look away; these were *her* rooms, after all. Let Nico be the one to look away in discomfort.

But Nico did no such thing; instead, he leaned in closer. Nehal was too surprised to react when one of his hands cupped her cheek and the other fell on her waist, pulling her closer to him. Then he pressed his lips to hers.

He was addled by the sweet wine, surely that was all this was, and yet perhaps Nehal was addled too, for she opened her mouth to him and reached up to wrap her arms around his neck. She had never been kissed before, at least not like this; Nico was holding on to her like she was the only thing in the world he needed. No—he *wanted* her, that much was certain, and that alone was enough to thrill Nehal. She had not considered herself particularly attracted to Nico, but Nehal had never been one to turn down a pleasurable activity.

Nico's breathing was heavy when he pulled back to trail his lips down Nehal's neck, pulling her nightgown down her shoulder and breast. She fell back against the cushions, Nico moving atop her and pinning her beneath his larger frame. The water beside her had not yet stilled; had she wished, she could have easily resisted him with waterweaving.

But Nehal had no wish to resist.

Nehal buried her fingers in Nico's soft, wispy hair and pulled him back to her mouth; his tongue was all salt and sweet wine, and his hand was trailing down Nehal's body—

Then came the sound of glass shattering.

Nehal and Nico wrenched apart, Nico startling so violently he slammed into the bowl of water beside them, spilling half of it onto the cushions. Nehal adjusted her nightgown and sat up, lips pursed, and glanced at the door, where Ridda stood, eyes wide and pale face bright pink.

"I—I'm so sorry, I didn't mean to— I didn't realize—" She averted her eyes and made to kneel to pick up the shards of the cup she had dropped, but then hesitated, so that she was awkwardly hunched. "I was only bringing you your hilbah, like you asked—"

Nehal sighed. "Yes, I did ask, didn't I? I completely forgot. It's all right, Ridda, no harm done."

Ridda looked up. "I—should I—"

"Why don't you go fetch the broom and dustpan?" said Nehal patiently. "You shouldn't touch the glass with your hands; you'll hurt yourself."

"Yes, yes, I'll—yes."

When Ridda left, Nehal turned to Nico, who had backed away from Nehal and stood by her bed looking like a cornered animal. His gaze was unfocused, and he directed it anywhere but at her.

"I—I shouldn't have—we shouldn't have—" The words slurred together.

Nehal raised an eyebrow, amused and a little disappointed. "We're both well within our rights. I *am* your wife, you know," she said wryly.

"I don't *want* you to be my wife." The words came out harsh, a growl Nico could not take back.

Nehal's chest stung with a mixture of rancid emotions that she had no wish to examine. She hadn't wanted to be Nico's wife either, and yet here she was, tied to a man who did not want her and felt guilty when he did. They had never explicitly spoken about whether they would consummate their marriage, but, presupposing Nico's arrangement with Giorgina, Nehal had assumed it was a nonissue. Now that there *was* no arrangement, and Nico himself believed their relationship over, could he not allow himself to move on? With his legal wife, at that? If they were going to be stuck with each other for the rest of their lives, they might as well enjoy themselves.

"What exactly is your plan?" snapped Nehal. "Remain celibate for the rest of your life?"

Nico said nothing. He did not even have the grace to look at her.

"Get out," said Nehal in disgust.

Nico obeyed immediately, and when Ridda returned to clean what she had broken, she made no comment on his absence.

16

GIORGINA

MALAK MAMDOUH LIVED ON THE BORDER OF MAYADI AND Fustat. The former was a wealthier district containing mostly stately homes, while the latter held most of Alamaxa's administrative buildings, including Parliament and the university. Thankfully, Malak's house was not too far from Giorgina's bookshop; on days when the weather was pleasant, she could usually walk there. Since early that morning, the sun had been beating down on Alamaxa, and heat waves danced in the air like worms. Giorgina had started to sweat through her galabiya, so when it came time to head to Malak's, she paid to hitch a ride on a mule cart.

Giorgina shared the cart with another woman and three men. One of the men was leering at her insistently, but she decidedly looked away and refused to meet his eyes, thankful that her distinctive hair was tucked well beneath her veil. Without it she mostly looked like any other Ramsawi woman, and she suffered the leers as they did.

After a few minutes, the leering man got off, walking past Giorgina as he did so. His hand swept her knee as he passed; she flinched and shrunk away. She could not be certain if he had done it purposefully, but even if he had, he would deny it if she said something, call her a hysteric or roll his eyes, so she said nothing. The man continued to leer at her as the cart drove away. Shuddering slightly, she sat closer to the only other female passenger and stared at her feet until the cart stopped at the entrance to the lane that led to Malak's building.

As far as Giorgina knew, Malak had inherited the house from her father, and its size made it the perfect place to host meetings. It helped that the building sat at a corner at the very end of the dead-end lane, making it easily overlooked. From the outside, it was not particularly spectacular, but the inside reflected the wealth Malak came from.

After being let in by Malak's servant girl, Nadra, Giorgina made her way to the second-floor parlor, where meetings always took place. Inside, about forty women lounged on cushions and divans. Most had removed their shawls and veils and were comfortably smoking shisha, munching on roasted sunflower seeds, or sipping tea. As always, being inundated with the volume of the chatter startled Giorgina, but also as always, she steeled herself against it and made her way forward. Her eyes quickly found Malak, and she approached her table to deposit her latest writing assignment for the magazine.

Malak was chatting with two women, both of whom had their backs to Giorgina. When she came close enough for Malak to notice her, the women turned as well. One of them was Carolinna Farino, who had only spoken to Giorgina directly once, to comment on her hair. The other woman was far shorter and darker and—it was Nehal Darweesh.

Giorgina stopped in her tracks and blinked, feeling some heat rise to her cheeks as she recalled their previous encounter.

Nehal showed no discomfort whatsoever. "Nice to see you again, Giorgina."

"How in the world do you two know each other?" Carolinna looked from one woman to the other. Giorgina could discern exactly what Carolinna was thinking: how could two women from such vastly different classes be acquaintances?

Nehal and Giorgina both hesitated, and it was Malak who lied smoothly, "They met briefly at the Opera House, during the protest."

"Oh, right." Carolinna sighed. "I wish I could have been there."

"Carolinna and Nehal are both students at the Academy of the Weaving Arts," continued Malak. "Nehal expressed a desire to join the Daughters of Izdihar."

"How . . . how nice," said Giorgina lamely. "Um, Malak, I only wanted to give you my latest piece."

Malak smiled at her. "Of course! Thank you, habibti."

Nehal raised her eyebrows. "You write for the magazine?"

Something in Nehal's tone piqued Giorgina's irritation, but before she could do more than shrug, Malak said, "Giorgina's one of my best writers. You should read her pieces, Nehal. Initials G.S.?"

Nehal smiled. "I intend to."

Malak's attention was then drawn by another woman. Giorgina retreated, looking for Labiba, but her friend didn't seem to have arrived yet. She made her way to an empty cushion and somehow wound up seated beside Nehal, who had followed her and sat far too close, oblivious to Giorgina's discomfort at her overly casual intimacy. At least she was immersed in the latest issue of *The Vanguard*.

To avoid looking at Nehal she cast her eye across the rest of the women in the room. She recognized most of them, by face if not by name. When she had first started attending meetings, Giorgina had been surprised by the diversity of the attendees. There were women like Nehal and Carolinna, dressed in the fine cotton robes and heavy jewelry that marked their wealth and status, but they were far outnumbered by more ordinary women like Giorgina, in simple galabiyas and shawls. And still others were in threadbare garments, with dirty feet and knotted hair. They varied in age too; the youngest attendee was a teenage girl who Giorgina was almost certain was homeless, while the oldest, Rauwya, had to be in her sixth decade at least.

Out of the corner of her eye, she finally saw Labiba and Etedal walk in. Labiba immediately caught Giorgina's eye, and there was an open question in her glance as she nodded toward Nehal, whose eyes were still buried in the magazine. Giorgina shrugged and gestured for Labiba to join her, but she and Etedal were tugged away by someone else.

"I had no idea they did all this," said Nehal.

Giorgina turned back to her reluctantly. Nehal was still flipping idly through *The Vanguard*. "I have a subscription back home, but I have to admit I never read it cover to cover. A free health clinic for the poor . . . food drives, soap drives, used clothing, childcare supplies . . . literacy initiatives . . ."

Giorgina resisted the urge to sigh. A free health clinic was where she had met Labiba and the very discreet female physician who had performed Giorgina's abortion. During one particularly difficult month, she had availed herself of two free bean packets from one of the food drives. The charity drives were fairly well known; it was part of the reason why the Daughters of Izdihar had built a certain amount of goodwill among the Ramsawi populace. But of course a woman like Nehal would be unaware of charity initiatives.

After a moment, Giorgina chided herself for such an unfair thought; Nehal, after all, was not a native of Alamaxa. She had only been in the city for a little over a month and already she was here, attending a meeting. That was far more than could be said for most of the women in her social circle, who had lived in Alamaxa all their lives.

"Oh!" exclaimed Nehal. "There's a public secondary school for girls opening next year!"

Giorgina smiled a little at Nehal's excitement. Giorgina herself had only been able to attend primary school, since only boys could attend public secondary school. Had she wished to continue her studies further, as a woman, she would have needed to enroll in an expensive private school. Even if her family had possessed such exorbitant funds, Ehab would never have spent it on his daughter's education. The new secondary school was a direct result of Malak's negotiations with Parliament, donations, and, it was rumored, a significant contribution of her own personal funds.

Nehal started to speak again, but before she could, the room quieted; Malak had taken a seat at the head of the room, behind a low table laid with neat piles of papers. She stared at the crowd for a moment, like a queen surveying her subjects, before she addressed them.

"Welcome, all, and thank you for attending." Her voice, deep and throaty, commanded the room even at its low decibel. "We have much to discuss today. First, magazine sales have increased, which bodes well. The rally we held at the opera last week was well-attended and rather more . . ." Malak's mouth twisted into what Giorgina thought might have been a smirk, ". . . polite than expected."

Several women chuckled, while Etedal snorted loudly.

"However, Parliament has yet to cede to any of our demands, nor has there been any improvement whatsoever in local cases involving women. Some of you might remember Umaima Fawwaz—she was a young girl I worked with some weeks ago, who had been coerced into sex and became pregnant as a result."

"Coerced how?" asked Nehal, frowning.

"The man she bedded claimed to be in love with her and promised to marry her." Malak sighed. "Once he had gotten what he truly desired, however, he abandoned her."

Giorgina sat back, her stomach churning, hoping that her twisting insides did not seem obvious. Umaima's case in particular always troubled Giorgina; the girl may as well have been Giorgina herself. She had thought herself in love, thought herself loved, and been duped and betrayed, left to deal with the evidence all on her own. If not for Labiba's discerning eye, Giorgina might have been in Umaima's position.

"What happened to her?" someone asked.

"She was convicted in court," said Malak.

"For what?" said one woman in disgust.

Malak glanced down. "According to the judge, 'she enabled a distasteful deed, by giving herself to whoever it was that committed the act in her, without informing any of her family members or contacting the authorities until her pregnancy became visible.' In other words, the court chose to hold her accountable for having extramarital relations."

"In other words," Etedal spat, "she was convicted for not being a man."

"But there's . . . there's no law about that, is there?" a young girl named Aleyya asked hesitantly.

"Not technically." Malak's eyes glinted. "But the court believed the girl still deserved to be punished. For violating her own honor. And her family's honor, I suppose." Malak shook her head. "Her father even attempted to argue on her behalf, but the court was insistent."

"But that's . . . that's not fair, then!" someone said.

"No shit," said Etedal. "That's why we're here."

Malak gave Etedal a look, and Etedal shrugged but quieted.

"You're right, Aleyya," continued Malak. "It's not fair that this girl will spend the next six months of her life in prison. Nor is it fair that Qanawiyya Fahmy's murderer has been acquitted."

There were gasps and hisses around the room, and Etedal cursed.

"Who's Qanawiyya?" asked Nehal.

Malak's steady gaze landed on Nehal. "She was a young woman from a village just outside Alamaxa. She was discovered to be with child, and she was unmarried. Her brother murdered her—and her unborn child."

As always, a chill ran down Giorgina's back at the reminder of this case. These types of killings were not especially common among Ramsawis, but they were not unheard of either, particularly in more rural villages. Giorgina was almost certain her father condoned these types of punishments.

"The judge was not ambivalent in his opinion." Malak held up a paper and began to read off it, her voice soft. "'It could not have been easy for the closest one to her to commit any acts against her unless she had done some terrible deed that led him to do what he has done to protect his honor, and that of the family.'"

There was silence in the wake of Malak's words, until Etedal cursed again, followed by other mutters agreeing with her. Malak allowed the anger to flourish, to build up before speaking again.

"A reminder of what we are working against, and how far we have to go." Malak sat up straighter. "Which brings me to our main issue: suffrage. Parliament refuses to grant women the vote, and we cannot truly make change if we cannot vote, if we cannot hold judicial and parliamentary positions. We've petitioned, we've argued, we've debated . . . now I'm afraid it's time to take the fight to them. I propose a march. A march that will take us to Parliament's doors, and to the office of the prime minister. We don't leave until he gives us what we are owed, what is ours by right."

Malak's voice carried into the corners of the room, echoing throughout the chamber like the proclamation of a goddess. Yet she still exuded calm; she sat straight, shoulders thrown back, head held high, a perfect portrait of regality. When Malak spoke, even ludicrous suggestions like marching on Parliament seemed sane. Giorgina envied her the ability to command a room of people so easily.

A small, uncertain voice interrupted the silence. "They'll arrest us." This was a middle-aged woman Giorgina did not recognize, dressed in a cheap galabiya with a faded flower pattern.

"We've been arrested before," Labiba reminded her.

"Not me," said another woman more confidently. "Unlike you, I don't have Malak to bail me out. I haven't got anyone."

"Malak." This came from a woman only a few paces from Giorgina, a diminutive young woman with deep brown skin and steely gray eyes. Malak's assistant and secretary, Bahira, was unfazed as all eyes turned to her. "A march like this could turn violent."

"Perhaps that is precisely the point," said Malak. "Sometimes it is necessary to use violence against those who only understand the language of violence."

Now there were more mutters. Giorgina could not help but agree with Bahira's concerns; with Malak's infamy, such a march could potentially draw hundreds. Once they all gathered at Parliament, it would only take a small spark to fan the flames of chaos.

"What are you suggesting, Malak?" asked Labiba uncertainly. "Are you suggesting we . . . we hurt someone?"

Malak waved her hand in the air. "Of course not. The Daughters never resort to violence unless we are attacked first. I only mean that the prospect of potential violence should not be enough to deter us."

"I think it's an excellent idea," said Nehal. "This way they can't ignore us or claim we're too delicate for politics."

"All due respect, miss," said a woman dressed in a ragged old galabiya. "It's all well and good for you being high-and-mighty and married to the richest man in the city. You don't gotta worry about being dragged off to prison and left to rot."

Privately, Giorgina agreed, and she winced when Nehal retorted, "Don't be so certain of that. You can't let fear stop you from doing what you want."

"Come on, you cowards," said Etedal loudly. "I'm not rich or fancy, and I think this is a good idea. How long are we going to keep begging for what we're owed? You'll wear your face veils, hide your faces like you always do. If the police come, well, we have weavers on our end. We'll fight them off if it comes to that."

"But hopefully it will *not* come to that." Malak raised her voice and her hands to quiet the rising tide of mutters. "The march will be peaceful. If nothing else, it will make all the papers."

"When do you want this to happen?" asked Bahira.

"Five weeks," said Malak. "That should give us enough time to plan and advertise. Who's with me?"

"I am," said Nehal immediately. She was followed by Etedal, and Labiba, and more and more voices until the room became a cacophony of agreement.

Giorgina thought of the child she might have had and the man who had abandoned them both. She thought of Lorenzo Baldinotti, who held her reputation in his hands. She thought of the late nights she spent poring over books pilfered from Anas's shop, trying desperately to educate herself. She thought of how often in her life she felt she was being suffocated. She took a deep breath, unclenched her fists. Then she added her voice to the chorus.

Malak smiled at them all. "Excellent. We'll need to spread the word, but we'll want to be discreet in doing so. I don't want Parliament expecting us. We'll tell only those we know we can trust—to everyone else, this will just be advertised as a lecture at the university auditorium. Once everyone is gathered there, we'll march, and those who don't want to join us can leave."

Giorgina could only admire the genius of this plan. It gave them the element of surprise, but it also likened the chance of the march drawing greater numbers. There would be women present who thought they were only attending a lecture that was safe and controlled, if not entirely respectable, given the speaker. When it turned into a march, even if they did not want to march, they would struggle not to be swept up in the camaraderie of like-minded women. Giorgina had felt this herself many times. There were so many people in her life, women included, who conspired to make her believe she was mad for believing in egalitarianism. Being among women who shared her values inspired her to do things she would not have otherwise considered.

"We'll need volunteers to distribute handbills advertising the lecture," Malak continued. "We also need more volunteers to sell the magazine. I know it's not a particularly pleasant task, but it is a necessary one." She set out the sign-up sheets as she spoke.

Giorgina had distributed handbills several times, though she didn't relish the task, but at least she didn't necessarily have to distribute anything to people; she could simply plaster handbills on whatever flat surface she could find, or leave a sheaf where they might be found. Selling the magazine was a far more aggressive and involved task. Giorgina was not surprised when those who signed up for the latter task were those least likely to be accosted—like elderly Rauwya—or those who weren't afraid to be accosted—like Etedal.

To her surprise, Nehal got to her feet and stood behind Rauwya and Etedal to sign up to sell the magazine. Giorgina felt a mixture of respect, awe, and bitter jealousy.

The remainder of the meeting was devoted to some administrative updates regarding distribution schedules and charity drives, followed by a reading and critique of two scholars' recently published essays on the status of Ramsawi women. When it was time to leave, Giorgina's gaze was drawn to Nehal, who appeared to be lingering, but then Labiba hooked her arm through hers, and she followed her and Etedal out.

17

NEHAL

IT TOOK A GREAT DEAL OF EFFORT FOR NEHAL TO LINGER casually until everyone had left. Many women wanted to have a private word with Malak, but finally, only Bahira remained. She and Malak were discussing something in low voices, and Nehal did her best to try to appear occupied with the burgundy curtains hanging across the wall.

When Bahira left, she gave Nehal a strange glance, but Nehal could discern nothing from the other woman's expression. Malak, on the other hand, gave a short exhale, like she was setting down something heavy, and smiled at Nehal.

"Thank you for waiting," she said softly. "I assume you wanted to discuss something in private?"

Nehal opened her mouth, could think of nothing to say, and so only nodded. She was not entirely sure why she had not left, only that she wanted a moment alone with Malak, for reasons she couldn't explain to herself.

A servant girl entered the room and looked at Malak questioningly.

"Let's leave Nadra to clean up," said Malak.

Malak led Nehal into a different parlor; this one was much smaller and cozier, more like a small personal office. It was decorated tastefully in gray-and-blue geometric designs that lined the tiled floors and cushions. Mashrabiyas set into the windows of the seating area cast a honeycomb of light onto a low table littered with books and papers.

Malak gestured for Nehal to take a seat on one of the cushions, then sat across from her, so close they grazed one another's knees. Malak's long braid fell forward across her chest; the dappled light from the mashrabiyas highlighted the blue-black sheen of her hair.

Nehal cleared her throat to shake off her thoughts, though it was difficult with Malak smiling at her and giving her such undivided attention. "I . . . hadn't realized the Daughters of Izdihar do so much."

Malak nodded encouragingly.

"Particularly all this charity," Nehal continued, her thoughts quickly catching up to her. "Where do you get the funds for it all?"

Malak leaned her elbow against the table. "Magazine sales help, but it's donations, mostly. There are many who believe in our cause but are too afraid to support us publicly. We had just started to hold funding drives at Lotfy Templehouse, but . . . we've run into some problems there." She shrugged, and Nehal could not help but notice how Malak seemed a different person in the absence of her rapt audience, less like an untouchable figure and more like the reserved woman Nehal had spoken to at the opera.

"I see." Nehal nodded and made a quick decision. "I'd like to contribute funding as well." Nehal's funds were tied up with Nico's at the moment, but she would untangle that mess and donate what she could.

Malak's lips parted for a moment. "Are you certain?" she asked softly. "I do my best to ensure all donations are confidential, of course, but I can't guarantee—"

"I'll put out an announcement in the paper myself if I have to!" said Nehal, a bit too loudly.

Malak's soft laugh bubbled out of her. "Well, there's no need for that, though I appreciate your enthusiasm."

There was a moment of silence, and then Malak asked softly, "How is your husband?"

Nehal rolled her eyes and laughed. "Giving me the silent treatment, at the moment. You know men."

"Fighting already?" said Malak. "You're newlyweds, aren't you?"

Nehal shrugged. "It was an arranged marriage that neither of us wanted," said Nehal bluntly. "I don't dislike him, but . . ." She trailed off, suddenly unsure of what she wanted to say. Malak was surprisingly easy to confide in, but Nehal wasn't sure she wanted to share such intimate details with anyone.

Malak hummed in thought. "I'm sorry he isn't what you expected."

"I never wanted to get married at all," said Nehal. "But at least he gave me his signature to attend the Academy." She couldn't bring herself to say the word *permission,* which sounded so utterly infantile. "It's only been a week, but it's been . . . awe-inspiring."

Malak's eyes glittered. "I can imagine. My own father was rather invested in my education, thankfully. I had a weaving tutor from Karatzia."

Nehal raised her eyebrows. "That's impressive."

"And expensive," Malak joked. "Our family wasn't particularly pleased with my father's priorities."

"I wish my father were more like that," said Nehal. "He's both traditional *and* financially irresponsible."

Malak winced. "A bad combination."

"*Terrible.*"

Nehal was surprised at the ease with which their conversation flowed; they moved from one topic to another like sandweavers gliding across the dunes, with never an awkward moment or pause. Nehal had never been shy or reserved, so she had many friends back home, but Malak was different. She was a weaver, like Nehal, and a revolutionary, both of which automatically endeared her to Nehal, but it was more than that. Malak invited confidence; she made Nehal feel as though she could tell her anything at all without judgment.

When Malak's servant girl came in to ask if she should set out dinner, Nehal was startled, but when she looked out the window, she realized the sky had grown dark without her noticing. She'd told Medhat to come pick her up in two hours, but it was closer to four now. She scrambled to her feet and crossed the room to look out the opposite window; indeed, a brightly colored palanquin was parked in the lane.

"Stay for dinner," Malak offered.

Nehal turned to her; she didn't want to leave. "I would, but . . . my palanquin driver's been waiting for so long already. I completely forgot about him," she added sheepishly.

Malak laughed. "I distracted you." She cocked her head at Nehal, a small smile playing across her lips. "Are you coming back to the city next weekend?"

"I am," said Nehal. "I'll be here for the meeting."

"Well, that's good, but I was thinking perhaps we could continue our conversation?" There was a subtle note of hesitation in Malak's tone Nehal had never heard before. "Have you been to Fishawy's Teahouse yet? It's quite something."

Nehal stared into Malak's glittering dark eyes and tried to keep the heat from rising to her cheeks. "I'd love to go."

As was customary, Malak kissed Nehal's cheeks in goodbye, the orange blossom scent of her causing Nehal's stomach to flutter.

NICO'S SILENT TREATMENT did not take very long to become irritating.

When she returned from Malak's, Nehal marched toward his study, intending to—she wasn't entirely sure what. To tell him about the meeting? To tell him she had spoken to Giorgina? She decided to figure it out when she looked at him.

In his study, he was, as usual, bent over a book. He glanced up when she entered and, predictably, blanched and swallowed heavily, then looked back down at his book.

Nehal taunted him, called him a child, a fool, a hopeless romantic, but she could not manage to provoke him into any kind of response. He only looked on blankly, so she huffed and left, making sure to slam the study door behind her, and sequestered herself in her rooms, intending to enjoy her final day in luxury before her return to the Academy the following afternoon.

But Nehal could not stop thinking about what had almost happened. She had never been with a man before, never really kissed one, and the feel of Nico's lips against hers had stirred within her something that she had never quite experienced before, not even when she satisfied her own needs. There was an added spark to having Nico clinging to Nehal as though she were his only salvation. There was, she thought, a kind of power in the hold she had over Nico at that moment, and it was intoxicating.

Nehal's thoughts suddenly wandered to Malak, but she stopped herself before she could get carried away.

The following morning, as Nehal was preparing for her departure to the Academy, her routine was interrupted by the arrival of an unexpected visitor requesting to see Nico. Because Nico had apparently told the servants he was not to be disturbed, it was left to Nehal to greet the guest while Ridda went to fetch Nico under Nehal's orders. Ridda had led the guest into the parlor and presented him with a cup of tea.

When Nehal entered, the man jumped to his feet. He was light-skinned but weathered, like someone who spent too much time in the sun, with a large aquiline nose that looked as though it had been broken several times. Unlike most of the men Nehal met in Alamaxa, he was clean-shaven, displaying a wide, square jaw. He was clearly still of the upper class, though; his galabiya and turban were spun of the finest cotton.

He waited for Nehal to approach and extend her hand. "You must be Lady Nehal," he said, bowing slightly.

"You introduced yourself to my maid as Raouf Metwally, but I'm afraid I don't recognize the name." Nehal settled down onto the cushions and gestured for Raouf to do the same.

"I am a friend of your husband."

Nehal cocked her head, running her eyes along the man's face and perusing her memories. "I don't recall seeing you at the wedding."

"I've only just been granted leave." He chuckled. "Nico just had to go and get married in the middle of a campaign."

Nehal was puzzled. "Campaign?"

Raouf sat up straighter. "I'm a general in the army."

Nehal raised her eyebrows in surprise. A soldier! She was immediately thrilled at the prospect of peppering Raouf with questions, but before she could formulate even one, Nico appeared.

He looked utterly disheveled, as though he had slept in his clothes on the floor of his study, which wasn't entirely unlikely. He blinked rapidly at Raouf, eyes bleary behind cloudy spectacles, and then his face broke into a smile.

"Raouf!" Nico approached with open arms; Raouf met him halfway and the two men fell into an embrace. "I couldn't believe it. What are you doing here?"

Raouf, who was smiling, said, "I was granted my request for leave! It's my first night back. I can't stay long, but I had to stop by."

"I'm so glad to see you, my friend!" Nico laughed. "You must have tea, let me—"

"Already taken care of!" Raouf gestured to his half-empty cup of tea. "Sit down, sit down!"

Nehal looked on at this display of Nico's gregariousness with pursed lips, but said nothing as Nico continued, "Tell me, how is life in the army?"

Raouf shrugged. "Fine. A bit dull for my tastes."

"Loraq's aggressions not exciting enough for you?" Nico chuckled. "Anyway, I think most people would be happy for things to remain dull."

"I don't think they will be for long . . . my superior officers seem to be convinced we're heading for war any day now!"

"Not with Loraq, surely?" asked Nehal. For decades, their eastern neighbor had been attempting to advance on the mines that made up the border between the two countries, but Loraq's army was small and weak, and had only ever been a nuisance, never a true danger.

Raouf shook his head. "Zirana."

Nico shook his head. "Don't say that. Parliament will work it out. Nobody wants war with Zirana."

"King Hali wants war," said Raouf bluntly. "Or at least that's what everyone says about him. Bloodthirsty, warmongering, tyrannical, all that. His government's already put forward a draft requirement for soldiers. If that happens and we go to war, they'll overwhelm us with their sheer numbers—"

"How can their army overwhelm us?" Nehal interrupted. "We have weavers in the army now, don't we?"

"We have weavers, that's true, but not as many as we would like, since the Academy's only just started training them properly." Raouf turned back to Nico. "If you ask me, they ought to create a regiment of weavers, fund it properly, but no, instead Parliament decides to waste its money on that silly women's division—"

"What do you mean, silly?" interrupted Nehal sharply.

The two men turned to her. Nico looked somewhat apprehensive, as though he knew what was coming, while Raouf blinked in surprise, but recovered quickly.

"I only meant— Well, obviously, they're women." Raouf looked genuinely confused. "I mean, you understand, women can't be soldiers, it's just not in your nature. The division isn't going to *accomplish* anything."

"That's ridiculous," Nehal snapped. "Women can fight just as well as men can, if we're trained properly. And female weavers fought just fine in the war against Talyana."

Raouf looked at Nico in bewilderment, but Nico's eyes were

averted. "Well, that— Those were extraordinary circumstances—we had no choice! Not to mention those were weavers, not ordinary women—and look what happened when Edua Badawi was allowed to gain too much power; it overwhelmed her nature."

Nehal ignored this.

"You just said our army would be overwhelmed by Zirana," she argued. "It seems like you need all the soldiers you can get, men or women."

"Or we could institute a draft of *men,* like Zirana," argued Raouf. "Before forcing women from the safety of their homes."

"You don't need to force anybody anywhere," said Nehal. "I said you should allow women to volunteer, not grab them by the hair and drag them out of their homes. Or is that how you're used to dealing with women?"

Raouf's mouth fell open and his eyes grew comically wide. "Lady Nehal—"

"Nico agrees with me." Nehal turned to her husband, glaring savagely at him. "Don't you?"

Raouf and Nehal both stared expectantly at Nico, who finally looked up, but did not directly meet anyone's gaze. "I . . . I suppose I think women should be given the choice to do what they like, just as men are."

"And have women roaming among our soldiers?" asked Raouf incredulously. "Will they be fighting or courting?"

"I thought soldiers were supposed to be disciplined," said Nehal icily. "Now you're telling me they won't be capable of handling themselves among women?"

"Lady Nehal, I truly don't mean to offend you," began Raouf. "But as a general—"

"I find I no longer trust your opinions on this matter, *General,*" said Nehal. "Not when you hold such regressive views."

"I find," said Nico very loudly and very pointedly, "that this has become a rather controversial issue among many. In fact, I've recently finished reading a rather magnificent tome on the subject of the psychological toll of warfare, and it spoke in great detail about Edua Badawi's motivations. Quite fascinating, really! Come, come to my study, I must show you—"

Somewhat forcefully, Nico linked arms with Raouf and led him out of the parlor. Nehal stayed put, nostrils flared, listening to their footsteps and muffled conversation as they ascended to Nico's study. The slam of the door sealed Nehal in isolated silence. On the table in front of her, Raouf's cup of tea trembled; the remaining liquid in it shook to the rhythm of Nehal's uneven breathing. She sat there, too furious to move, until her feet began to tingle beneath her, growing numb, and yet still she sat, measuring her breath and struggling to control her anger.

After some time, a door creaked open, and Nehal once again heard muffled footsteps and conversation, growing louder as they came closer and closer, then fading once more as they walked past the parlor and toward the front door. Nehal heard goodbyes, followed by a closed door, and then fast, furious footsteps approached. When Nico came into the parlor, Nehal stood.

Nico's pale face, which flushed rather easily, was now blotched pink. Nehal said nothing; she was going to force Nico to be the one to shatter the silence between them, and it seemed he was finally eager to do so.

"I know it's practically impossible for you to be civil," Nico fumed. "But you might at least *try* to behave like a lady rather than someone I picked up off the street."

Nehal narrowed her eyes. "If you'd like me to sit quietly behind you and simper while the men talk, you married the wrong girl."

"I'm *well aware* I married the wrong girl." Nico spoke through gritted teeth. "And I don't need you to *simper*. But I would hope that you would at least treat my only friend with some courtesy even if you disagree with him."

"Oh, I'm *sorry*," said Nehal sarcastically. "Should I be expected to apologize for your friend's inferior opinion of me? *You* don't even agree with him!"

"That's not the point, Nehal!" Nico balled his hands into fists. "You could have disagreed with him like all friends disagree—"

"In a palatable way that wouldn't ruffle his sensibilities?" snapped Nehal. "Politely and demurely so he wouldn't actually have to confront his prejudices? Why, is that what *Giorgina* would have done?"

An icy silence stretched between them until Nehal felt herself shiver. Nico's face paled; he stared at Nehal as though she had struck him. The silence seemed to carry everything they needed to say, but Nehal spoke anyway.

"First of all," Nehal hissed, "your darling Giorgina has been part of the Daughters of Izdihar for longer than she's known *you,* so I very much doubt she would appreciate your complacency. Second, it is not *my fault* that she refused you. It is not *my fault* that we were forced into this marriage, and it is *certainly* not *my fault* that you kissed me. If you feel guilty, I suggest you actually *do something* about it instead of locking yourself in your room and hiding like a coward."

As Nehal shoved past Nico, Raouf's cup of tea finally tipped over.

18

NEHAL

NEHAL HAD ALWAYS BEEN SMALL: SHORT AND THIN AND diminutive, and not particularly strong. The running joke in the family was that she appeared to be half of her twenty-two years, and while Nehal resented being made to feel like a child, she could not help but privately agree that her overall appearance was far from intimidating.

So she, far more than any of her classmates, deeply appreciated her strength training at the Academy. Though initially taxing and tedious, and leaving Nehal sore all over, the results of her exercises were too beneficial to ignore. At the close of her second week at the Academy, she could already feel the changes in her body: her muscles tore and tightened, her arms and legs grew leaner, and her stamina increased. The results on her weaving were astonishing; whereas before manipulating a few liters of water would exhaust her, now she could weave triple that, and for far longer.

She threw herself into training; after dinner and before curfew, she would wander out to the banks of the River Izdihar and practice. Once or twice, she encountered Nagi, who was only too pleased to watch her and point out improvements where he could. He was impressed by her progress, Nehal could tell, and it was gratifying in a way Nehal had never experienced before. This was all her—her progress in weaving—all her own strength and determination, and nothing at all to do with her name or her family reputation or their wealth. This was just Nehal and her element.

She had even begun to tolerate her nonpractical classes, though holding all the information in her head was a struggle. Yuri was intent on ensuring his students thoroughly understood the scientific principles behind weaving, of which there were many, theories developed over the years by scholars, but it never escaped Nehal that they were all essentially educated guesses. Weaving came from the gods, and Edua Badawi had certainly defied all laws of weaving when she exhibited prowess in all the elements. What was the point, then, of studying all these theories that could eventually be disproved?

History and Geopolitics of Weaving was more interesting, but Akram was a truly terrible teacher, in Nehal's opinion: there was no rhyme or reason to his instruction. He lectured like he was chatting with his inebriated friends, jumping aimlessly from one subject to another depending on what grabbed his interest. At their last class, he had, apropos of nothing, begun with the question, "How did weaving influence the implementation of a Ramsawi parliament?"

For a moment everyone simply stared at him blankly as they settled into their seats, while Akram looked back thoughtfully at them.

As usual, it was Shaimaa who answered; her studiousness reminded Nehal very much of Nico.

"Talyana took advantage of a weak and foolish Ramsawi king, Ratib Galal, who allowed the Talyanis to begin colonizing Ramsawa. When Ramsawa fought back with weavers, the king was so horrified by Edua Badawi's actions that he abdicated, not wanting to bear any responsibility for the catastrophe, and decided to hand power over to his advisors, who eventually became Parliament." Shaimaa paused. "I suppose the connection isn't that direct, but . . ."

"No, no, no, that's fine," Akram mused.

"I'm more interested in today's war," said Talaat.

Loath as Nehal was to agree with Talaat, whose attitude toward her had decidedly not improved, she had to admit she cared more about the looming threat of Zirana than the ancient history that was Talyana.

"*Is* there a war?" asked Akram.

"Oh, come on," Talaat scoffed, "the whole reason the Academy was reopened was to prepare for war against Zirana. Everyone knows it's coming sooner or later."

"Do they?" Akram looked around at them all with wide-eyed innocence. "And what makes you say that?"

"It's everywhere, isn't it?" said Talaat. "The papers talk about it, Parliament talks about it, that ambassador is here—"

"Why now, though?" interrupted Waseem. "I know they've never gotten over what happened, but that was two hundred years ago."

"Well," started Zanuba hesitantly, "they think we owe them land—compensation for what Edua destroyed."

"But why demand it now?"

Fikry piped up, "Their king is—" Then he whistled twice and twirled his finger by his temple.

Some chuckled, while others shook their heads.

"That's all you need sometimes, I suppose," said Akram. "A single individual with enough power and determination can change the course of history."

Talaat shook his head. "This is why monarchies are disasters."

Nehal perked up. "Precisely why *all* of Ramsawa's citizens should be permitted to vote."

Talaat only scoffed and rolled his eyes.

"I agree," said Carolinna. "If you're going to disenfranchise one group of citizens, what's to stop you from disenfranchising another just as easily?"

"Oh, come on!" said Talaat. "If anything your lot's just making things worse! Malak Mamdouh only shows people how destructive weavers are; you think that's gonna endear the citizenry to us? You think it's gonna help cool things down with Zirana?"

"Are you saying the Daughters of Izdihar are responsible for the war?" demanded Nehal.

Talaat waved her off. "You're oversimplifying things. I'm just saying that all these demonstrations with weaving aren't exactly helping us look like a safe, stable country. Malak Mamdouh reminds people of Edua Badawi." He shrugged. "So yeah, when we ask, why now, maybe she's part of the reason. Maybe if you all stood down for a while, we'd have a chance to talk Zirana down."

"You're being completely absurd," said Carolinna. "With or without the Daughters of Izdihar, Zirana wants war. It doesn't matter how much we try to compromise; they hate weavers enough that nothing will pacify them."

There was a silence at Carolinna's words, broken only when Akram cleared his throat and said, "So, who wants to tell me about the economic impact of weavers on Karatzian merchant guilds?"

With that, Nehal groaned inwardly and put her head down until the class was over.

Never far in her mind was her upcoming meeting with Malak. She was so excited that even Nico locking himself in his study immediately upon her arrival home did not bother her.

The following evening, Nehal took pains with her appearance, while still trying to dress sensibly. She eschewed heavy cosmetics, as she never felt quite herself with them, but she did allow Ridda to dab some kohl on her eyelids. She wore her simplest outer robe and then, after some consideration, decided to leave her veil behind. She tucked her hair into a loose knot at the base of her neck.

She left without informing Nico. He certainly had no right to inquire after her whereabouts if he was going to continue behaving so childishly.

Medhat and the palanquin could only take Nehal as far as the entrance to Khalili Souk, the oldest bazaar in the city; the palanquin was too large to enter the market's tiny, labyrinthine cobbled streets. Nehal told Medhat she would find her own way home, and after a moment's hesitation, he nodded.

Khalili Souk was a popular tourist attraction in Alamaxa, but Nehal had never been here before. The narrow lanes were lined with merchant stalls selling all sorts of things: brightly colored galabiyas with garish flowery designs, cheap shawls, incense cones, pungent spices, little statues of the Tetrad. As Nehal walked, her pattens clicking against the cobbled stones, merchants shouted out to her if she so much as glanced in their direction.

"Here, my lady, you could use a pair of earrings!"

"A lovely altar for you, miss, and I'll throw in an incense cone for free!"

"You seem to be missing a veil, habibti, how about a new one?"

Nehal almost wanted to smile, but then the merchants might think she was flirting with them, so she averted her gaze and walked on, losing herself in the crowd, and in the bazaar. There were shops and stalls tucked everywhere, even in the alleyways so narrow that Nehal could extend her arms and touch both sides simultaneously. Twice Nehal found herself lost and had to ask for directions, until finally, she found Fishawy's.

A mixture of rickety wooden chairs, high tables, cushions, and low tables lined the lane in which the cafe was tucked, making it difficult to walk without brushing up against someone. The crowd was enormous in such a small space, and the syrupy sweet smell of tobacco was overpowering. Nehal walked through entire clouds of shisha smoke and hot tea fumes until she found herself at the entrance to the teahouse: a large archway with a dangling chandelier in its center. To her right, on the stoop, was a musician playing an oud and singing what sounded like Basim Almahdi's epic ballad "Weavers on the Wind."

Inside, there were more chairs and cushions; glittering lanterns dangled from the ceiling, casting the customers in bright light. Here it was the smell of strong coffee that inundated Nehal, a pleasant aroma that reminded her of late nights on the beach in Ramina.

She immediately spotted Malak, who was easily recognizable without a robe or veil. Nehal maneuvered her way toward Malak and tapped her on the arm. Malak turned, then grinned. "You're here!"

"Is it always this crowded?" Nehal shouted to be heard above the din.

Malak laughed. "Always. It's a tourist attraction, after all." She gestured for Nehal to sit and then ordered them both coffee and kunafa. The coffee, piping hot and with a thick layer of foam, nearly burned Nehal's tongue, but she loved its bitterness, especially when contrasted with the kunafa, which was dripping with sweet syrup.

They could barely hear each other talk in Fishawy's, so Malak quickly took Nehal's arm and led her out. They wandered the lanes of the souk, and Nehal walked past more and more shops selling all sorts of merchandise: glittering lanterns of every shape and size, glass cases of heavy golden necklaces and brass earrings, enormous carpets with intricate geometric designs, rows of silver shisha pipes, and sequined robes.

There was so much that Nehal wanted to stop and see it all, and Malak smiled and slowed her pace.

"I can't believe you've never been here before!" said Malak.

Nehal bent down to examine a golden headdress. "We've never stayed in Alamaxa for very long, so there was never time, I suppose."

"Well, that won't do!" Nehal looked up to see a playful smile on Malak's lips. "You've left me no choice, Nehal."

And so they explored the souk, wandering from shop to shop. Malak pointed out her favorite places: a tiny stationery store and an even tinier bookshop. At a shop with a smiling toothless vendor, Nehal purchased a lovely violet vest with sequined buttons and a new water gourd. Malak bought them two glasses of ice-cold sugarcane juice.

After some time, they wandered out of the souk. Nehal followed Malak down twisting dark alleyways and cobbled lanes. They left the cacophony of central Alamaxa behind, the clamor of the bazaar fading gradually until they walked in silence. Mashrabiyas looked down on them, the dim light from within casting honeycomb carpets of light beneath their feet. When they emerged from an alley onto a main street again, Nehal could smell the Izdihar; they were steps from the corniche.

Nehal leaned against the railing and reached out, arresting the flow of the river. She lifted a ribbon of water, the minute ministrations of her fingertips causing it to twirl in midair. Moonlight winked against the dancing liquid.

"Glad to see the Academy is doing its job." Malak leaned her elbow against the railing, facing Nehal with a half-smile.

Nehal laughed. "It's the best thing that's ever happened to me. Except, I don't care much for all the science and history lessons."

"Oh, I remember all that!" said Malak wistfully. "Air currents, the molecular structure of water, the ratio of muscle mass to weaving strength . . ."

"All terribly dull," Nehal pointed out. "It should come naturally."

"It's useful, though," said Malak thoughtfully. "You're a better weaver when you understand your element." Her gaze slipped toward the Izdihar; a lone felucca glided across the banks.

In the far distance, crickets sang a crooked melody. The moon was a glittering white orb in a starless sky. Under its pale light, Malak's hair shimmered a deep, velvety blue. Its sheen made Nehal want to reach out and run her hands through it. As though sensing her stare, Malak turned. Her smile was slow and small, tinted with something a little like grief. A silent understanding seemed to rise between them, communicated in tentative smiles and intense gazes.

Malak was as beautiful in the shadows as she was in the light; it was the kind of haunted beauty that made Nehal's knees go weak and her heart flutter. She felt the urge to close the distance between them.

Instead, Nehal cleared her throat and looked away. "Your father must have loved you very much," she teased. "To hire you a tutor all the way from Karatzia."

"He did," said Malak softly. "He was a very progressive man in many ways. In others, not quite."

"And your mother?"

Malak looked away, stiffening slightly. "She died when I was young."

"Sorry," said Nehal quietly, marveling at how much she wanted to reach out and touch Malak. With anyone else she might have already pulled them into a playful hug or put an arm across their shoulder, but it was different with Malak, and she was not entirely certain why that was.

Malak shook her head, smiling sadly. "It was a long time ago. All she wanted was for me to marry and settle down."

"Is that why you were engaged twice?"

Malak turned to Nehal with a wry smile and quirked eyebrow; Nehal shrugged sheepishly. "Apparently it was in the papers."

Malak laughed softly. "I'm sure it was." She sighed and looked up at the moon. "My first engagement was to my cousin. The match was brokered before I was even born, and he and I grew up together. By the time we were sixteen we were more like siblings than anything else, and we decided to stay that way. I assume the papers didn't think to mention the separation was amicable and mutually agreed upon?"

Nehal shrugged again. "Bastards."

Malak chuckled. "At university, the year before I graduated, one of my classmates went to my father to ask for my hand, and I thought, why not? He was kind, intelligent. I thought perhaps I should try to better fit in with my countrywomen, to not be such an enigma to my surroundings. So I agreed to an engagement."

Nehal was listening quietly, not trusting herself to speak. When Malak paused for a long time, Nehal thought she was done with her story, but then she slowly leaned forward and turned to look directly at Nehal.

"I tried to fall in love with him," said Malak quietly. "I really did. I thought if I could fall in love with any man it would be him. But I couldn't. It wasn't fair to him, so I broke it off. I stopped bothering with men after that."

Nehal blinked. She felt like she had just been given an important revelation, but she wasn't certain how to address it just yet, so she steered the conversation into a different territory.

"The papers said your family disowned you," said Nehal, echoing what Mahitab had told her all.

Malak shrugged. "They make it sound more dramatic than it was. My mother was dead, my father died soon after I broke off my second engagement, and we had never been especially close with the rest of our family. They just . . . slowly stopped speaking to me."

"I couldn't imagine not having any family," said Nehal wonderingly. "It must be lonely."

Malak looked slightly surprised, like she hadn't considered that before. "Sometimes," she said hesitantly. "But I have the Daughters of Izdihar. I have friends. I've made my own family."

It seemed terribly sad to Nehal. She missed the company of her family nearly as much as she missed the sea. True, she hadn't seen or spoken to any of them, not even her parents and siblings, since her wedding, but she comforted herself with the knowledge that they were *there,* that they loved her and would welcome her back whenever she returned, and they would all fall back on old patterns. She could not imagine how she would fare if she had no one.

"You two look cozy."

Nehal and Malak broke apart. Malak tensed immediately, her shoulders rising up, her arm moving into a defensive stance, ready to weave. The words had come from a man standing just a few steps away from them, leaning casually against the railing, one hand loosely hovering over his waist, from which a khopesh dangled. He was bald but sported a full beard.

With a sneer, he said, "Always interesting to see Malak Mamdouh walking among us mortals."

"Is that why you've been following us, Attia?" asked Malak mildly. "Hoping for a glimpse?"

Nehal glanced at her in surprise. She hadn't noticed the man—Attia—at all, and Malak had given absolutely no indication that they were being followed.

Attia laughed harshly, then straightened and began to approach them. His hand never left his khopesh.

"Just what is it you think you're going to accomplish with that?" asked Malak, nodding to his rustic weapon.

"With this?" Attia tapped his khopesh. "Not much. But I can do more with this." Suddenly, a different weapon was in his hand, something Nehal had never seen before; it looked like a musket, but it was small enough to be held in one hand. She blinked at it, confused, but with a growing awareness of just how dangerous that strange weapon was.

"The Khopeshes have pistols now?" Malak asked the question as casually as if she were discussing the weather. "Now where would you be getting those? I know the police don't have the funding for that."

Attia frowned, likely annoyed Malak wasn't displaying the fear he expected. "That's none of your business."

"Are you going to kill me, then?" Malak shrugged. "Or are you just trying to scare me? Having a bit of fun?"

"Don't have to kill you." The Khopesh took a step forward. "A bullet in the leg will do just fine."

Nehal had heard enough. She sidestepped out from behind Malak and twisted toward the river. Engaging every newly scarred muscle in her body, she pulled the Izdihar to her, drawing forth a wave as large as a palanquin. She raised it high, until it blocked the moon, casting a deep, dark shadow across them all.

Attia turned to the wave in horror. He fumbled the weapon in his hands, unsure whether to shoot or run. Before he could make a decision the wave attacked him with a racking crash, sweeping him back from the corniche. When the water trickled away, he lay flat on his back, spread out like a starfish, his pistol gone.

Malak took a step forward, her eyes fixed on the prone man. "Nehal—you shouldn't have done that."

Nehal turned to her in shock. "He was going to shoot you."

"And I would have stopped the bullet in midair."

Nehal was awed. "You—you can do that?"

Malak turned back to her, smiling gravely. "I can do a lot of things. Most of them more inconspicuous than . . . this."

Nehal tucked her hands into her trousers, feeling a bit ashamed of her actions now, but still convinced the man deserved what he'd got. "He'll be fine." She nodded toward Attia, who was already sitting up, coughing and disoriented. "Perhaps he'll have learned his lesson."

"Or perhaps he'll be even more motivated to seek us out again," said Malak. "In any case, we ought to go." Malak took Nehal's hand and pulled her away before Attia could come to his senses, guiding them between buildings and through twisting alleys, where they could hide far more easily than on the broad corniche.

"I don't understand why you were humoring him," said Nehal as Malak continued to pull her along. "You're so much stronger; you could have swept him aside like a gnat."

Malak stopped walking and turned to Nehal, dropping her hand and looking at her wryly. "Yes, I could have. But that man—Attia Marwan—happens to be a policeman who could easily arrest me—arrest us. It's all far more trouble than it's worth. I've learned to pick my battles." She sighed. "And there's always a battle when you're as recognizable as I am. I'm sorry he ruined a nice evening."

"Are you serious?" Nehal grinned. "I got to use my weaving to knock down a Khopesh of the Tetrad—and a policeman. What could be more fun than that?"

Malak shook her head, smiling ruefully. "You enjoy courting trouble, don't you?"

Nehal shrugged. "I like a little excitement. What's wrong with that?"

Malak's eyes twinkled in the moonlight. "Nothing. Nothing at all."

19

GIORGINA

GIORGINA WAS PACKING A SATCHEL, PREPARING TO LEAVE for her morning shift at the bookstore, when she felt Sabah shuffle up behind her. Giorgina could always recognize Sabah's walk; when she was a young girl, her left leg had been mangled in an accident at the factory where she worked, and it had never been quite right since.

Sabah sat beside Giorgina with an exhausted sigh.

Giorgina looked up from her bag, careful to keep the handbills for Malak's lecture tucked away. "Does your leg hurt?"

"Don't bother trying to hide them," said Sabah with no preamble. "I saw them in your bag yesterday."

For a moment, Giorgina could not process her sister's words, and then once she realized what Sabah had said, she had no idea how to respond. Her hand hovered over her satchel protectively.

"You think I don't know you've been hanging around them?" said Sabah, keeping her voice as low as a whisper.

"I don't—"

Sabah scoffed. "Please don't bother denying it. But you're advertising for them now? If Baba finds out—"

"He won't if you don't tell him, Sabah," said Giorgina. "How did you even—"

"And I *know* it's not a lecture," said Sabah, ignoring Giorgina's question. "I know you're planning to march on Parliament."

"I—how—"

"Basna," said Sabah simply. "She heard about it from a friend, and she's planning to attend."

Giorgina was stunned into silence; Basna was their neighbor and Sabah's close friend. She had gotten married at fifteen and had her first child by sixteen. Giorgina recalled Basna being rather complacent about the engagement and had not heard her complain in all the years since.

Sabah pulled on her dark brown locks, twirling the waves tightly in her fist. "I don't know what she's thinking. Or what you're thinking, for that matter."

"You talk all the time of how unfair things are! The Daughters of Izdihar are actually trying to do something about it—"

"That's not the point!" Sabah snapped. "Danger is always following them! They're always involved in riots or being arrested. Marching on *Parliament,* Giorgina? How can you think that will end well?"

Giorgina swallowed; she was unused to fighting with Sabah like this and did not know how to structure her defenses. "This is how change happens—"

Sabah scoffed. "Hah! Change! You think men will change their minds when women force their hands? At best they'll ignore you. At worst they'll call you agitators and terrorists and throw you in prison. Or they'll spite us by taking away what few rights we *do* have."

"So, what then?" demanded Giorgina. "We do nothing and wait for them to give us our rights when they feel like it?"

"You sound like Malak Mamdouh," accused Sabah. "Just parroting her words."

A flame of anger flared in Giorgina's chest. "I don't *parrot* anyone's words; I have a mind of my own."

"Yes, and I thought you were smarter than this—"

"Malak won't let the march spiral out of control—"

"Oh, we trust *Malak* now?" Sabah's voice was steadily rising. "What, did she become part of the family when I wasn't looking?"

"She has a plan," said Giorgina, a little desperately. She wasn't quite certain why convincing Sabah of this mattered so much, but it did. Perhaps Giorgina was convincing herself as well. "She just wants Parliament to pay more attention, to . . . to see our issues as important ones."

Sabah shook her head. "I don't understand you. I don't understand why you think you need to be a part of Malak's games, you and Basna—"

"How can it be a march if no one attends?"

"Then there won't be a march! Or you could leave the marching to Malak and her ilk," Sabah snapped. "Her high-bred ladies with husbands who . . . who own the factories *we* work at. *Those* ladies have nothing better to do, and they have people who can keep them safe. Who do you and Basna have?"

"You're being unfair!" said Giorgina. "Not everyone in the Daughters of Izdihar is rich. I was there! Some women are even poorer than you and me. And Malak isn't playing games—she holds charity clinics and helps the poor and petitions for girls to have secondary schools, and I can't believe you think so little of me that you think I haven't thought this through—"

"*Giorgina.*" Sabah leaned forward and placed her hands atop Giorgina's. "Of course I don't think little of you. I'm *worried* about you. You have a respectable, wealthy suitor, and instead—"

"So you think I should just marry him, then?"

Sabah stared hard at her. "Why wouldn't you?"

Giorgina was quiet, and Sabah took advantage of her silence.

"You've always been such a romantic," she said quietly. "You need to grow up, Giorgina. Be realistic. A good marriage is all girls like us can hope for. And your presence at that march isn't going to make any difference to anyone."

Giorgina tugged her hands out of her sister's grip. "It will make a difference to *me*." Her eyes burned with unshed tears.

Sabah sat back. For a long time, the two only stared at one another quietly. Giorgina could not bear this angry silence between them. She and Sabah had always been close; only eleven months separated them, but Sabah took her role as eldest sister seriously. They hardly ever fought.

"I feel like I don't know you anymore," said Sabah softly. "This past year . . . you've kept so many secrets from me."

Giorgina tensed, her heart hammering. What else did her sister know? "What are you talking about?"

Sabah only shook her head. With a grunt of effort, she got to her feet and shuffled out of the room, leaving Giorgina to stew in her uncertainty.

IT WAS NOT without some trepidation that Giorgina arranged the newsstand in the bookshop that morning. Her argument with Sabah was still on her mind, making her far more aware of the risks she was taking.

Alongside the usual newspapers and pamphlets, Giorgina had added a new item: the handbills advertising Malak's "lecture" at Alamaxa University. Though it was black-and-white and as nondescript as the other publications, it still seemed to stand out among the rest.

Giorgina shook her head to rid herself of that ridiculous notion; her nerves were letting her imagination run wild. It was unlikely Anas would even notice, and yet Giorgina still felt as though she had started a small rebellion. It was not a feeling she disliked. There was power in it.

Giorgina was possessed of little in life that made her feel powerful. She was a woman, and a poor one at that, with no means and few prospects. Even her weaving was not accessible to her; it only plagued her with anxiety. Were she to sit down and truly consider her station in life, it would infuriate her. Usually, she was too exhausted or too sad to think about her misfortunes so clearly.

The Daughters of Izdihar seemed to revel in that, however. Malak's strategy hinged on reminding women of their misfortunes in life, to stoke the fires of their anger until they were ready to burn everything to ash. It frightened Giorgina, but it exhilarated her as well.

She could hardly concentrate on anything for the remainder of her shift. In the middle of all her tasks her gaze would swivel back toward the newsstand, where Malak's handbills sat like a beacon. Word of the march had already begun to spread, the way open secrets did: from one woman to five, and on and on. How many women would be there? Malak was the most formidable person Giorgina knew, but could even she contain such a crowd? Was Sabah right; would the march inevitably spin out of control?

When Anas arrived for his shift, it was a relief; Giorgina had lunch with Labiba to look forward to. When he came in, Giorgina pushed her books aside and picked up her shawl, ready to leave. Then Anas froze. His abruptness might have been comical, if his gaze were not focused so incredulously on the newsstand.

With a deep breath, Giorgina approached Anas, gripping her shawl tightly between her fingers.

"It's been a rather quiet day—" Giorgina began.

"What is this garbage?" Anas pointed at the newsstand.

Giorgina swallowed. "What do you mean?"

Anas picked up the handbills and waved them in Giorgina's face. "Since when do we advertise trash like this?"

"It . . . it's not trash," said Giorgina in a small voice. "I thought—I thought it was interesting."

"I don't recall paying you to think," Anas snapped.

But you do, thought Giorgina. *You value my thinking and my judgment.*

"Have you forgotten yourself?" continued Anas. "I pay you to do as I tell you to do. You don't make decisions around here without my say-so."

Giorgina tried to speak but her voice snagged in her throat, tears pooling in her eyes as flames licked up her gut.

Anas snapped his fingers. "Are you listening?"

Giorgina attempted speech once more. "If you would just—"

"Are you telling me how to run my own shop now?" Anas sneered. "You think I don't know that she calls men idiots who are enslaving their own country? Throw these in the trash where they belong."

Giorgina stared at the newsstand so she wouldn't have to meet Anas's glare. It was true that Malak's language could be inflammatory, but how could any decent person be so upset about respectability when women were suffering so much abuse? Didn't the reality of oppression matter more than the language they used to fight it?

"Girl!" Anas snapped his fingers again, this time so close to Giorgina's nose she felt the sound waves bounce off her. "Throw them in the trash, or you're fired. There are plenty of others in this city looking for work. Don't think I can't replace you in a day." Anas walked over to the counter, pulled out a bin, and set it in front of Giorgina. Then he stood back and crossed his arms.

Giorgina stared at him.

"Hurry up!" he barked.

A spark of defiance momentarily flared in Giorgina, making her pause, but it was swiftly put out by rationality. Moving quickly, she tossed every single handbill into the bin.

"That's better." Anas shook his head. "I was under the impression you were a decent girl from a good family, not a hooligan shouting in the streets. If you give me another reason to doubt you, you *will* be out of a job. Is that understood?"

Stiffly, Giorgina nodded.

"Speak up, girl!"

"It's understood," she said.

Giorgina exited the shop trembling, the ground beneath her feet echoing her emotions. She was not certain if it was fear or fury. Likely both. The injustice of it was like scalding water pouring down her back. It was *not fair* that she was forced to choose her job over her dignity. It was *not fair* that she had to spurn the man she loved to preserve something as nebulous as a reputation. It was *not fair* that she was forced to care so damn much about preserving her reputation when men could do whatever they liked without a care in the world. She took a moment to calm herself down before she continued down the alley.

When she met up with Labiba, the other woman frowned. "Oh no, what's wrong?"

Giorgina gave a hollow laugh. Labiba had developed an uncanny ability to read Giorgina's moods, though normally she was adept at keeping her feelings hidden from everyone else, including her family. Although, given that Sabah had been aware of Giorgina's involvement with the Daughters of Izdihar all along, perhaps Giorgina wasn't as canny as she thought.

"It's been a long day," said Giorgina finally. "Did you manage to speak with Nasef?"

Labiba had intended to go to King Lotfy Templehouse that morning. At Giorgina's question, her lips downturned into a sad pout. "He won't see me. He said he was too busy, but I could tell he was lying."

They walked together to a favored lunch spot; it was a small, old-fashioned restaurant with a partition down the middle to separate men and women. Giorgina relished being able to sit and eat without her shawl, without having to worry about men leering at her. She and Labiba sat on the floor, a low table between them. There was a single lantern in the entire women's section and no windows, so the restaurant was cast in shadows. It was comforting, however; Giorgina felt thoroughly hidden.

Unlike the new, fancy restaurants Nico had taken her to, there was no waitstaff here; Giorgina and Labiba had to go to the counter to order their food. They each ordered falafal and fava bean sand-wiches, which came in piping hot flatbread, and with an assortment of mezze: olives and torshi, yogurt dip and cold cucumbers. They ordered two cups of black tea to wash down their food; Labiba plied hers with four spoons of sugar.

"So tell me," said Labiba, biting into her fava bean sandwich, "why was it a long day?"

Giorgina tapped her finger against her steaming hot tea, winc-ing from the pain. Labiba had quickly become the person to whom Giorgina told all her secrets, and more, the person to whom she *wanted* to speak her secrets, whereas before she had simply buried them all within her. Perhaps it was because of the way they had met, Labiba having rescued her from a crisis, already privy to Giorgina's most dangerous secret. Or perhaps they were simply bound together in the way that some people were. Sometimes it surprised Giorgina, that such a strong intimacy could be fostered between two people in the short space of a year, whereas with others decades could not create any such affinity. As it was, Giorgina could no longer imagine her life without Labiba there.

So, after a brief moment of hesitation, Giorgina told Labiba about her arguments with Sabah and Anas.

"It doesn't matter what Anas thinks," said Labiba immediately. "It's all right, just do what he says, keep your job safe. As for your sister . . ." Labiba shrugged. "It's harder with family."

Labiba knew this all too well; she and Etedal were both from Upper Ramsawa, farther south, and had run away to Alamaxa when their families had attempted to force them both into arranged mar-riages with older men. As far as Giorgina knew, neither of them had spoken to their parents since, nor did their parents have any idea where their daughters were.

"There's something else." Giorgina looked down at her food, which was suddenly turning her stomach.

Labiba waited patiently until Giorgina found her words.

Giorgina's voice was a strangled whisper. "I have a suitor." She glanced up at Labiba through her lashes. Her friend's eyes were wide, her mouth shaped into a perfect circle of surprise.

"Not . . . not Nico, I assume?" said Labiba weakly.

"His name is Zakariyya Amin," replied Giorgina miserably. "He was a customer at the bookshop. He spoke to my father already; they've decided it between them."

"What are you going to do?"

"What *can* I do?" Giorgina waved her hands. "I have no say in any of this. I can't even sign my own marriage contract without my father as a witness. And he's *rich*, Labiba. He could help my family. What possible reason could I have to refuse?"

Labiba was quiet. All too quickly, Giorgina realized the implications of what she had said.

"Oh—no, I didn't mean—I wasn't—"

"I *know*, habibti," said Labiba gently. "To be honest, if it weren't for Etedal . . . I would have stayed. I would have married a strange man older than my father and been miserable. There's no way I would have left everything behind and fled to another city all alone." She winked then, her melancholy quickly dissipating into a grin. "And my suitor wasn't even that rich."

"I hate that I have to just . . . surrender," said Giorgina quietly. "Marriage is so final. Permanent. He doesn't even want me to work, Labiba. He just wants me to sit at home and be his wife."

Labiba placed her hand atop Giorgina's. "What about Nico?" she asked, so softly Giorgina had to strain to hear her. "Are you sure you won't take him up on his offer?"

Giorgina sat back, slipping out of Labiba's grasp, but Labiba was earnest as she leaned forward.

"I know women in those arrangements," said Labiba. "They're happy enough. They're secure and free. They have friends."

"And they're shunned," said Giorgina a little shrilly. "No family, no respect. And their children? Bastards with no legal rights, not even a proper last name? Not to mention what it would do to my family. My sisters would never be able to marry. My parents wouldn't be able to show their faces in their own neighborhood."

"All right," said Labiba quietly. "I understand."

For the next few moments they were both quiet; Giorgina's food had grown cold, and she only picked at it. She would wrap it up to take with her and eat later, when her stomach was no longer in knots.

"Just so you know," said Labiba slowly. "If anything ever happens with your family, or if you change your mind about this suitor . . . you always have a place with me and Etedal. You can always stay with us, for as long as you like." Labiba's eyes were warm and bright, amber orbs in the shadows. "You wouldn't be alone. We've got you."

It took all of Giorgina's willpower not to burst into tears.

20

NEHAL

BY NEHAL'S FOURTH WEEK AT THE ACADEMY, HER SKILLS had improved to a degree of which she had only ever dreamed.

Nagi had begun teaching them how to affect water pressure and physical state in order to grasp objects. Nehal liked Nagi very much—he didn't condescend to her or Shaimaa, treated them the same way he treated the men, and made no special allowances for them. And he even managed to make scientific jargon interesting, as he related it to weaving in a practical way that made Nehal embrace the knowledge and yearn for more. He'd spoken quite a lot about molecular structure and the shifting states of matter, then paired each of them with a rather large rock. Nehal was quite eager to perfect this new skill: a length of water in her hands, swirling it around her like a snake as she grasped at its molecular state, as Nagi had told them.

Beside her, Waseem lashed out with a splash, his water spilling all over the ground. With a smirk, Nehal turned away, then began carefully maneuvering her own water toward the rock. As she willed it, she felt the water shift in her grasp, solidifying, and it was as natural as breathing—she wrapped the water around the rock and lifted it into the air.

Nagi whistled. "Nice."

Talaat, who, like Waseem, had only managed to splash around unsuccessfully, shot her a dark look. Nehal resisted an extremely childish urge to stick her tongue out at him. Shaimaa, who stood at Nehal's left, gave her a gentle shoulder tap and a smile.

"Let's try something, Nehal," said Nagi. "I think you're ready for it. The rest of you, keep at it!"

Nagi took Nehal aside and gestured for her to sit down. He pulled a small amount of water out of the Izdihar and held it up between them. Then, within moments, he shifted it into a solid ball of ice.

Nehal could not help the delighted sigh that escaped her. Nagi grinned at her pleasure, shifted the ball of ice back to water, then pulled his arms apart and transformed it into steam.

Nehal could not help but gasp. "Amazing!"

"Perhaps. But also something *you* can do," said Nagi. "It's only an extension of what you just did. Just keep going."

Encouraged by his confidence in her, Nehal took the water from him and held it up, then began to solidify it, and, as Nagi said, simply kept going . . .

Until she was holding a ball of ice.

She and Nagi shared a surprised laugh, and then Nehal, wanting to impress him further, focused all her will and energy into the ball of ice and shifted it back into water.

"*Excellent!*" Nagi beamed. "Now we try steam."

It took Nehal several tries to turn liquid into steam, but by the end of the lesson, when some of her classmates were still dropping their rocks halfway through, she was effortlessly shifting large amounts of water from ice to liquid to steam and back again.

Basking under the glow of her success, Nehal walked off arm in arm with Shaimaa, Waseem trailing behind them.

"How'd you do all that so quickly?" he asked, jogging after them.

Nehal waved her arm in the air. "One can't explain natural talent," she joked.

Shaimaa rolled her eyes, but Waseem frowned as if confused.

Talaat continued to glare at her poisonously, but Nehal could not be bothered with his jealousy. In fact, it delighted her. Everything about the Academy delighted her—the company, the instructors, the sense of achievement and purpose. It seemed unbelievable that she might have been denied this opportunity to be where she clearly belonged.

WHEN NEHAL WAS off the island and back in central Alamaxa, she showed Malak her newfound skills.

She and Malak had been meeting regularly every weekend now. Sometimes they went to Khalili Souk, sometimes to a new restaurant, or sometimes they would just spend time in Malak's house, where just being near Malak felt like a dare. Every casual brush of fingertips, every exchanged glance, every shared laugh, held within it a kind of thrill Nehal had never felt before.

Nehal had had *friends* before, of course, but it was different with Malak. There was something in the intensity of her gaze, in the way her touches lingered. Sometimes, Nehal wondered if she was imagining it, this unfamiliar intimacy between them. Nehal had grown up among women, among cousins and family friends, but there was something about Malak that was . . . different.

In the deep recesses of her mind, Nehal knew what this feeling was, but she tried to ignore it. Nehal did not need another reason to be excoriated by her society. She had courted rebellion all her life, but this . . . people who walked this path were disowned, beaten, killed. If weaving was frowned upon by many, *this* . . . this was almost universally abhorred.

Nehal told herself she was not afraid, that she was only weary of having to fight all the time, for everything, but—she was a little afraid, too.

When they were not simply enjoying each other's company, most of their time was taken up with activities involving the Daughters of Izdihar.

Nehal had had no proper conception of what they actually did. There were so many events, so many rallies and riots and speeches given impromptu in the middle of the street or in Parliament's public forums, written and practiced in advance and delivered by adept speakers. Nehal thought she might graduate to this eventually; she was a lady, after all; the rabble on the streets would be much less likely to accost her or throw things at her.

The Daughters sold their magazine, *The Vanguard,* for revenue, but the handbills were distributed free of charge, with snapshots of the magazine's content to entice people to buy it, but also for the poorer classes who could not afford to purchase the magazine. Malak was always conscious of the lower classes, and it had gotten Nehal to think more of them too. She had not thought of the magazine as particularly expensive, and she had a renewing subscription, but she supposed she had never had to worry about money before.

Even handing out handbills was strictly scheduled and organized; Malak was careful never to oversaturate a particular street or locale.

And then there were the charity events, food drives and soap distribution, used clothing markets, distribution of childcare supplies. There were "literacy initiatives" that amounted to members of the group volunteering their time to tutor young girls who could not otherwise afford it. She also attended meetings with the Daughters of Izdihar, meetings which Malak held at least once every weekend.

Through it all, Nehal was by Malak's side.

Malak, and her soft laugh, and the gentle caress of her ever-lingering touches. Nehal wanted nothing more than to spend this entire weekend with her again, as she had been doing for the past few weeks—but unfortunately, this particular weekend found Nehal and Nico invited—or, more accurately, summoned—to join Nico's parents for dinner at the Baldinotti estates. Nehal was forced to cancel a planned outing with Malak, and instead suffer a night with Lorenzo Baldinotti.

Nico was, if anything, even less enthused by the prospect. The night of the dinner, Nehal thought Nico looked like he wanted nothing more than to drink himself into a stupor and crawl beneath the covers of his bed. The two did not commiserate, however; the frost between them still persisted. They had said little to one another since their argument the previous month, after Raouf's disastrous visit. When Nehal was home from the Academy, Nico did his best to avoid her; as it was, they had barely even been in the same room together in weeks.

When Nehal met Nico on their way to the palanquin, she saw him freeze, his eyes trailing over her body. Nehal wore no outer robe, only her vest, and a short vest at that, cinched around her waist and tight around her chest. Her hair was loose about her shoulders, the curls spilling freely with no veil or even chignon to contain them. Nico opened his mouth, but words withered on his lips when Nehal glared at him coldly. He hastily looked away. Nehal knew she was provoking trouble with her attire, but she was done inconveniencing herself for others' sensibilities. Nico should have been grateful Nehal had not yet mustered up the courage to remove her undershirt and bare her arms freely, like Malak did.

They rode to the Baldinotti estates in steely silence, sitting on opposite sides of the palanquin, both taking care not to draw the other's attention in any way. When they arrived, a servant led them into the parlor, where Nico's parents were waiting. The smiles slipped off Lorenzo and Hikmat's faces when their eyes landed on Nehal.

"By the Tetrad, girl, *what* are you wearing?" asked a scandalized Lorenzo.

Nehal stiffly greeted Hikmat with two kisses before answering. "I'm wearing my clothes, Uncle." She made to greet him but Lorenzo held back, his eyes trailing up and down her person.

"Where is your robe? Your veil?" Lorenzo turned to Nico. "How could you let her wear that?"

Nehal responded before Nico could. "I'm quite capable of dressing myself, thank you, Uncle." She took a seat beside Hikmat and crossed her arms, staring defiantly at them all.

"Well, she was only in the palanquin," Hikmat said to Lorenzo.

Nico cleared his throat twice. "Hello, Mama, I've missed you. How is your pomegranate tree coming along?"

Nico's terrible attempt at changing the subject did not go unnoticed. Lorenzo raised a single pale eyebrow and glared at his son as Nico took a seat beside Nehal.

"Nehal, you're dressed inappropriately," said Lorenzo curtly. "The only women who walk about the street like that are . . . well . . . dancers and the like."

Nehal smiled sweetly, hoping Lorenzo could see the mockery behind it. "Then perhaps we could all learn from dancers and the *like*."

Lorenzo huffed out a breath through flared nostrils but said nothing more. He raised a hand to one of the servants, who sprung into motion and began to arrange the dinner. Nobody spoke while the servants came and went. They set down steaming bowls of yellow rice cooked with golden raisins and pine nuts, sizzling lamb kofta dressed with parsley, cold yogurt-cucumber dip, and a jug of icy mango juice. Through it all Lorenzo glared at Nico, his eyes occasionally wandering over to Nehal.

"I've been meaning to speak to the pair of you," said Lorenzo as he sliced into his kofta with unnecessary force. "About who you associate with."

Nico, who had already begun to eat, paused with a utensil halfway to his mouth. "What do you mean?"

"Yusry Sarhan." Lorenzo pointed his fork toward Nico. "I'd advise you to stay away from him."

Nehal's set her cup of juice on the table with a slam. "What's wrong with Yusry?" she demanded.

Beside her, Nico winced, but Nehal ignored him.

Hikmat leaned forward, her gaze falling on Nehal sympatheti-cally—or patronizingly. "There are unsavory rumors swirling about him, habibti, that's all. We just want you to be careful."

Nehal wrinkled her nose. "What sort of unsavory rumors?"

"They say he is—forgive my language—a queer." Lorenzo shud-dered.

"Excuse me?" Nehal's voice was a whisper.

Hikmat answered in a voice just as low. "It means he associates with men in unnatural ways."

"I know what the word means," Nehal said stiffly.

"Well then, it should be quite clear to you that an association with him can only harm you." Lorenzo patted his mouth with a handkerchief. "You were with him at the opera, and then dinner at his house! Nico, you especially will want to be careful around him."

Nico said nothing, but apparently his father required no encour-agement.

"Who knows how that sort of proclivity spreads," Lorenzo continued. "You'll not want to be too close to him. I suppose cer-tain meetings will be unavoidable, given his connection to Nagat Shawkat. She and her husband are both respectable people, at least, though I can't understand why they continue to associate with that man. Cousin or not." He shook his head and returned his attention to his food.

Nehal grit her teeth so tightly her jaw clicked. The words she wanted to say were coming far too fast for her to process them; if she opened her mouth all that would emerge would be a nonsensical tirade of shouts and curses.

She opened her mouth anyway.

But before she could speak, Nico, who had apparently been watching her, covered her fist with his large hand. It was the first time he had touched her in weeks. She turned to him in surprise. Not quite meeting her eyes, he leaned toward her and said, for her ears only, "Don't bother. You won't change his opinion."

Nehal's eyes widened with fury. "Do you share his views, then?"

"No," Nico replied, doing his best to keep his voice low. "You know I don't. But—"

"But you're a coward," Nehal breathed. Their faces were nearly close enough to touch; it was an unwelcome reminder of the last time they had been so close. "You would rather keep the peace than speak up for what's right."

"I told you, you're not going to change his—"

"There are times when you *must* speak, Nico," Nehal said through gritted teeth. "Even if you can't change the other person. If you don't speak, then they have succeeded in changing *you*."

"Is something wrong?" asked Hikmat.

Nehal looked up; Lorenzo and Hikmat were both staring at them. Their whispers must have grown in volume.

"Yusry is our friend," said Nehal furiously. "He has been nothing but gracious. I have no intention of discarding him because of rumors, which, even if they happened to be true, would not bother me."

Lorenzo stared blankly at Nehal before exchanging a look with a bewildered Hikmat. "You cannot be serious."

"I am *quite* serious."

Lorenzo chuckled, but there was no amusement in the gesture. "You behave as though I've said something out of the ordinary. Surely you realize it is *your* opinion that is outlandish?"

Nehal said nothing but poked her tongue into her cheek, attempting to keep her anger reined in.

"If I recall correctly, Nico shared these ridiculous views too." Nico's breath quickened as his father's gaze landed on him. "When you eventually stopped arguing with me about them, I assumed you had finally matured and realized your errors. Was I wrong?"

Nehal turned to Nico with some satisfaction; Lorenzo had just proved her point. To her immense irritation, however, Nico only shrugged.

Lorenzo scoffed. "In any case, we should move on. That's not all I wanted to discuss."

Nehal then realized what she should have known all along; this dinner invitation was not at all that of a father and father-in-law wishing to spend time with his family, but that of a family patriarch keeping his house in order. The sour taste of anger stuck in the back of Nehal's throat.

"This is to do with you specifically, Nehal," said Hikmat gently. Hikmat's hands had settled in her lap and her attention was directed completely toward Nehal. Lorenzo looked on out of the corner of his eyes, maintaining a mild expression.

Nehal looked at the pair of them with narrowed eyes. This was clearly a setup, and Hikmat's gentle tone only raised her suspicions. "What is it?"

"Well . . ." Hikmat hesitated. "There's been talk. You've been seen several times with Malak Mamdouh. At her home as well."

"Yes. What of it?"

"Well, habibti, surely there can be no argument regarding *her* reputation. The way she dresses, the things she says—"

"What's wrong with the things she says?" Nehal interrupted. "She's fighting for our rights. Yours and mine."

Hikmat sighed. "But the way she does it? Calling Parliament 'a bunch of imbeciles'? Starting riots in the streets? Putting women in the army?"

"Women can fight as well as men, if they're trained," countered Nehal.

"That's hardly the point." Hikmat frowned. "There are certain things no respectable women should engage in, no matter her abilities."

"But—"

"Nehal." Hikmat smiled kindly. "The world is not so unfair as Malak Mamdouh claims. Men and women are simply created differently, and we are meant for different things."

"So we're meant to have no say in our own futures?" argued Nehal. "No ability to vote, to influence the laws that affect us?"

"The world of politics is not for us—"

"But politics affects everything!" Nehal burst out. "If politicians don't want to provide funds for schools, girls can't learn. If judges are willing to let men who murder women go free—"

"Habibti." Hikmat reached across the table for Nehal's hand. "Please, calm down. There's no need for this kind of talk. All I'm saying is if you continue to be seen with that woman, your reputation will be at stake. I'm sure you've seen the things they say about her. You are a prominent woman whose every move is observed. Your name will be in the papers."

"I don't care about my reputation," said Nehal. "If I did I wouldn't have enrolled at the Weaving Academy."

"I beg your pardon?" Lorenzo looked up sharply, his cup of sharbat hovering above his lips. "The Weaving Academy? Your father allowed this? With what money?"

Nehal shrugged. "It was Nico who signed the papers."

Lorenzo turned to Nico, fire in his eyes. "You did *what*?"

Nico looked like he wanted to crawl under the table, though Nehal would have immediately dragged him back out. Instead, he sighed wearily and said nothing.

"It's a miracle this hasn't been in the papers yet! The *Weaving Academy*. What in the Tetrad's name for? What exactly do you plan to do with your ridiculous affliction?"

"It's not an *affliction*," snapped Nehal. "And for your information, I plan to enroll in the army. The Izdihar Division."

Hikmat clapped a hand over her heart rather dramatically, and Lorenzo dragged a hand across his beard. "My daughter-in-law is going to be the death of me," he muttered. "You are going to ruin yourselves. And you will drag this family down with you. I will not have my name ridiculed in the papers, do you understand, Nehal?"

Nehal turned to him, nostrils flared.

"You are a member of this family now. We'll deal with this ridiculous army business later, but for now, I will *not* have you in Malak Mamdouh's company. Is that understood?"

"I will do what I like," Nehal hissed.

Lorenzo slammed his hand down on the table; Nico jumped and looked at his father in shock, and even Hikmat's eyes went wide. "You will do as I say, you silly, ignorant girl! You've *no* idea. You admire this woman, is that right? Have you any idea how she accomplishes these things you speak of so highly? That ridiculous female military unit only passed because she bedded the minister of defense. She's a common whore! Is that what you want people to say about you?"

"That's enough!" Nico shouted. His voice thudded against the walls.

Nehal, who had momentarily paled, staring at Lorenzo in stunned silence, turned to her husband in even greater shock. She did not think she had ever heard him raise his voice before. Lorenzo scowled at him, but surprisingly, Nico did not back down.

Nico swallowed audibly, his hands trembling at his sides. "You *will not* speak to my wife in that manner."

"*You* will not tell me how to speak in my own home, boy—"

"Fine!" Nico yelled. He got to his feet and held his hand out to Nehal. "Then we're leaving."

"Niccolo!" shouted Lorenzo. "Sit down!"

But Nehal had already taken Nico's arm and pulled herself up, and there was no stopping her as she marched out of the parlor. Lorenzo shouted again, but they ignored him as they put on their shoes. The pair quickly escaped into the cool night breeze.

In the palanquin, Nehal was quiet, sitting in the corner with her arms wrapped around herself. She could not stop thinking about what Lorenzo had said about Malak. Out of the corner of her eye, she saw Nico, who, after some hesitation, moved closer and put a hand on her knee. "Are you all right?"

She turned to him with a frown. "It's not true, is it? What he said about her?"

Nico sighed. "I don't know. I wouldn't trust my father very much, though."

"He's horrible!" Nehal burst out. "I know he's your father, and I'm sorry, but he's absolutely horrible!"

Nico laughed, then laughed even harder at the bewildered look on Nehal's face. "I'm sorry—it's just—you don't have to apologize. I'm quite certain I hate my father even more than you do."

Nehal shook her head. "Why do you always do as he says, then?"

Nico sighed, leaning back against the palanquin. "I don't always. I just . . . to be honest . . ." Nico paused for a long time, as though deciding how to best word his revelation. "The thing is, I'll do almost anything to avoid confrontation. It's not one of my best qualities, I know, but it is what it is. Once my father's back is turned I usually do what I like anyway. There's just no point in drawing his ire."

"Sometimes drawing ire is precisely the point," said Nehal.

Nico rolled his eyes, but he was smiling. "You *would* think that."

"So is that why you agreed to marry me?"

Nico's laughter slipped away. "No. I didn't have a choice."

"What does that mean?"

Nico looked to be contemplating, then he sighed heavily. "He threatened Giorgina."

Nehal reared back. "To—harm her?"

"Not physically!" said Nico hurriedly. "He has . . . information about her."

"What kind of information?"

Nico hesitated. "I . . . I can't say." He held a hand up, staving her off. "And before you try to bully me, it is not my secret to divulge. I can only tell you that it would ruin her."

"Well, how does he have this information? And is it even true? You just said you shouldn't trust him—"

"It's true. Giorgina confirmed it. As for how . . . he knows people, my illustrious father," said Nico bitterly. "Plenty of them would be willing to do anything for his favor."

"He's horrible. *Horrible.*" Nehal peered up at Nico, eyes narrowed. "And what about Yusry? Do you share your father's views at all?"

"I'm certain I don't share *any* of my father's views on anything," retorted Nico. "I like to think it's my father's views on the matter that will soon become outlandish."

Nehal said nothing for a few moments. Then: "Nico . . . thank you."

"You don't have to thank me for—"

"No," interrupted Nehal. "Not for what you just said. For standing up to your father. For defending me against your father." Nehal grinned. "Even with your desperation to avoid confrontation."

"Oh." Nico smiled back. "I suppose you are my wife, after all."

WHEN THEY RETURNED home, Nico did what he apparently had been wanting to do all evening, and retired to his room to sleep. This left Nehal to pace the parlor somewhat like a madwoman. She could not get Lorenzo's words out of her head. His coarse language thundered in her skull. He had instilled a new sort of fear in her, but there was anger there too. She had so much energy buzzing through her. In Ramina she would have thrown herself into the ocean at night and fought against the rough waves during high tide, but there was no ocean here, only the polluted Izdihar. It may have been the lifeblood of Ramsawa, but to Nehal it was a poor imitation of the sea.

Finally, Nehal decided. She called Ridda to order Medhat to bring the palanquin around as she hurried to slip into her shoes and pattens. When she was in the palanquin, she directed Medhat to Malak's house.

It was nearing ten in the evening, so this was rather foolish and for all Nehal knew Malak could be out or asleep, but Nehal knew she could not rest until she spoke to her.

There was a light shining through Malak's mashrabiya when Nehal arrived. She told Medhat to wait for her inside the palanquin in case she stayed for some time, and he nodded gratefully as she walked past him to Malak's apartment.

When Nehal knocked, Malak opened the door.

"Nehal?" Malak stepped back and gestured for her to come inside. "Is everything all right? We'd canceled tonight, hadn't we?"

"Yes, we had, everything's fine—" Nehal paused as she realized Malak was fully dressed. "Sorry—were you going out?"

"Oh, no!" Malak chuckled. "I just got home. Come in, sit down. I'm glad you could make it after all. I can make us some tea?"

Nehal looked around the empty, quiet apartment. "Where's your servant girl?"

"She's only here a few days a week."

Nehal nodded somewhat distractedly. "It's all right. Can we sit?"

Malak nodded and led her into their usual parlor. As Nehal settled into the cushions, Malak unbuttoned her vest and tossed it aside. She wore only a thin sleeveless undershirt and trousers. She sat down beside Nehal, swung her long braid over her shoulder, and began to unbraid it as she stared intently at Nehal.

"Are you sure you're all right?" Malak asked again.

"I . . . I had an unpleasant evening. With my father-in-law."

Malak made a face. "Lorenzo Baldinotti? I hear he's somewhat unpleasant, yes."

"He said awful things about you," Nehal blurted out, unable to hold it in any longer.

Malak paused, her fingers hovering in and around her braid. "Like what?"

"He said the only reason the Izdihar Division was created was because you . . . bedded the minister of defense." Nehal paused. "He used those exact words."

To Nehal's surprise, Malak only laughed and resumed unplaiting her hair. "He sounds charming." Then she shrugged. "It's a common enough rumor. In retrospect my meetings in Hesham's private office probably shouldn't have run so late, but people in this city will talk no matter what."

"I hate that people think that of you," said Nehal furiously. "Like . . . like you haven't earned everything you've accomplished. Like you haven't worked hard for it. Or you're not clever enough to accomplish it without feminine wiles or bullshit like that."

Malak ran her fingers through her hair, which was now strewn in long, loose waves that fell to her waist and framed her face. Nehal had never seen Malak with her hair down before; she was momentarily disarmed by the effect.

"Did you come all this way because you were indignant on my behalf?" Malak asked teasingly.

"I—I don't know why I came here, exactly," said Nehal, because it was true; as usual she had made a decision without entirely thinking it through.

"Hmmm." Malak cocked her head, her downturned eyes intense, then reached out and pulled lightly on one of Nehal's corkscrew curls. "You're wearing your hair down. Have I ever told you how lovely it looks?"

Nehal blinked at the abrupt change of topic. "As does yours," she said quietly.

Malak's touch lingered, twirling Nehal's hair around her finger. The two women looked at each other for a brief moment, a quick meeting of the eyes, and then Malak's arm slowly returned to her side.

"Does your husband know you're here?" asked Malak softly.

"He's not really my husband, you know," said Nehal slowly. "Not in any way that matters."

Malak said nothing, but her gaze was intense.

Nehal heard herself swallow her nerves and her misgivings and her fears, and then she was leaning forward, toward Malak, and Malak was closing the gap between them and orange blossoms filled Nehal's nose.

Malak's lips tasted of coffee. It was a soft kiss at first, a careful and tentative brushing of lips. Then Malak buried her hand in Nehal's curls, pulling her closer, kissing her with a desperate intensity.

Nehal cupped Malak's face in her palms, her fingers brushing soft strands of hair. She was so warm and soft and *right,* and Nehal pressed against her until the two were tangled in one another.

Nehal dared to part Malak's lips gently with her tongue, and Malak responded eagerly, insistently, pulling Nehal down on top of her. Hands were lost in each other's bodies as their gentle kiss grew fierce and fervent.

Nehal's mind went blank when Malak ran her hands along Nehal's thighs, her waist, her breasts. She was filled with an impossible warmth. She pulled back for a moment to breathe, rested her forehead against Malak's.

"Are you afraid?" whispered Malak.

"Never," said Nehal, and kissed her again.

21

NEHAL

NEHAL SPENT THE FOLLOWING WEEK AT THE ACADEMY somewhat distracted, holding the secret of her tryst with Malak close to her heart. But her distraction did not affect her weaving: Nehal had gotten very good in a very short period of time. At week's end she went home shining with pride, and eager to see Malak again after five days at the Academy. She spent her evening luxuriating in her private bath and then went to sleep, exhausted from days of weaving practice. The following morning, she dressed and break-fasted quickly, fully intending to depart as soon as possible, when she heard voices in the parlor. She didn't go to see who was below. She didn't need to.

Nehal was rather good at eavesdropping.

As a young girl she would often stand at the door and listen in on her parents' conversations with their friends. This was the only way she could get any information about anything, since her parents were so often unwilling to share important details with her. In fact, eavesdropping was how she had first discovered her father's debts and her parents' plan to marry her off.

It was a habit she was fond of. People tended to be much more honest about what they thought of you when they didn't have to say it to your face.

So, when Nehal quietly crept to the parlor and spied Nico's friend Raouf, looking very much like a man on important business, Nehal decided to delay her trip to Malak's. Instead, she watched from afar as Nico led him into the parlor and closed the door. Then she looped around into the stairwell that led into that parlor, tiptoeing carefully and gently taking a seat on the steps. She leaned her head toward the door and was pleased to discover she could hear every single word as though she were in the parlor with the two men.

"Nobody seems worried that our peace treaty with Zirana is a hair's breadth away from collapsing," Raouf was saying. Nehal heard an intense bubbling sound; Raouf must have been smoking shisha. She smirked at that as she pictured Nico's dismayed expression; he loathed the smell of shisha.

"Most people aren't prone to living their lives in fear of war." Nico's voice was slightly strained, as though he were holding back a cough.

Raouf sighed. "Perhaps. I've become a bitter and terrible bore, haven't I?"

"Not at all."

"In my defense, it's all anyone can talk about at the army camp." Raouf took another drag on his shisha. "I should talk more of the type of gossip the city prefers. How is your very spirited wife?"

At this Nehal sat up and leaned even closer to the door, as close as she possibly could without tipping over.

She heard Nico hesitate. "She's well."

"Are you happy with her, then?"

"She's—I—we're quite—"

"Because last I recall," interrupted Raouf, "you were rather besotted with the lovely Giorgina, weren't you? I never took you for a man who would take on a concubine."

"And I haven't. I have certain duties as the only Baldinotti heir," said Nico stiffly.

Nehal grimaced at the obvious posturing.

Raouf laughed. "Careful, Nico. You're beginning to sound like your father."

"What about you, then?" said Nico quickly. "When can I expect to attend your wedding?"

"Oh, I'm in no hurry. I'm quite enjoying the life of a bachelor—my sister has some lovely friends."

Raouf laughed. Nehal rolled her eyes so far back they ached.

"Speaking of my sister," continued Raouf. "Do you know what she's been talking about for the past week?"

Nico shook his head.

"There's to be a march. On Parliament."

There was a pause. "What sort of march?"

"A march of the Daughters of Izdihar," said Raouf. "Imagine that! These girls want to go shout at Parliament to let them vote. This is what I mean when I say women are frivolous."

If Nehal had not been so intent on remaining silent and unobtrusive, that would have been the moment she banged the door open and punched Raouf in the throat to shut him up. As it was, she had to satisfy herself with digging her nails into her thigh as she endured his casual disdain for women.

"These women should be in their homes, taking care of their husbands and brothers," Raouf was saying. "Not wasting their time with politics! What do women need the vote for?"

"I think they only want to be represented, to have their voice heard," said Nico softly. "And it's not just the vote, Raouf—there are other important changes to the laws—"

"Oh, that's right," Raouf interrupted, chuckling. "You side with your wife on this, don't you? Will you be escorting her to this silly march, then?"

Nehal heard the frown in Nico's voice and cheered him on silently. "I don't think it's as ridiculous as you make it sound," said Nico, keeping his tone even. "There's precedent for women having the vote and expanding legal rights—in other nations—and it's hardly surprising that they should want more freedoms."

Raouf was clearly unconvinced. "Women don't need freedoms, they need protection from what freedoms bring."

"Like you?" Nico said pointedly. Nehal snorted.

But Raouf was unfazed, laughing the jibe away. "Anyway, I don't see what they hope to accomplish by disturbing the peace and antagonizing Parliament. Proper women aren't meant to be so rowdy; this behavior will hardly convince lawmakers to change their minds."

"'There are times when violence is necessary to rouse the oppressor from the comfort of his throne,'" Nico chanted solemnly.

There was a beat of silence, and then Nico spoke again.

"It's Qasim Wagdy. He was one of Ramsawa's leading generals during the Talyani occupation—"

"I *know* who he is, Nico. I just can't believe you're comparing Ramsawa's rebellion against Talyani imperialism to this."

"Is it not a rebellion of its own?"

Raouf snorted. "I should hope not. It's hardly comparable. Nobody is oppressing women; we're only keeping them safe from harm. They ought to be protected, in their homes, among their families. Not walking the streets and shouting at the top of their lungs."

"It seems your own sister is invested in this march, though," Nico said. "Surely if Nazira sees its value, you can as well."

Raouf sighed heavily. "Not quite. She only brought it up because of what she heard her friends gossiping about. It seems your wife's name came up quite a bit."

Nehal shifted; she had always expected her presence among the Daughters of Izdihar to stir gossip. She had grown up accustomed to this, to having her every move observed and dissected, and she had grown adept at ignoring it. Frankly, it was a wonder her attendance at the Weaving Academy was not yet on the front page of the *Alamaxa Daily*. But whatever Raouf was getting at . . . was this something she might need to worry about?

"I already know Nehal has become involved with the Daughters of Izdihar," said Nico.

"And are you aware of . . . the extent of her involvement?"

"Raouf, you've never been coy—what are you getting at?"

Raouf seemed to hesitate. "It's mostly gossip, and salacious gossip at that. Likely untrue. But you know how people in this city talk. Especially when the woman is someone as prominent as your wife. Perhaps you should speak with her about modulating her behavior."

Nehal dug her nails farther into her thigh, and it was only the cloth barrier that prevented her from drawing blood. *Modulating her behavior*—the phrase pounded in Nehal's head.

"I don't like to think how that conversation would go."

"I'm only worried for the both of you," Raouf said. "Talk about your wife will inevitably shift to talk about you and yours. You know I detest gossip, so you must understand the gravity of this situation for me to bring it up."

"Raouf, I have no idea what you're saying to me," said Nico.

Raouf was quiet for a moment. "You . . . you do know what they say about Malak Mamdouh, don't you?"

Nico hesitated as well. "I—I've heard rumors about . . . her methods. But they're only rumors. Like you said, salacious gossip."

"Well, there are other rumors. More persistent ones. Even among her little circle, not everyone is quite so pleased with her. Word spreads quickly among women, you know. And of course the doormen are always eager to talk with one another."

"Why are they displeased with her?"

Nehal could almost see what was coming. Part of her wanted to simply walk away. She knew she would not like what she heard next. And yet, she knew she needed to hear it.

"Well, they say—they say she behaves unnaturally. With other women."

The silence was like a thud. Nehal recalled the feel of her lips on Malak's and for a single moment felt like crying.

"No one speaks this aloud, mind you," said Raouf. "Nazira only whispered it to me and urged me to tell you, because your wife was seen visiting Malak Mamdouh at night."

At Nico's silence, Raouf quickly continued, "Of course, no one means to cast aspersions on Nehal. It's just as likely she's unaware of these unpleasant rumors. Which is why Nazira thought I should speak with you. So you can inform her, and she can modify her behavior appropriately. I daresay even she wouldn't want to be caught in this particular tide of rumor."

Nehal scowled, the possibility of tears long gone, replaced now by rage. What did the stupid bastard know about what she wanted?

After Raouf said his piece, he seemed eager to change the subject. Nehal remained hidden, in case he said something else she would do well to hear. But talk quickly turned to the sort of politics that didn't interest Nehal: diplomatic relations with Zirana, new economic regulations, trade laws . . . was this what Nico discussed with Giorgina? It was a wonder the pair of them didn't die of boredom. But still Nehal remained, just in case.

Finally, Raouf indicated he needed to go, and Nico called for a servant to escort him out. Like most Ramsawis tended to do, the pair lingered by the entrance of the parlor, chatting for an irritating amount of time before finally bidding one another goodbye. When Nehal was certain Raouf was gone, she swung open the door of the stairwell and stepped out.

Nico spun around, his eyes wide in shock.

"Nehal!" he cried. "What are you— How long have you been there?"

Nehal's lip curled in disdain. "So which is it? Is Malak a politician's whore or a queer? This city can't seem to make up its mind."

Nico blinked, then shook his head slowly as he took a seat. "You shouldn't eavesdrop. I would have told you what he said. You, on the other hand, seem keen to keep me in the dark. Is that where you disappeared to last weekend? Malak Mamdouh's home?"

Nehal went still, keeping her face neutral. "So what if I did? It's not unusual for women to stay at one another's houses."

"It is when they share a house with their husband in the same city," said Nico.

Nehal's eyes narrowed. "What are you saying?"

"Well, I just—it's just—that is, I—"

"Stop *stammering*, Nico, and ask what you want to ask."

Nico stared at her intently. "Fine. Is there—truth to the rumors?"

Nehal glared and said nothing, which seemed to make Nico even more uncomfortable.

"When you and I—" He blushed, pausing. "I assumed—you seemed quite—but I could be wrong—"

Nehal pursed her lips. "I *was* 'quite.' That doesn't mean I don't have other interests."

Nico blinked. "Oh. Right. So you and Malak are . . . ?"

Nehal looked away. "I don't know what we are."

Nico paused, then leaned forward, staring at Nehal intently. "Nehal. You have to be careful. Not because of rumors but—well, yes, because of rumors, actually. I know you know I don't care, but—this is serious. You could be arrested for indecency."

Nehal scoffed, but she could not deny the truth in Nico's words. There was, technically, no law against queerness itself, but there were many laws against indecency and debauchery that were so nebulously constructed they could mean anything the police wished them to. Nehal and Malak were both high-profile women, known to nearly everyone in Alamaxa. It would be frighteningly easy for them to become mired in a nest of rumor and legal arguments if they weren't careful. Even if Nehal were simply caught in the crossfire of it all, there would be no walking away from it all without Malak's enemies taking advantage, and no way Nehal's and Nico's families would escape entirely unscathed.

But Nehal was not the sort to let the possibility of disaster dissuade her from the reality of her desires, so she shrugged Nico off and left without telling him where she was going. Despite her best efforts, however, his words of warning rang in the back of her head all the way to Malak's house, only dissipating when Malak swung her door open with a bright smile and pulled Nehal inside.

22

GIORGINA

THE DAY OF THE MARCH ARRIVED FAR QUICKER THAN Giorgina would have liked. She woke early, nerves nipping at her bones, but remained beneath the covers, listening to her sisters' steady breathing. She had arranged her shift at the bookshop to fall after the march, which was scheduled to begin at nine, just as Parliament began their session, and informed her family that it was her work shift that began at nine. If she escaped the march unscathed and free, she would then go to work, though she could hardly see why she should bother.

What was the point of any of it for her anymore—her job, the march, the Daughters—when she was to be married so soon? Further talks with Zakariyya had confirmed that he absolutely did not want Giorgina to work.

"You will have no need to," Zakariyya had said to Giorgina, and Giorgina's parents had been delighted. It was true; rich women had no *need* to work, and it was highly insinuated that they should not have a desire to work either. Zakariyya would make her a rich woman. Giorgina should have been glad of it. Zakariyya seemed polite and well-meaning, if old-fashioned and steely about his opinions. For their engagement, he had presented her with an elaborate shabka, a sparkling set of golden jewelry that her younger sister

Nagwa couldn't stop preening over. It probably cost more than their entire house.

But Giorgina did not just want a rich, polite man. She wanted Nico. She wanted a man who saw her as an intellectual equal, not a man who wanted a pretty young wife to cook him meals and share his bed. She wanted to keep her position in the bookstore, to continue writing for the Daughters of Izdihar. But what was freedom worth when compared to the safety and security of wealth?

Giorgina tried her very best not to think about any of it. She was operating in a kind of half-daze, focusing only on the present, and attempting to forget entirely that she was soon to be a married woman, to a man she barely knew.

For now, however, there was the march. If this was to be Giorgina's last month as a free woman, she would certainly do something more worthwhile with her time.

Breakfast was not the usual subdued affair. To celebrate Giorgina's engagement, Ehab had splurged on halawa, a soft block of sweet sesame paste the girls all loved. The excitement in the Shukry household was palpable. Nagwa and Hala could not stop smiling, and even Ehab was cheerful. Only Sabah was slightly subdued, and often gave Giorgina pointed looks, as though she wanted to say something to her. Giorgina was almost certain her older sister knew more than she had insinuated, but it was too much for Giorgina to worry about right now.

After eating only a plain half of flatbread, Giorgina quietly slipped out. She wrapped her shawl around her to shield herself from the chill in the early-morning air. The alley was slowly coming alive: Giorgina walked past Hamdy the grocer as he set out overripe apples and tiny bananas spotted with dark circles. A man with a mule dragging along a cart of lemons walked past her, ringing a bell and shouting "Lemons! Lemons! Two for a piastre!" at the top of his lungs. A little farther down, at the corner of the street on which Giorgina lived, was the bakery. The scent of freshly baked bread and sweets trailed Giorgina as she walked past and toward the intersection. Suddenly she wished she had eaten something more substantial; she had a long way to go yet.

She walked on.

When she arrived at the gates of Alamaxa University, the giant clock tower in the center of Tarar Square read eight-thirty. There were other women ahead of her, walking toward the university, some alone, some in pairs, some in groups. Hurriedly, Giorgina followed them as they strode confidently to the central domed building. Giorgina's own gait was not so steady. Her gaze could not help but be drawn to the campus surrounding her: the thick shrubbery lining the paths, the impossibly tall palm trees scattered throughout vast expanses of green, the packs of young students, mostly male, wandering about with books in their hands, unaware of the blessing handed to them—just one more thing denied to her, and so many other women.

Inside the main building was the Qasim Wagdy Lecture Hall. As Giorgina approached, padding along on thick carpet, she was surprised to hear a buzz of noise and activity. There was something about this time of the morning that seemed to decry sound and crowds, but the lecture hall did not appear to obey that particular dictum. It held more people than Giorgina had ever seen. Or, she should say, more women.

The lecture hall was an enormous modern auditorium, lined with chairs rather than cushions or sitting poufs, clearly meant to hold an impossible number of people. Giorgina tried to locate Labiba and Etedal, or even Malak or Nehal, but it was impossible. If she had to guess, there were at least three hundred women present in the room, some seated in the modern chairs, some clustered in chatting groups, some old, some young, some rich, some poor. Sprinkled among them were many men as well.

Giorgina allowed the door to slam shut behind her, but even that sound did not register among the cacophony in the lecture hall. She walked carefully to an empty chair, took a seat, and waited.

Soon enough, Malak took the stage. As always, her presence

alone was enough to dispel the chaos in the room. She did not have to shout or even speak; as soon as the women noticed her standing on the stage, they began to quiet. In less than a minute the lecture hall was submerged in utter silence.

Malak smiled at them before she spoke. "Welcome, my friends." There was a murmured response, then quiet again. "I hope most of you, by this point, know why we are here. A country cannot be free if its women are not. Do you agree?" A cheer rose into the air, hundreds of voices coming together. "Parliament does not. They do not believe that we deserve rights. Independence. Freedom that is owed to us as human beings."

Giorgina had to hand it to her; Malak had promised a lecture, and she delivered it. In a steady voice, she outlined all the demands with which Giorgina was now familiar. The right to vote. The right to run for office. The right to sign papers independently. The right to independently obtain a divorce without a husband's agreement. The right to maintain custody of children. She wove her words together as brilliantly as ever.

The crowd cheered again. Malak raised her voice. "We've been polite. Respectable. We've asked for what we're owed. What rightfully belongs to us. And Parliament has continued to ignore us, like we're worth nothing more than the dirt beneath their shoes. So here is what I propose: we bring the fight straight to them. We *demand* our rights. Today, I'm marching into Parliament and demanding what I am owed. Who's with me?"

The resulting cheer was so thunderous Giorgina's chair shook.

"Well, then, let's go and give it to them straight, shall we?" Malak grinned. "Onward to Parliament!"

The final cheer was kindled by roaring applause. Malak leapt off the stage, windweaving herself to the floor. She strode toward the doors, a trail of women in her wake. Most covered their faces with veils held in place by wood, but nearly as many women chose to go entirely unveiled, just as Malak did. Giorgina, with her distinctive coloring, had not been so brave, and so she adjusted her own face veil before following the crowd, adrenaline rushing through her as the cheering rose.

Parliament was only a short walk from the university. As they marched, the women held up their signs and shouted their slogans, drawing the attention of passersby. Giorgina caught a variety of reactions. One man raised his eyebrows, clearly impressed. A young woman, barely of age, looked longingly at them before being pulled away by her mother. One older man spit in their direction. Others jeered and made lewd gestures.

Giorgina detected their hostility but could not feel it. She walked in the center, surrounded on all sides by women who formed a protective shield. She could not help the exhilaration that ran through her bones, replacing nerves, the adrenaline that rushed through her veins like a drug. She found herself smiling, and then, shouting along with the others.

The marching women slowed as Parliament came into view. The building was an impressive structure; a columned, two-story building, once likely white, now a dusty brown. It was wider than it was tall, with a fat dome sitting in its center, a Ramsawi flag flying high atop it. The women congregated at the gates, which were shut, guarded by two skinny boys with muskets. Giorgina tensed as the guards hesitantly drew up their weapons. From her vantage point, Giorgina could just barely see Malak approach one of the guards. She had no idea what Malak could have said to him, but soon the gates swung open, and they poured into the courtyard, marching forward until they reached the doors of the building.

There their shouts intensified, coalescing into a single unified voice, a single powerful woman demanding justice. Giorgina gazed up at the Parliament building and thought she saw one of the shuttered windows open, then close again.

She was not the only one who noticed. Someone threw a stone at the window, eliciting an involuntary gasp from Giorgina.

"Come out and face us, cowards!"

Giorgina followed the familiar voice and found Etedal, her robe and veil abandoned, gearing up to throw another stone. Beside her, Labiba was more circumspect, holding back her cousin's wrist. Giorgina quickly walked over to them and tapped Labiba on the shoulder. Labiba turned and smiled when she saw Giorgina, who had briefly lifted her face veil. Labiba gave her a quick hug.

"I was looking for you!" exclaimed Labiba. "How are you doing?"

"Better than I thought," replied Giorgina.

With Labiba distracted, Etedal had taken the opportunity to hurl another stone at the shuttered window, which opened with a slam this time, drawing Labiba and Giorgina's attention. A middle-aged man stuck his head out, spectacles dangling off his nose. He was saying something, but he could not be heard above the shouts of the women in the courtyard.

Just then, a strong breeze overtook the women; Giorgina felt it blow back loose strands of her hair. Malak's unnatural wind was instantly recognizable. The crowd quieted.

"Speak, Senator Tariq," said Malak to the man leaning out the window. Her tone held more than an undertone of mockery.

"This is your only warning," the senator snapped. "Vacate the premises immediately or else."

"Or else what? Isn't this our government too? Parliament will hear us out first." Malak's voice was firm and steady, carrying to the entire courtyard.

"Parliament is concerned with important matters," said the senator. "We do not have time to waste on a bunch of impertinent wenches who clearly weren't raised right!"

"This is *your* final warning, Senator," said Malak. "We have a right to be heard. We have every right to be here."

The senator only scoffed. "Go back to your house, woman," he said scornfully. "Find something useful to do with your time."

To Giorgina's surprise, Malak smiled, though she showed no teeth. It was a smile that held only bitterness.

Malak turned, her back to the crowd, and held both up both

arms. Even as far back as she was, Giorgina could feel Malak's inhalation of breath as she drew the air to her, and then—she pushed it at the doors.

Giorgina started as the wooden doors began to rattle on their hinges. There was another inhalation, another feeling of tension in the air, and then Malak's wind grew stronger than Giorgina thought should be humanly possible, and the doors were blasted open, broken free of their locks.

The cheer that erupted nearly burst Giorgina's eardrums, and she was swept forward with the crowd, into the halls of Parliament. Giorgina was consumed with anxious thoughts—Malak had broken into Parliament. She had used weaving to break down the doors. This was no longer a peaceful protest, but what could easily be interpreted as a violent attack by weavers.

Labiba grasped Giorgina's arm to keep her from stumbling, her fingers too warm on Giorgina's skin.

"Are you all right?" asked Labiba, peering anxiously at Giorgina.

"Isn't this going too far?" asked Giorgina. "We've broken in!"

"They locked us out. Malak just unlocked it for us. It's public property," Labiba assured her. "All citizens have a right to be heard in Parliament Hall."

That may have been technically true, but the line they were treading was a thin one. In any case, there was no retreating now, not for her or anyone else. The women were all trapped within in their own momentum, which continued to propel them forward.

They marched down a wide, carpeted hallway hung with portraits of Ramsawi men in elaborate turbans. At the head of the line, Malak threw open another pair of doors, and the women spilled into a large, high-ceilinged meeting room. The floor was covered by a plush, intricate rug, the walls lined with heavy red curtains. Above them was the dome, a masterpiece of stained glass through which sunlight filtered into the space. An array of decadent seats circled them as they poured into the room.

Three men, who had been seated within, rose to their feet, shock and anger inscribing itself over their features. "What is this?" said one of the men, who looked to be the oldest. "What the hell do you think you're doing, barging in here?"

"You know what we're doing." Malak's voice rang clearly in the cavernous hall. "We are here to demand our rights."

A younger man stepped forward, shaking his head. "You've gone too far, Malak. Much too far. Leave now, and we can try to forget—"

"Forget?" Giorgina was surprised to hear Malak snap. "How easy it would be for you to simply forget, Senator. You are not the one who has to live with the daily consequences of this injustice."

"Ha! Injustice!" the older senator laughed. "Do you hear yourself? Injustice! Are all women so melodramatic?"

Malak's eyes narrowed. "We are not leaving until we are heard."

The senator continued to laugh, but Malak only chanted, "We—demand—the vote!"

A chorus of voices rose up to join her, drowning out the men's laughter and disbelief. Giorgina was not certain how long they stood there, chanting and roaring and stamping their feet, and there was nothing for her to do but join in, shouting until her throat was raw.

A shove at her back cut her off, and then the chanting behind her faltered, interspersed with shouts and a scream. Giorgina turned, but she did not have to look for the source of the disturbance for long. She choked back a gasp.

At the very back of the crowd were at least twenty uniformed men wielding muskets.

The Alamaxa Police.

They elbowed and shoved their way through the crowd, raising their voices above the women's, many of whom tried to shove them back. Giorgina wanted to scream at Malak and the others, beg them to stand down, for their own good, but no one would hear her, or listen.

In the crowd of policemen, Giorgina spied a familiar face, with a pale bald head and thick beard: Attia Marwan, the officer who had taken the time to taunt her and Labiba in their cell. He stood oddly still among his compatriots, who were pushing and shoving. Then, with no hesitation, he raised his musket at the ceiling and fired.

The explosive sound of the shot itself was followed by the sound of shattering glass as a hole erupted in the glass dome above them, raining down sharp shards. Before Giorgina could even consider raising her hands to shield her face the glass was blown backward by a wide-eyed Malak. But in her haste, the shards raced straight toward the group of senators who had remained standing, observing the chaotic scene. Glass rained down on them. They panicked, their screams rising above the cacophony, and drew the attention of the police, who rushed forward, muskets held aloft.

Labiba was no longer beside Giorgina; instead, somehow, she had wound up in Attia Marwan's periphery. Giorgina planted herself in the middle of the chaos and watched in shock as Labiba was accosted by Attia, the butt of his musket striking her in the face. Labiba stumbled back, stunned, and Attia took the opportunity to strike her again, this time in the ribs. Instinctively, Giorgina rushed forward, fighting her way through bodies, but she was tossed back, stumbling.

When she looked up again, she met a terrifying sight: long licks of flame shot from Labiba's fingertips. She was on her knees, and the flames caught at the dry carpet.

Giorgina saw Labiba's mouth move, could almost hear her gasping as she frantically patted at the carpet in a desperate attempt to quench the flames. Blood was spilling freely from her mouth, splattering the carpet as she chased her own flames, which fled her easily. They raced across the room to lick at the curtains. In a blink, the fire devoured them entirely. Smoke poured into the room like overflow at a riverbank.

Screams erupted anew, and the chaos heightened to a delirious frenzy. There was a race to escape through the doors before the flames reached them. Giorgina fought to make her way to Labiba, who was still attempting to put out her flames, alternately slapping at the carpet and making gestures with her hands, all to no avail.

In the midst of this screaming chaos, Attia Marwan stood strangely still. He raised his musket and carefully took aim. Giorgina blinked, following his gaze. But before her eyes could land on his target, she heard him shout.

"Fireweaver!" he screamed, suddenly animated.

Then he fired his musket directly at Labiba.

23

NEHAL

WHEN THE FLAMES CAUGHT HOLD OF THE CARPET, NEHAL reacted immediately. With her thumb, she opened the flask of water she always carried at her side and directed it forward. It was not enough. Of course it was not enough; the paltry amount in a tiny flask could not be enough to put out those flames. She dared to close her eyes and cast out her awareness, searching for the River Izdihar, begging it to hear her call, but she felt nothing. The river was too far, and Nehal was not powerful enough to call it to her. She drew the water back into her gourd.

Then she spied Carolinna. Nestled beside her was Zanuba, nursing what looked like a broken wrist, but Carolinna had both her arms up and pointed at the flames. As Nehal looked on, Carolinna carefully maneuvered them away from the doors, allowing women to escape. She was scowling in concentration. Nehal could guess at her frustration; Carolinna had learned to control flames, but tamping them down entirely was still beyond her power, especially when they were spread this far out of control.

One of the policemen noticed Carolinna weaving; his eyebrows drew into a scowl as he began to approach her, musket raised.

Nehal uncorked her gourd again and maneuvered a string of water toward the policeman, changing its state while wrapping it around his musket: in moments the musket was frozen entirely in ice, and therefore completely useless. Scowling, he tossed it aside, then dug out *another* weapon, a much smaller one, much like the one Nehal had seen months ago, wielded by one of the Khopeshes: a pistol. The policeman pointed it at Carolinna.

Nehal tackled him.

She had caught him utterly by surprise, otherwise her small frame would hardly have caused him to stumble. Instead, given her angle and her momentum, she knocked him down. They landed together in an ungainly heap. Nehal made to stand, but before she could find her footing the policeman backhanded her.

The force of his assault was shocking. She had not thought a backhand could carry so much strength. She was knocked backward, collapsing onto her back as dots of black danced before her eyes. Pain dazed her as her cheek split open. The warm blood that began to trickle down her cheekbone only made her angrier. She shot forward toward the policeman, who had gotten to his feet and was once again raising his weapon. She hooked her hands around his arm, which was all she could reach.

"She's trying to help!" Nehal shouted at the policeman. "She's keeping the fire away from the doors!"

He shook Nehal off roughly. She stumbled back. The policeman raised his pistol again. Nehal growled in frustration. She needed *water*. This was the problem with waterweaving; if she was not near a usable source of water, she was utterly powerless.

"Carolinna! Carolinna!" Nehal screamed until Carolinna turned to her. Nehal saw her face change as she caught sight of the policeman pointing his weapon at her. She panicked, letting go of her control on the fire, and stumbled back.

But Malak had also heard Nehal scream. Moving quicker and with more grace than Nehal had thought possible, Malak directed one hand toward the fire, shooting forth a gust of wind that swept the flames back from the doors. With her other hand she shot a gale of wind at the policeman, knocking him off his feet. He slammed roughly into a wall and crumpled to the floor in a heap.

Carolinna wrenched Zanuba off the floor and ran for the doors.

Nehal raced to Malak, who had blown the flames far from the doors, only for them to engulf the rest of the hall.

"Your face!" cried Malak.

Nehal shook her head. "It's fine. We have to leave. Now." Nehal pulled her away, and after a moment of resistance, Malak allowed herself to be led forward.

Most of the women had managed to escape the fiery room, making it easy for Nehal and Malak to run to the exit. But then a shock of red hair forced Nehal to stop.

Giorgina was kneeling down beside Etedal, arguing with her. Both of Giorgina's hands were wrapped around Etedal's upper arms, pulling at her. Nehal blinked and tried to see through the smoke. She walked closer, coughing, chest burning. The sight she was confronted with made her breath catch in her throat.

Etedal's face was screwed up in a scream of anguish as she clung to a limp figure in her arms.

Labiba's eyes were open but sightless, her mouth frozen in what might have been a question. The front of her chest was soaked with blood.

Malak stumbled. "No . . ." Her voice trembled, and that frightened Nehal more than anything.

Giorgina looked up as Malak and Nehal approached. Malak collapsed to her knees across from Labiba.

"We have to go!" Giorgina's voice was hoarse and scratchy.

"I'm not leaving her!" Etedal screamed.

"Of course not." Malak's tone was calm, flat. "She's leaving with us." She grasped Labiba's arm and looked to Nehal, who understood immediately, and ran forward to grab one of Labiba's legs. Giorgina needed no encouragement.

Together, the four of them awkwardly sped forward, Labiba's

weight pulling at them, the smoke invading their lungs, all of it slowing them down. The exit seemed to stretch farther away with each
passing second. Nehal's vision grew hazier, her chest burning with
every step.

Then they were through the doors. Nehal wanted to stop, to collapse for a moment, but Malak and Giorgina were pushing and pulling them forward, forward down the long hallway they had walked
down earlier, going farther and farther, faster and faster, until Nehal
could hardly breathe.

Finally, they emerged onto the steps of Parliament. The cool
breeze hurt when Nehal inhaled it; she collapsed into a coughing
fit. Three women and a policeman ran forward to help them de-
scend the steps with Labiba. Once they were in the courtyard and
far enough away from the flames, Nehal allowed herself to fall to
her knees. Malak collapsed beside her, cheeks covered in soot, eyes
blank. On Nehal's other side, someone squeezed her wrist. Nehal
looked up at Giorgina's stricken face, tear tracks cutting through the
smoky detritus on her cheeks.

"I have to go," said Giorgina. "I can't be arrested again."

Dazed, Nehal barely felt herself nod, and then Giorgina was
gone, face veil in place as she ran through the gates, along with hundreds of other hidden women who sought to escape police custody.
The police and the fire brigade were concerned only with containing
the flames and ensuring Parliament's senators and prime minister
escaped the building safely.

"What happened?" Malak was asking. "Etedal, what happened?"

"I don't know!" Etedal sobbed. "I lost her, I lost her, I didn't
see!"

Malak reached forward to embrace Etedal. "It's all right."

Etedal shook her off violently, causing Malak to stumble back.
"She's dead! Labiba's dead; nothing is fucking *all right*!"

Malak tried to speak, but Nehal pulled her back. She held on to
her tightly, startled to feel a tremor in Malak's hands. For the first
time since she had met her, Malak looked bewildered and utterly

lost. Nehal pulled them both to the ground. As Etedal sobbed, holding Labiba in her arms, Malak and Nehal watched the flames.

In Edua Badawi's day, waterweavers and fireweavers, expertly trained, would have been called to the scene to douse and control the flames. Now, as Shaaban had once told Nehal, the fire brigade relied on steam-powered engines to power their water hoses. It was an utterly inefficient way to control something as powerful as fire.

Nehal might have stood up and helped direct the water, had her knees not felt so weak, and had she not feared being shot for weaving. So instead she merely sat and observed until the flames began to die.

She did not have an opportunity to rest. When Parliament was finally nothing more than a smoky husk, just as Nehal thought she might close her eyes and lay down for a moment, she felt rough arms pulling her up. Another policeman wrenched Malak even more violently; Nehal saw her wince but offer no resistance. Etedal, who screamed like a madwoman whenever anyone attempted to pull her away from Labiba's body, was left alone.

Nehal and Malak had their hands tied behind their backs. The policemen took them to an open cart with the word POLICE painted on its side. A black horse at its head flicked its tail restlessly. The police shoved them roughly into the cart, then joined them inside it. Nehal struggled to maintain her balance as the cart rumbled forward, its giant wheels bumpy on the uneven roads. She tried to meet Malak's eye, but Malak seemed lost, her eyes on Parliament, which was growing smaller and smaller.

At the police station, they were separated before they had a chance to speak. Malak was taken to the cells belowground, but one of the policemen at the station recognized Nehal; she knew this by the way his eyes nearly popped out of their sockets at the sight of her. He shook his head at his colleague.

"That's Lady Nehal Darweesh," the policeman whispered loudly to his fellow. "Take her to the commander's office. And for the Tetrad's sake, untie her hands."

Nehal was taken to Shaaban's office, but he was not there. She was told to wait. Once the policeman left, the unmistakable sound of a lock clicking behind him, Nehal collapsed. Her knees had not yet stopped trembling. The open cut on her cheek throbbed angrily, refusing to let her rest. She leaned her head back, strands of her hair falling out of her chignon and sticking to her sweaty neck. She wanted to bathe. She wanted to sleep. She wanted to scream.

They had only wanted to be heard. They had done little that could be deemed violent, and yet someone had called in armed policemen, who had then dared to fire into a congregation of unarmed women! The gall of it, the utter cowardice! Labiba was dead, the Daughters of Izdihar were scared and scattered, Malak was imprisoned, and their goal was even farther away than it had been when the day had begun.

Labiba. In the quiet of Shaaban's office it struck Nehal; she had not truly felt it before. Labiba was *dead.* Labiba had been killed. Nehal had not known her very well, but she could recall the way Labiba always smiled with her whole face, and her chest ached.

Nehal sat up when she heard the lock turning. Shaaban slammed the door open so hard it hit the wall, cracking the paint. He slammed it shut again behind him. Without looking at Nehal he walked around to his desk, sat down, and put his head in his hands.

Nehal could not bear the silence. "Uncle—"

"What were you thinking?" Shaaban thundered. "I'm sorry—that's a stupid question, because clearly you *weren't* thinking at all!" He had never yelled at Nehal before, but it was not in her nature to cower. Especially as it was *his* men that had turned the day violent.

"Us? What were *you* thinking, sending armed police, granting them leave to fire into a crowd of unarmed women?" said Nehal furiously. "One of my friends is *dead*—"

"Parliament is *gone*," shouted Shaaban. "One of *my* men is dead, three senators suffered severe injuries, and—"

"None of that would have happened if you hadn't sent in your police with weapons!" Nehal matched his volume. "We didn't want *anyone* to be hurt, and no one would have been if that oaf of a policeman hadn't fired his musket into a *fucking glass dome!*"

Shaaban hesitated for a moment, then sighed. "Fine, Nehal. You tell me exactly what happened, then."

Nehal recounted her version of events to him, making sure to emphasize that Malak, both times she had deployed her windweaving, had been attempting to prevent injury.

"That's not what my men told me," said Shaaban.

"Then they're liars," Nehal snapped.

"And the fire?" Shaaban said wearily. "You're telling me that wasn't one of yours?"

Nehal hesitated. She had not seen what had caused the flames to erupt. Shaaban did not seem to want to wait for her answer, however.

"Nehal, why are you mixed up in this?" said Shaaban. "You could have been *killed* today, do you realize that? You would have left me to deliver your body to your parents."

Nehal ignored his transparent attempt to make her feel guilty. "All we wanted was a chance to be heard," said Nehal. "An attempt to convince the prime minister—"

"*Nehal!*" Shaaban interrupted. "Your father didn't send you to Alamaxa for you to become entangled with Malak Mamdouh of all people! Look at you! Look at your face!"

"You can thank one of your policemen for that," snapped Nehal. "When I tried to stop him from firing his weapon and killing an innocent woman he backhanded me. *Splendid* police force you've got here. I wonder why we could possibly want the right to vote with such men protecting us."

Shaaban rubbed furiously at his temples.

"Where's Malak?" asked Nehal.

Shaaban's expression darkened. "In a cell, where she belongs. She's exhausted this city's goodwill. This is the end for her."

Nehal's stomach dropped. "What does that mean?"

"It means she's going to remain in prison pending trial," said Shaaban.

"She didn't *do* anything!"

"Once again I remind you that Parliament was *on fire,* and two people are dead—"

"None of that is her fault—"

"She is the one who decided to force her way into Parliament along with hundreds of other women who were willing to do anything she said!" shouted Shaaban.

"But—"

Shaaban held up both of his hands. "*Enough,* Nehal. I've had enough. Your husband should be here soon to pick you up, and after that I expect you to remain at home and *for once* behave like a proper lady."

Nehal glared at Shaaban, but his attention was no longer focused on her. He left without a word, locking Nehal inside his office once more. She seethed, her right leg jiggling uncontrollably.

When Nico arrived, he was without a turban, his yellow locks disheveled and his eyes bloodshot. His eyes widened when they landed on the cut on her cheek. He knelt beside her, so tall that his head reached her shoulder.

"What happened?" He touched her cheek gently, but Nehal still winced away from him.

"One of these pigs hit me," said Nehal roughly. "It doesn't matter. Let's go."

"Nehal, the city's in an uproar—they're saying Parliament's burned down!"

Nehal said nothing.

"Where's Giorgina?" asked Nico frantically. "Did you see her? Was she there? Was she hurt?"

"She's fine." Nehal shrugged. "She was there. She ran to avoid arrest."

Nico visibly relaxed, exhaling slowly as his shoulders fell. Then he shook his head. "What happened? You told me this was meant to be a peaceful march—"

"It would have been, if Parliament hadn't decided to call in armed police who were only too happy to fire into the crowd!" snarled Nehal. "This wasn't our fault."

"All right," said Nico, who appeared stricken by Nehal's venomous tone. "All right, it's all right, let's just take you home and find a doctor for your face."

Nehal thought of Malak, trapped below in a dungeon-like cell. But short of breaking her out, there was nothing Nehal could do for her at the moment. Reluctantly, she stood, only to fall into Nico when her legs would not hold her.

He caught her gently, supporting her like she weighed nothing at all, which to him she probably didn't. "Are you all right?"

"I'm *fine*."

But Nico had to keep his arm around Nehal's waist to hold her up; she was furious with herself for it. She could not seem to transmit this anger to any of her limbs, however, so she reluctantly leaned on Nico and allowed him to lead her out and into their palanquin. He practically had to lift her into it. The warmth and quiet of the familiar palanquin was a strange comfort after the events of the day.

Nico could only look at Nehal with concern. Tears of smoke and fury pricked her eyes, but she angrily wiped them away before they dared fall.

"Everything is ruined, Nico," said Nehal. "They've ruined it all."

24

GIORGINA

GIORGINA RAN THROUGH PANICKED CROWDS. SHE IGNORED questioning looks and ugly glares. She ran until her face veil stuck to her skin with sweat. She ran until she could not breathe. She ran until her shawl slipped from her shoulders and tangled in her feet, forcing her to come to a clumsy halt. She leaned against a wall of cool exposed brick, struggled to catch her breath. She ripped her face veil off and tossed it to the floor, the wooden bit clunking loudly against the cobblestones.

She drew in ragged breath after ragged breath; she was drawing stares again, most worried, some hostile. She tried to force her breathing to come slower, quieter, but she needed to *breathe,* and she couldn't, her heart was racing so fast and her thoughts were speeding along faster than she could process them and there was a strange pressure growing in the back of her skull like a rotten fruit threatening to burst and the ground was trembling—

Giorgina fell to her knees, with no choice but to be heedless of the stares directed at her. She crawled into a corner, pulled her knees to her chest, and tried to calm herself down. She was spinning. She was spinning away like she hadn't in years.

Images played over and over in her mind. Labiba, wide-eyed. Labiba, confused. Labiba, falling backward, a bloom of red blossoming out of her chest, like spilled ink on parchment. Labiba, pale and still. Labiba, wide-eyed and still. Labiba, Labiba, Labiba. Gone. Dead and gone forever.

There were tears coming now, heaving sobs that felt as if she was being cracked open from chest to throat. She had no control; her body was taking over her entire self and she felt like the world was slowly vanishing into an abyss.

Then something tugged at her sleeve.

She startled, gasping, and found herself face-to-face with a skinny young girl. She was no more than thirteen, with dirty skin and matted hair. She blinked up at Giorgina with eyes far too large for her scrawny face.

"You okay, miss?" asked the girl uncertainly.

Giorgina swallowed and blinked at the child across from her several times. The girl's clothes were ragged, her feet bare and covered in muck. Likely homeless. Giorgina tried to speak, but only stutters came out. The girl was unperturbed, however; she simply crouched in front of Giorgina and stared, her unblinking eyes oddly steadying.

Finally, Giorgina could take a single calm breath, then another, and another. With each breath her panic dissipated slightly, until it had almost subsided entirely.

"I'm—I'm sorry," mumbled Giorgina. "I'm—I'm—" But she did not know what to say.

"You coming off that march?" asked the girl.

Giorgina only stared.

The girl shrugged. "They're saying the fire's real bad. Smoke get to ya?"

Giorgina could not speak; she did not know what to say. She shrugged, then leaned against the wall so that she could crawl to her feet. The girl mimicked her movements, her eyes eerily unblinking as she did so.

"I have to go," mumbled Giorgina. She turned her back on the girl and began to walk as fast as she could.

———

GIORGINA HAD TO be at work in less than thirty minutes, but she was dirty and sweaty and covered in soot. She thought fast and made a detour down Hilawi Lane, walking fast to the small textile factory by the river where Sabah worked. She entered through a back door that Sabah had showed her many years ago, when she had first started working here.

Nobody paid her any attention; the overseers kept their eyes on the assembly lines, which rang with the clangs of heavy machinery. The factory floor was dark and airless, heavy with cotton fibers. Giorgina would not have been able to locate Sabah if she tried, and she would not have been able to pull her off the assembly floor with the overseers watching and docking pay for a single missed minute.

Instead Giorgina directly maneuvered her way to the bath chamber and locked herself in. She took deep, steadying breaths, then dared to look at herself in the mirror.

Her cheeks were ringed in soot; her pupils dilated unnaturally. Her hair, which had been neatly arranged that morning, had escaped its braid, half of it falling awkwardly against her dirty cheeks. Her clothes were rumpled and dirty. With another slow, steadying breath, she methodically began to put herself back together.

She unbraided her hair, ran water through it, then carefully re-plaited it. She splashed cold water on her face again and again until the soot was gone and only pale cheeks remained. She washed out her mouth to get rid of the taste of smoke, though she was only partially successful; the smoke continued to sting the back of her throat. She turned her black shawl inside out to hide the mud that painted it. When she looked at herself in the mirror again, she looked almost normal, but for the stricken look on her features, which she could not seem to control.

She whispered a prayer of thanks to the Tetrad when she did not run into anyone on her way out. She walked at an even pace, her steps brisk but measured. She arrived at the shop only a few minutes late.

When she walked in, Anas looked up and frowned at her. "You're late."

"I'm sorry," said Giorgina mechanically.

Anas peered at her critically. "You weren't caught up in that chaos at Parliament, were you?" He almost sounded as though he cared.

Giorgina shook her head.

Anas heaved a dramatic sigh, then departed. Giorgina took her seat slowly behind the low counter. She ran her fingers over the manuscripts Anas had left behind, finding comfort in the familiarity of their weathered leather pages, ignoring the panic crawling at the edges of her subconscious.

How was she supposed to stand there and work when Labiba was dead? When Giorgina would never speak to her again, never hear her laugh, never be hugged by her? How could she simply be expected to go on with her day when her best friend was gone forever?

But she had no choice. So Giorgina did her work. She organized books and cataloged new arrivals. She smiled at customers, answered their queries mechanically. By the time she closed up shop she was exhausted, with barely enough energy to walk home. She wanted so desperately to sleep. If she slept, none of this would exist. In her sleep, she would have some reprieve from the reality of Labiba's death, which racked painfully in her chest whenever she allowed herself to think about it.

In sleep, she could believe that Labiba was simply sleeping too.

GIORGINA WOKE IN the middle of the night struggling to breathe, and desperately wondering what had happened to Labiba's body.

Etedal had been cradling her cousin when Giorgina fled—and oh, the shame that skittered over her skin when she remembered how much of a coward she had been. She should have stayed with Etedal. She should have helped her. But Giorgina had been so afraid—if she had gotten arrested again, there was no guarantee anyone would be able to get her out. She couldn't risk it, and Labiba was already dead—

Giorgina sucked in a rattling breath and slid out from under the covers. Beside her, Nagwa and Sabah both slept soundly. Giorgina's clothes stuck to her skin with sweat, but she was shivering as well. Her breath came in short gasps. She felt trapped: she wanted so desperately to open the door to their home and run outside and suck in deep gulps of air, to ground her feet into the rough earth and settle her nerves—but if her father found her in the street in the middle of the night, he would flay her alive.

So instead, Giorgina opened a window and stuck her head out as far as she could without falling out. Her hair slipped over her shoulders and hung on either side of her head as she took slow, even breaths.

Malak was in prison; that much Giorgina knew. It was all anyone could talk about, how the great Malak Mamdouh had finally fallen, how she had finally gone too far, and was now in prison where she belonged.

Was Etedal in prison? Giorgina ought to seek her out. She should find Etedal, find out where Labiba was, if there would be a funeral. Etedal and Labiba had been estranged from their families; who would help Etedal with the funeral arrangements, with Malak in prison? Strangers? Who would pay for it all?

And then there was Attia Marwan. Giorgina saw his face whenever she closed her eyes. The way he had sought out Labiba, beat her, made her bleed and spark, and then, finally, ended her, as though he had been following a written set of instructions.

As these thoughts all collided in Giorgina's head, they simply increased her heart rate, so she did her best to push them away, to slow down the avalanche of worries and anxieties filling her brain.

Tomorrow, Giorgina decided, she would find Etedal, and in doing so, she would find Labiba.

25

NEHAL

NEHAL DID NOT PERMIT HERSELF TO REST UNTIL NICO
pressed her. In the palanquin, she had recounted to him in detail the
events of the march, angrily explaining that the Daughters of Izdihar
had not instigated the violence. Nico had little to say in response.

When they arrived at home, Nehal paced relentlessly while Nico
sent one of the servants to call on a physician.

"Nehal, please," said Nico. "Will you sit down and rest?"

Nehal ignored him.

When the doctor, an elderly man with a bushy mustache, arrived, Nico finally had to take Nehal by the shoulders and guide her
to the parlor so she could sit still. To both their surprise, she let him.

Her injury required stitches. While the doctor sewed up her
cheek, Nico sat beside her and told her to squeeze his hand, for which
she was grateful. When the doctor was done, he held up a small mirror to show her a neat line of stitching.

"Rest assured, my lady, the scarring will be minimal!" the doctor announced proudly. His smile faltered when Nehal completely
ignored him. Nico thanked him instead.

After the doctor had taken his leave, Nico ordered the servants
to bring lunch. Nehal picked at her food, managing to swallow only
a few morsels. After they had eaten, Nico urged her to go to her

room and sleep, but she only continued to pace the length of the parlor.

"How do trials usually go, Nico?" Nehal asked as she walked the length of the room. "Will they really keep Malak in prison for long?"

Nico sighed. "It depends. They might deem her a danger to public safety—"

"She's not!"

"They don't know that—"

Nehal stopped pacing and turned to stare at Nico. "And then what? What happens at trial?"

"Well, there will likely be an initial trial to convict or acquit. If she's convicted, there'll be a sentencing trial, to determine her punishment."

"Is there anything we can do to help?"

Nico sighed. "She'll need a lawyer, though I don't know who would be willing to represent her."

Nehal stuck her thumbnail between her teeth and took up her pacing once more. Nico sipped his tea and watched her.

The day grew long and dark. Nehal exhausted herself and sank into the parlor cushions. She drew her knees up to her chin and closed her eyes. Just before she fell asleep, she felt Nico draw a blanket over her.

When the sun's rays began to filter in through the mashrabiya, Nehal was only marginally aware. She was pleasantly drowsy, still caught in the throngs of sleep, savoring the warmth cast on her face. Then a series of thuds jolted her awake.

She yawned as she sat up, rubbing the sleep from her eyes with the heels of her palms. Beside her, Nico, his hair disheveled, looked like he was awaking from his own rest.

The banging was coming from the front door. Nehal heard it creak open, then heard an odd combination of voices, one hushed, the other raised. Heavy footsteps approached the parlor.

Lorenzo Baldinotti strode into the messy space, his eyes taking everything in before landing on Nico and Nehal. In his hands was a crumpled newspaper, which he smacked against the door.

"Get up!" he snapped. "Get *up*, the pair of you!"

"What's wrong?" Nico fetched his spectacles and put them on.

Lorenzo scowled. "Why are you always so utterly oblivious?" He threw the newspaper at Nico, but it hit Nehal in the chest instead. With a scowl of her own, she picked it up and unfurled it. Nico leaned toward her to see.

Splayed across the front page of the paper were four enormous photos: one each of Malak, Nehal, Nico, and Lorenzo. In bold, incriminating letters, the title of the article read: "BALDINOTTI HEIR'S WIFE INVOLVED IN PARLIAMENT ARSON" and then, beneath that in smaller letters: "LADY NEHAL OF THE HOUSE DARWEESH IMPLICATED ALONGSIDE DAUGHTERS OF IZDIHAR AND MALAK MAMDOUH."

Nehal quickly scanned the article. "They make it sound like it was planned!" she protested. "There was no arson; it was an accident!"

Lorenzo marched toward them and snatched the newspaper from her hands. "As usual, you fail utterly to see the point. Did I not warn you against associating with Malak Mamdouh? You were seen being carted off to prison with her, you complete fool! You did the exact opposite of what I said!"

Nehal leaned back on her palms. "What in Tefuret's name made you think I would do anything you said?" she asked coolly.

Lorenzo cursed, then kicked away the low table standing between him and Nehal. Nico started as empty cups of tea and a water jug clattered to the floor. The jug of water shattered, soaking the carpet.

"Baba, stop!" Nico tried to pull his father back, but Lorenzo shook him off and advanced on Nehal. She remained seated, observing Lorenzo with barely concealed contempt. If he thought he could frighten her, he was so utterly wrong.

"What does it take to get through to you, you stupid girl?" Lorenzo demanded. "Those whores you insist on associating with have burned down *Parliament*. What more will it take to convince you? You are dragging my family's name through the mud, and I won't allow it. And you!" Lorenzo turned on Nico. "What sort of man cannot keep his wife in line?"

Nico took an involuntary step back. The fear in his eyes was unmistakable. Nehal got to her feet, eyes narrowed and nostrils flared. She raised her hand from her side.

"If you cannot keep her under control, I will do it for you, do you understand?" Lorenzo turned back to Nehal. "I will keep you under lock and key if I have to—"

Nehal raised her arm. There was a whisper of gurgling water coming from the carpet, which was no longer wet. Then a hardened, icy stream of water shot out from Nehal's hand, straight at Lorenzo's chest.

Lorenzo was thrown off his feet by the force of the impact, hurled back toward the opposite wall. He slammed into it roughly and slid to the floor. Water soaked the front of his chest, which would likely begin to bruise. He stared blankly at Nehal, who slowly lowered her arm but kept her eyes locked on Lorenzo.

"You've lost your mind," said Lorenzo hoarsely. "You've gone mad. Utterly mad."

"Get out of our house," said Nehal calmly.

Lorenzo scrambled to his feet, swaying as he did so. Clutching his chest, he cried, "No wonder your parents were so eager to be rid of you. I see now they've burdened me with a madwoman."

"Get. *Out!*" Nehal's roar was accompanied by another stream of water, this one striking Lorenzo across the cheek. Idly, she wondered if *he* had ever felt the sting of a palm cutting across his cheek. Red-faced and furious, Lorenzo made his way to the exit. When he left, he slammed the door so hard the entire building shook with reverberations of his fury.

Nehal's chest rose and fell with her harried breaths. She shouted for a servant, who came running.

"That man who just left?" said Nehal. "You will no longer permit him to enter."

The servant bowed his acquiescence and departed.

"We—we can't do that," Nico stammered.

Nehal whirled on Nico. "Do you want him in your life?"

Nico looked between Nehal and the parlor door. "No, but—"

"Then it's settled," said Nehal fiercely. "This is *our* home, Nico, *our* life. They already forced us to marry. From now on, we can do whatever the hell we like."

IT HARDLY SEEMED possible that Nehal needed to return to the Academy that very afternoon. The school seemed far away, like something that existed in an altogether different world, especially after the events of yesterday's march. Malak was imprisoned, and all Nehal wanted was to go to her, to help her somehow. Leaving for the Academy without at least attempting to visit Malak felt like abandonment, so Nehal ordered Medhat to take the palanquin to the police station first. She had to try to do *something* or she would go mad.

At the police station, Nehal ignored the stares and whispers directed at her, and simply marched toward Uncle Shaaban's office.

A gangly boy with a wispy mustache stood guard outside; he startled when he saw Nehal.

"Miss, uh, my lady, please you can't—" He held out his arms as if to try and stop her, but Nehal walked right past him and opened the door.

Shaaban looked up from his papers and stared at her, slack-jawed, as though she were an apparition.

"Hello, Uncle," said Nehal, closing the door behind her, straight into the face of the panicking police boy. "May I come in?"

Shaaban's lip curled. "You're already in."

Nehal ignored him and took a seat. "I'm sure you can guess why I'm here," said Nehal carefully. "I want to speak to Malak."

Shaaban heaved a sigh and leaned back. "And why is that, Nehal?"

Nehal took this curiosity as a good sign and tried to soften her response, to appeal to Shaaban's sensibilities.

"We've become close friends," replied Nehal. "I only want to make sure she's all right. Please. It would put my mind at ease."

Shaaban ran his hand across his beard and looked away. Nehal said nothing; she knew when Shaaban was contemplating. "Five minutes," he said finally. "And I will be there, observing."

Nehal started; she had not truly expected Shaaban to acquiesce so quickly. She'd had several more arguments prepared. But only five minutes! She supposed it would have to do. She smiled at Shaaban. "Thank you, Uncle."

With a weary sigh, Shaaban motioned her toward the door. She followed him around the corner and into the stairwell, where they descended into the cells. Nehal had never been down here before. The cement floors were filthy and uneven, forcing Nehal to tread unsteadily. The air was dank and chilly, despite the warmth of the day outside these walls. Nehal hoped they had supplied Malak with a blanket, though the few other inmates down here did not appear to be kept warm. Many of them stared at Nehal and Shaaban as they walked past, but few did more than curse or spit. She thought most of them might have been prostitutes, judging by the way they were dressed, though there were a few that looked altogether too young and too defeated to be in prison. She wondered what their crimes could possibly have been.

Shaaban stopped at the very last cell and gestured for Nehal to go forward.

A lone figure was seated on the floor of the cell, shivering.

Malak had no blanket, and they had even taken away her shoes. She had undone her braid and wrapped it around her shoulders in a clear attempt at warmth, but it did not seem to be helping.

"Malak?"

Malak looked at Nehal. Her eyes were bloodshot, the bags under her eyes prominent. She struggled to her feet and approached the bars. Nehal reached inside to hold her hand. She turned to Shaaban angrily. "What are you thinking? She's freezing!"

"If she wants to walk around with no proper clothes, she should be prepared to bear the consequences," said Shaaban flatly.

Nehal squeezed Malak's cold fingers.

"What are you doing here?" Malak whispered hoarsely.

"I had to see you, of course," said Nehal. "I'm sorry I couldn't come sooner—how are you? Do you know what's going to happen?"

Malak leaned her forehead against the bars; Nehal forced herself not to lean forward and kiss her, or at least wrap her in her arms to try and warm her up a bit.

"I'm awaiting trial, I suppose." Malak threw Shaaban a dirty look. "Though I've been given no opportunity to speak to a lawyer about bail."

"Under the Ramsawi Penal Code, you have been deemed a domestic terrorist, which means you're not entitled to bail . . . or a lawyer, for that matter." Shaaban shrugged. "I suppose if one desperately wants to represent you, they can appeal to the courts."

"Terrorist," said Malak mildly. "I always preferred 'dissident.'"

"Dissidents don't burn down government buildings!" Shaaban shot back.

Malak only sighed, as though she'd had this argument many times before and was tired of it.

Nehal was dismayed. "So you're just going to keep her in this cell until trial? When is *that* going to be?"

But Shaaban had turned away and was staring at the ceiling. "Four minutes."

Malak tried to smile. "They've been searching for an excuse to lock me up for years. They finally have it."

Nehal shook her head. "Tell me what to do. Tell me how to help."

Malak sighed and closed her eyes, then gazed at Nehal. Their hands were still entwined. "Have you seen Etedal?" Malak whispered.

Nehal flinched. Consumed as she had been with thoughts of Malak, she had not spared Etedal or Labiba much thought.

"I haven't seen her," said Nehal hesitantly.

"Could you go to her?" asked Malak. "She lives at 657 Nasr Street. The third floor. Giorgina knows where it is. Please, make sure she's all right. And there'll have to be a funeral—" Malak's voice faltered.

"I'll make sure she has everything she needs," Nehal vowed.

Malak nodded absently, then flinched as a shiver racked through her. Nehal could stand it no longer.

"Here." Nehal removed her robe and forced it through the bars of Malak's cell.

Malak did not hesitate to wrap the robe around herself; it was too small and too short, but it did not matter.

"Nehal, you can't—" Shaaban protested.

"Why not?" Nehal demanded as she unhooked her veil from her hair and passed that to Malak as well. "She's already locked up; must she freeze to death as well?"

Shaaban shook his head in defeat. "Your time's almost up."

Nehal turned away from him and locked her fingers with Malak's again. She was pleased to see they were slightly warmer. Only very slightly, but still. Malak pulled Nehal closer, until their faces were only a breath apart.

"What can I do?" Nehal whispered. "What do you need?"

Malak closed her eyes for a moment. "The Daughters of Izdihar need to clear our name. We need to put out an issue of *The Vanguard,* or give an account to the *Alamaxa Daily,* if they'll hear us. Giorgina can write it. Find Bahira—you've met her, remember? She'll know who to speak to. You'll find her in Bulaq, an establishment called Zubaida's. We can't let this derail everything we've worked for. Promise me, Nehal."

Nehal nodded. "I promise." Nehal was grateful for Malak's instructions; she needed this direction.

Malak smiled and squeezed her hand.

Nehal glanced at Shaaban, who had begun to tap his foot rather loudly. "I don't know if I'll be able to see you again. I'm sorry."

"It's all right." Malak shook her head. "I'll be all right."

"Your time's up," said Shaaban, turning to the women. "Let's go."

Nehal did not want to leave Malak behind. She glared at Shaaban with as much venom as she could muster, but she knew she was powerless to accomplish much else. She wished she could walk through the bars and embrace Malak, but they were so narrow even her wrist could barely fit through them. She did not know how to say goodbye.

Malak did it for her; she let go of Nehal's hand and walked farther back into her cell, wrapping her arms around her waist. She smiled sadly at Nehal, who stood immobilized until Shaaban took her by the arm and led her away.

By the time Nehal was aboveground, she had decided: she would go to the Academy and inform them that she needed a very brief leave of absence, two days at most—she would sort everything out with Bahira and Etedal and Giorgina, and then she would go back to the Academy, and she would continue working with the Daughters of Izdihar on the weekends.

She left Shaaban with a curt nod of thanks; he seemed only too glad to be finally rid of her.

The ride to the banks of the Izdihar, and then across the river to the Academy, seemed to take triple the time it normally did. There was no part of Nehal that wanted to take even a single day away from the Academy if she didn't have to, but she owed this to Malak. She had given her word. Nehal reminded herself that the reprieve would be as brief as she could make it. First, however, she needed to inform . . . whoever it was she needed to inform.

On her way to the administrative offices, she ran into Fikry, who was bouncing off the walls, literally: he used his windweaving to propel himself up toward the sky-high ceiling and then zoom across toward the opposite wall.

"Nehal!" exclaimed Fikry. "You're here! Everyone's talking

about it!" He dropped himself to the floor gracefully and grinned widely at her. "Did you really burn down Parliament?"

"No," said Nehal tersely.

"But the papers—"

"Do I look like a fireweaver to you?" Nehal waved him away. "I'm in a hurry."

"Bye, Nehal!"

At the administrative office, a harried-looking man sat at a low desk, surrounded by stacks of papers. Spectacles were sliding down his nose, and he kept pushing them back up. The nameplate on his desk read SAMEH RUSHDY.

Nehal knocked but did not wait for him to respond before she entered.

Sameh Rushdy looked up, eyes wide and mouth open. "Oh— Lady Nehal Darweesh, yes?"

Nehal raised an eyebrow; she was accustomed to being recognized on sight, but it never ceased to be a little disconcerting. "Yes, hello. I needed to speak with—my instructors, I suppose? Concerning my attendance."

Sameh blinked at her, then removed his spectacles and wiped them down methodically on his galabiya. After he placed them back on the bridge of his hooked nose, he cleared his throat. "I'm afraid . . . that won't be necessary."

Nehal frowned. "Excuse me?"

"I was just preparing the paperwork—Miss Nehal, I'm afraid you've been expelled from the Academy."

Nehal's stomach dropped, but she only frowned. This man was obviously a fool. Though her hand suddenly felt weak, she raised it anyway, to emphasize her point as she said, "That's not possible."

Sameh cleared his throat again. "Word of your exploits at Parliament were deemed to be unacceptable conduct by an Academy student."

"You're a liar," Nehal choked out.

"I'm a secretary." Sameh sighed. "I do as I'm told, my lady."

Words crumbled to dust on Nehal's tongue, but it did not take her long to regain her voice. She slammed both her hands down on Sameh's desk; he startled back.

"I am Nehal of the House of Darweesh. My father is Khalil of the House of Darweesh. I am married to Niccolo Baldinotti of the House of Baldinotti, who has already paid the Academy's exorbitant tuition fees. You're going to expel *me*?"

Sameh shuffled some papers. "The paperwork has already been put in place to refund the larger portion of your tuition fee—"

"I do not want a *refund,* you absolute fool!" Nehal shouted. The knots in Nehal's stomach surged like the waves of an implacable sea. The gourd of water she always wore began to beat against her side. Sameh's eyes slid to it uneasily as it visibly trembled. "I want to speak to someone with some *semblance* of authority!"

The door to one of the offices behind Sameh cracked open. "What is this racket—ah." Yuri Saroukan sighed. "Lady Nehal. Of course."

"I demand—"

"Why don't you step into my office, Nehal?" said Yuri politely.

Nehal rose to her feet and marched past Yuri, who pulled the door closed behind them, but did not shut it entirely. He made his way around Nehal to kneel behind his desk. He gestured for Nehal to sit. She was too tense, her fists curled at her sides, but Yuri clearly would say nothing until she acquiesced, so she sank to her knees in front of him.

"What's the meaning of this? Expulsion?" Nehal spat. "For what?"

Slowly, Yuri pulled out a newspaper and held it out to Nehal. It was the same nonsense Lorenzo had batted at her and Nico earlier that day. She peered down at it with barely concealed disgust.

"What of it?" Nehal bared her teeth. "I'm a waterweaver; I had nothing to do with any arson. Clearly it's all lies. I attended a peaceful march that turned violent at the hands of overzealous policemen!"

Yuri clasped his hands together, steepling them below his chin. He looked at Nehal for a long moment, while she stared at him impatiently.

Finally, Yuri said, "Do you have any idea how difficult it was for Parliament to reopen this Academy?"

Nehal blinked at the abrupt change of subject. "I—of course I do."

"Do you really, though?" Yuri peered at her; his eyes, a murky green, seemed sad. "Do you have any idea how much the Khopeshes of the Tetrad lobbied against it? How much the Police Union lobbied against it? Do you know how much anti-weaving sentiment is flowing through this city as we speak?"

"What does this have to do with—"

"Listen, Nehal," interrupted Yuri. "Do you ever truly *listen*? You toss your family name about because you know it means something. You know you are one of the most recognizable women in the city." He nodded at the newspaper. "If you'd bothered to read through the paper, you'd have seen that the entire city now knows you are also an Academy student. An Academy student embroiled in a scandal the likes of which Alamaxa hasn't seen in decades. Weavers attacking government property. Domestic terrorism. Parliament might very well decide to shutter our doors again, and all because a group of women—"

"It wasn't our fault!" Nehal protested loudly. Her stomach roiled with the injustice of it all. "We deserved to be heard! It was all we wanted! If it weren't for the police—"

But Yuri only held up a hand. "It doesn't matter, Nehal. Are you not listening? Don't you *see*? It doesn't matter what the truth is; what matters is what people perceive." He shook his head. "If we didn't expel you, it would be as good as us condoning your actions at Parliament. No. We had to take a decisive side, and yes, we chose the Academy's well-being over your own. This country needs trained weavers, and sacrificing you for the many is simply no question at all."

"Who is 'we'?" Nehal managed to utter. "Who made this decision?"

Yuri sat back. "The instructors took a vote. It would have been unanimous if not for Nagi. He fought for you, claimed you were his best student, that it would go against everything we stand for to squander your talents. And to a certain extent, I agree with him." Yuri sighed. "But Nagi is nearly as young as you are. He struggles to understand the larger picture. I *am* sorry, Nehal, but I am afraid you are no longer permitted to be on the premises. If you attempt to resist, I will have you escorted out—"

Nehal stood and drew herself up to her full height. "I've not sunk so low that I need to be *escorted* off the premises. I don't stay where I'm not wanted." Nehal took a step closer toward Yuri and peered down at him with as much disdain as she could muster. "You're on the wrong side of this, Yuri. You should know that."

Yuri sighed wearily. "I am truly sorry, my girl. You have so much potential. This is not a choice I wanted to make."

Yuri's concession took all the fight out of Nehal. Tears of fury pricked her eyes, so she whirled away from Yuri, her vest flaring out behind her as she rushed out of the office and past Sameh, into the cavernous empty hall, and onto the hot sand of the Academy courtyard. She stood quite still, until she noticed the felucca that had transported her, which she had instructed to wait, since she had not intended to stay the day. How foolish those plans felt now. The irony of it all ate at her.

The Academy had been the only thing Nehal ever truly wanted. It had been the only thing she'd ever been truly good at. And now it was gone; it had slipped through her fingers like the water she yearned to master. Regret inundated her, even as she desperately struggled to keep it at bay, to dam it up with righteous anger. This was not *her* fault; she had only wanted to help fight for the rights Ramsawi women deserved.

But. *But.* It was difficult not to wonder where she might be now if she had simply not gotten involved, or if she had been more circumspect, more cautious . . . she could have worn a face veil to the march, like Giorgina. She'd thought it cowardly at the time, but it was clever too, and safe. Or she could have stayed away from the march entirely. Cowardly, again, and Nehal hated cowardice, but . . . how many times had Nehal mistaken prudence for cowardice?

Nehal had to clear her name. She had always intended to help Malak prove the Daughters of Izdihar were innocent; now Nehal's own fate was tied up with theirs. If she could clear all their names, establish the truth of what happened at Parliament and get the newspapers to print it, the Academy would have to rescind their expulsion. They couldn't expel her if the newspapers declared her innocent, if the city was on her side.

She *had* heard what Yuri said. And so she would take action.

Nehal was going to fix everything that had broken, even if it killed her.

26

GIORGINA

GIORGINA WAS FORCED TO POSTPONE HER VISIT TO ETEDAL. In all the chaos of the march, she had entirely forgotten that today was the day she was supposed to meet Zakariyya's mother, Ferial, who had invited Giorgina's mother and sisters along as well.

Nagwa and Sabah fussed over Giorgina, carefully oiling her hair and braiding it elegantly in a crown around her head. They applied kohl to elongate her eyes and painted her lips a soft rose. Nagwa lent Giorgina her best galabiya, a shapely sea-green garment. Nagwa's velvety moss-green shawl complemented the look; Giorgina's sisters draped it over her hair and shoulders. When Nagwa left the room, Sabah rested her palms on Giorgina's shoulder and gave her an encouraging smile in the mirror.

"I know this isn't what you wanted," said Sabah softly. "But it's going to be good for you. You'll see."

Giorgina was too tired to argue, and truly . . . she was too practical not to see Sabah's point. After everything that had happened . . . Labiba was gone, Malak was in jail, and the Daughters of Izdihar were likely finished. Nico was still married. What was the point in resisting Zakariyya Amin?

Giorgina had spent countless nights envisioning herself lying beside him, waking up to him, greeting him when he came home from work . . . she had thought of it so often the prospect no longer seemed suffocating, but . . . ordinary. Banal. Tolerable. Giorgina would simply be . . . a wife, like so many other Ramsawi women. Only she would have the privilege of wealth. It was what Nico would have afforded her.

Except Zakariyya was not Nico, and it was that recollection that always twisted Giorgina's stomach in knots.

But Giorgina could not afford to sacrifice reputation and stability for love.

So she did her best to smile back at Sabah, and tried to be happy—if not for herself, then for her family.

Nagwa and Sabah had insisted on spending their weekly earnings to rent a palanquin to take them to Ferial's house. Giorgina lamented the expense and attempted to argue against it but was brushed off.

"You have to arrive elegantly!" Nagwa admonished. "They're already wealthier than us; you mustn't give them another reason to look down on us."

The palanquin was not as grand or as clean as Nico's, nor were the camels' hides as shiny. The driver was a skinny young boy with dirty bare feet and torn trousers. Giorgina wasn't entirely sure the expense would dispel any preconceived notions Ferial might have of her and her family, but she kept any further protests to herself.

Giorgina's sisters, who had never been in a palanquin before, giggled excitedly as they looked out the windows at the people on foot. And though the palanquin was a novelty for Hala as well, she only smiled quietly. When her gaze met Giorgina's, she reached out and squeezed her daughter's hand.

"Why aren't you excited?" asked Hala, softly so Nagwa and Sabah would not hear. "This is your moment, habibti. The Tetrad has finally blessed us."

Giorgina mustered up enough energy to shrug one shoulder. Ehab had asked around about Zakariyya, and his reputation was sterling. He was fair to his workers and did well by his mother. By all accounts, Zakariyya Amin was a decent man. Another girl in Giorgina's position would have been ecstatic at her good fortune. So how could she explain any of her feelings to her mother, when she was struggling to understand them herself? That even though she knew this was her best option moving forward, she simply could not muster the energy to feel happy about any of it?

As though sensing her daughter's somber thoughts, Hala only patted Giorgina's hand and said nothing more.

Ferial did not live far from the Shukry household, though in a wealthier, more fashionable area. Here, the streets were cobbled, cleaner, the buildings less shabby and more modern. The palanquin dropped them off directly in front of Ferial's door, which was opened by a pale-faced servant the moment Hala knocked. They removed their shoes and followed the maid into the parlor.

Ferial was waiting for them, a wide smile thinning her plump cheeks. "Welcome, welcome!" she said, struggling to her feet.

"Oh, don't get up, Auntie!" Nagwa, ever the charmer, knelt beside Ferial and kissed both her cheeks in greeting. Hala followed, then Sabah, then Giorgina.

"You are as beautiful as my son said!" Ferial exclaimed, cupping Giorgina's cheek gently. "Such lovely hair!"

Giorgina struggled to smile at her future mother-in-law. Ferial was a short, stout woman, with a wide, cheerful face and graying curls poking out from beneath her veil. She had her son's striking green eyes.

"Thank you so much for having us," said Hala politely.

"Of course, of course!" said Ferial. "We're to be family, after all. Now, what will you be drinking?"

As decorum dictated, the Shukry women at first refused any and all offers of food and drink, while Ferial heartily insisted. Finally, they all gave in, as they knew they would, and the maid was called in with a tray of tea and a platter of ghraybeh. Giorgina was not the least bit hungry, but she reached for one of the shortbread cookies regardless. She forced herself to swallow it, though it felt like sand in her throat, and the almond studded in its center was too soft.

Ferial asked Giorgina about her work in the bookshop, about her cooking skills, how many children she wanted, and if she kept a clean house. They were all typical questions, but Giorgina struggled to answer any of them. Luckily, Hala and Nagwa supplemented Giorgina's answers, while Sabah kept her palm resting idly on Giorgina's knee.

Ferial seemed pleased. After the tea was drunk and the ghraybeh was eaten, Ferial cleared her throat and plastered an apologetic smile on her face.

"I'm glad we've become such good friends, Hala." Ferial leaned in conspiratorially toward Giorgina's mother. "Because there's just one more thing, and it is better done between friends than strangers."

Hala smiled, but Giorgina knew her mother well enough to see the confusion hidden behind it. "Of course. What is it?"

"Well." Ferial brushed ghraybeh crumbs off her galabiya. "There's just the matter of—well—the virginity examination."

A fist clenched around Giorgina's heart. She kept her face calm, stoic, but then she thought it was too stoic, too unnatural, that Ferial and her mother would surely see through her—and it did not help that Sabah's face stilled and her hand on Giorgina's knee stiffened.

Hala cleared her throat. "Is that absolutely necessary? I can assure you my daughter is the pinnacle of propriety."

Ferial reached out to take Hala's hand. "Of course, habibti, of course! I don't doubt it! But in these situations, one has to make sure, you know . . . if you had sons you would do the same."

Hala's smile was frozen in place. Giorgina silently willed her mother to argue further, to refuse such a heinous invasion. Virginity examinations, though not uncommon before marriage contracts were drawn up, were not a requirement either.

"I have a midwife on hand," Ferial said, in what she must have thought was a comforting tone. "I wouldn't dream of making you go down to the police station."

Wisps of anger curled in Giorgina's belly. Ferial had a midwife ready? This was no longer a negotiation, then. It never had been. Ferial smiled apologetically at Giorgina, who felt suddenly that she wanted to slap her. Everything she might have said to her—the invasiveness of virginity tests, the injustice, that several leading medical experts now doubted their accuracy—stuck in her throat. Sand coated her tongue. Sabah squeezed Giorgina's knee even tighter.

Hala licked her lips. "I suppose if the midwife is already here . . ."

Giorgina turned to her mother so quickly she felt her neck crack. "Mama . . ."

It was Ferial who answered. "It'll only take a moment, habibti, you have nothing to worry about. Really, it's just a formality."

Giorgina was trapped. The midwife might determine that Giorgina was not a virgin, which was in fact the truth. But if Giorgina refused the test, Ferial would grow suspicious and come to her own conclusion that Giorgina was not virginal. They would discover it all, and everything Giorgina had sacrificed to keep her reputation intact would be for naught.

"Your mother and sisters will be right here with you," Ferial was saying as she struggled to her feet. "It will be quite quick."

Giorgina allowed herself to be led forward by her mother, toward a staircase, up into a small bedroom. It was furnished warmly, with dark blue curtains, brown rugs, and several sparkling lamps. The bed, which was tucked into a corner against the wall, was covered in plush blue bedding. The bedroom looked completely ordinary, comforting, even, utterly at odds with what was about to ensue. Sabah, who had not left Giorgina's side, rubbed the small of her back.

"It'll be all right," she breathed, so softly that only Giorgina could hear her. "It'll be all right. These things are unreliable. You told me that."

Giorgina did not look at her sister, who knew far more than she had any right to and yet had never said a word about any of it.

Near the bed, a broad-shouldered older woman was hovering, a satchel in her hands. She had wide shoulders and a square jaw. The lines around her mouth indicated she was prone to smiling, as she was doing now.

"This is Rabia," said Ferial, leading Giorgina to the bed. "She delivered my Zakariyya."

Rabia laughed. "And I'll deliver Zakariyya's child as well, if the Tetrad wills it." She helped Giorgina sit on the bed and shooed Ferial away. Ferial went to stand at the back of the room, where she was joined by the Shukry women. This way, they could only see the back of Giorgina's head.

Giorgina clenched her hands into fists to keep them from trembling, to keep herself from making the ground beneath her tremble. She felt like she had stepped through a doorway into an alternate reality; her grasp on her surroundings was fading quickly, but simultaneously growing far too clear, like she was looking at it through a spyglass. Her skin was clammy. Her breath came in short spurts.

"Now, habibti," said Rabia as she rubbed something onto her hands. "I'll have you remove your undergarments and lie back."

Wordlessly, Giorgina obeyed. She lay down on her back and shut her eyes tight, willing herself to fade into oblivion. She was unsuccessful.

Rabia's cold hands lay on Giorgina's ankles. "Now, Giorgina, lift up your legs like this, that's right, ankles together—now drop your knees on either side—that's it, that's right, perfect, now relax, habibti, relax—"

But Giorgina could not relax, not when Rabia's fingers were forcing their way inside her and she was struggling to keep a grip on her weaving. She clenched involuntarily. Her palms curled into tight fists. Rabia paused.

"Relax, habibti, it's all right, this won't hurt a bit, but you have to relax."

Giorgina forced herself to take a deep breath, but it was ragged. She heard Rabia sigh and go forth with the examination. Giorgina squeezed her eyes shut but could not prevent the tears that leaked through and slipped into her hair.

An eternity later, Rabia instructed Giorgina to sit up. Giorgina sat up so fast she felt dizzy. Before anyone could tell her otherwise she reached for her undergarments and slipped them on.

Ferial's cheerful face came into view. "Well? Good news, I assume?"

Rabia's face was troubled. "Well—it's—it's inconclusive, I'm afraid, Ferial."

The way Ferial's smile slipped from her face might have been comical in any other situation, but now it only made Giorgina sick. "What do you mean, inconclusive?"

Giorgina saw her mother and sisters approaching, their faces stricken.

"Just that," said Rabia flatly. "Inconclusive. I can't make a determination one way or the other."

"Well, Rabia, that can't be!" said Ferial. "The girl is either a virgin or she isn't."

Rabia shrugged.

"Fine, fine." Ferial waved her off. "Then I'm afraid I'll have to ask you to recommend a colleague so I can get a second opinion."

"I'll save you the trouble." Giorgina trembled as she got to her feet, her mind curiously blank as she stared down Ferial. "I'm not a virgin. I haven't been for years."

Giorgina did not know whether it was her words or her harsh, hoarse tone that made Ferial flinch.

"Giorgina, stop!" Hala cried. "What are you saying?"

But Giorgina was overtaken, panic and fury thrumming in her veins. There was a dull throb of pain between her legs. "It's the truth."

Ferial clucked her tongue. "Well, then. That's that." She sighed and turned to Hala. "I'm afraid I will have to ask you to leave now. The betrothal is off, obviously."

They were ushered out of the house without another word. Outside, Giorgina blinked at the sun's glare. Everything looked different, somehow. Giorgina took a deep breath, and for that single moment, she felt free.

Then the panic hit.

Oh gods, what had she *done*? How could she have been so rash? In front of two perfect strangers Giorgina had exposed her most dangerous secret, everything she'd worked so hard to conceal, and now her reputation was shattered. But it was not just her: the stain would follow Nagwa and Sabah as well. Her sisters would struggle to find respectable marriages. Her parents would be the joke of the neighborhood. Their friends would look down their noses at them, shun them. Her sisters might lose their jobs, their friends. All because of Giorgina. She had known all this, and she'd done what she'd done anyway.

Giorgina's mother looked dazed. "Why, Giorgina?" she asked sadly. "Your father won't let you back in the house."

Hala's resigned grief hit Giorgina hard. She wished her mother would have yelled at her, slapped her, cursed her—anything but this deep well of disappointment and helplessness.

"Maybe we can tell him something else," Sabah said desperately. "We can tell him they called it off for another reason—"

"With the way word spreads in this city?" said Hala. "Even if Ferial doesn't say anything, that midwife will. By tonight everyone will know." She shook her head. "You're ruined, all of you."

Sabah clutched Giorgina's arm. "Go stay with Basna," she said. "Until we can convince Baba—"

"You think Basna's husband will let her stay once he finds out?" said Hala.

"Then what, Mama?" Sabah asked. "Where can she go?"

Giorgina looked at her sisters, Sabah with her stricken but calculating expression, Nagwa with the look of an animal caught in rail tracks. She had ruined them, utterly. But . . . the pain and humiliation of that virginity test. Shouldn't Giorgina have been spared that? Shouldn't her sterling reputation have protected her? Why should she any longer deny herself what she wanted, when everything she'd done to preserve her reputation had not served her in the least? She'd had an abortion to hide her supposed shame, a child she had grieved over for months. She'd hid her involvement with the only women who felt like home. She'd given up the man she loved. And in the end, she was still suspect. She was still humiliated and violated. What did reputation matter if it did not keep you safe?

And what did *any* of that matter when Labiba was *dead*?

Giorgina gently extricated herself from Sabah's grasp. "Don't worry." Her voice sounded utterly hollow, and she could not discern if she was calm or in the grip of a terrible panic. "I have somewhere to go."

Hala looked at her daughter as though she were a stranger. "Why, Giorgina?" she asked again. "Why would you do this to us?"

Giorgina shook her head. She had no answer that would satisfy her mother. She hadn't done this *to them*. She had done this *for herself*. Admitting to her lost virginity in front of Ferial had been utterly selfish. But despite the panic Giorgina felt, she couldn't entirely regret her actions. That was a terrifying revelation.

"Mama, people are looking!" Nagwa whispered loudly.

Indeed, not only was Ferial's doorman staring with unabashed interest, a small crowd of people had gathered across the street, casually glancing over their shoulders.

"I'm sorry," said Giorgina, so quietly she was not even sure if she had been heard. She turned her back on her family and walked away. She found herself caring very little as eyes lingered on her form, as whispers trailed her down the street. She had always thought she would care, that the taint to her reputation would slither into her chest and make itself a filthy home that would consume her from the inside out. Instead, she felt everything more vividly than ever before: the wind on her cheeks, the pebbles beneath her feet, the smell of jasmine trees drifting in the breeze. It was not happiness; of that she was certain. It was a curious thing, something Giorgina had never experienced before.

Giorgina wondered if this is what it felt like to have nothing left to lose.

Her feet carried her across Alamaxa, toward Nico. She ignored the curious stares when she entered his neighborhood. She knew she did not fit in with its wealthy denizens, but she kept walking anyway, kept walking until her feet hurt, even though she could barely feel the pain. At Nico's door she knocked three times.

The door was opened by a young woman who must have been a servant.

"Can I help you?" she asked hesitantly.

"I'm here to see Nico, please," replied Giorgina politely.

The woman stepped back and allowed her to enter. "Follow me." She led Giorgina into the parlor, then left to call Nico. Giorgina did not sit down.

She heard Nico before she saw him, his footsteps coming down the stairs, the creak of the door, his sharp intake of breath at the sight of her. She took him in as he walked to her: his hair, longer than it had ever been, his glittering blue eyes, his tender smile.

"Giorgina," Nico breathed. "What's— Are you all right? What's happened?" He looked at her as though she might disappear at any moment.

The sight of him cracked something open in Giorgina, brought her back down to reality. But she could not put words to what happened. Her lips trembled, her throat closed up, the tears she had been holding back trickled out of her eyes, and she found different words bubbling out of her: "Labiba's dead. Labiba's dead, and I— I—" The sobs burst out of her, heavy and violent, forcing her to her knees.

"Oh, Giorgina." In seconds Nico was on the floor beside her, his hands wrapping around her and holding her tightly against him. Giorgina collapsed into the warmth of him, the familiarity—he smelled like dried flowers and old books, of joy and laughter and hope. Giorgina never wanted to let him go.

If this was shame, if this was dishonor, then Giorgina would embrace them both.

27

GIORGINA

GIORGINA FELT HOLLOW.

She had cried for what seemed like hours, until there was nothing left in her, until her throat was raw and her eyes were as dry as the desert. Nico brought her mint tea, which she sipped at halfheartedly, and tried to convince her to eat, but she refused all his offers. She could not stop thinking about what she had done. What had come over her? She was not rash and impulsive and willful; she was careful and circumspect. Wasn't she?

But she could not deny the sheer relief coursing through her. She was—free. Free of obligation, free of the burden of respectability, free to do whatever she liked, really. Giorgina had ruined herself, but within her ruination was liberation. She had lost her status, her reputation, and, likely, her family, but in turn had gained a new life. But what sort of life would it be? She had so disdained being a mistress, but what other avenues were open to her now? She had worked herself into a corner with no escape routes. And she could not deny the part of her that relished it.

Giorgina shut her eyes. She wanted to sleep. She wanted to sleep for years.

But just as the tension had begun to seep out of her limbs, she heard the front door open and shut, and she tensed again, opening her eyes to see Nico frowning.

Within moments, Nehal Darweesh marched into the parlor.

She looked somewhat disheveled—she was missing both her robe and her veil, her curls twisting out of the hasty knot she had pulled them into. Her expression looked even more mutinous and combative than usual. Giorgina, frankly, was too tired to wonder whether Nehal was irritated by her presence, with Nico, or something entirely different.

"Nehal," exclaimed Nico. "Shouldn't you be at the Academy?"

"Yes, I should," Nehal snapped. "But they've expelled me."

"*What?* Why?"

Nehal began to pace. "My involvement with the Daughters of Izdihar. My face all over the papers. They claim they have to *choose sides* or some such nonsense." She was rapidly increasing speed as she paced around the room, her hands gesturing wildly. "Fine. *Fine.* I'll show them. I'll prove them all wrong." She paused, then turned to the pair of them. "Hello, Giorgina. I'm glad you're here. You saved me a trip."

Giorgina blinked—this wasn't at all the reaction she had expected. "I did?"

"I saw Malak," said Nehal.

Nico stood. "Shaaban let you see her?"

"Only for a few minutes." Nehal shook her head as she continued to pace. "She's not well. It's so cold in those cells and they gave her nothing to wear, I had to give her my robe! Shaaban says since she's been declared a domestic terrorist she can't apply for bail, and a lawyer would have to jump through hoops to defend her. Is that true, Nico?"

Giorgina's heart fell. If they were already deeming Malak a domestic terrorist, her trial would be a show at best.

Nico licked his lips, considering his words. "If they've designated her as such, I'm afraid so."

"Completely ridiculous," muttered Nehal. "Well, one thing at a time. She asked me to visit Etedal, see about the funeral expenses—Giorgina, you know where she lives?"

Giorgina got to her feet, her stomach lurching in guilt at the thought of Etedal. "I do. I've been meaning to go see her—"

"Good, we'll go together right now," Nehal declared. She turned to the young woman who had let Giorgina in, snapping her fingers. "Ridda, have Medhat bring the palanquin around."

Ridda left hurriedly.

"Wait a minute, Nehal—" Nico began.

Nehal ignored him. "And then we'll have to go see Bahira. We have to challenge the narrative the papers are putting out; we can't have Alamaxa thinking the Daughters set fire to Parliament on purpose. Malak said Bahira would know who to talk to; she has contacts."

"Nehal," said Nico more forcefully. "Wait. Giorgina's in no state to—"

Giorgina touched his arm. "No, Nico, it's all right. I can't just sit here. I need something to do, and I need to see Etedal. I haven't even paid my respects yet."

Nico turned to her hesitantly. "Are you sure you're all right?"

Giorgina tried to smile. "I will be."

NEHAL WASTED NO time. Giorgina hardly had a moment to catch her breath before Nehal was pulling her along as soon as she had a new robe and Medhat was ready with the palanquin. Nehal's energy did not fade when they were in the palanquin; in fact, she buzzed with an excess of it, her fingers drumming on her thigh as she hummed an off-tune melody.

"So what's the matter with you?" Nehal asked suddenly.

Giorgina startled. "What?"

Nehal waved her hand impatiently. "Nico was asking if you were all right. You look as though you've been crying. You were at our house after vehemently denying Nico several times." Her expression softened somewhat. "Is it Labiba? You two were friends, yes?"

Giorgina swallowed heavily. "Yes." She could have left it at that, allowed Nehal to think it was only grief affecting her, but Giorgina needed to tell someone, and she suspected Nehal's outrage on her behalf would be cathartic. "But—this morning, I . . . I left my family."

Nehal raised her eyebrows and waited.

"They found me a suitor," Giorgina explained haltingly. "But his mother demanded a virginity examination."

Nehal's scowl betrayed her disgust. "Ugh! Please tell me you refused."

Giorgina almost laughed at Nehal's willful naïveté. "I couldn't. It would have been as good as an admission of guilt. Not that my compliance did me much good in the end." Giorgina paused, recalling the feel of the midwife's fingers between her legs, all too aware that her family was watching her endure this humiliation. "The midwife said the result was inconclusive. So the suitor's mother said we would do another examination, get a second opinion."

Nehal swore loudly.

"I refused." Giorgina shrugged. "And then I told her I wasn't. A virgin, that is."

Nehal's eyes grew wide. "That's . . . I don't know whether to be impressed or . . . I don't know. You were so adamant about protecting your reputation. What changed your mind?"

Giorgina bit her lip and looked out the window of the palanquin. "I thought if I kept my reputation pristine, I would be . . . I don't know. Protected? Rewarded? But I still ended up being prodded at by a stranger."

"Reputation is meaningless," Nehal declared. "With the way people gossip in this country? Half of it is lies. I never waste time worrying what people are saying about me."

Giorgina bit back a retort. Nehal was a lady of the House of Darweesh, a woman with wealth and means who could afford to sit back and let her reputation fester if she so desired. For Giorgina, her reputation was all she had. Was it any wonder she had nursed it so carefully? But it had meant nothing for her in the end. It had not protected her.

"Are you agreeing to Nico's offer, then?" asked Nehal. "To be his concubine?"

"I—I don't know." It was not a decision to be taken lightly. Though, when Anas heard the rumors and fired her, as he surely would, Giorgina would have no income, and then what would become of her?

"Stay with us until you decide," said Nehal firmly. "You'll be *my* guest."

"I—" Until then, Giorgina had been readying herself to ask Etedal if she could stay with her for a bit, though in truth she dreaded the prospect of living with Etedal's grief. Not to mention they had never been close; Labiba had always been there as a buffer between them.

Before Giorgina could formulate a proper response, the palanquin came to a halt. The man leading the palanquin—Medhat, to whom Giorgina had given directions to Etedal's building—helped them both out. The familiar sight of the butcher and the dilapidated exposed brick had Giorgina's stomach sinking, knowing that Labiba would not be inside, that she would never be inside again.

Etedal lived on the third floor, the stairs to which were lumpy and uneven, worn in random places. Nehal muttered complaints under her breath as she navigated them. Dust coated the handrail, as though it had never been cleaned. There was hardly any light.

On the third floor, Giorgina pointed out Etedal's apartment, and Nehal immediately began to pound loudly on the door before Giorgina had the wherewithal to stop her.

"What?" asked Nehal.

"You sound like you're coming to arrest her," said Giorgina.

"I just want to make sure she can hear us."

"She's grieving, not hearing-impaired," replied Giorgina, then bit her lip at the sharpness of her retort.

Before Nehal could respond, the door swung open with a long creak.

Etedal was wearing a plain black galabiya covered in dirt. Her curls were unusually puffy, undefined and sticking out in random directions, and her face was covered in soot, as though she hadn't washed since the day of the march.

"What?" Etedal demanded.

"Etedal—" Giorgina reached for her, but Etedal drew back violently, startling Giorgina.

Nehal frowned. "Malak sent us to make sure you're all right."

"Oh, I'm wonderful," said Etedal in a thick, sarcastic tone. "My only family in the world was murdered in front of me a few days ago, so I'm fucking *excellent*."

"May she rest in the Tetrad's embrace," Nehal intoned. "I wanted to help with the funeral."

"I don't want anything from *you*," Etedal snapped. "And there's not going to be a funeral; the police took her body and won't give it back."

"Etedal," said Giorgina softly. "Please, can we come in?"

Something in Giorgina's expression must have softened Etedal, because she threw up her arms in defeat and walked back, leaving the door open for them to follow her. Nehal marched inside, and Giorgina gently shut the door.

On a table just inside the entryway were sheafs of papers, mainly funding materials for the Daughters of Izdihar. Giorgina was suddenly reminded of Nasef, the young Sheikh who had been so obviously taken with Labiba. She wondered if he knew she was dead, and if Labiba's family knew she was dead, and a powerful wave of grief struck her hard.

Nehal was holding herself stiffly, her hands clasped together at her waist. "I can speak to Commander Shaaban. Have him release her body."

Etedal kicked a worn sitting pouf so hard it struck the wall. "Have him wrapped around your finger, do you? While you're at it, then, get him to arrest the pig who killed my cousin. *Attia Marwan,*" she spat. "Labiba told me how he gloated when she was locked up in prison with you. I bet he was fucking *gleeful* about shooting her."

Nehal looked startled. "Attia Marwan?"

"Do you know him?" asked Giorgina.

"I—had a brief run-in with him." She paused. "Malak was with me. He was following us—her."

"Because he has it out for us," said Etedal.

"He targeted Labiba," Giorgina said quietly.

Etedal and Nehal turned to her.

"What?" asked Nehal blankly.

"I was standing by her." Giorgina swallowed, her voice trembling. "I saw him—he went right for her. He hit her in the face with his rifle, twice, until she started fireweaving by accident. Then he just—he just *stood* there, staring at her, waiting, watching her panic, and then he shot her." Giorgina looked up. Etedal's face was frozen into a mask of fury. Nehal looked bewildered. "I think he planned it. All of it. He was the one who shot into the ceiling. He knew Labiba was a fireweaver who couldn't control her power. He wanted to create chaos."

"There's no way he could have predicted everything would happen the way it did," said Nehal slowly.

"Maybe not," said Giorgina, growing more convinced of her theory the more she spoke. "But what was there to plan? He knew if he hit Labiba hard enough she might start a fire. If she didn't, well, then he had nothing to lose. But if she did, it would ruin us. Even if Parliament hadn't burned down like it did, we would have still looked like instigators so long as Labiba sparked."

She had thought it might sound crazy when she said it out loud. But it didn't. It made the strangest, cruelest sort of sense.

Etedal strode past Giorgina and Nehal, toward the door. Giorgina rushed after her, latching on to her galabiya.

"What are you doing?" Giorgina gasped with the effort of holding Etedal back.

"I'm going to find him," said Etedal, her eyes blazing. "And I'm going to *kill* him."

"No. Stop. Etedal, stop!" Giorgina wrestled with Etedal until her arms were practically wrapped around her. Giorgina twisted around and blocked the door. "You can't. He'll only hurt you too!"

"So what then?" Etedal shouted, shoving her back. "We do nothing?"

"No." Nehal walked up to them and laid a hand on Etedal's arm, carefully controlled fury evident in her every taut movement. "I'll tell Commander Shaaban about this policeman too."

"And what, he'll sacrifice one of his own officers for us?" Etedal sneered. "Are you that naïve?"

"It's not naïve; it's practical. We have to try speaking with him first," Giorgina insisted. "Before we do anything reckless. If he can't help, then we can think about what to do next. All right?"

Etedal said nothing.

"Etedal," Giorgina urged, "I need you to tell me you agree with this."

Etedal raised both hands and vigorously rubbed her hair, as though she could scrape it off if she tried hard enough. "Fine. *Fine!* But you do this today, do you hear me?" She whirled on Nehal. "You speak to him *today*."

Nehal nodded, her eyes bright. "I swear on the Tetrad."

WHEN NEHAL INFORMED Medhat of Bahira's whereabouts, he hesitated. "Bulaq?" he repeated uncertainly.

"What of it?" Nehal asked impatiently.

"It's a slum," said Giorgina when Medhat hesitated. "Not exactly a place for lords and ladies." Giorgina herself had always been instructed to stay far away, for it was said to be teeming with thieves and brothels. Bahira must be very poor indeed if she lived there.

"I don't care." She turned back to Medhat. "Take us there."

Nehal was, if anything, angrier and more tightly wound than

she had been before. Her finger tapped an incessant, uneven rhythm on the window of the palanquin.

"Do you think the police commander will believe you?" Giorgina ventured to ask.

"I'll make him believe me," Nehal said shortly.

Giorgina bit her lip. Nehal's confidence was comforting in the way a mother's reassurance to her child would be, but that was also what made it frustrating, because Giorgina was not a child, and she knew it would be very, very difficult to get the police to turn on one of their own. She wanted to ask Nehal what other options were open to them if Commander Shaaban refused to listen, but she suspected Nehal was the sort of person who would not entertain even the possibility of her failure until it was staring her in the face, so Giorgina kept her own counsel.

They did not speak again until they arrived in Bulaq.

They could smell it even from within the palanquin: garbage rotting in the heat, excrement and dried urine, moist sweat. She wrinkled her nose and started to wrap her shawl around her mouth, only to remember that she had left it behind. Nehal, who had no robe or veil, instead held up the length of her sleeve to her nose; Giorgina did the same with her galabiya sleeve, though she had much less fabric to work with. She did not want the palanquin to stop. She certainly did not want to venture forth into this miasma unprotected.

But the palanquin did stop. When Medhat came around, his brow was creased with worry.

"The lanes are too narrow for the palanquin, my lady," he said.

"We'll walk," Nehal said shortly.

"But—"

"You stay here with the camels." Nehal made her way out of the palanquin, forcing Medhat to help her down. "Make sure nothing gets stolen."

Giorgina followed her out. Nehal strode confidently toward the first alley in front of them, leaving no time for Medhat to protest. Here the streets were neither cobbled nor properly paved; the road beneath Giorgina's feet was lumpy and squishy with mud, and likely other unsavory substances she had no wish to think about. Her shoes squelched loudly in the filth. There was a humid moistness to the air that clung to Giorgina like a second skin, making her feel dirty and unwashed as she walked through a stench that was almost tangible.

The alley was alive with activity. They walked past a coffeehouse that was nothing like the luxurious places Nico had taken Giorgina to, but rather a loud establishment filled only with brawling men playing tawla and smoking shisha. They stumbled through the cloud of smoke emanating from the door toward a shop with screaming chickens and geese. The ground in front of the shop was thick with dried blood and sticky feathers. Giorgina narrowly avoided stepping in the mess; she was forced to lift her galabiya up to her ankles as she walked.

Nehal stopped so suddenly Giorgina nearly walked into her. When Nehal turned, she was frowning.

"I don't know where anything is," said Nehal.

"Then where have you been walking toward?" asked a bewildered Giorgina.

"I thought once we got into the neighborhood things would make more sense." Nehal gestured to the street on which they stood, from which several other lanes, even narrower, branched out. "As it stands, nothing makes sense."

With a sigh, Giorgina looked around. She approached the friendliest-looking person she could find, a plump elderly woman in black sitting in front of a veil shop.

"Pardon me," said Giorgina. "Could you please tell us where to find Zubaida's?"

The old woman peered up at Giorgina with suspicion. "Why're you looking for that?"

Giorgina started to say, "We're looking for a friend," just as Nehal said, "That's none of your concern."

The woman glared at them both, then rolled her eyes. "Keep

walking straight till you see Gamal's Coffeehouse. Make a right. The brothel'll be at the end of the alley on your right."

Giorgina flinched. "The *what*?"

The woman raised a pair of thick dark eyebrows, but Nehal dragged Giorgina away before she could say anything.

"All right, so it's a brothel," said Nehal with obviously false bravado. "So what?"

Giorgina looked down at Nehal in disbelief. Not only were they in a slum in one of Alamaxa's most disreputable neighborhoods just as the sun was setting, but they were heading to a brothel, of all places. There was bravery, and then there was stupidity.

And then there was whatever they were doing.

But Giorgina was certain there would be no deterring Nehal, so she reluctantly followed her. At one point they encountered a huge, muddy puddle too large for them to jump over, so Nehal held out her hand and weaved the water in it to the sides, drawing curious eyes.

"Stop that!" Giorgina admonished. "We don't need to draw attention."

Nehal grumbled something unintelligible but released the sludgy liquid, allowing it to once again pool into the depression in the middle of the street. They slogged through.

When they came to Gamal's Coffeehouse, they turned into a crooked alley so tiny not even a mule cart could squeeze through. At the end of the alley stood a two-story building. While it was not particularly pleasing to the eye, it was sturdy and relatively clean, unlike its neighbors, and painted bright red. A small, dangling sign read *Zubaida's* in messy script.

A group of three men lounging around the door leered at them as they approached.

Giorgina grabbed Nehal's arm to slow down her confident march. "Should we be going inside?"

"How else are we to speak to her?" Nehal shook herself free of Giorgina. "Don't worry. If they try anything, I *will* make them regret it." She touched the gourd of water at her waist.

As it was, there was no need for any weaving; the men continued to leer very conspicuously, their mouths hanging open, but did not approach them as they crossed the threshold.

A wave of heat and stale beer attacked Giorgina the moment she entered. She blinked, adjusting her eyes to the poorly lit and over-crowded room. Toward the back was a bar filled with sloshing cups of cheap beer. The air was heady with the cloying scent of incense, mingled with the smoke of shisha and tobacco. In one corner was a man sitting on a cushion with his arm around the waist of a woman who wore an obscenely unbuttoned vest with nothing beneath. Gior-gina averted her eyes.

On her right was a group of low tables surrounded by cushions. Men and women sat scandalously close, imbibing beer and shisha and black coffee, and laughing at the top of their lungs.

"What now?" said Giorgina loudly to Nehal.

Nehal's eyes were carefully scanning their surroundings. With-out a word she strode toward the center of the room; Giorgina hur-riedly followed, not wanting to be left alone.

"Pardon me," said Nehal to a young woman serving drinks. "Where might we find Bahira Naguib?"

The girl tucked her tray against her chest and looked them up and down; she could not have been older than sixteen.

"Who are *you*?" she asked somewhat rudely.

"Friends," said Nehal shortly.

The girl only stared, but Nehal matched the intensity of her gaze with an expectant glare of her own; it was the look of a woman ac-customed to always getting what she wanted. Giorgina was glad of Nehal's company then; she herself would likely have wilted under the girl's gaze.

After a moment, the girl shrugged and pointed to the staircase in the back of the room. "It'll be the last door on your left."

Though much quieter than the first floor, the second floor's silence was nevertheless punctuated by the various sounds of passion com-ing from within the locked rooms. Heat warmed Giorgina's cheeks.

Reluctantly, she continued to follow Nehal down the hallway. When they were standing in front of the last door, Nehal knocked loudly.

The young woman who opened the door was long-limbed and gray-eyed, with russet-brown skin and tight black coils pulled back into a low ponytail. Giorgina relaxed a little at the sight of someone familiar.

"Bahira," said Nehal. "Malak sent us."

With a sigh that seemed like it was a long time coming, Bahira stepped back and gestured for them to step inside. Grateful for a reprieve from the obscene sounds in the hallway, Giorgina shut the door behind them.

She was surprised to find a rather sparse room that smelled mildly of soap. In one corner there was a low desk stacked with a mess of papers. In the other corner was a ratty sleeping mat with a flowery coverlet.

Bahira gestured to the mat. "Have a seat."

Giorgina hesitated, but Nehal said, "Is that where you . . . entertain clients?"

Bahira frowned. "I'm not a prostitute."

Nehal pointed to the roof atop their heads. "Are you quite certain about that?"

Bahira raised an indignant eyebrow. "I do the finances for the brothel."

Nehal gaped. "Are you honestly telling me you're an *accountant*?"

Bahira narrowed her eyes. "Why are you here?"

"Malak sent us," said Nehal again. "She said we need to publish a new issue of *The Vanguard*, with our side of the story—"

Bahira scoffed. "Leave it to Malak to organize from her jail cell." She turned and settled behind her desk on the floor. She motioned for them to do the same. "We can't publish anything."

"Why not?" Nehal demanded as she sat down.

Bahira smiled grimly, a closemouthed, crooked thing, full of bitterness. "We've been banned."

"Banned?" Nehal repeated. "What does that mean?"

"Parliament just released an edict. For the time being, *The Vanguard* is banned from circulation."

"We'll circulate it anyway," said Nehal automatically. "They can't arrest all of us."

Bahira rubbed her forehead. "I considered that. The printing press I work with refused."

"So we find another one."

"Do you think I haven't tried that?" said Bahira. "Do you think it was so easy to find a printing press willing to work with us in the first place?"

"Then we try to speak to someone at the *Alamaxa Daily*—"

"My contact there refuses to speak to me."

"*Fine*. Then we hold another rally—"

"Another rally? *Now?*" Bahira shook her head. "Are you insane? Everyone hates us. We'll be murdered in the street."

"I won't let anyone—"

"Stop!" Bahira held up both hands. "You're not going to convince anyone else to march, not now, not when one of our own *died* at the last march we attempted for Malak. It was a mistake then, and it's even more so now."

"Excuse me?" Nehal's cheeks reddened. "Do you march for Malak or for yourself?"

"I tried to tell her marching on Parliament was a bad idea," Bahira insisted. "But as usual, Malak listens only to herself."

"Don't you dare blame her!" said Nehal. "Labiba was targeted by the police—"

"Labiba set Parliament *on fire*," interrupted Bahira loudly.

Startled, Giorgina said, "Bahira, it was an accident. One of the policemen provoked her."

"Irrelevant," said Bahira flatly. "Parliament still burned down, and everyone still blames us. We may want to consider distancing ourselves from weaving elements—"

"And do nothing while Malak rots in prison?" Nehal sneered. "Are you angling for a coup?"

"Don't be a child," snapped Bahira. "Do you think this is just about Malak? You think I'm doing nothing? Do you know how many women depend on us? Our charity drives? Our health clinics? I'm struggling to keep it all organized—"

"*What about Malak?*" Nehal demanded.

"*Oh,* I see." Bahira sneered, leaning toward Nehal. "This isn't about the Daughters of Izdihar. For you, it *is* about Malak. You *like* her."

Nehal stilled, until she was stiff as a rock. "We all like her."

Bahira cocked her head. "You like her the way most women like men."

Nehal's gaze flickered toward Giorgina, who wanted to tell Nehal not to worry, that she already knew about Malak, that she would never reveal Nehal's secret or judge her, but before Giorgina could form the proper words, Bahira continued, "It's understandable, really. I've certainly been there. She's beautiful, charismatic, makes you feel like the most important person in the world. Until you're not. The work always comes first, with Malak."

"Bahira," said Giorgina sharply when Nehal stayed quiet. "That's enough."

Bahira sat back with a shrug. Giorgina exhaled silently, the tension in the room stiffening her limbs. She shifted in place with a grunt.

"Perhaps we can get someone to speak on our behalf?" Giorgina suggested. "What about the senators who were there? They were witnesses—"

Bahira barked out a laugh. "One of those dogs, helping us? Hardly."

"It's something to try," Giorgina insisted. "Do we know who they were?"

"Yes," said Bahira grudgingly. "I can give you their names, but you're crazy if you think they'll speak to you."

"They'll speak to my husband," said Nehal, her tone flat.

Bahira snorted. "Depending on a man for help is like depending on a sieve to hold water."

"Nico will help," said Giorgina. "The *Alamaxa Daily* might speak to him as well. I'm sure Nico has a contact or two there."

"Then I guess we're done here." Nehal shot to her feet. "Give us the names and we'll leave you alone."

Bahira scribbled the names on a piece of paper and handed it to Giorgina without once looking at Nehal, who turned and walked away without a word.

THEY LEFT THE brothel under the cover of darkness; the sun had faded entirely, but its departure had not heralded the usual cool breeze that came with desert nights. The air was still thick and muggy, heralding a nascent storm. Though the walk back to the palanquin was somewhat harrowing, what with all the leers they received, they made it back unaccosted.

Nehal decided to detour them home so she could drop Giorgina off before going to see Shaaban, and so that she might have something to eat before gearing up for an inevitable confrontation. Giorgina had not been able to fathom accompanying Nehal and finding herself once again in the presence of the commander to whom she had lied so blithely about her involvement with the Daughters of Izdihar. It was best to let Nehal speak to the commander herself, without Giorgina's unwelcome presence intruding. Besides, Giorgina was exhausted, and hungry—she had not eaten since breakfast—and she looked forward to a bath and a night's sleep. Somehow, along the way, Giorgina had decided to accept Nehal's offer, and stay with her—and Nico.

Unfortunately, when they entered the home, they were greeted by raised voices. Nehal froze, her expression practically comical: her nostrils flared and her eyebrows drew together into a crinkled scowl.

"That sounds like my mother," she said slowly. "But I obviously must be hallucinating, because what would my mother be doing in Alamaxa?"

The woman's voice came again, far more clearly this time. "What sort of errand?"

Nehal cursed and marched toward the parlor.

As they approached, Giorgina heard Nico's tentative response: "Visiting a friend?"

"You sound uncertain," the woman said. "Which is it, Nico? Is she running an errand or visiting a friend? Don't you know where your wife is at this time of night?"

"Leave the boy alone, Shaheera," came a man's voice. "You know what Nehal is like."

Nehal opened the door to the parlor, with Giorgina hovering hesitantly behind her. "What am I like, Baba?"

Nehal's parents both stood in the center of the parlor, facing Nico. Nehal's mother, Shaheera Darweesh, was at first glance the image of her daughter, sharing her dark skin, curly hair, and wide eyes, but Nehal's features were more exaggerated, more striking, whereas her mother was more regal. Her father, Khalil Darweesh, was a thin, lanky man with a slight paunch and thick beard. Three very similar-looking small children, all with wiry curls, rose to their feet and ran to embrace Nehal. She ran her hands through their hair fondly, but distractedly, her eyes never leaving her mother's.

Giorgina wanted to crawl under the rug. She had absolutely no desire to have anything at all to do with Nico's *in-laws*. But Nico caught her gaze, gave her an encouraging look, and Giorgina sidled into the room, not quite standing beside him but hovering in a corner.

"Where have you been?" Shaheera snapped at Nehal.

Nehal scowled at her mother. "Out. Are you here all the way from Ramina to question me about my whereabouts?"

Shaheera's expression hardened. "What happened to your face?"

Nehal shrugged. "Armed policemen happened. I'll ask again: why are you here?"

Shaheera's scowl matched Nehal's.

"No fighting," said one of the boy children.

"Ridda, please take the triplets to bed," said Shaheera. Ridda, whom Giorgina had not noticed hovering in the opposite corner, nodded.

"But I'm not sleepy!" protested the girl. She held on to Nehal's robe. "I want to stay with Nehal!"

Nehal knelt and gave her younger sister a light peck on the nose. "I'll be up to see you in a bit. I'll show you some new tricks."

The girl did not look entirely satisfied but went along with Ridda quietly. Shaheera waited until their footsteps faded before speaking.

"Your father-in-law sent me a rather incendiary letter regarding your behavior. I am loath to believe a word of it, so I came to speak to you in person."

"What sort of letter?" asked Nico apprehensively.

"A *very* strongly worded letter claiming Nehal *attacked* him," said Shaheera. "Please tell me he's exaggerating."

Nehal crossed her arms. "He deserved it."

Shaheera's hands flew to her hair. Her husband stepped forward and placed his hand on his wife's shoulder, but she flinched away toward Nehal.

As Nehal stepped forward to meet her mother halfway, Shaheera finally noticed Giorgina, who was doing her best to remain inconspicuous.

"Oh," said Shaheera, lowering her hands. "Hello. Are you a friend of Nehal's?"

Giorgina hesitated, so Nehal simply said, "Yes, Mama, she's our friend."

"Perhaps your friend could give us some privacy?"

"Of course." Giorgina hurried to leave, but Nehal caught her arm.

"That's not necessary." With a frown, Nehal pulled Giorgina into the parlor and drew the door shut. Giorgina cringed, longing to escape, but Nehal gripped her arm like a vise.

"*Nehal.*" The warning in Shaheera's tone, and in her glare, was as obvious as a sandstorm, but it did not seem to affect Nehal in any way.

"You should have heard the way Lorenzo spoke to me, Mama!" Nehal exclaimed. "And to Nico! If you were here to witness his behavior you would not be criticizing mine."

Nehal finally released Giorgina, who slowly backed away until she was against the wall.

Shaheera turned to her husband with a look of wide-eyed consternation. She motioned for him to speak. He cleared his throat, and began, "Habibti, there are ways to resolve conflicts that don't involve weaving—"

"Oh, but of course," said Shaheera, voice dripping in sarcasm. "Our daughter is an Academy student now. What else can we expect? We *explicitly* forbade you from going anywhere near the Academy, so you go behind our backs—"

"Behind your backs? How could I be going behind your backs? I thought I belonged to my husband after marriage," Nehal shot back acidly. "If he consented, what's the problem?"

Shaheera shot Nico a glare; he immediately blushed and looked away.

"And that's not even all of it!" exclaimed Shaheera, waving her hands in the air and pacing, looking very much like her daughter had earlier that very day. "Running around with the Daughters of Izdihar, getting caught up in *domestic terrorism*, dear Tetrad—"

Nehal rolled her eyes. "Why does everyone keep using that term? The fire was an accident, one that never would have happened if Uncle Shaaban hadn't thought it wise to send an entire armed police squadron after us!"

"You cannot behave like this." Shaheera shook her head. "Nehal, when I receive a letter from your father-in-law *demanding* that we rush to Alamaxa because of your behavior, that is a problem."

Nehal shrugged. "A problem for who? It's certainly not *my* problem."

Shaheera closed her eyes and took a deep breath. When she opened them again, she glared at Nehal and asked, "How many parties have you held here?"

Nehal stared back at her blankly, and even Giorgina was surprised at the abrupt turn of subject.

"What?" Nehal looked at her mother as though she'd gone mad. "What in Tefuret's name are you talking about? Who cares how many parties we've had?"

"It is *expected* of you," said Shaheera through gritted teeth.

"That's ridiculous—"

"You will hold a grand party," Shaheera continued as though Nehal had not spoken. "Right here, in the courtyard. You will invite all the right people, and then some. You will invite Lorenzo—"

"I will *not*!" cried Nehal.

"*You will!*" shouted Shaheera. "You will have a party, and it will be seemly and elegant and it *will* dispel any further rumors about you."

Nehal seethed. "I am not going to waste my time planning parties."

Shaheera sneered at her daughter. "Your time is so valuable, is it? Playing weaver at the Academy?"

Nehal swallowed, and Giorgina saw how it was costing her to hold back that she had already been expelled.

"In any case," continued Shaheera, "I will help. Your father and I will be staying here with you and Nico for the time being."

"*What?* Why?"

"Because you clearly need the supervision," Shaheera snapped. "Now show us to one of the guest rooms." Without giving Nehal a chance to argue further, Shaheera turned to Giorgina. "I am sorry you had to witness all this, habibti. We haven't even been introduced."

"This is Giorgina Shukry," said Nico quickly. He glanced at Nehal, who only offered him a shrug.

"And how do you know my daughter?"

Giorgina said the first thing that came to mind. "Through the Daughters of Izdihar, Auntie."

Shaheera's expression darkened. "I see. And how do your parents feel about your involvement in all that?"

Nehal groaned and started to pull her mother away. "Let Giorgina be, Mama, and go settle in if you insist on staying."

Shaheera gave her daughter a look that, were it directed at anyone but Nehal, would have made the recipient wilt. "As you can see, Giorgina, my daughter has no sense of propriety." She narrowed her eyes at Nico's prone form. "Nico, *join us,* please?" she said pointedly, her eyes flickering to Giorgina.

Giorgina blushed. Of course. She and Nico could not be left alone together.

"Giorgina's staying with us for a bit, by the way," said Nehal.

Shaheera gave Nehal a look that made Giorgina dig one of her fingernails into her thumb with mortification. It had been one thing for Giorgina to stay when it was just Nico and Nehal, though even that was just bordering the bounds of propriety, but to do so with Nehal's parents under the same roof? But she had nowhere else to go.

"The house is yours, habibti," Shaheera said to Giorgina coolly. "Nico, now, please."

With an apologetic glance at Giorgina, Nico followed his mother-in-law, leaving Giorgina standing alone in their parlor, uncertain and unsure.

28

NEHAL

AS SOON AS HER PARENTS WERE ENSCONCED IN THEIR ROOM, Nehal informed Nico that she was leaving to see Shaaban.

He was startled. "What? Now? Nehal, it's the middle of the night."

She waved him off without quite looking at him. "Don't exaggerate. It's only just past sunset. If my parents ask, tell them I'm visiting a friend."

"Wait, Nehal, of course they'll *ask*—"

Nehal ignored him. She'd hoped to change and eat something before going to see Shaaban, but she had to seize the opportunity to escape her parents, so she simply stopped by the kitchens on her way out for a loaf of bread, which she chewed on in the palanquin on the way to the police station. When she was finished, she wiped her fingers against her trousers, covering them in a light dusting of flour.

Medhat set them down across the street from the police station, which stood stark against the dusty landscape, the squat, freshly painted building staring at Nehal mockingly. Her fingers drummed an unsteady rhythm on her thighs as she stared across the road. She had purposely set aside her fury for Attia Marwan, and now her anger was vibrating off her in waves.

Nehal liked her uncle Shaaban well enough, but it was no secret that the police were corrupt. Certainly, there were some like Shaaban who were honorable and dedicated to maintaining the peace, but then there were others like Attia Marwan who entered the profession for the unbridled power it granted. The police harassed the public with impunity, and Nehal had frequently witnessed them accepting bribes, or turning a blind eye to the illegalities of the wealthy and privileged.

But she had never imagined that a policeman's corruption would reach so far that he would murder an unarmed woman. Labiba. Nehal had only spoken to her a few times, but she'd been kind. Warm. She certainly didn't deserve to be killed, and Attia Marwan needed to pay. He needed to be punished.

Nehal jumped out of the palanquin, landing heavily on her feet. A thick conglomeration of clouds clustered to hide the moon from view. The streetlights were shrouded in a haze of fog. The air felt thick enough to cut through. It did not rain often in Alamaxa, but Nehal could feel the water clinging to the clouds, waiting for a chance to break free. She breathed in the invigorating scent of it before striding purposefully into the police station.

She walked past various policemen and administrators who called after her as she made her way toward Shaaban's office. Soon enough, they quieted, and Nehal assumed someone had finally informed them of her identity.

Nehal knocked on Shaaban's door once but did not wait for a response before entering. He looked up angrily when his door swung open, but when he saw Nehal, he sighed.

"Barging in again, Nehal?" He set down his pen. "We need to discuss your knocking etiquette."

"No, we need to discuss something that's actually important." She shut the door behind her and leaned against it for a moment, steadying herself. "I'm here for two reasons. First, I'd like to ask you to release Labiba Wagdy's body to her cousin, so she can give her a proper funeral."

Shaaban gripped the bridge of his nose between forefinger and thumb. "Nehal. Since Malak is in prison, Labiba's body can only be released to her closest male relative. Once we find them—"

"She's a corpse," said Nehal harshly. "What possible danger could there be in releasing her body to her female cousin?"

"It's not about danger; it's about propriety—"

"Fuck propriety!" Nehal's voice rang in her ears. Shaaban's eyes widened comically. "Why is it always about propriety and tradition? Who do those things serve? What do they serve? Is that why your policemen go around murdering women? To preserve propriety?"

"Murder? What are you talking about?" Shaaban asked tersely.

Nehal forced calm into her voice, though she thought she did not sound entirely like herself. "I've learned something about one of your policemen. Attia Marwan?"

Shaaban opened his mouth, but Nehal barreled over him. She told him everything: that Attia Marwan knew Labiba and recognized her, that he had purposely targeted Labiba hoping to make her spark. She described his targeted assault on an innocent woman, and when she was finished, she waited for her uncle Shaaban's righteous fury. Or indignation. Or even disquiet.

Instead, she received a tired sigh and a grave look.

"Have you heard anything I've said, Uncle?" Nehal demanded. "This man needs to be held accountable!"

Shaaban waved his hand in a motion one might use to quiet a child, a gesture that only infuriated Nehal more. "Why don't you sit down?"

"I don't *want* to sit down!" exclaimed Nehal. "I want you to *do* something with the information I've just given you!"

"You see, the problem is that I have ten policemen who have testified that it was Malak Mamdouh who shattered that ceiling—"

"That's a lie!" snarled Nehal. "I was with her, she never—"

"Even the senators said they witnessed her using her abilities to manipulate the glass—"

"That was *after* Attia Marwan shattered it!" said Nehal. "Malak was only trying to keep it from falling on us."

Shaaban smiled at Nehal indulgently. She had the distinct sense he was humoring her, and she *despised* being humored. "I understand you want to protect her. But inventing wild conspiracies—"

"I'm not *inventing* anything!" Nehal's shout caught in her throat; her vocal cords felt ragged. She knew, on some level, that shouting would not help her convince Shaaban of her veracity, but she couldn't help it. "I'm telling the truth! I was *there*! Do you really not believe me?"

Shaaban leaned back with a sigh. "Your behavior as of late hasn't been particularly trustworthy, Nehal."

"Fine!" Nehal spat. "I can bring in Giorgina; she witnessed everything. And Etedal Wagdy, she'll—"

"Attia is one of my best, and he does his job well," said Shaaban firmly. "The Daughters of Izdihar are always wreaking havoc, and Attia does his best to contain it. He's already explained the incident to me. He was defending himself against a rogue fireweaver who wished to burn him."

"I told you Labiba sparked *accidentally*," said Nehal acidly. "And she was nowhere near attacking Attia when he shot her."

"That's not what Attia said," replied Shaaban evenly. "He insists it was self-defense."

Nehal's nostrils flared. Her hands turned into fists, nails digging deeply into soft skin. "I could bring you a hundred women to tell the same tale and you still wouldn't believe us, would you?"

Shaaban sighed heavily. "Unless Attia himself walks into my office and confesses, I'm afraid not." He leaned to the right as though to look over her shoulder. "Are you here unchaperoned? Where is your husband? And your father? I heard he's here in the city—"

The rest of Shaaban's words faded away. *It's meaningless to him,* Nehal thought. Her words, their plight, their fight, all of it was utterly meaningless. To Shaaban, Nehal was only playing at politics, the Daughters of Izdihar a gaggle of women with nothing to keep them better occupied. Shaaban had not taken her seriously for a moment. Here was a man who had watched her grow up, who was like a brother to her father, who she called Uncle—and even he had no faith in her.

Though he was still talking, Nehal turned on her heel and marched out of his office without a word. He called after her, but she ignored him. The gourd of water at her side was shaking, but Nehal ignored that too.

Outside the station, she took a deep breath to steady herself. Then she realized she did not want to be steadied. She did not want to lose this anger, this fuel. Instead, she descended the steps of the police station, crossed the street, and instructed Medhat to go home. He balked at first, but backed down when Nehal shot him a glare. When he had turned around, Nehal tucked herself into a dark alley across the street from the police station. There she waited.

He emerged sometime later, chin tucked. He looked just the same as the last time Nehal had seen him, and attacked him: pale and bald, with a thick, neatly trimmed beard.

Nehal peeled herself out of the darkness and followed him.

It was not a difficult pursuit. Attia Marwan walked with careless abandon, a spring in his step, the walk of a man confident that all would step out of his way to let him pass. He was sure-footed and held his head high, never once pausing or looking back.

If Nehal wished to corner him she would need to wait until they approached a quieter street. She had no plan in mind. All she knew was that her veins were throbbing with rage, a sensation that was spreading through her limbs and controlling her every move. She had no sense of what she might do once she caught him, but she had to catch him.

So she pursued.

The sky cracked open. Thunder growled as rain fell by the bucketful, turning the streets into sludge. Nehal lost her pattens in the muddy alleys, leaving her with cloth slippers that immediately became soaked. Her hair, weighed by water, tumbled out of its chignon and stuck to her like a cape.

She delighted in it.

Alamaxans scrambled to avoid getting wet, squealing with equal parts delight and dismay at the rare bout of rain. To Nehal, the rain was energizing. It was not only on her skin that she felt it, but in her blood, in her fingertips, within her grasp. She was confident with the knowledge that all she had to do was reach out and the rain would be at her command. It roared in her ears, blanketing all other sounds.

As it continued to pour, the streets cleared. They also grew cleaner, and cobbled: Attia was moving north, toward the Talyani Quarter.

After some time, the downpour eased, and then stopped completely, leaving behind a chilly breeze. Nehal slowed her pursuit, lest Attia Marwan hear her.

When he turned right into a narrow alleyway, Nehal followed carefully, looking over her shoulder to make sure they were alone. The street behind her was deserted. Carefully, she leaned forward, looking for Attia.

He stood on a threshold; he was speaking to someone, but Nehal could not see who. The alley was not quite an alley either, but a kind of alcove between two buildings, so that Attia was only steps away from her. Hurriedly, she flattened herself behind a thick vine of flowering gardenia. The smell was overpowering, but Nehal forced herself to remain still.

Who was he talking to? Did he live here, with someone? Was he planning on spending the night? Her heart thudded; there was no way she would go back home without confronting him. She leaned into the gardenia bush, straining to listen to what Attia was saying.

"You're really not going to let me in?" said Attia, somewhat surly.

The answering voice was cool and spoke in a Zirani accent. "You're covered in mud. Not to mention I warned you against coming to my home; this is an unnecessary risk. If you're seen—"

Nehal frowned. That smooth voice was familiar, but she could not place it.

Attia sighed loudly, performatively. "You haven't been answering my requests for a meet. You know, you could be a bit nicer to me, given all I've done for you."

"You've done nothing for *me*, Mister Attia," replied the Zirani. "All you've done, you've done for money."

"At your behest," replied Attia testily. "*You* sought me out."

Nehal peeked through the gardenia leaves. She could see Attia, but the Zirani man was still standing in the doorway, and entirely hidden.

"I'm not some mercenary," Attia argued. "I believe in this. I connected you with the Khopeshes because I believe in your cause."

"Yes," replied the Zirani dryly. "That *was* helpful. Less helpful is the girl who was shot at Parliament."

Nehal tensed. They were talking about Labiba? *Who* was this man? She dared lean forward a little farther, willing the man to shift so she could see him.

Attia's expression twisted into an ugly sneer. "Not helpful? Parliament burned to the ground and they're blaming it on weavers."

"They're blaming it on rogue women—"

"*Weavers*," Attia insisted. "You think Parliament isn't going to be amenable to more severe restrictions after weavers burned their house down?"

Finally, Attia's companion moved, taking a step outside his doorway so that Nehal could see his profile, and her eyes widened. She recognized him easily; she had, after all, seen him up close at the opera.

Naji Ouazzani.

What was Attia Marwan doing having this conversation with the *Zirani ambassador*?

"And why, precisely, Mister Attia, was it necessary to kill the girl?" Naji asked. "As I understand it, she had already set the place aflame when you shot her."

Attia shrugged. "What does it matter? She's a nobody. A woman. A weaver. You're the last person I thought would give a shit; you're the one whose king rounds up weavers and throws them in underground prisons—"

"But does not murder them needlessly, or so *publicly*," replied the ambassador smoothly. "You've created a mess that did not need to exist because you have a grudge against the Daughters of Izdihar—"

"You hate them yourself; I know you do!"

"My personal feelings on the matter are irrelevant, as yours should have been," said Naji. "Such acts of wanton violence are exactly what we condemn in weavers. I'll not have you turn me into a hypocrite. I only asked you to ensure the march went poorly, not to murder a girl who might one day have been cured of her affliction. I will not work with someone so volatile. Our partnership ends here."

Naji made to step inside, but Attia reached for him. "You don't think you're a hypocrite? You've been giving the Khopeshes money for pistols and ammo; what is it exactly do you think they're doing with that? What about the weavers *they've* killed, huh? You don't think that's on you? Don't get all high and mighty with—"

Naji Ouazzani wrenched himself free of Attia Marwan's grip and retreated, shutting the door loudly in Attia's face without another word. Attia stood frozen, his hands closed into shaking fists, which gave Nehal a moment to ponder the conversation.

Naji Ouazzani was funding the Khopeshes of the Tetrad, a gang of fanatics who created chaos and murdered weavers. Naji Ouazzani was also working with Attia Marwan, who had just admitted to murdering Labiba in cold blood.

Nehal was beyond rage. Her fury was bubbling over, threatening to spill out of her.

Attia Marwan walked right past her and did not see her. She did not hesitate. There was a puddle of water at her feet. She held out her hands, gripped the water, hardened it until it hovered in a state somewhere between liquid and solid ice, and shaped it into a whip, which she then thrust forward to wrap around Attia Marwan's ankle. When she pulled, he sprawled on his belly with a shout.

She was about to congratulate herself, but Attia had a policeman's reflexes. He twisted onto his back and shot to his feet, his hand on his belt, where his pistol sat. When his gaze found Nehal, his eyes widened in recognition.

"*You*. You were that girl with Malak. The one who nearly killed me." He pulled out his pistol and pointed it at Nehal. "I ought to shoot you on sight."

Nehal took a step closer to him, unafraid, and he held his pistol higher. "Careful, girl. There's no river here for you to use."

"You're a murderer. You killed my friend."

Attia stared at Nehal quizzically, a curious smile spreading slow over his lips.

"Is this a joke?" he said finally.

"Her name was Labiba," said Nehal, her voice shaking with rage. "You shot her after you forced her to lose control of her fireweaving. You're going to walk back to the police station with me right now and confess to the police commander."

At that, Attia laughed, long and loud. "Why don't you run home, girl, and find something useful to do with your time."

He started to turn away, but Nehal wrapped her water whip around his wrist and wrenched him back. He stared at her in disbelief, and, she was pleased to see, a little fear. "Let me go, freak."

"That's Lady Nehal of House Darweesh to you!" Nehal spat. "You know what you did. And I just heard you admit it to the Zirani ambassador. You need to confess."

Again Attia smiled as though he were thoroughly amused. "Well, sorry, *my lady,* but you can't prove a thing."

"Do you not feel an ounce of remorse?" Nehal seethed through gritted teeth. "You killed an innocent woman."

Attia shrugged. "I did my duty. Commander's been wanting your sorry lot put down for months."

Nehal narrowed her eyes. "Malak Mamdouh isn't going to rot in prison for what *you* did. You're going to confess."

Attia sneered. "And you're going to make me?" He brandished his pistol again. "I'm not afraid of you or your weaving, girl."

Nehal was too angry to be afraid. "Are you going to kill me too? Is that your answer to everything?"

"I'm giving you a chance to walk away," said Attia. "Run along home and forget about all this."

Nehal moved, and Attia cocked his weapon. The sound echoed unnaturally in the empty alley.

"Hands behind your back," Attia instructed.

Nehal could hear her own blood pulsing in her veins. It left a thunderous roar in its wake, drowning out all coherent thought. All Nehal could hear was the pounding of her blood, and—and— another rhythm. Another song. Her eyes found the thumping vein on Attia's neck as his heart beat fast, her elemental awareness crying out to it, wanting to reach for it, to seize it—

So she did.

Attia clutched at his throat and fell to his knees, gasping. His grip on the pistol weakened until the barrel was pointed at the ground. Instinctively, Nehal sought the veins in his wrist, took hold of the blood inside, and wrenched his wrist back until he dropped the gun.

Nehal had a hold on Attia Marwan from the *inside,* and it filled her with a thrill that was like a hurricane. This was like nothing she had ever felt before. It was a rush, a high that filled her own veins with sticky sweetness. She cast out her senses further, feeling inside the rest of Attia's body, the wet slick blood that filled him from head to toe.

Of course. *Of course.* Blood was just water, after all, water of a different kind.

She found the blood in his palms, grasped them. She *pulled,* ignoring Attia's shallow gasp. She forced his arms to his sides. Then she found the blood in his feet, and she worked her way up to his ankles, his calves, his thighs. She forced him to stand, though he did it jerkily, like a marionette puppet on strings. His had grown ashen.

"*Confess*," Nehal hissed. She relaxed her grasp on his throat so he could speak.

"I did it," he gasped. "I did it, I shot at the ceiling, I provoked the fireweaver, it was me, just let me go!"

"Not until you tell Commander Shaaban," said Nehal. "Let's go. *Walk*."

Nehal granted Attia just enough leeway to walk on his own, but she kept a tight hold on his abdomen, a hold she knew he felt with every aching step.

She walked a small distance behind Attia, careful not to let his movements grow too jerky lest someone notice. She did not know how long it took for the police station to come back into view, but when it did, she tightened her grip. Attia spasmed in pain, and Nehal grimaced in satisfaction, then pushed him up the stairs.

Nehal felt stares as always, but there was no move to stop either party as they made their way forward. At Shaaban's door, Nehal reached down for Attia's palm, pulled it up, and slammed it against the door. It swung open after a few moments, Shaaban on the other side, his face turning ashen at the sight before him.

"Attia, son, what—" But Shaaban froze when he caught sight of Nehal. His eyes trailed down to her fist, which was shaped into a tight claw at her side.

He gasped, a look of horror twisting his features into a grotesquerie, and launched himself toward them.

"Get in!" Shaaban hissed. "Get in, right now!" He made no move to touch her, Nehal noticed, to pull her in, so she pushed Attia inside and followed. Shaaban locked the door behind them.

Attia stood stiffly in the middle of Shaaban's office. Nehal did not release him. "Tell him," Nehal commanded, giving Attia a shake just to see him wince. "Tell him what you just told me."

Shaaban looked from Nehal to Attia, his eyes wider than Nehal had ever seen them. He held his hands at his chest, palms open, as though expecting to catch something.

"I destroyed Parliament's ceiling," groaned Attia through gritted teeth. "I shot it when I arrived, hoping to provoke the fireweaver. When that didn't work I attacked her. I knew she was prone to sparking."

He paused, so Nehal shook him again, watching his body twitch. "And you killed her even though she wasn't attacking you! *Admit it!*"

Attia drew a shaky breath. "Yes. And I killed her. Please, please, let me go!"

Nehal ignored him. "You heard him, Uncle?" said Nehal.

Shaaban was staring at Nehal with something very close to fear. "Nehal." He spoke slowly, carefully, as one might speak to a madwoman. Nehal frowned at his tone. "Just . . . let him go, habibti. Release him."

"Did you hear what he said?" Nehal repeated. "He confessed!"

"Yes, yes, I heard," said Shaaban hurriedly. "Just . . . please, just let him go."

Nehal released her grip. Attia collapsed to his hands and knees. He was trembling all over.

Serves him right, Nehal thought venomously. The thrill of energy animating Nehal rushed out of her limbs slowly, leaving her suddenly exhausted. Her bones felt like cotton, but sheer will kept her standing.

Shaaban kneeled beside Attia and placed a tentative hand on the back of his neck. Attia flinched away.

"What in the name of the Tetrad was that?" Attia's voice was ragged. He would not look at Nehal, though his next question was clearly directed at her. "What did you do to me? What the fuck kind of weaving is this?"

Shaaban glanced up at Nehal and shook his head rapidly, warning her to say nothing. He needn't have bothered. It wasn't as though she were about to explain herself to Attia Marwan.

"Well, Uncle?" asked Nehal again. "He's confessed. What more do you need?"

Shaaban ignored her as he helped Attia to his feet. "Wait here, Nehal."

"But—"

"For once in your life, *do as you're told*!" Shaaban's roar, so unlike him, surprised Nehal, but if he thought it would cow her, he really didn't know her at all.

She narrowed her eyes. "Don't you shout at me," she hissed. "Do you think you'll scare *me* with a raised voice? After what you've just seen me do?"

Shaaban blinked, then shook his head, and returned his tone to a normal decibel. "I need to speak with Attia. Just . . . just wait for me here. Please."

Slowly, Nehal nodded. Shaaban led Attia out, balancing his weight on his shoulders. When they were gone, Nehal allowed herself to collapse, leaning on Shaaban's desk for support. Her every muscle felt deflated, like she had just gone swimming in the ocean for hours and hours. Everything in her ached, and her head was beginning to pound like it did when she was terribly hungry or hadn't slept. But she could not forget the way she had felt when she had Attia under her control so completely. The power that had thrummed in her veins was intoxicating. She swallowed, her throat dry, aching for another taste.

She grew impatient waiting for Shaaban and considered leaving the office to find him. Just as she began to stand, the door opened, and Shaaban stepped in. He was curiously stooped, and he did not look at Nehal. Even after he closed the door he continued to stare at the floor, one hand on the doorframe.

"Uncle?" said Nehal.

"What have you done?" Shaaban said to the floor.

"I did what you were unwilling to," said Nehal firmly. "I got him to confess to what he did."

Shaaban leaned against the door and put a palm to his forehead. "And you think a confession given under such duress will hold? For all I know he said what he did to release himself from your grasp."

Nehal's mouth opened, her nostrils flared. "You're determined not to believe me! What more could I have done—"

Shaaban spoke over her. "I've convinced Attia to remain silent about what you've done, for now. But Nehal—I have to arrest you."

Nehal's shoulders drooped like a wilting flower. "What?"

Shaaban shook his head. "You assaulted an officer of the law. In full view of his peers. You see that, don't you? Even you must understand the gravity of what you've done."

There was a low buzzing in the back of Nehal's head. Her limbs were growing heavier by the minute.

Nehal had not really considered the aftermath of her actions. She had been singularly focused on making Attia confess. She had assumed it was Attia who would face consequences afterward, not her. Surely his crimes trumped her own? Surely the ends justified her means? She stared blankly at Shaaban, who approached her slowly, as one might a wild animal. Then he gripped her shoulders. Nehal startled. Shaaban had never touched her before.

"Listen very carefully, Nehal," said Shaaban slowly. "Attia won't say a word, but neither can you, do you understand? You mustn't tell anyone what you just did."

Nehal frowned. "Why—"

Shaaban shook Nehal roughly, startling her into silence. "*Please*, Nehal, tell me you understand me. This is for your own safety. Trust me. Please, habibti."

Shaaban's wide, frightened eyes and his quiet flustered words perturbed Nehal far more than his raised voice. She moved her lips wordlessly for a moment, until Shaaban squeezed her shoulder.

"Swear to me."

Nehal just wanted him to let her go. "I—I swear."

Shaaban's grip relaxed as he sighed heavily, but he did not let go of Nehal's shoulders. "All right. All right." He nodded, then looked up with a pained expression. "Now—I'm sorry, Nehal, but you've left me no choice. You're under arrest, and I have to take you to the jail cells now."

With his hand firmly gripped around her elbow, Shaaban led Nehal out of his office and toward the underground jail cells.

"You'll be all right," Shaaban muttered, mostly to himself. "You'll be just fine."

The cells were quieter than they had been earlier that day—had it really been just this morning when Nehal visited Malak? It felt like a lifetime ago. She had still been an Academy student then. Her return felt even further out of her reach now.

Tonight, most of the occupants were asleep, and those who weren't sat quietly, their shawls drawn around themselves for warmth.

Shaaban was taking her down a corridor that looked vaguely familiar. She looked up at him. "Isn't this where—"

"I'm doing this so you don't have to be alone," said Shaaban shortly. "Try not to destroy the prison."

With that, he gestured toward the cell they had arrived at, which held Malak, who was sleeping soundly on the floor, wrapped up in Nehal's robe. For a moment, Nehal simply looked at her, then she turned to Shaaban, who was unlocking the cell door. Nehal stepped inside and waited for him to lock it.

"What happens now?" asked Nehal quietly.

"I go see your husband," said Shaaban. "He'll come in tomorrow, apply for bail, and wait for a judge to sign off on the request. Just try to sleep, Nehal. You look exhausted."

Nehal *felt* exhausted. She'd been running on pure adrenaline this entire time, and now that Shaaban was walking away, leaving her to the silence and darkness of these cells, she felt the weight of everything that had happened today. She sank to the floor against the wall opposite Malak, who had not woken up. Nehal smiled a little, to learn Malak was a heavy sleeper.

Malak slept on her side, her hair unbraided and falling across her cheek, her chest rising and falling slowly. Nehal lay on the ground facing her across the cell and tried to match her breath to Malak's. In moments, she was fast asleep.

29

GIORGINA

GIORGINA DRUMMED HER FINGERS IN HER LAP NERVOUSLY. She sat in the parlor with Nico and Nehal's parents, who were pacing the room.

When Medhat had come back with an empty palanquin, Shaheera and Khalil Darweesh had narrowed their eyes and demanded to know where he had left Nehal. Shifting nervously, Medhat explained that Nehal had ordered him to go home and leave her at the police station.

"So she's with her uncle Shaaban," said Khalil, clearly relieved.

"But why is our daughter spending her time at a police station in the middle of the night?"

"It's hardly that late—"

But when midnight came and went and Nehal still had not arrived, Nehal's parents began to question Nico, and when he did not yield any satisfactory answers, they turned on Giorgina.

"Does this have to do with the Daughters of Izdihar?" Shaheera demanded. "What is my daughter involved with?"

Giorgina shrunk from the woman's gaze, wondering if she ought to tell them why Nehal had gone to visit Shaaban, because now Giorgina was beginning to fret as well. She strongly suspected that Nehal's conversation with Shaaban had not gone well, and it was not beyond the pale to imagine that Nehal had decided to take things into her own hands, circumventing Shaaban entirely and seeking out Attia Marwan herself.

Might there have been an altercation between them? Could he have harmed her, even shot her, like he had shot Labiba? The thought made Giorgina's stomach curdle, but she could not bring herself to give voice to her fears.

Nehal was fine. She had to be.

Giorgina glanced at Nico, who was very pale, eyes red from lack of sleep. Every now and then, he would glance nervously at Shaheera, who continued to pace the parlor, muttering.

"This is ridiculous," Shaheera finally announced. "I'm not just going to sit here and wait. Khalil, let's go see Shaaban."

Her husband nodded, and Giorgina wilted in relief to see them go, but a loud, insistent knock at the door gave them pause. Every occupant of the room stiffened, listening to the sound of mumbled conversation and footsteps.

Shaaban strode into the parlor, still in his work clothes, the epaulets on his uniform swaying as he shifted his shoulders. He looked grave. Giorgina went cold.

Khalil stepped forward and embraced his friend, but Shaheera stood still, white-faced. "Where is my daughter? Is she hurt?"

"Nehal is safe," said Shaaban hesitantly.

"Then where is she?" demanded Shaheera.

There was a long pause.

"In jail," said Shaaban finally. "She's been arrested for assaulting a policeman."

A more delicate woman might have swooned or at the very least sat down, but Shaheera only narrowed her eyes. Not for the first time, Giorgina could see the resemblance between mother and daughter.

"I beg your pardon?" said Shaheera acidly.

"It seems she was convinced that one of my officers was involved in some sort of conspiracy against the Daughters of Izdihar. She came to me about it earlier tonight, but when I didn't act on her suspicions she sought out the officer in question and . . . persuaded him to confess."

There was something about Shaaban's tone that made Giorgina's neck prickle.

"How did she persuade him?" Nico ventured.

Shaaban hesitated, then drew a restless hand across his hair. He turned to Giorgina with a little nod of the head that told her he remembered her. "Would you grant me a few moments of privacy with Nehal's husband and parents?"

Giorgina blinked, then nodded hastily, managing to ease out of the parlor without stumbling. It was an unwelcome reminder of her foreign position in the household, and it turned her stomach. For a moment she thought to listen at the door, then shook herself at her silliness. She was not a child, and besides, Nico would likely tell her anyway.

She waited for him in his study warily, knowing Nehal's parents would not be pleased if they found her here, but their minds would likely be on Nehal. She paced restlessly as she waited. Finally, Nico appeared, brow furrowed, though his expression softened when he shut the door of the study behind him.

"Is he gone?" asked Giorgina.

Nico walked to his desk and sank heavily beside it, gesturing for Giorgina to do the same. She did so, sitting some distance away on her knees, so that she might stand at any moment if they were interrupted. "Yes. We're to go see Nehal in the morning."

"What happened?"

Nico opened his mouth, then closed it. "Nehal . . . she used waterweaving on the officer in question. A very particular branch of waterweaving that's not especially well known."

Giorgina shook her head. "What sort of branch?"

Nico sighed through his nose, looking weary. "Well, weaving

disciplines have various iterations, yes? You're not just an earth-weaver; you're a sandweaver or a woodweaver; waterweavers can become iceweavers and steamweavers . . ."

Giorgina knew all this, and Nico knew that she knew all this; he was stalling, but Giorgina nodded encouragingly anyway.

Nico continued, "There's one particular iteration of waterweaving that isn't spoken of very much, partly because of how rare it is. But I think also because weavers hoped they might be able to drive it out of existence."

Giorgina was growing irritated with his cryptic tone. "What *is* it, Nico?"

"Ah—they call it bloodweaving."

Giorgina frowned. "How does that . . . how is it useful? Unless you're already standing in a pool of blood . . . ?"

Nico shook his head, a bitter smile curling his lips. "Not if you can weave the blood when it's still inside living things."

Giorgina reared back.

"Do you recall the marionette show we went to last year?" Nico asked gravely.

"That shouldn't be possible," said Giorgina slowly. "You can't weave something you can't see, or . . . or feel in some way."

Nico ran a hand through his tawny waves, forcing them to stand on end. "In theory. Not so for bloodweaving, I suppose. Again, it's a very rare branch, and it hasn't been studied very well." He paused. "It's what got Edua Badawi expelled from the Alamaxa Weaving Academy."

Edua Badawi's expulsion from the Alamaxa Weaving Academy was common enough knowledge, but it came without any contextual details. Schoolchildren simply learned that Edua Badawi was expelled for some grievous offense, but no books ever detailed what the grievous offense was.

"How do you know this?" asked Giorgina. "Is it in those letters you found?"

Nico shook his head. "I haven't read the letters yet. No, I've just seen certain documents in the National Archives not accessible to the public—all the internal communication of the Weaving Academy, back in the day."

"And you're saying Nehal . . . Nehal is a bloodweaver? Like Edua?" The words felt foreign in Giorgina's mouth.

"She likely wasn't even aware of what she was doing," said Nico hurriedly. "I doubt she knows the history behind it, or how spectacularly illegal it is. You know Nehal, she rushes into things with hardly a speck of foresight." Nico sighed. "Shaaban said the officer gave his word not to say anything."

"Attia Marwan? I wouldn't trust that man's word at all," said Giorgina.

Nico shrugged and shook his head at the same time. "All we can do is trust Shaaban knows what he's doing."

"Which is what, exactly? How long is Nehal going to stay in jail?"

"I doubt her parents will let her stay there long," said Nico. "Someone of her status—but I suppose we'll still have to post bail and wait for a judge to sign off on the process."

Giorgina sat back on her haunches, hands curled tightly in her lap. Could Nehal really have done something like this without being fully aware of it? Giorgina was no stranger to the impulses of weaving, the lack of control, but to do something so very deliberate—that required deliberation, didn't it? Weavers were not at the mercy of their element. Or at least, they were not supposed to be. Giorgina swallowed thickly.

"Nico," she started. "I'll sleep here tonight, since it's late, but I'm leaving tomorrow."

Nico startled. "What? Why? I know we haven't had a chance to speak much about the future, but—"

Giorgina shook her head. "It was one thing to be here as Nehal's guest, but she's not here anymore. I can't just be here with you and her parents; they'll suspect something."

"Maybe . . . maybe I should tell them—"

"No!" interrupted Giorgina. "They have enough to worry about right now, Nico. It's not the right time."

"But where will you go? You said you can't go back home—"

"I'll go to Etedal," said Giorgina. "She should know what happened with Attia Marwan. I'll stay with her until . . . until something changes." She paused. "You didn't read Edua's letters."

"I wanted you to be there with me when I did," replied Nico. "Will you be?"

Giorgina opened her mouth, but no words came; all she felt was a fierce rush of affection for Nico that left her momentarily speechless. She pursed her lips and looked away.

"Will you meet me at Farouk's Teahouse at noon tomorrow?" Nico broached hesitantly.

"All right," said Giorgina softly. "At noon."

WHEN GIORGINA WOKE, she was comfortable, which was unusual, but troubled, which was not. She sat up slowly, blinking away the fog of sleep. How strange it was to wake up in a room that wasn't damp but pleasantly warm, in a bed as soft as feathers, in a room all her own. Even her washroom was private: she could spend as much time in there as she wanted. She could wash her hair with luxurious scented soaps and slick it through with expensive oils. She could fill up the bathtub with warm water and scented oils and rose petals and soak in it for as long as she desired.

The ache in her chest accompanied her as she splashed her face with water. She had dreamed of the march, and Labiba. How many more nights would she be forced to bear witness to her dearest friend's murder? How long would it take to stop feeling like her chest was being cleaved in two?

With a sigh, she made her way back to her room. It was barely dawn. Giorgina stepped out onto the balcony that faced the inner courtyard, watching the glistening sky fade from pale gray to hazy pink. The date palms in the courtyard swayed lazily in the gentle morning breeze. Two birds landed on the rim of the fountain and dipped their beaks in for a sip, then began to chirp.

Giorgina wished she could simply stay here forever, in this warm, comfortable place, in this particular moment, and it did not escape her that this might have been her life. *Should* have been her life. If Nico had married her as intended, this would have been how Giorgina greeted every morning. This would have been *her* home, not Nehal's. Instead, she was a barely welcome guest.

She shook those acrid thoughts away as she dressed and combed her hair, then quietly stepped out of her room, determined to sneak out of the house without disturbing any of its occupants. Unfortunately, she ran into Shaheera on her way to the exit. Apparently Nehal's mother was a fellow early riser.

"Good morning." Shaheera smiled, but there was a stiffness to it. Giorgina smiled back as politely as she could.

"Good morning, Auntie," said Giorgina.

"Did you sleep well?"

"Very well." Giorgina paused. "Please give Nehal my regards. I should be getting home. I'm sorry to have intruded."

Shaheera's expression did not soften. "I'm afraid we can't spare the palanquin," she said.

Giorgina's skin prickled. "That's all right. I don't have very far to walk."

When Giorgina was out on the street, she allowed herself to breathe a sigh of relief. She walked out of the alley containing Nico's house and leaned against the wall, allowing herself a moment to take stock. The main street was quiet since shops had not yet opened. Giorgina liked Alamaxa most like this, in the waking hours, before the cacophony of mule carts and crowds and street peddlers. It was quiet enough to think.

She recalled that she had a morning shift at the bookshop today. With everything that had happened in the space of one day, the bookshop felt very far away, but Giorgina needed to see if she still had a job. She needed to see how far word of her actions had spread.

With each step she took toward her old neighborhood, her stomach tightened, until it was in knots. Giorgina's heart refused to stop thudding, and she was unsurprised to feel the ground shaking beneath her feet. She stopped, took a breath to steady herself, and kept walking.

It took her nearly an hour and a half, by which time her shift was due to start. If the bookshop was quiet, waiting for Giorgina to open it, then all was still well. If Anas was there . . .

Giorgina turned the final corner that would take her to the bookshop, then walked down the lane until she was at the doorway. She placed her hand on the door, and her heart fell to her feet when it swung open.

Anas stood behind the desk. He peered up at her when she walked in, and his expression went cold.

"Did you really think you could come back here?" said Anas.

Giorgina's heart was leaping into her throat, but she made herself calm, steady. *Breathe,* she told herself. *Everything will be all right if you just breathe.*

"I don't understand—"

"Don't play dumb with me," Anas snapped. "And after I vouched for you to Zakariyya Amin? To find out that you're—" He shook his head. "You're fired, obviously. Don't come back here."

"Mister Anas, I—" Giorgina swallowed. "I need this job. My family needs this job."

"Perhaps you should have thought of that before you gallivanted around with various men," said Anas. "Do you think I want my shop associated with you more than it already is?"

Had Giorgina really expected any other reaction? Had she thought to find sympathy from Anas, of all people? She'd known that this was the outcome of her actions. But just because she was not surprised did not mean she was not angry; there was a roaring in her head, growing louder by the second.

"What's the matter with you?" Anas demanded, a thread of fear in his voice.

Giorgina looked up at him, startled to find that her hand was shaking violently, and with it the entire bookshop.

"Are you doing that?" asked Anas in astonishment. "Are you a *weaver*?"

Giorgina pulled her shaking hand into a fist and drew it to her belly. Instead of answering Anas, she turned and stumbled out, wanting to get as far away from him as possible. The thoughts spiraling in her head continued to tumble atop each other with a ferocious speed, so Giorgina stopped and fell to her knees, heedless of the stares directed at her; she'd been stared at so much recently that it no longer mattered anymore. She dug her hands into the ground, into sandy earth, and tried to let it comfort her, root her. She took one slow breath after another, pushed all her intrusive thoughts away as best as she could. Yet they still hovered on the edges of her periphery, taunting her with what she had done, with her stupid, rash decisions.

Enough. Giorgina needed to pull herself together. Even if all she wanted to do was sob and fall apart, she couldn't. She thought of good things: Nico was there for her. He would help. He would help her fix this. There was no other choice.

I'm ruined, but I'm not dead, Giorgina thought. *And I* am *free.*

For now, she needed to go see Etedal, who deserved to know what had happened with her cousin's murderer. Giorgina would direct all her attention to this one task, and afterward, she could deal with all the rest of it.

30

NEHAL

NEHAL WOKE NEARLY AS EXHAUSTED AS SHE HAD BEEN the night before, only now her back was stiff from having slept on the floor. She shifted under a robe that hadn't been there last night. Blinking blearily, she sat up in confusion, until her world adjusted, and her eyes found Malak.

Malak leaned cross-legged against the opposite wall. Her eyes were closed, her head resting against the wall, her dark hair pulled into a loose braid across one shoulder. For a long moment, Nehal just looked at her quietly. Then she stood and closed the gap between them.

Malak opened her eyes at the sound, her eyes following Nehal as she sat down across from her and threw the robe atop them both. Malak smiled her slow, small smile, the one that showed a mixture of amusement and resignation.

"Did you land yourself in jail *just* to see me?" Malak teased.

Nehal half-laughed, half-scoffed. "You tell yourself that." Then she sobered. Up close, Malak did not look well: she was pale, dark circles painted under her eyes, her hair absent its usual sheen. A bone-deep exhaustion seemed to cling to her movements. "You look ill," Nehal said bluntly.

Malak shifted, shrugging one shoulder. "Jail isn't the most hospitable environment," she said wearily. "But Nehal, what happened? Why are you here?"

Nehal heaved a heavy sigh, then began to explain. Malak listened carefully, her focused expression unchanging until Nehal told her about the Zirani ambassador.

"He's funding the Khopeshes?" Malak frowned. "That's . . . astonishing. Oh, how I wish we had proof of that. It would completely undermine Zirana's position in negotiations." For a moment she drifted, her gaze becoming unfocused. "I doubt any of it would be in writing, if he was laundering the funds through Attia Marwan . . . that's probably why he was working with him in the first place . . . sorry, continue. How did this lead to your arrest?"

"Attia Marwan," said Nehal. "We had an . . . altercation. I made him come back and confess everything."

Malak raised an eyebrow. "And just how did you manage that?"

Nehal hesitated, Shaaban's warning echoing in her mind. But this was Malak, so Nehal leaned forward, unable to contain her excitement. "Malak, I did something I've never done before. I'm not quite sure I understand it, but I— His blood called out to me, and I reached for it. I controlled him from the inside out."

Rather than looking pleasantly surprised, as Nehal might have expected, Malak only looked dismayed, her lips parting in surprise.

Nehal frowned. "There's something I don't know, isn't there? Uncle Shaaban was frightened too, when he saw."

Malak nodded tightly. "That's because bloodweaving has a rather . . . unpleasant history. Edua Badawi was a bloodweaver. They say at the height of her power she could control an entire military regiment. You can imagine what this sort of ability can do."

Nehal's eyes grew wide. "A regiment? I can hardly imagine controlling more than one person."

"And you *shouldn't*." Malak squeezed Nehal's hands firmly within her own. "If people knew you could do this, it would put you in danger."

"That's what Uncle Shaaban said. But I don't see how it's different from any other kind of weaving," insisted Nehal stubbornly. "How is what I did worse than burning someone with fireweaving? Or an earthweaver burying someone alive?"

"People aren't always so logical about these things," said Malak carefully. "And also . . . surely you see how bloodweaving can be used to assault women without leaving a mark?"

Nehal blushed and reared back; this thought had not crossed her mind.

"But I would never—that's not—"

"Of course not." Malak tucked one of Nehal's curls behind her ear, smoothing it down gently. "But these are the connotations it comes with."

Nehal looked away. She felt a sense of creeping shame that she very much had no desire to feel, and she didn't want to argue with Malak. "Well, in any case, it didn't work. Even after Attia confessed, Shaaban wasn't convinced."

Malak sighed. "No, I doubt he was. So you're charged with assaulting a policeman? Nehal, that's a serious charge."

Nehal shrugged. "Nico and my parents will get me out."

"They'll bail you out easily enough, but . . ."

"I'll be fine."

Malak shook her head somewhat ruefully. "I hope so. How did it go with Bahira?"

At the mention of Bahira's name, Nehal scowled, her skin already prickling with irritation at the reminder of Bahira's attitude. "She was useless. It was like she was being deliberately unhelpful. Her strategy was to do nothing."

"Bahira likes to be cautious. Overly cautious, sometimes." Malak ran a hand through her hair. "What about our next issue of *The Vanguard*?"

"Well, apparently it's been banned from circulation," admitted Nehal grudgingly. "And Bahira can't find a printing press to work with her."

"Banned from circulation." Malak shook her head. "Parliament's overreaching. But I can't do anything about any of it from in here." Frustration leaked into Malak's normally placid tone.

"Do you know how long until your trial?"

"Ah, that." Malak smiled wryly. "They want it over and done with as quickly as possible—before the new constitution is signed. I was told it'll be held next week."

Nehal was confused by Malak's tone. "But that's—that's good, isn't it? Instead of waiting for months?"

Malak shrugged. "It gives me no time to appeal to a lawyer or build a defense. In all likelihood it'll be a sham trial designed to toss me in prison for years."

Nehal blinked, stunned. "But that's—no, that won't happen. It can't."

"I'm afraid it's exactly what's going to happen. It's just the opportunity they've been waiting for. Not only will Parliament get rid of me, but they'll demonize everything I stand for. Now they'll feel no pressure to grant women the vote—or anything else we've asked for."

Approaching footsteps put a halt to their conversation. A skinny police officer, who couldn't have been older than seventeen, came up to their cell, a ring of keys in his hand.

"Back up!" he barked loudly.

Malak raised a single eyebrow and didn't move. She stared the teenager down until his ears turned red. He looked away from Malak and nodded instead at Nehal.

"Stand up," he ordered. "You're going to come with me."

Narrowing her eyes at his tone, Nehal stood.

"Commander Shaaban requests your presence upstairs," he said as he unlocked the cell doors.

Nehal exchanged a final glance with Malak before following the boy out and down the long, damp corridor, up the uneven stairs, and into Shaaban's office.

Nehal had but a moment to register her mother's presence before Shaheera swept her up into a tight but brief hug.

"Have you lost your mind?" Shaheera demanded the moment she let Nehal go. "What have you done?"

"Shaheera, give her a moment," said a weary voice. Nehal looked over her mother's shoulder to see her father leaning on Shaaban's desk. Nico sat in the chair beside him; he gave Nehal a small smile.

"Give her a moment?" said Shaheera. "She's in *jail*, Khalil. Jail. Our daughter is in jail."

Nehal looked straight at Shaaban, who was seated behind his desk. "Is Attia Marwan in jail?" she asked loudly.

Shaaban looked up warily. "He's been suspended, but—"

"But he's free to do what he likes, while Malak and I rot in a cell," Nehal sneered.

"Would you *stop* with that woman! You have far more pressing things to think about," Shaheera snapped. "I don't want you associating with her any longer."

That will be difficult when we share a cell, Nehal thought, but in a moment of uncharacteristic foresight, she kept the thought to herself. She bit her lip to force herself to remain silent, which was not difficult when Shaheera appeared unable to stop talking.

"When will you release my daughter from this hole?" demanded Shaheera as she whirled to face Shaaban.

"I can't just release her," replied Shaaban somewhat tersely. "Half of my officers watched her assault one of their coworkers—"

"Nehal is not some criminal you picked up off the street," said Shaheera icily. "She is a lady of the House Darweesh *and* the House Baldinotti and she deserves treatment worthy of her stature."

Shaaban sighed and dug his fingers into his eyelids. "It's not quite that simple, though, is it, Shaheera? I can't brazenly release her when she's committed a crime. Things don't work like that anymore."

"Like what?" said Shaheera acidly. "Like the name Darweesh means something to this country? Are you telling me a bribe to the right judge wouldn't—"

"Don't use that word around me!" Shaaban said indignantly. "Don't tell me you plan to do something illegal and pretend I can unhear it. I can't sidestep the law for a family name, no matter how much I want to."

"Can't or won't, Shaaban?" Shaheera retorted.

Shaaban placed a palm across his chest. "Shaheera, Nehal is like a daughter to me—"

"You wouldn't have thrown her in here if she were," snarled Shaheera.

"I'm left with no choice!" Shaaban stood, pacing to one corner of the room and back. "She was *seen*, Shaheera, and"—his voice dropped to a whisper—"she was seen *bloodweaving*! Do you want *that* to be the talk of the city? Because if I release her, it will be."

Shaheera's lips thinned. Nehal knew her mother's expressions well. Shaheera was preparing to admit defeat.

"I promise you I will do everything in my power to fix this," said Shaaban. "But Nehal hasn't made this easy."

"Oh, I'm sorry," Nehal snapped. "Did I inconvenience you by trying to bring a murderer to justice? You won't ignore the law for me, but you will for Attia?"

Shaheera slapped Nehal's bare shoulder. "Mind your tone!" Shaheera flared her nostrils and widened her eyes, another expression Nehal was all too familiar with. When she was a child, this disapproving expression would be enough to convince Nehal to cease whatever activity she was engaged in.

But Nehal was a child no longer.

"My *tone* is hardly the most pressing issue here," said Nehal, dancing out of her mother's reach. "Attia Marwan's a *murderer*. Do you really not see that? Do none of you care? He *killed* a woman. A woman who was good and kind and who was causing no harm. He hit her and then he shot her and watched her die. Does that really not matter to any of you?"

Shaheera sighed, and Khalil and Shaaban only looked away.

"*Fine*. He's also a traitor to this country. Do you care about that?"

This captured their attention once more.

"What are you on about now?" asked Shaheera sharply.

Nehal told them about the conversation she had overheard between Attia and the Zirani ambassador.

Shaheera was unusually silent. Khalil turned to Shaaban, who was shaking his head. "I don't believe that."

"You mean you don't believe *me*," said Nehal icily. "You really think I would make something like that up. You really think *so* little of me."

"I don't think you would make it up—"

"Either that," Nehal interrupted loudly, "or you think I misunderstood, which means you think I'm either a brazen liar or an idiot, and frankly I don't know which is worse."

"Nehal, habibti, *please*," said Shaaban. "Please believe I'm doing what is best for you and for the city."

"You're doing what's best for your rogue police force," said Nehal coldly. "And for the men of this city who can't stand the *idea* of a woman having a voice. Well, I *do* have a voice. And the moment I can, I'm going to tell the entire city what Attia Marwan's done."

Shaheera threw her arms in the air. "This is madness. All of this. And you!" She whirled on Nico, who looked alarmed. "You've not said a word. You have nothing to say to your wife?"

Nico hesitated; for a moment Nehal thought he might simply bow his head to Shaheera, but then, in an unusually firm voice, he said, "I support my wife's decisions."

Nehal smiled at him, but then Shaheera said, "Is that right? And is your support genuine or are you simply glad Nehal is gone so you might enjoy your trysts with that girl Giorgina?"

Nico paled; his lips moved wordlessly, looking very much like a cornered animal. But Shaheera would not be stopped.

"Do you think me a fool?" she snapped. "Do you think I haven't noticed the way you two are together? How *dare* you—"

"Do you think *I'm* a fool?" interrupted Nehal. "That I would let my husband just cavort around without my knowledge? I *told* him to, Mama. I changed my wedding contract so Nico could have a concubine."

Shaheera just stared at her, her mouth flopping open and closing several times in an attempt to speak. "Help me understand if I am in fact going mad," she said very slowly. "You *willingly* granted your husband the right to a concubine?"

Nehal shrugged. "In exchange he signed the papers for my entrance to the Weaving Academy. And paid the tuition." She did not mention her recent expulsion, which was still too raw to talk about, and not particularly relevant to the current conversation.

"You—" Shaheera looked from Nico to Nehal in disbelief, then took a step back, leaning on Shaaban's desk for support. "That *is* madness. You've gone mad. Both of you." Shaheera turned to her husband. "Khalil. Say something to your daughter. Talk some sense into her."

Nehal turned on her father, who shrugged helplessly. "I suppose if Nehal is happy with the arrangement—"

"Oh, never mind!" snapped Shaheera. "One disaster at a time, I suppose." She turned back to Shaaban. "Where are those damn bail papers?"

"Hang on," said Nehal. "I want to talk to my husband. Alone."

Shaheera narrowed her eyes. "Oh, now he's your beloved husband, is he?"

"He's my husband, and that's all you need to know. It's my legal right to speak to my legal husband in private," Nehal shot back.

"Let's just give them a moment," said Shaaban in resignation. "The bail papers aren't here, anyway. I'll take you. Come on."

The moment they were gone, Nehal sat across from Nico, close enough that their knees were touching.

Before Nehal could speak, Nico asked softly, "How are you faring?"

Almost reluctantly, she felt some of her anger ebb at this genuine concern for her. He may not have been her beloved, and their marriage might be a complete sham, but Nico was no longer simply a stranger. She felt a small rush of affection toward him, and for a moment, this overtook her anger.

"I'll be fine," said Nehal. "We have more pressing concerns than my well-being. You have to tell the papers about Attia and Naji. Expose them both. And then there's the senators who were there at the fire—Giorgina has their names. You have to speak to them, convince them to testify, to tell the truth—"

"Nehal," Nico interrupted loudly. "Just—slow down for a minute, will you? I need to—to process all this—"

"Well, hurry!"

Nico rubbed at his golden beard. "I'll—I'll go see the senators, all right? I will. But—you have no proof of Ouazzani's misdeeds. Nobody will print that; it would be libelous."

Nehal looked at him blankly. "It's the truth. I *heard* them."

"It doesn't matter if it's the truth, Nehal," said Nico. "What matters is that you've no *proof* it's the truth. You can't just say—"

"Of course I can just say! You can, too. Have you forgotten who we both are, Nico?" Nehal demanded. "You think our word doesn't carry power? If we both say it's the truth—if *you,* Lord Niccolo Baldinotti, say it's the truth, then it will *be* the truth."

"No one will print it," said Nico weakly.

"You're telling me you can't find a single publication willing to run with this? I see how many different subscriptions you get. It doesn't have to be the *Alamaxa Daily.* Surely someone will see this as an opportunity to sell some copies, if nothing else." Nehal shook her head. "You're just too much of a coward to go through with it."

Nico's head snapped up. His cheeks had gone pink, but he said nothing.

"No, you can't even deny it, because you know it's true," said Nehal.

"It's—it's not *smart,* Nehal!" sputtered Nico. "I'd be putting myself in the spotlight, making an enemy of the Zirani ambassador, angering Parliament, and for *what*?"

"For the truth!" said Nehal. "For justice!"

Nico scoffed, and Nehal felt her earlier affection for him melt away. "Truth and justice? This isn't a quaint little folktale where the heroes win because they're supposed to. If something like this is printed with our names attached to it, it'll ruin both our reputations, and then where will we be?"

"I'm already in jail," said Nehal acidly.

"Exactly! But you don't seem to care! You ought to be cautious, not throwing caution to the wind!"

"It's because *you* have nothing to lose," said Nehal. "This isn't your fight. You're not a woman, you're not a weaver, so you don't give a damn—"

"That's not fair," protested Nico. "Of course I care, but—"

"If you cared, you would *do* something, instead of just sitting on your hands on the sidelines! It's not enough to *say* you care, Nico!"

"There's nothing I *can* do!"

"Rack that big brain of yours and I'm sure you can figure something out! If you won't do it for silly notions like truth and justice, do it for me. Or, better yet, do it for Giorgina."

Nico looked like he'd been punched in the stomach. Before he could reply, the door to the office opened, revealing Shaheera, who looked from Nico to Nehal with disapproval. "I heard you two shouting—"

Nehal shot up. "It's nothing. Just my husband proving he's useless."

Shaheera stared at her. "What now?"

Shaaban and Khalil appeared behind Shaheera. "We just require your signature, Nico, as Nehal's husband—"

"Can I go back to my cell now?" said Nehal loudly. "The company's better."

Shaheera narrowed her eyes and looked ready to deliver a scathing retort, but Nehal turned away from her mother, her father, and her husband, and looked pointedly at Commander Shaaban, who shrugged and waved one of his officers in to take her back to Malak.

31

GIORGINA

FAROUK'S TEAHOUSE WAS A BALM OF FAMILIARITY. AT noon, it was quieter than it usually was, for which Giorgina was grateful. She chose a table tucked away in the far corner, where she waited patiently for Nico. She perused a menu she was already familiar with in an attempt to distract herself from last night's conversation with Etedal.

Unsurprisingly, Etedal had been furious to learn Attia Marwan had slipped through their fingers.

"I told you so," Etedal shouted. "I *told* you it's no use trusting the police. They take care of their own. I should just take a knife to his back—"

"Etedal, *no*," said Giorgina as firmly as she could. "Nehal is already in jail because she tried to take him on herself. What good will it do if you join her?"

"It'll make me feel better," Etedal said flatly.

When Giorgina left Etedal this morning, the other woman had still been fuming, pacing around the apartment and slamming things around. Giorgina, who was simply grateful Etedal was letting her stay in the apartment, had tried to be as unobtrusive and accommodating as possible. She had never been close with Etedal like she had been with Labiba, and she wasn't quite sure how to behave around her, especially when she was furious and grieving. In an attempt to be helpful, Giorgina had made them tea and breakfast that morning, but Etedal had spurned it all, choosing to go hungry, and Giorgina was unwilling to push her.

Giorgina had reached the final page of the menu when Nico finally arrived, looking weary. He seemed to collapse into the chair opposite Giorgina, and immediately motioned over the waiter and asked for a glass of sweet wine.

Giorgina gave him a worried look. "Nico, it's noon."

Nico unwrapped his turban and let it fall loose around his neck. "It's necessary."

"And for you, miss?" asked the waiter politely.

"Tea and kunafa, please."

The waiter departed with their order.

"How is Nehal?" Giorgina asked carefully.

Nico's expression darkened further. "Her usual self," he said shortly. "You'd think being in jail would subdue her a bit, but no."

"I'm glad she's keeping her spirits up," said Giorgina.

Nico heaved a heavy sigh. "Yes. I'm sorry. She—we fought."

That partly explained Nico's attitude and his desire for wine—he hated any kind of confrontation; it wreaked havoc on his nerves. Nehal was a formidable opponent in any situation, but Giorgina doubted being in jail had done anything to soothe her temper.

"What about?"

Nico glanced around them once to ensure the waiter was nowhere to be found, then lowered his voice. "When she followed that policeman, Attia Marwan, she caught him meeting with Naji Ouazzani. Apparently, he's been working with Attia to fund the Khopeshes of the Tetrad."

Giorgina sat back, stunned. "That's how the Khopeshes are getting their weapons."

"And he asked Attia Marwan to ensure the march went disastrously," said Nico. "He's trying to make sure negotiations go his way, that Parliament puts in anti-weaving restrictions in the new constitution. And after everything that's happened, I'm given to believe it'll work."

"Did he—did he tell Attia to kill Labiba?" Giorgina asked hoarsely.

Nico hesitated. "I—I don't know. Nehal wasn't clear. Her focus was on trying to get me to go to the *papers* with this insane story. Like anyone would believe me without proof!"

Giorgina felt a spark of irritation. "Nico," she said, "sometimes I think you're ignorant of your own powers."

Nico sat back in surprise. "What?"

Giorgina treaded carefully, keeping her tone mild. "It's just . . . you're Lord Niccolo Baldinotti. People care what you have to say."

His expression shuttered. "That's what Nehal said."

"That's why you fought, isn't it?"

"It's a ridiculous idea, Giorgina," Nico insisted. "Putting my name to what everyone will think is an unfounded, unsubstantiated rumor . . . and about the Zirani ambassador, no less!"

"Nico—"

"I told her I would talk to the senators," said Nico bitterly. "The ones whose names you're supposed to give me? Can't that be enough?"

Nico stared at her pleadingly, which only filled Giorgina with a mixture of pity and irritation. She struggled to put her feelings into words. She loved Nico; she loved his kindness and his sweet gestures and his indifference to hierarchy—but, if she were being truly honest, she resented him just a bit for his lack of initiative. He had *so much* power at his fingertips, but he refused to use it. Most of the time, Nico's resentment of his own privilege was one of his most endearing traits, but not now, not when it was his privilege that could make so much difference.

Giorgina sighed. "Nico . . ."

"Are you angry with me?" he asked miserably.

He looked so lost, almost like a little boy, and Giorgina wanted to comfort him. But Nico was not a little boy. He was a powerful, wealthy young man who had the world at his fingertips. Giorgina loved him too much to be cruel, but she had to make him see the reality of his circumstances.

"I'm not angry," said Giorgina gently. "Nico, I know you don't like confrontation, or politics, or being in the spotlight. But you're caught up in all this whether you want to be or not. Don't you see that?"

Nico was no longer looking at her; he seemed intently focused on his signet ring. "You think I'm a coward," he said flatly.

"No—"

"Nehal does," said Nico bitterly. "She told me so herself, loudly enough that I'm sure half the police station heard."

"Well then, you'll just have to prove her wrong, won't you?" Giorgina reached for Nico's hand. "I'm not saying you have to hold a rally in the midst of Tarar Square. But you have honorable convictions and ideals. Be true to them."

"The *Alamaxa Daily* won't print something like this, Giorgina," said Nico. "And I can't bully them into it. I *can't.*"

Giorgina thought fast. "All right. I can see your point. But there's still something you can do." Giorgina leaned forward. "*The Vanguard* has been banned from circulation, and no one will speak to us, no one wants to hear our side of the story about what really happened at Parliament. But they'll listen to *you.*"

Nico looked at her questioningly. "So you want me to . . ."

"Give an interview to the *Alamaxa Daily,*" said Giorgina.

"I told you, they won't print—"

"They will, if you go about it properly. Go to your contact there. Tell them what really happened, what Attia Marwan did. Throw your support behind us, behind Malak and Nehal. And then allude to Attia's patron without mentioning Ouazzani's name." Giorgina did things like this all the time when she wrote her own articles, alluded to things without saying them outright, allowing her readers to come to their own conclusions.

"That'll be tricky," said Nico.

"I'll coach you," replied Giorgina. This, she could do easily, and through Nico it would be her words that the public would read.

GIORGINA RETURNED TO Etedal's feeling somewhat lighthearted. She had walked Nico through what to say, and thankfully, he had an exceptional memory, so she was confident he would deliver exacting statements with aplomb. After, when she told him of her dismissal from the bookshop, he had wordlessly slipped her a wad of money. He didn't even count it, like it didn't matter. She had hesitated, at first, pride warring with gratitude, but Giorgina was not the sort to let ego interfere with practicality.

When she saw Sabah sitting stiffly on the stoop of Etedal's doorstep, Giorgina nearly stumbled.

"Sabah." Giorgina gripped the handrailing as she stared at her sister. "What are you—how—"

Sabah stood up slowly, gingerly stretching out her bad leg and grimacing. "I followed you here once or twice."

"You—you followed me?"

Sabah shrugged. "You're my little sister. Who else is going to follow you to make sure you're okay?" She motioned impatiently to the door. "Well? Are you going to let me in?"

Giorgina fumbled with the key Etedal had given her—Labiba's key—and let Sabah inside. She hovered awkwardly as her sister limped into the shabby room, which was not too unlike their own home, only dimmer. Sabah lowered herself onto one of the three poufs in the room and gestured for Giorgina to do the same.

"How are you?" asked Sabah once Giorgina had settled stiffly across from her.

"I'm well," said Giorgina. "Did . . . did Mama send you?"

"Nobody knows I'm here."

"How . . . how is Baba?"

Sabah's pause was so lengthy Giorgina thought her sister would say nothing at all. "He's . . . sad."

This Giorgina had not expected to hear. She had anticipated fury from her father, but grief?

Then Sabah continued, "He was so calm when he told Mama you were dead to us. That he has only two daughters, not three."

Now that sounded more like Ehab Shukry. Giorgina wanted to slap herself for having thought otherwise.

"Was it worth it?" asked Sabah.

"Yes," said Giorgina simply.

"This Niccolo of yours must be amazing," said Sabah. "If you've ruined your life—and mine and Nagwa's—for him."

Giorgina pursed her lips. "You know about Nico."

Sabah sighed. "Yes, Giorgina, I know. Like I said, I keep an eye out for my little sister."

"And you never said a word?"

"I hoped you would tell me on your own, in time, but . . ." Sabah gestured to the room around her. "I suppose you found other friends to tell."

"You're angry with me."

"Shouldn't I be?"

Giorgina did not know how to respond to that, so she pivoted. "This isn't just about Nico."

"No?"

"No," said Giorgina firmly. "It's about me. I can finally do a little of what makes me happy without having to worry about hiding from everyone around me. Do you know what that sort of freedom is like?"

"No, I don't," said Sabah. "But then, we don't all have rich lovers to support us when we throw everything away."

Giorgina reared back, stunned at the bitterness lacing her sister's words. "Sabah—"

"Sorry. That was petty." Sabah ran a hand roughly through her dark hair. "But Baba's been insufferable lately. His temper . . .

money's going to be tight without your salary . . . and you should see the way the neighbors look at us now. Basna's husband won't even let her speak to me."

Unshed tears blurred Giorgina's vision. "I'm . . . I'm sorry," she whispered. "I know it was stupid, it was rash . . . I know I could have just left without saying what I said, but I was . . . I wasn't in my right mind. I made a mistake, Sabah."

"And now all of us are paying for it," said Sabah wearily.

"I—I'll fix it," said Giorgina earnestly. "I'll make things better."

"Oh? Is he going to divorce his wife and marry you, then?" asked Sabah. "Because that's the only thing that will even come close to fixing this, Giorgina."

Giorgina swallowed the burgeoning lump in her throat. "We haven't—so much has happened, we haven't had a chance to—to talk about everything—"

Sabah sighed. "Right. I just hope you haven't put your trust in the wrong man. Again."

Giorgina went cold. "What?"

Sabah's look was pointed, but there was pity in her eyes too. "That teacher who got you pregnant."

Giorgina stilled. She had guessed after their last few conversations that Sabah knew about this, but it was still a shock to have it spoken of so bluntly. "How long have you known, then? How long have you been—been spying on me and keeping it all to yourself— you said nothing, and I was *desperate*—"

"I told you I like to keep an eye on you—"

"What good is that if you don't *do* anything about it?" asked Giorgina. "Or do you just like to gloat over my mistakes?"

"You clearly didn't want to share your secrets with me!" Sabah retorted. "I didn't want to force them out of you. But for your information, when I found out about your condition, I started looking for midwives who could help. I had to ask the other girls at the factory, who all started looking at me like I was dirt on their shoe, and in the end you took care of it all by yourself. Just like you always do," added Sabah bitterly. "Why would I talk to you when you clearly had no desire to talk to *me*?"

Giorgina had nothing to say to that. She let out a hard breath, and a silence fell between the sisters.

"I should go," said Sabah finally. "I just wanted to make sure you weren't sleeping on the streets. I'll tell Mama and Nagwa you're all right." Slowly, Sabah got to her feet, and Giorgina had to stop herself from instinctively helping her up. Sabah limped to the door, opened it, then paused, turning very slightly. "You know where to find us, Giorgina."

SEEMINGLY OVERNIGHT, NICO got his interview.

His acquaintance at the *Alamaxa Daily* had given him over to an up-and-coming young journalist named Mohsin Hafiz, widely praised for his journalistic objectivity and integrity. The words Nico fed him were an echo of what Giorgina had coached him to say, and when she saw his account in print—extolling the virtues of the Daughters of Izdihar, accusing Attia Marwan of escalating the march—she felt a swell of pride, both for her and Nico. She missed writing for *The Vanguard,* and for now, this was the closest she could get to that.

Gossip always spread like wildfire in Alamaxa, but with Malak's trial only days away, the interview circulated even faster. Within hours, it seemed to be on everyone's lips. Bahira, who had come to visit Etedal, told Giorgina that it was all anyone in the brothel could talk about, a respectable young lord like Nico Baldinotti throwing his support behind the Daughters of Izdihar, standing by their account of the Parliament fire.

Nico's words carried weight, as Giorgina knew they would. Murmurs of doubt now rippled throughout the city, carried on notes of sympathy for the Daughters of Izdihar and their fallen soldier. It was jolting, to see and hear Labiba's name spoken by strangers, but at least it meant she would not be forgotten.

Furthermore, while Malak was a controversial figure, Nehal was more unknown, and easier to sympathize with: a young, innocent upper-class lady with a cause she was willing to go to jail for. It spoke to her determination and reflected kindly on the importance of the Daughters' mission.

But it wasn't enough, Giorgina knew, and she needed to do something to *make* it enough. She had given her entire life away in pursuit of this—her reputation, her family, any semblance of stability she could rest on—and now she could not simply sit still and wait for something to happen, especially not when her own future rested on one of the demands the Daughters had asked of Parliament: the right for women to represent themselves in contractual agreements.

If Nehal could sign her own papers to attend the Alamaxa Weaving Academy, she would no longer require Nico as a legal husband. She would be amenable to divorcing, and then, at least, Giorgina and Nico would have a path to walk, even if that path would be fraught with threats from his father to jail Giorgina for her past. They could deal with that obstacle together, when it met them.

But what could Giorgina *do* to make her goals a reality? Her lack of ideas frustrated her as much as the lack of cooperation around her. She had tried, and failed, to get Bahira to bring together the Daughters for a rally. Bahira was the only one aside from Malak who knew how to contact all their members; Giorgina was at her mercy, and Bahira continued to insist that it was too dangerous to act.

So at night, shivering beside Etedal in their damp apartment, Giorgina thought, and thought, and thought, and struggled to sleep, until, before she knew it, the day of Malak's trial was upon them.

32

GIORGINA

THE ALAMAXA SUPREME COURT WAS HOUSED IN AN OLD, crumbling building desperately in need of repair. It was squat and round, the roof of the entrance held up by four columns carved in the likenesses of the Tetrad. Inside, it seemed almost like an arena: circles of ascending benches surrounded what looked like a giant, sunken pit. At one end, three judges sat on a high dais, looking down on Malak, who was made to stand below them, her hands shackled, two policemen on either side of her. Rectangular windows filtered in strong sunlight, casting shadows across the occupants.

The building was surely not meant to hold as many people as it currently did, but Alamaxans had come far and wide to witness Malak's trial. Giorgina, Etedal, and Nico struggled to make their way through the crowd, but were finally able to find room to stand and watch. Giorgina spotted many members of the Daughters of Izdihar, including Bahira, dotted throughout the crowd.

Once they had settled in, Giorgina finally noticed the bench directly below the judges, where their witnesses sat. As she had expected, the three senators who had been at Parliament the day of the march were there. To her surprise, one of them was seated apart, on the judges' left side, indicating that he would be testifying in Malak's defense rather than against her. He looked nervous and couldn't stop fidgeting.

"That's Kamal Zaghloul," said Nico wonderingly. "He wasn't very keen on helping when I spoke to him. I didn't think he would change his mind."

According to Nico, none of the three senators he'd visited had been willing to testify on Malak's behalf, but it seemed Kamal Zaghloul's conscience had caught up with him, even if he didn't seem especially happy about it. She wondered if Nico's interview—and the subsequent outcry—had helped sway him.

If *Giorgina's* words, in Nico's mouth, had swayed him.

But any nascent pride at that thought was mitigated by the sight of another unexpected surprise: Naji Ouazzani.

Giorgina's chest thudded in alarm. What was *he* doing here? He had been nowhere near Parliament that day, and as far as Giorgina knew, Malak had no dealings with him. What could he possibly have to say? Had he concocted another scheme with Attia Marwan?

One of the judges, a wiry man with a mustache too large for his face, banged his gavel and held up one hand, signaling silence. Once the audience fell into a hush, he began, "May the Tetrad grant us their blessings on these proceedings. We are here today to determine a course of justice against one Malak Mamdouh, who stands accused of inciting a riot, destruction of government property, intent to cause grievous bodily harm, domestic terrorism, and two counts of negligent homicide."

Giorgina gasped, as did several others in the gallery. *Two* counts of negligent homicide? One was for the policeman who had died in the fire, but the other . . . they were charging *Malak* with Labiba's death.

Beside Giorgina, Etedal had gone stiff, her hands clasped so tight around the railing her knuckles had gone white. Her jaw was clenched so painfully Giorgina winced in sympathy.

All those charges . . . was it at all possible for Malak to work her way out of them? Was this trial anything more than a formality leading to Malak's life imprisonment?

The trial began with witness statements; first, the two senators on the judges' right gave their account of the events of the march. Giorgina was not surprised to find their testimony very carefully neutral: they described the Daughters' entrance into Parliament, led by Malak, and the chaos that followed, but they carefully avoided details as to who instigated what. When directly questioned by the judges about the shattered glass dome, the fire, and the deaths of Labiba and the policeman, they claimed they had not seen or could not recall.

Then it was time for Kamal Zaghloul to speak.

When he stood, Giorgina could see him more clearly. He was utterly, perfectly ordinary, the picture of a quintessential Ramsawi man: of average height and build, his features plain, stiff curls poking out from beneath his turban. Even his clothing was drab, simple, unadorned, and dark gray. She could not even determine his age. He might have been only a few years older than she was, but he might also have been as old as her father.

Giorgina should have been heartened that a senator was testifying on Malak's behalf. Unfortunately, Kamal Zaghloul looked like he would rather be digging his own grave than testifying. He was sweating profusely, so much so that dark stains soaked through his galabiya, and he was fidgeting nonstop. As he stood in front of the judges, his fingers tugged again and again on his sleeves, then went to adjust his turban. He cleared his throat twice, then smoothed down his girdle. Giorgina bit her lip. The man couldn't look more suspicious if he tried. It was unsurprising that he was an unelected member of Parliament; he came from the House of Zaghloul, though Giorgina could not comprehend why they had chosen him of all people to represent them.

Despite his pedigree, the judges peered down at him with barely concealed disdain.

"Is your name Kamal Zaghloul?"

Kamal cleared his throat again. "I—I am. I mean, yes, that is my name."

Etedal rolled her eyes. "Malak's fucked."

But Kamal's testimony was surprisingly coherent: the senator had clearly practiced what to say, and once he started speaking, he relaxed some.

"So, you claim it was one of Commander Shaaban's officers who shot at the glass dome, shattering it?"

Kamal swallowed. "Yes."

"Can you point this man out today?"

Kamal raised a slightly shaking finger and pointed; Giorgina drew a sharp breath. Couched in shadows on one of the lower benches, arms crossed tightly and forehead set into a scowl, was Attia Marwan. His expression was unchanging as Kamal pointed to him.

"I see." The judge scribbled something down, then looked up again. "What of Labiba Wagdy, the fireweaver who died?"

Gently, Giorgina clasped Etedal's hand. Etedal did not move.

"I—I did notice her, yes." Kamal tugged at his collar. "It was—it was chaotic, but I—I think what I saw—"

"You think or you know?" interrupted another judge.

Kamal cleared his throat. "I—what I *saw* was this woman— Labiba, she was—well, that is to say, the very same policeman I just pointed out—" He nodded to Attia Marwan. "He attacked the young lady with his musket. Twice, in fact. It—it was savagely done, quite, quite savage. And then all I could see were the flames, and I— that's when I started running."

The judges scribbled while Kamal Zaghloul stood fidgeting, waiting for direction or dismissal. Finally, one of the judges looked up and said, "Thank you for your testimony, Lord Kamal. You may be seated."

Kamal's sigh of relief was audible throughout the gallery. Giorgina's hand on Etedal's felt clammy. This testimony was good: Malak might still be indicted on minor charges, but if it could be established that it was Attia Marwan who had incited the violence and chaos, the charges of homicide could be dropped.

But would Kamal's testimony alone be enough? None of the Daughters of Izdihar had been called as witnesses, having been deemed too prejudiced, and the trial had been put through so quickly that Malak had had no time to prepare a defense strategy or gather any other witnesses who might speak for her. The deck was purposely stacked against her.

Giorgina had been glancing intermittently at Malak throughout the witness testimonies; Malak's expression was familiarly placid and unchanging, as though she were only mildly interested in the proceedings, or like she had better places to be. Giorgina admired her restraint, but she also wondered if it was a hindrance; perhaps it might be better to show some emotion, for sympathy?

"And now," said the judge, "we have a statement from Mister Naji Ouazzani, the Kingdom of Zirana's ambassador to the Ramsawi Republic. Please proceed, sir."

Naji stood languidly, his deep-set dark eyes trailing across the judges. He was impeccably dressed in richly embroidered moss-green robes, with a matching turban and girdle. His gold-slippered feet made no sound as he glided across the floor to stand in front of the judges. He gave a respectful incline of his head.

Giorgina tensed. It was still unclear on what grounds he was speaking here.

She knew, though, that his words were not likely to be in Malak's favor.

Naji turned slightly, so that he faced the gallery, while still angling himself toward the magistrates. "Thank you, judges." Giorgina had never heard the man speak before; his accent had a strong Zirani lilt. "And I would like to thank my colleagues at Parliament, for granting me this opportunity to speak. This is a matter that concerns both our countries, and as such, I felt it necessary to address you all today.

"It is no secret that the Kingdom of Zirana and the Ramsawi

Republic have been on the precipice of war for some time." Naji ignored the frowns and tense glances that attended his words. "That is why I am here: to divert this threat, and to bring peace between our two nations." He paused. "I do not wish to dwell on unpleasant history. But it is important to acknowledge that the strife between our nations lies at the feet of Edua Badawi, the most destructive weaver in known history—and a woman."

The ambassador continued, "All weavers are, of course, destructive; such divine abilities are not meant to be housed in human vessels. But women in particular are predisposed to far more . . . expansive emotions. They are more fragile. They are more volatile. The proof is before us." He spread his hands, motioning to the proceedings, and inclined his sharp chin at Malak, whose expression had gone from placid to stony. "Parliament was destroyed due to the volatility of female weavers, just as Talyana and Zirana suffered destruction at the hands of Edua Badawi. You, the citizens of Ramsawa, deserve better than destruction at the hands of weavers. I leave it to you to judge whether such volatile elements deserve to wander freely among you."

Etedal jerked forward, but Giorgina yanked her back and shook her head silently. She squeezed Etedal's hand until the other woman stood still, though her nostrils were flared.

Naji turned back to the judges with another polite incline of his head. "Judges. Respectfully, I hope you will find it within your wisdom to set an example today, a hard line. Malak Mamdouh is a woman who believes her weaving makes her invincible, beyond the values that govern polite society. She endangers our values, our traditions, and our peace. In my humble opinion, her imprisonment can only serve to strengthen us, and keep both our nations safe."

Giorgina swallowed, though her throat was dry. Naji Ouazzani had somehow managed to incontrovertibly link the Daughters of Izdihar with the dangers of weaving, and he had done it through Malak, while simultaneously linking her imprisonment with the political futures of Zirana and Ramsawa. And he had done it in a shifting, circuitous manner that left little room to poke at his arguments, because they were as nebulous as a desert mirage.

The judges declared a recess, presumably to deliberate and return with a decision.

"That's it?" said Etedal blankly. "That's the whole trial?"

Giorgina barely heard her; she was focused on Naji, who was slipping out through one of the corridors between the benches.

"Giorgina?" Nico pressed, trying to follow her gaze.

"I'll be right back." She stood abruptly and waded her way through the crowd, until she found her way to the corridor Naji had disappeared into. She was not altogether certain what she wanted to say to him, but she wanted to say *something*. According to Nehal, it was this man's actions that had led to Labiba's death, whether that had been his intention or not.

He was alone when Giorgina found him, striding purposefully. Giorgina hurried after him and called out, "Mister Naji?"

He stopped mid-stride and turned, looking at Giorgina with utter disinterest. "Do I know you?"

"No, I—" Giorgina paused, momentarily at a loss for words. Why had she followed him? What could she say to him that would make any sort of difference? "I know you're funding the Khopeshes," said Giorgina.

For a moment Naji Ouazzani simply stared at Giorgina, and she stared back, hardly daring to believe the words that had come out of her mouth. Then he threw his head back and laughed: a short, cynical huff of breath that was over quickly, and then his face comported itself into a sharp scowl.

"Are you one of them, then?" he drawled.

Giorgina did not know what he meant; was he asking if she was a Daughter of Izdihar or if she was a weaver? Not that it mattered; she was both. But Naji Ouazzani did not need to know any of that.

"It doesn't matter who I am," said Giorgina slowly. "But surely— surely you see the danger in helping a group like the Khopeshes?"

Naji sneered. "I'm not going to waste my time discussing this with a random woman I don't know." He started to turn away, but Giorgina ran after him and blocked his way. Her heart was thudding so fast she was certain Naji could hear it, and there was a strange ringing between her ears.

"What about Attia Marwan?" Giorgina cried. "He murdered an innocent woman. I know you know about that. Her name was Labiba. Do you care at all?"

"Get out of my way," said Naji evenly.

"You're helping to send Malak to prison for something she isn't responsible for," said Giorgina in a trembling voice. "You *told* Attia Marwan to cause chaos at the march. This is your responsibility as much as it is his; if you had any sense of honor you would admit that, instead of allowing Malak to shoulder it all on her own."

Naji was shaking his head, his scowl deepening. "Get out of my way, girl."

"You should confess," said Giorgina. "Confess before someone else exposes you."

The ambassador's eyes widened slightly, and for a moment Giorgina thought she saw a hint of alarm in them, but then he laughed, and cruelly. "Expose me? You think anyone would believe *you*? Take your word over mine? Who do you think you are? Now *get out of my way*."

Naji Ouazzani struck out and shoved Giorgina aside, sending her sprawling into the wall.

At that moment, the ringing in Giorgina's ears grew cacophonous. Red and black spots danced in her vision. She felt entirely off-kilter. She had endured so much these last few days—this entire past year. She had been shoved and bruised and sexually harassed and humiliated. She had lost her very best friend in the world. And now, this man thought he could abuse her with impunity, because she was nothing and no one.

Her hand lay flat against the wall, to support her, keep her standing when her legs were trembling, but her fingers found purchase within the bricks, her fingertips sinking into the wall. She stared in wonder at her half-buried hand. Vibrations passed from her fingers into the wall.

As Giorgina watched Naji Ouazzani carelessly walk away without a second glance, a strange feeling engulfed her. It took her a moment to recognize that it was uncontrollable fury, an emotion she was mostly unfamiliar with, an emotion she had grown accustomed to clamping down and ignoring. But now it inundated her like a flood, like a furious sandstorm, filling up every inch of her limbs, skittering under her skin, and it found its focus in the Zirani ambassador.

When the ground started trembling, Naji stopped and turned back. His arrogant sneer had been replaced by a befuddled frown that quickly turned to alarm. His glance at Giorgina's fingers, now half-buried in the wall, was enough to have him stumbling backward and running.

He wasn't fast enough.

Giorgina was not thinking straight. Giorgina was not thinking at all. She was simply feeling, and all she knew was that she wanted this man—this powerful, callous man—to feel some of her pain, her rage, and her fear.

So she unleashed it all.

The ground shook so hard Naji stumbled and fell to his knees. The wall at Giorgina's side crumbled into chunks, each nearly the size of a mule cart, and overtook the ambassador, barreling into him without mercy and sending him reeling to the opposite wall. He crashed into it with a resounding thud, and then that wall began to tremble too, cracks climbing upward like fleeing spiders. If Naji cried out, she didn't hear it amid the cacophony of falling stones and the roaring in her head.

The roaring grew, and grew, like a solid pressure pushing back against Giorgina's brain, until it coalesced into a chorus that made her shudder.

Giorgina fell to her knees, the sudden exhaustion coursing through her overpowering. She blinked several times, staring at the pile of rubble sitting atop the Zirani ambassador. She could only see his feet.

"No," Giorgina whispered.

And yet . . . her regret and panic could not quite eclipse the shameful feeling of triumph rushing through her.

She struggled to her feet and ran to the ambassador, struggling to stay upright. She stumbled into the rubble and started trying to dig him out, but the bricks were too heavy, and she succeeded only in slicing open her fingers. Her blood dripped onto the pile—Naji Ouazzani's cairn. Giorgina stared at it blankly. Then screams drew her attention away.

Dazed, Giorgina stumbled away from the buried ambassador and desperately sought her way back to the courthouse arena. She emerged from the corridor just in time to watch the cracks she had caused reach up into the courthouse's high ceiling. Dust and rubble dribbled into the arena, and for a moment, everything seemed suspended in time.

Then the ceiling broke open.

It was Malak who reacted first. In seconds both her hands were raised to the sky. Gusts of wind flew out of her palms, slowing the fall of the rubble from the ceiling, but not stopping it entirely.

Then someone else stepped forward: a stout Ramsawi woman ran into the arena, took on a wide stance, and raised her arms. She moved so quickly Giorgina could hardly keep track, but she quickly identified the older woman as an earthweaver who had taken control of the falling debris. She grasped what Malak was struggling to hold on to, and moments later, she was gently laying down chunks of brick and mortar on the floor of the courthouse arena.

The screaming hadn't quite stopped, only now it was interspersed with panicked shouts and sobbing and cries of pain. Giorgina glimpsed a wailing girl whose leg had been crushed by debris, and an older man on the upper benches who had been trampled.

I did this. Bile rose in Giorgina's throat; she turned and retched, but nothing came out, only her own ragged breathing.

Nico and Etedal. She tried to look for them where she had left them, but the chamber was chaos. Though the courthouse had stopped shaking, and the stout earthweaver was working to stabilize it further, the crowd was rushing to leave, pushing and shoving at one another, and Giorgina could not find Nico or Etedal anywhere.

Her breathing was so shallow her stomach was beginning to hurt; Giorgina felt as though snakes were crawling through her belly. She walked out into the arena, snaking around the fallen debris, and did her best to stay clear of the stampede; she only followed the wave of panicked people rushing toward the exit.

Outside, the sun glinted harshly in Giorgina's eyes, causing her to squint. She swayed unsteadily as she held up a hand to shield her gaze from the sun's glare. For a long moment she felt completely re-moved from her surroundings, as though she had escaped her body and was watching herself from above. Though disorienting, it was comforting as well, and Giorgina wanted to linger in this liminal space, free from panic and fear and guilt.

"Giorgina!"

That panicked cry brought Giorgina hurtling back into her body. Suddenly Nico was in front of her, blue eyes wide and pan-icked behind his spectacles, which were covered in dust. Etedal hov-ered behind him, peering at Giorgina.

"Where did you go? Are you all right?" Nico rested his hands gently on her shoulders to keep her steady.

Giorgina blinked once at him, then again, struggling to keep him in her vision as he began to blur and fade—and then Giorgina felt her knees buckle, and everything went dark.

33

NEHAL

NEHAL PACED HER CELL RESTLESSLY. SHE HAD NO IDEA how long Malak's trial was meant to last, but morning had already trickled into afternoon. An hour ago, a skinny guard had brought Nehal lunch, simple fare consisting of unseasoned fava beans, stale bread, and tea that resembled dirty dishwater more than a proper strong drink, but Nehal was so hungry she devoured it all. More than anything she wanted a bath; she had not changed her clothes in days. They were sticky with sweat and mud, and she was beginning to itch.

With an angry sigh, Nehal threw herself to the floor and looked up at the ceiling. Without Malak it was so desperately *boring* in here; she almost wished Uncle Shaaban would put her in a cell with some of the other prisoners, loud and uncouth though they were, just so she would have someone to talk to. She could hear the echoes of their laughter and shouting, but could not quite make out what they were saying.

Then she heard footsteps, growing louder by the moment, and the clinking of chains. As quickly as she had sat down Nehal jumped to her feet, and soon Malak came into view.

Nehal startled at the sight of her. It was not because Malak's wrists and ankles were chained; that was how the police had led her out of the cell this morning. It was not even because of the way the policemen on either side of her were gripping her so roughly, practically dragging her forward. It was the bedraggled look of her, her face covered in dust, her hair disheveled, a streak of blood on her cheek.

The police unchained her and unceremoniously pushed her into the cell. Nehal hurried to steady her, shooting a glare at the policemen, but they ignored her entirely, and departed without a single word.

"What happened?" Nehal helped Malak sit down.

"Nothing good." Malak sighed heavily. "It was a disaster from start to finish."

"But—what was the verdict?" pressed Nehal. "And why are you covered in—dust?"

Malak leaned her head back against the wall and closed her eyes, sighing again. "There was no verdict," she said without opening her eyes. "The courthouse collapsed while the judges were deliberating. Though I can't say it looked promising for me either way."

Nehal stared. "The courthouse . . . collapsed? What?"

Malak opened her eyes and leaned forward, her face so close to Nehal's that her breath fluttered against Nehal's cheek. "It may have been an earthquake. But given that the courthouse was the only building affected, it was most likely an earthweaver. What's that silly old rhyme?"

"*Quaker, quaker, earthshaker,*" replied Nehal automatically. It was a common refrain among schoolchildren seeking to torment earthweavers. "But why? How could they think that would help?"

Malak shrugged. "Maybe they didn't want to help. Maybe they wanted to make things worse. Or maybe it was an accident. I don't know. I don't know anything at all."

"But what about the verdict, then?" Nehal demanded.

"Like I said." Malak twisted her lips wryly. "I don't know anything at all."

THREE DAYS PASSED with no news. Shaaban did not come, only a cycle of unfamiliar policemen silently delivering food, quickly and efficiently. Nehal and Malak talked, and slept, and talked in circles, until Nehal was as knowledgeable about Malak's trial as Malak herself. Malak, whose memory was impeccable, recited the Zirani ambassador's speech for Nehal in its entirety, and Nehal's fury flared at the words, at the hypocrisy of it all.

Trapped as she was, there was nothing she could do. She spent much of her time pacing in an attempt to burn off the energy thrumming through her, while Malak looked on with a dryly amused smile. Malak had a spectacular ability to sit utterly still for long periods of time; it was a skill Nehal found herself envying after only a few hours in jail. The cell walls seemed to be closing in around her, the constant damp seeping under her skin and making her shiver. She longed for blue skies and sun and ocean; she had never been more homesick for Ramina, for her veranda and sand between her toes.

It was on the fourth morning after Malak's trial that there was a change in Malak and Nehal's routine, though it was an unwelcome one: at the break of dawn, before they'd even been brought their breakfast, Attia Marwan appeared before them.

When Nehal saw him she immediately shot to her feet, but he was prepared. There was a pistol held firmly in his hands, pointed directly at her.

"If I see your hands so much as twitch," said Attia quietly, "I will shoot."

"And how exactly will you explain that to your commander?" Nehal challenged. "Going to spin up another elaborate lie?"

But she stood still nonetheless, her hands at her sides; she wasn't stupid enough to get herself shot over nothing. In the corner of her eye she saw Malak slowly untangle her limbs and climb to her feet to stand beside Nehal.

"You don't think he'd believe me, after the stunt you pulled?" Attia sneered at her, never lowering his weapon. "Messing with my *blood* like that, turning me into your puppet." He lowered his voice. "I've told people about your freakish little trick, you know. You oughta watch your back."

"Oh, how *honorable* of you," Nehal said. "Especially after you gave Shaaban your word that you would keep quiet."

"There's more honor in everything I do than you could possibly understand, *woman*."

"Are you just here to make threats?" Malak asked Attia wearily. "I assume you came here for a better reason than that, Attia."

"That's Mister Attia to you," snapped Attia.

Malak shrugged. "I'll call you what I like," she said simply.

Attia's pale face started to turn red, but he took a deep breath to steady himself. His weapon was still held aloft, steady as a tree.

"I thought you'd want to know the result of the chaos you created," said Attia. "Who'd you convince to bring down the courthouse? Because they're a murderer."

"I had nothing to do with that," said Malak, a slight edge to her voice. "And nobody died."

Attia laughed harshly. "That's where you're wrong. The Zirani ambassador's dead. Found buried under a pile of rubble."

There was a long silence.

"Good riddance," said Nehal.

"You understand *nothing*," Attia said scornfully. With his free hand, he dug into his pocket and pulled out a crumpled newspaper. He tossed it into the cell, where it landed at Nehal's feet, the words *Alamaxa Daily* splashed across the top. Beneath that was the announcement of Naji Ouazzani's death, and Zirana's outrage, and—

"Zirana's declared *war*?" said Malak. She knelt to retrieve the newspaper, her eyes quickly scanning the report.

"Negotiations completely fell through," said Attia angrily. "And why wouldn't they, when a weaver murdered their ambassador on Ramsawi soil? Chaos, Malak. All you do is leave chaos in your wake. Your rallies, your riots, and now this. It all leads back to *you*."

Malak was still on her knees, her attention focused entirely on the newspaper. At Attia's declaration, she looked up slowly, but for the first time, she seemed at a loss for words.

Nehal, however, had no such problem. "This isn't Malak's fault," she said angrily. "Lay the blame at the feet of the idiot who killed the ambassador—"

"You don't get it, do you?" interrupted Attia. "She inspires fanaticism. All you women who follow her are crazy, and here's the proof! One of your own has escalated to murder—"

"Oh, you're one to fucking talk!" snapped Nehal. "Did you forget I heard every word you said to Naji Ouazzani? *What does it matter, she's a nobody.* That's what you said."

"I did what I did to maintain peace in my country," said Attia coldly. "I killed a worthless woman to lead Parliament in the right direction. Killing the Zirani ambassador has started a war."

"*You fucking hypocrite!*" Nehal's sense left her entirely; heedless of Attia's gun, she swung up her hand, curling her fingers into a claw. She recalled the feeling of seizing Attia's insides, the thrill it gave her, and the ability came back to her as smoothly as water flowing through a stream. Attia was too slow, far too slow, and Nehal had him in her grasp before he had even realized what she was doing.

Attia's body went as stiff as a statue. Nehal twisted his wrist, and the pistol tumbled from his hand. Then she *pulled,* dragging him forward with a thrust until he smashed against the bars of her cell so hard the meat of his cheek wedged between the bars.

"Nehal!" said Malak warningly.

Nehal ignored her. She squeezed Attia, pulling at him harder against the bars while he struggled—or tried to. His limbs were at her mercy; all of him was at her mercy, and Nehal relished it.

"You think you can just come here and torment us?" Nehal hissed. "You think we're at your mercy?"

Malak's hand closed tightly over Nehal's wrist.

"Nehal, *stop.*" Malak's voice was harsher than Nehal had ever heard it. "Let him go. *Now.*"

Nehal did not want to let Attia Marwan go, but Malak's grip on her wrist was a vise, and the harshness of her voice a whip. Nehal's breath stuttered, but she let Attia go. He crumpled to the floor, then began to crawl toward his pistol. Malak whipped out a hand, emitting a loud gust of wind that sent the weapon skittering to the far reaches of the dark corridor and out of sight.

"No," said Malak firmly. "No more violence. No more threats. You're going to leave, Attia. *Now*." Her hand was held up, a warning of windweaving to come.

For a moment Nehal thought he would argue, but he only swallowed and unsteadily got to his feet. With one last poisonous look at Nehal, he hurried away.

Malak lowered her hand slowly, watching him depart. When she turned to Nehal, her expression was troubled.

"You *cannot* keep doing that," said Malak.

"There's no water in here," argued Nehal. "It was the only thing I *could* do."

"You didn't need to do anything at all," said Malak evenly. "You could have simply let him prattle on. People like Attia Marwan just like to hear the sound of their own voice. Not every idiotic soliloquy requires a response."

Nehal scowled at being made to feel like a child who had misbehaved. "And let him think he can get away with anything he wants? *No*."

"Nehal," said Malak. "He already hates weavers, and it's because of this. Because weavers have a power he doesn't, a power that can be used to hurt him—"

"And he has his pistol!" Nehal interrupted loudly. "And his uniform, and the power of the entire police department behind him. Why shouldn't we use whatever we've got? Just because it's unpalatable? *I don't care*, Malak. I'm going to use whatever powers I have at my disposal."

"This isn't helping." Malak shook her head. "The Zirani ambassador is *dead*, Nehal, murdered by a weaver, at a trial for a weaver. Surely you can see the implications of that?"

"You weren't being tried for weaving," countered Nehal.

"It doesn't matter." With a sigh, Malak sank to the floor, looking up imploringly at Nehal. "It all blends together in the end. Suffrage, weaving, marching . . . it all turns into a single, formless crime, and laid at *my* feet. Tell me you see that."

Nehal looked away, swallowing roughly. Quietly, she sat beside Malak, who reached for her hand. Nehal let her grasp it.

"Do you think I don't feel your anger?" asked Malak gently. "But there is strength in restraint, in acting decisively and purposefully rather than simply lashing out."

Nehal pulled away from Malak's grasp. "I'm not a child," said Nehal evenly. "I wasn't just lashing out. I was making him *afraid*."

"There's strength in being feared, too."

34

GIORGINA

GIORGINA WOKE TO A DARK ROOM. FOR A MOMENT SHE panicked, but then her eyes adjusted, and she recognized Etedal's apartment, and the thin cot she had spent the past week sleeping on. And there, huddled beside her, a broad-shouldered figure resting his chin in his palm and doing his best not to drift off into sleep.

"Nico," Giorgina whispered.

Nico sat up, startled awake. He heaved a sigh. "Finally. Thank the Tetrad."

Gingerly, Giorgina tried to sit up. Nico rushed to help her, grasping her hand in his own and gently pulling her into a seated position. He reached for an ewer sitting beside him and poured water into a beaten aluminum cup, which he handed to Giorgina.

She found she was desperately thirsty, and starving as well. She downed the water and asked for more.

After, she asked, "What did you mean, finally?"

Nico took the cup from her and set it down. "You've been sleeping for nearly four days. You've been . . . feverish. Delirious."

"Four . . . four days?" Giorgina repeated blankly.

"I had a physician come examine you," said Nico. "He said there was nothing he could do, that you would either come out of it or . . ." He trailed off. "Giorgina, what happened?"

Giorgina shook her head. She felt curiously drained, but at least there was no weaving in her. No destruction. It was as though she had expended it all. She relished it, the momentary freedom from the burden of uncontrollable weaving. But it would come back, of course. It always did.

"Naji Ouazzani died," said Nico carefully. "They found him in the rubble."

Giorgina looked at her fingers, which were dry and pale. There was dirt buried under her fingernails from when she had dug into the wall.

Nico's hand on hers was so gentle. "Was it you?"

Giorgina could not look at him. "I didn't mean to." She spoke so quietly she was not sure if Nico had heard her. "I didn't mean to."

But that was a lie, wasn't it? Perhaps she hadn't meant to kill the ambassador, or to cause the destruction of the courthouse, but she had certainly intended to cause harm, to hurt, to inspire fear in Naji. She had been reckless and malicious and now a man was dead at her hands, and so many people were injured. The shame was excruciating.

The thrill of having wielded that power was even worse.

"I know you didn't," said Nico softly. "You just lost control. It's all right. It's not your fault."

But Giorgina did not want his sympathy. She did not deserve it. She took her hand out of his grip and ran her dirty fingers across her cheek. "What's been happening?" she asked stiffly. "With the ambassador dead . . . who are they blaming?"

"Giorgina . . ."

She finally turned to Nico, who shifted uncomfortably. "Please just tell me, Nico."

"Zirana's convinced it was a deliberate act of aggression by a Ramsawi weaver," he said finally. "They've declared war."

WHILE ZIRANA WAS convinced the death of their ambassador was a deliberate provocation by the state, many Ramsawis were content to blame the Daughters of Izdihar, convinced one of them had destroyed the courthouse to avenge Malak, and that Naji Ouazzani had simply been collateral damage. This was certainly the narrative Parliament was desperate to convince Zirana of, in order to avoid war.

Giorgina was not sure which theory was worse.

Bahira, who had come to visit Giorgina, seemed to think it was the latter.

"It's just so stupid," Bahira was saying irritably. "Why would we destroy the courthouse? Why would we make things *worse* for Malak? If anyone took two seconds to think about it, they'd realize how ridiculous it is."

"They don't think." Etedal set down a tray holding three cups of tea. "They just want someone to blame, and we're the easiest target."

Between them, Giorgina was silent. Technically, they *were* to blame, or at least Giorgina was, and she was a member of the Daughters of Izdihar, wasn't she? The blame was hers to bear, but neither Bahira nor Etedal knew about Giorgina's weaving, and she was not prepared to tell them.

"Have either of you heard of Nabawiya Shafik?" said Giorgina suddenly.

They both looked at her blankly.

"She was an activist during the Talyani occupation," explained Giorgina. "When her brother was unjustly imprisoned for defending her against a Talyani officer, Nabawiya went on a hunger strike to shame the Talyanis into releasing him. She spent ten days without food and nearly died, but her brother went free in the end."

"That's nice, but . . . why are you telling us this?" asked Bahira.

"Are you feverish again?" Etedal made to feel Giorgina's forehead, but Giorgina gently caught her palm and set it down. She had been considering this since last night, after Nico had left her and Giorgina had had nothing to do but think, think of something, anything she might do to atone for her actions.

"We could do that," said Giorgina. "A hunger strike at Parliament's doors. The signing is a week from today, but Parliament will be in session every day until then, so they'll see us standing there. They won't be able to look away."

"To strike at what, exactly?" said Bahira incredulously. "You think they care about giving us the vote when we've just had war declared on us?"

"I want to get their attention," said Giorgina. "Convince them we had nothing to do with the collapse at the courthouse, show them we're on their side, that we're patriots in the fight against Zirana, that they should make use of us instead of ignoring us. Work with us and not against us."

"You *are* feverish," said Bahira. "You wouldn't be suggesting madness like this otherwise."

"Hold on—" started Etedal.

"No." Bahira's spirals of dark hair bounced as she shook her head. "What world are you living in? Did you not just hear me say everyone hates us even more than they did?"

"I'll speak," said Giorgina, hardly daring to believe her own words. "You wouldn't have to do anything except stand there."

Bahira turned to Etedal. "Please talk sense into her."

But Etedal only shrugged. "You know I've hated just sitting here doing nothing. I say we do it. What do we have to lose?"

"What do we have to—" Bahira looked at them both like they were mad. "How about everything? How about this is *dangerous,* and it will accomplish nothing. If you think you can shame Parliament into doing the right thing, clearly you don't know those men at all."

"It's still something to do, instead of just sitting on our hands," snapped Etedal. "My cousin *died* for this, Bahira. You think I want to let her death be in vain just because you're a coward?"

Bahira's eyes widened in outrage. "I am *not* a coward—"

"Just tell everyone," Giorgina cut in. "You're the one who knows how to get in touch with the others. Tell them and let everyone make their own choice. You don't have to come."

"Oh, I'll come," spat Bahira. "But this is a bad idea, and it's not going to work."

TWO DAYS LATER, just before dawn, Giorgina stood with Nico and Etedal at the doors of Parliament. The makeshift building, with its peeling paint and cloudy windows, was a rather disheartening sight. Nico was pacing nervously, shifting his weight from one foot to the other. He was to stand on the periphery of their protest, not close enough to mar the spectacle they intended to be, but near enough to help if necessary. He had also ensured Mohsin Hafiz, the journalist who had published Nico's interview, would be present, along with a photographer.

As Giorgina eyed the squat building, she heard footsteps, and turned to see Bahira approaching. Like Giorgina, she was dressed entirely in white, her curls peeking out from beneath her shawl. She looked at Parliament warily. Giorgina was just grateful Bahira was there, despite her misgivings.

Giorgina, Etedal, and Bahira stood beside one another quietly as dawn rose around them. Soon enough, they were joined by others. Not all the Daughters of Izdihar came, but by the time the sun was burning on the back of Giorgina's neck, there were ten women on either side of her, all dressed in white. Their garments attracted stares and whispers from passersby: women were discouraged from wearing white, as it revealed the shape of their bodies, and was bright and eye-catching. Which was precisely why Giorgina had encouraged it.

A crowd began to loiter around them, expectant, waiting to see what the Daughters of Izdihar would do as senators sidestepped them and entered Parliament. Some of them lingered beyond the gate, watching warily and whispering among themselves, and this was what Giorgina had been hoping for.

She broke away from the others and approached the senators. She recognized Kamal Zaghloul hovering alone, but she directed her words to three senators gathered in a knot just behind the closed gate. One senator looked at her with tired suspicion, the other angrily, and the third with clear distaste.

"Good morning, Senators." Giorgina paused. She had practiced what to say, but this sort of thing was not her strong suit; this was Malak's skill set. But this had been Giorgina's plan, and so it was up to her to implement it. This was not going to be a private conversation either, not with the observers who had gathered close to hear what Giorgina had to say, so she made sure her voice carried.

"What are you doing here?" snapped one of the senators. "Haven't you all done enough?"

"We're not here to antagonize you," said Giorgina as amiably as she could. "We intend a hunger strike to show you the seriousness of our resolve. When you see us here again tomorrow, and the day after that, know that we're willing to suffer for our rights. Know that we welcome death for the sake of freedom."

The senators exchanged a glance, and Giorgina continued, "We're going to deliver a speech at sundown. We would be very grateful if you would only listen."

With that, Giorgina nodded at them and returned to her place with the Daughters of Izdihar.

Bahira stood at Giorgina's right. "There's so many people now," she said.

"It's all right," said Giorgina. "We're not going to do anything, and neither will they."

Bahira muttered, "I hope you're right about that."

It was true that the crowd had grown, watching the silent white barricade the Daughters of Izdihar had formed around Parliament. But thus far nobody had approached them, and Giorgina could only hope it stayed that way.

As the day grew long, the crowd grew larger, and it had attracted unsavory observers, including policemen, who scowled at the Daughters of Izdihar but knew full well they could not arrest women who were simply standing in place. Then again, the police normally acted with impunity, so it was not unthinkable that they would find some small, silly excuse to make arrests. Still, there was nothing Giorgina could do about that. She could only stand firm.

Many in the crowd were not shy about making their opinions known. Giorgina heard all sorts of things.

"They should be at home taking care of their husbands!"

"Mind your own business; they're not hurting anyone."

"Making a spectacle of themselves . . ."

"Good for them; it's about time someone did something . . ."

"We're at war because of their antics!"

"They're bringing shame on their families!"

"They're really not eating?"

"Only loose women wear white!"

And on and on and on. Giorgina did her best to ignore the whispers, the shouts, whether they were pleasant or not. She was focused on standing upright and silent, like a statue. She kept her eyes carefully trained on the upper floor of the Parliament, where the senators were deliberating. Several of them made their way to the windows and hovered beside the curtains to stare at the line of women in white arranged before them. Giorgina hoped they were uncomfortable.

When the sun went down, the senators began to exit the building to make their way home. Many of them lingered, however, their eyes directed on the line of women in white surrounding the building. It was as Giorgina had hoped: the senators would not have come out just to hear the Daughters speak, but if they were already on their way out, they would have an excuse to linger and listen.

Giorgina's heart thudded in her chest as she made her way into the center of the crowd. Everyone was staring at her. She turned and caught Nico's eye; he gave her an encouraging smile. She glanced to her left; the senators had gathered at the gates and were eyeing her warily.

She had practiced this. She had written and rewritten the words, then rewritten them again, then memorized them word for word.

She may not have had Malak's charisma or elocution skills, but she had her words. And so she spoke.

"The Daughters of Izdihar had nothing to do with the collapse at the courthouse." The practiced lie slid smoothly off Giorgina's tongue. "Despite what some of you may think, we're not petty or irrational. Destroying the courthouse has only harmed us, driven a wedge between us and these honorable men of Parliament." Giorgina turned slightly and motioned to the gathered crowd of senators. She had their undivided attention now.

Honorable men, she called them. What an absolute joke. But it would appeal to their vanity, and soften them to her argument.

"The Daughters of Izdihar are not enemies of the people. Just the opposite—we stand here because we want the best for our people and for our country. As we speak, Parliament is attempting to stave off war. We want nothing more than to support Parliament—as *full citizens*. We wish to stand together against Zirana, who would enforce their own outmoded traditions on Ramsawis, and bend us to their whims."

Giorgina inflected her voice with indignation and continued, "We are all of us proud Ramsawis," she said, gesturing to not only the women gathered behind her, but the crowd that was listening. "Should we not all have the chance to show our loyalty to Parliament and country? To support those men who work so tirelessly on our behalf? To elect them and throw our support behind them, so that we can fight together against our enemies? Are we not stronger together than apart?"

Giorgina paused for a moment, the supportive murmurs of the crowd and their nodding heads buoying her. She turned and spoke to the senators directly.

"Senators." Giorgina gave them a genial smile and bowed her head. "We've been so at odds, and for what? The Daughters of Izdihar support you and your endeavors. We only hope that you give us the opportunity to support you even further. I implore you— when you put your pens to the new constitution, think of all the

Ramsawi women so desperate to work *with* you, and not against you." She smiled again. "Thank you for taking the time to listen to us." She turned back toward the crowd. "Thank you all."

THE FOLLOWING MORNING, their protest was on the front page of the *Alamaxa Daily,* a measured account detailing their hunger strike, along with a photograph, and a word for word dictation of Giorgina's speech. Giorgina smiled at Mohsin Hafiz's writing, which reminded her strongly of her own: he was entirely objective, detailing only the bare facts.

The Daughters of Izdihar had spent the night in front of Parliament, some sleeping in fits and starts. All night Giorgina's stomach had pained her, and now she swayed on her feet, balancing on Nico's elbow, but eventually steadied herself. After all, she had gone hungry before.

"I'm all right," said Giorgina softly. The sun was beginning to rise, and the senators would be here soon. "Go."

Her mind drifting as she shifted her feet, Giorgina wondered what her parents and sisters were doing. Were they thinking of her? Had they seen her in the papers? Had Sabah? Hala could not read well enough to read a newspaper, but surely she would see her daughter's face and recognize her. Would they be proud of her? Would they marvel that she had given such a speech to so many people?

The day went by without incident. The senators departed again, sidling out like rats, protected on all sides by an armed police presence. Some senators, Giorgina noted, looked at them with concern, while others could not look at them at all. Another night passed, and hunger was beginning to gnaw on Giorgina's insides.

The morning of the third day, a senator came out and walked directly toward them. He was a stately, handsome man, with a trimmed russet-brown beard and sharply upturned eyes. Giorgina recognized him. Hesham Galal was Alamaxa's elected representative, the Minister of Defense, and a very popular member of Parliament.

He stopped directly in front of Giorgina; he was a full head taller than she was. Her hunger seemed to have taken over her nerves, because she felt no fear or trepidation as she faced this man down. Only bone-deep weariness.

"What, here to negotiate?" said Etedal hoarsely.

The senator glanced at her with a frown, then turned back to Giorgina, speaking in a low voice.

"That was a clever speech." He stared Giorgina up and down assessingly. "Certainly quite different from what we're accustomed to hearing from Malak Mamdouh. A nice way to get people on your side."

Giorgina smiled. "I only spoke the truth."

Hesham Galal breathed what might have been a laugh, though it sounded entirely jaded. "We'll consider your requests. Now go home before this escalates."

"I'm sorry, Senator." Giorgina gave him a sincerely apologetic look. "But do you really think an empty promise to consider our requests will be enough? You think you can just brush us off so easily?"

"Parliament has enough to be getting on with—"

"And we want only to support you," said Giorgina. "As full citizens, who can vote, and sign our own papers—and perhaps even attend the Weaving Academy, just as men do."

Hesham frowned, but Giorgina pressed, "What if we do end up at war, Senator? Wouldn't you rather have more trained weavers, regardless of whether they're men or women? You signed the Izdihar Division into being, after all."

He looked at her somewhat quizzically, then glanced back at Parliament. "I don't entirely disagree with you, but I can't promise you anything. Some of my colleagues are quite . . . set in their ways."

"As we are set in our commitment to this strike." Giorgina's exhaustion and hunger had stripped her of all anxiety; her body could not muster up the energy to be nervous, or to think too much about her words. "We're going to stand here until the constitution is signed," said Giorgina. "We're going to starve and deprive ourselves of sleep, and you can continuously remind your colleagues of our resolve. Convince them that we're more useful working with them than against them."

With a long-suffering sigh, Hesham turned and walked away.

"I think that was the biggest concession we've gotten from a senator," said Etedal.

Grudgingly, Bahira nodded. "They're desperate, and they just want to be rid of us. This . . . may actually work."

But later that day, they were joined by the Khopeshes of the Tetrad.

They were immediately recognizable, the rusty khopeshes hanging from their belts prominently displayed.

Bahira eyed them warily. "I don't have the energy for them," she muttered to Giorgina. Three days without food had wreaked havoc on Bahira: her skin was sallow and blotchy, she swayed on her feet, and she complained of a persistent hammering in her head.

"It's all right," Giorgina assured her. "They just want to frighten us."

It was working. The Daughters of Izdihar, hungry and tired and tense, whispered among themselves and kept glancing at the Khopeshes, who did their absolute best to appear menacing, stalking around them and running their fingers along their weapons.

When Giorgina spied Attia Marwan in the crowd, smirking, she knew their presence was his doing. Something twisted in her chest; she sensed a plan in that smile.

Unhelpfully, the crowd around them was growing agitated.

"Good on you, standing your ground!" shouted one old woman at their backs, only to shrink back when jeers rose up to drown out her voice. Mutters rose from the spectators, and all eyes were on the Khopeshes, many of whom were large, burly men who looked like they could easily crush a watermelon between their palms.

Giorgina didn't see what started it. It happened suddenly: mutters turned to shouts, then came a scream, and then a scuffle broke out. A rush of sand flew at one of the Khopeshes, striking his skin with such ferocity that he began to bleed. Giorgina startled, falling to her knees, her heart thudding, before she realized she felt nothing in her fingertips. *It wasn't me.*

But it was the opportunity the Khopeshes had been waiting for: they rushed at the crowd, weapons held aloft.

The Daughters of Izdihar on either side of Giorgina scattered. Etedal cursed loudly, but Giorgina barely heard her over the shouts of the crowd around her. She held tightly on to Etedal and Bahira, and the three of them struggled to maneuver their way through the chaos of the crowd. Giorgina needed to get free of the mob, to get to Nico, to safety.

But when the three of them came face-to-face with Attia Marwan, smug and flanked by two fellow officers, Giorgina knew it was over. Attia Marwan had his excuse.

"Nice to see you again." Attia Marwan sneered. "I'm placing you three under arrest for disturbing the peace during times of war."

35

NEHAL

NEHAL'S BAIL HAD COME THROUGH. THE OFFICER WHO took her out of her cell was old enough to be her father, and he smiled kindly at her when he asked her to come upstairs with him.

"You won't be coming back, so take everything you need," he added pointedly.

Nehal turned, hesitated, then embraced Malak. "I'll come visit," she whispered into her hair.

Malak pulled back. "If they let you." With a meaningful glance at the officer, who was pointedly looking away as they said their goodbyes, Malak took a step back.

In Shaaban's office, Nehal found her parents waiting.

Shaheera grimaced. "You look awful."

Nehal raised an eyebrow. "Lovely to see you too, Mama." Shaheera herself looked more exhausted than Nehal had ever seen her. Her hair, usually sleek and shiny, was pulled back into a messy knot, escaped curls pooling at the nape of her neck. "Where's Nico?"

Shaheera's nostrils flared, her expression going cold. "He has more important matters to deal with, apparently."

"To be fair, his presence isn't required here," said Shaaban.

Shaheera gave him a withering glance, and looked ready to say something scathing, but Khalil placed a hand on the small of her back and smiled placatingly at her.

"What does that mean?" asked Nehal blankly.

"His . . . that red-haired girl's been arrested." Shaheera sniffed, then huffed out a breath. "He's applying for bail for *her*."

"He won't get it," said Shaaban bluntly. "They're treating her like Malak Mamdouh; she's considered a danger to the public."

"*Giorgina?*" asked Nehal incredulously. "A kitten is more dangerous."

"Your friend started a riot in front of Parliament," said Shaheera sharply.

"I think I'll wait to hear what happened from Nico," replied Nehal coldly. "I want the facts, not prejudiced distortions."

Shaheera threw up her hands, but she seemed more resigned than angry, as the roll of her eyes indicated.

"What about Malak's trial?" Nehal asked Shaaban. "She has no idea what's going to happen, no one's told her anything!"

"Everything is on hold for the moment, Nehal," said Shaaban testily. "Parliament is dealing with a war declaration; they have more important things to do than worry about Malak Mamdouh."

"So in the meantime she just rots in prison?"

"Yes," Shaaban said.

Nehal opened her mouth but Shaheera's hand clamped around her upper arm. "*Enough*. We're going home. *Now*."

Shaaban did not look like he had any intention of saying another word to Nehal, so she had no choice but to allow herself to be led away by her parents.

At home, Nehal rushed to her room, eager to finally be rid of her dirty clothes and soak in a rose-petal bath, but her mother followed her, and appeared to have no intention of leaving. She sat down on Nehal's bed, running her hands along the covers.

"Mama?" prompted Nehal.

Shaheera sighed and looked up. "We are always so at odds, you and I."

Nehal blinked; she had expected a lecture, not musings. She recovered quickly and said, "Well, that's because you never even try to see things my way."

Shaheera scoffed, but it was sad and tired, not scornful. "I could say the same for you. But I know your Baba and I haven't been entirely fair to you. Making you marry Nico . . . may not have been the right decision."

Nehal could not help herself from saying scornfully, "My dowry helped pay off Baba's debts, didn't it? So I suppose it was worth it, selling me to the highest bidder."

Shaheera did not flinch; she was much too accustomed to her daughter for that. Instead, shocking Nehal, she nodded. "Yes. You're right. It was a calculated decision. We sacrificed you to save everything else."

Nehal had known this. Still, hearing her mother speak it so bluntly was like being pierced in the chest with a rusty nail. "Glad to have been of service," said Nehal flatly.

"I worked hard on your marriage contract, you know," said Shaheera. "I made sure there was a clause forbidding Nico from taking a concubine. And then you went and undid it all, to go slumming at a school."

Nehal bristled; the reminder of the Alamaxa Weaving Academy hurt. The wound was still open and raw. She had barely been able to admit to herself that she was no longer going back, and she could not imagine telling her mother. Watching her gloat would be far too painful.

"Perhaps if you'd included me in your grand plans, we could have worked together," Nehal retorted. "Since apparently you're so disappointed we're always at odds."

"Sharing your husband with that girl will be harder than you think," said Shaheera, completely ignoring Nehal. "You may not love him, but he's still your husband."

Nehal scoffed. "I don't want any part of him."

"No," said Shaheera softly. "I suppose you don't. You wouldn't be happy being wife to any man, would you?"

Nehal looked at her mother sharply. There were several ways to interpret that question, and several possible answers. "I've never been interested in having a husband and children and . . . all that," said Nehal as carefully as she could. "You know that."

Shaheera nodded, her gaze finding the lantern beside Nehal's bed. Nehal watched her closely. She knew her mother to be both intelligent and secretive, and she had often wondered how much Shaheera kept to herself. And if Shaheera did know more than she was letting on, was it something she could put into words? Or would she and Nehal simply continue to speak in code and circles?

"You don't have to want it," said Shaheera flatly. "But you can pretend. Appearances are everything in this country." She stood. "Which is why tomorrow night, we're having a party, and you and Nico will pretend to be a perfect, happy couple."

Nehal stared at her mother as though she'd just grown a second head. "What?" she said blankly.

Shaheera gave her a look of annoyance. "You heard me, Nehal."

"A party? *Now?* Weren't we all just talking about how we're at war?"

Shaheera sighed so heavily Nehal could hear each and every one of her mother's years in that exhale of breath. "Why must you always be so contrary? Why can't you ever just do as I say?"

"Because what you're saying makes no *sense*—"

"Don't tell me what does or doesn't make sense when we've just bailed you out of *jail*. Whereas I have held this family together with my teeth for *years,*" snapped Shaheera, her momentary exhaustion flung away like a robe. "While your father spent his nights drinking and gambling, *I* was the one holding together our finances and our reputation. *I* was the one who found a way to salvage the debt he mired us in. I have *never* stopped thinking about how every single step we take affects our worth and our reputation. Maybe if you were a *bit* less self-centered, you wouldn't be so bothered by my suggestions."

Nehal scowled. "Sorry, Mama. I guess you'll have to teach me to be as cold and calculating as you are."

"Oh, you're already calculating, but you only know how to calculate for yourself." Shaheera threw up her hands. "You're an impossible child. You might *at least* thank me for trying to salvage your reputation."

"I don't care about my reputation!"

"Then you're a fool," said Shaheera. "Reputation equates to respectable acquaintances, which equate to connections, and connections make up the threads of power and influence. You are *nothing* without a respectable reputation. All this wealth could be gone if people no longer want to have dealings with the Baldinottis because of you. Try to think about that before you go off cavorting with people like Malak Mamdouh."

Nehal reeled back sharply, once again wondering at the extent of her mother's suspicions. But her pronouncement seemed constructed to prevent Nehal from asking her further questions. Whatever Shaheera knew or did not know about Nehal's inclinations, she did not want to discuss it.

"Say what you mean, Mama."

"You're selfish," said Shaheera bluntly. "You always have been. And your father and I certainly played a part in that; we've spoiled you. You're not doing what you're doing out of some altruistic vision for women; you're doing it for yourself. Be honest, Nehal—would you have embarked on this ridiculous crusade with the Daughters of Izdihar if your father and I hadn't made you marry Nico, if we had just let you go to the Academy? Would you have cared?"

Nehal winced, for there was some truth to her mother's words. But her argument was flawed. "But that's precisely the point, Mama." Nehal struggled to keep her voice level. "You *did* force me into marriage, and you *did* prevent me from attending the Academy. You took away my choices, and I wanted them back. Is that so wrong?"

"Women don't have the luxury of *choice,* not when so much

is at stake," said Shaheera. "Did you think about Nisreen and her husband? *Their* reputation? What about the triplets? The rest of the Darweesh family?" She gestured to the room around her. "You're a rich woman, safely ensconced in a beautiful home. Yes, I asked you to forgo one of your desires for the greater good. So what? Women in this country have been sacrificing their desires for the greater good for centuries. What makes you the exception?"

Nehal shook her head. How could she make her mother understand that this wasn't just about her? Perhaps it had started that way, but were not her anger and indignation born out of true injustice? Why *should* she be expected to sacrifice so much for the sake of tradition and propriety, when men could do whatever they wanted?

The trouble was, her mother's words hurt because they were true—Nehal *was* selfish. She sat with this for a moment, acknowledging this, absorbing it, wondering if she did in fact need to atone for it at some point—and decided she did not. Because her selfishness did not negate her actions. Her initial intentions were unimportant. Her personal crusade had become inextricably linked with that of all Ramsawi women. But Shaheera refused to see that.

So Nehal shrugged a single shoulder, plastered a careful smile on her face, and rolled her eyes, affecting the casual disdain with which her mother was so familiar.

NEHAL HAD LITTLE desire to be cooped up at home with her mother, but as it turned out, the conditions of her bail severely limited her movement. She was bound to her house until a date could be set for a trial, something that seemed to cast a shadow over Shaheera, who was determined to keep a very close eye on her daughter. And so, but for a brief reprieve, where Nico informed Nehal of the reality of Giorgina's hunger strike, and her speech, Nehal was forced to share in her mother's party preparations.

It was enough to drive her mad. A party. A party when Malak and Giorgina were in jail, Nehal was expelled from the one place she ever belonged, the Daughters of Izdihar were scattered, the signing of the new constitution was a mere two days away, and the entire country was at risk of war. But Shaheera seemed concerned only with ensuring that the party preparations went smoothly, and she had recruited all the servants to help transform the courtyard into her vision of an idyllic paradise. Baskets of colorful flowers painted the walls in shades of violet and pink. From every column dangled a giant fanous, casting so much light one could almost forget there was no sun. Garlands of jasmine were strung up from one end of the courtyard to the other, raining a pleasant scent down on them.

A high table the length of the entire courtyard had been purchased especially for this occasion, to hold a cornucopia of food platters: parsley-garnished hummus, sizzling kofta skewers, stuffed grape leaves, stuffed peppers, stuffed zucchini, rice studded with almonds and walnuts, roasted duck and chicken glazed with turmeric and paprika. Then there were the sweets, on the other end: basbousa dripping with honey, kunafa stuffed with cream, piles of ghrayba, stuffed dates, nut-filled qatayef, syrup-soaked zalabiya. Servants milled about the tables, ready to serve and replenish.

Shaheera had also procured the services of Nargis Taha, one of Alamaxa's most popular singers. The diva was situated on a raised dais with an entire orchestra seated behind her. In deference to recent events, Shaheera had not hired weavers, but had instead somehow managed to find a contortionist, a juggler, and, to Nehal's utter bafflement, a snake charmer.

Shaheera even commandeered Nehal's wardrobe, picking out her clothes and giving Ridda specific instructions for hair and cosmetics. When Nehal tried to protest Shaheera glared her into silence. Nehal glared back, but in the end she found herself stuffed into shades of periwinkle blue anyway, her face heavy with layers of paint.

Shaheera adjusted Nehal's headdress, then leaned down to place a soft kiss on Nehal's cheek. "Please behave tonight. No talk of Parliament, politics, or the Daughters of Izdihar. I've worked hard on this. All right?"

Would this be what it would take to prove that Nehal could rein in her selfishness? She could not quite muster an enthusiastic response, so she only shrugged, which seemed to satisfy Shaheera.

Her mother dragged her to the courtyard, where light chatter could be heard, along with Nargis Taha's high, clear voice rising above the noise.

"Well? Where is Nico?" asked Shaheera.

"How should I know?" replied Nehal. "I've been trapped in my room with you and Ridda all night."

Shaheera narrowed her eyes, then turned her gaze to the stairwell. Nico materialized soon after. He looked harried and distracted, like he had made no effort at all, and Nehal felt only satisfaction at her mother's displeased grimace.

"Good, you're here." Shaheera pulled Nico forward and linked his arm in Nehal's. "All you have to do tonight is greet your guests, mingle politely, and stay together as often as possible. We want people talking about what a lovely couple you are, not that one of you is a public menace and the other is too ineffectual to control her."

Nehal scowled again, while Nico's mouth gaped open. But Shaheera did not give them time to respond; she practically shoved them into the courtyard, where they were almost immediately accosted by a couple Nehal did not recognize.

As more and more guests began to arrive, Nico and Nehal barely had time to do anything other than greet everyone and respond to their exclamations about the lovely party. Shaheera was never too far away; she hovered near the couple with her husband trailing behind her.

Nehal was exhausted within moments. Her cheeks were sore from the false smile she plastered on her face. She wanted nothing more than to retreat to her room, until she caught sight of Yusry and Mahitab in the crowd.

Mahitab saw Nehal first and waved exuberantly at her as she approached. Yusry quickly noticed his sister's enthusiasm and looked up to meet Nehal's eyes. He shot her a smile, and she returned it, the first genuine smile she had given all night.

"Nehal!" Mahitab threw her arms around her. "I've missed you! When will you be back at the Academy?"

"As soon as I can," Nehal managed to mumble. "I'm confined to my home at the moment. A condition of my bail, I'm afraid."

Shaheera was close, immersed in conversation with an older woman, but not distracted enough to keep her from glancing Nehal's way every few moments. Nehal pursed her lips, then sidled closer to Yusry. "Can we speak in private for a moment, Yusry?"

He looked somewhat surprised but nodded anyway. Nehal led him casually away, keeping an eye on her mother, who for the moment was deep in conversation with the older woman.

Nehal, who was feeling somewhat claustrophobic, wanted to get as far away from the party and its noise as possible. She led Yusry up three flights of stairs and opened the door to the roof, which was the least adorned part of the house: it was a flat, dirt floor, with a very short brick railing that barely reached Nehal's knees. Here, the party felt like a distant dream; the music was a whisper on the night air, the chatter a mere caress.

Ignoring Yusry's clear hesitation, Nehal made her way to the edge. Yusry reached out and gently pulled her back onto safer ground.

"Careful!" he admonished. "Why are we up here?"

Nehal shrugged. "I wanted some air."

"I'm happy you're no longer in jail," Yusry offered. "It must have been frightening."

Nehal gazed upward; the full moon was so bright and large it might have been a doorway to another world. A better one. "Mostly just dull. But Malak was there, so it was bearable."

Yusry closed the gap between them. "Why did you bring me up here, Nehal?" he asked slowly.

She turned slowly and looked right at Yusry. "Nico's father said you're a known queer," she said quietly.

Though Yusry's eyebrows flew, his expression remained otherwise placid. "I see," he said carefully. "And that . . . disturbed you?"

Nehal kicked at a loose piece of rubble. "I think I am as well."

Yusry's expression softened, collapsing like a house of cards. "Malak, then," he said softly.

Nehal hesitated. She was not entirely certain what it was she meant to ask him. "I'm not . . . disgusted with myself or any of that nonsense they tell us we should feel. I know who I am, and I'm content with that." She looked up at him, her thoughts catching up to her words. "But do you ever wonder what sort of life you could have? You can't marry, you can hardly live out in the open unless you want to be arrested . . . what does it all come to?"

Yusry looked away, frowning. "Love, I suppose," he said. "Fulfillment. Satisfaction. Whatever you want to call it. If you're asking me if it's an easy life, I won't lie to you. It's not. You'll do your best to hide, but everyone will still find out and despise you anyway."

"Adil and Nagat don't despise you."

Yusry's smile was bitter. "They don't know. All they do is bemoan salacious rumors and try to find me a wife. I think they just don't want to admit it to themselves."

"What about the rest of your family?"

"I've only told my sister." Yusry sighed. "Our parents are dead. I never had to tell them. And I wouldn't recommend it, personally."

"Nico knows. Isn't that funny?"

Yusry looked alarmed. "What does he think?"

"He's quite progressive about these things, as it turns out." Nehal's lips twisted. "Not to mention he's madly in love with another woman. Nico has his own problems."

"Yes, but he could make her his concubine if he wanted to," said Yusry, a little bitterly. "Live in the open, and no one would say a word against him even as he betrayed his lawful wife. But for us . . ."

"Do you have someone in your life?"

"In a manner of speaking." Yusry sighed. "It's not . . . traditional, though."

Nehal laughed, though it was entirely devoid of humor. "No, I don't imagine it ever could be. It's not *fair*. None of it is."

Yusry reached out, took Nehal's hand in his gently. "No. It's not."

Standing this close to her, Nehal noted he smelled of lavender. She inhaled deeply, the scent helping to calm her.

They stood silently for a few moments, until Yusry said, "It all seems impossible at first. But it's not. It's difficult, and lonely, and dangerous, and overwhelming—" He laughed. "But it *is* possible, to be happy as we are. It's hard work, but not insurmountable. And it's worth it. I promise."

Nehal looked up at him, uncertain what to say to that, but before she could decide, a distant clanging interrupted.

She frowned. "What is that?"

Yusry was looking up at the night sky as though searching for the source of the sound. His brow was furrowed in concentration. "I think it's . . . bells?" Then he paled. "I think . . . but no. The bells of the Alamaxa Citadel? But—"

"What?" pressed Nehal. The Alamaxa Citadel sat on the western edge of Alamaxa, facing the desert. Nehal had never seen it, nor heard it spoken of except once or twice in school.

Yusry furrowed his brow. "The bells—well—they're only meant to ring when there's imminent danger—like an approaching army."

"But Zirana only declared war days ago." Nehal frowned. "Their ambassador *just* died."

"I don't understand it either." Yusry tugged Nehal away from the edge. "Let's go back downstairs.

But Nehal's thoughts were far too occupied. "You go," said Nehal. "I'll be down in a minute."

Yusry appeared to hesitate, but Nehal turned away, offering him no chance to argue, and after a moment she heard the tread of his footsteps walking away from her. She lingered on the rooftop for a few moments, frowning, the ringing bells swiftly producing a headache. But it was so nice to be here all alone, away from the

party, from her mother. Here there was only Nehal and the moon
and stars.

And those infernal bells.

A war. An army at the gates of Alamaxa. This was everything
Nehal had been preparing for, wasn't it? This was what her training
at the Academy was supposed to amount to. Would they mobilize
the students now? Would Shaimaa and the others join the Izdihar
Division . . . without Nehal?

No. She would not allow it. Now, when Ramsawa needed all the
skilled weavers they could find, the Academy would *have* to take Nehal back. Nagi claimed she was one of his best students. She would
be an asset. Surely no one would care about optics or the conditions
of her bail when the country was at war.

Thus resolved to return to the Academy, Nehal felt far more
settled than she had in days. She would tell Nico that night and leave
him to deal with her parents the following morning. They could not
stop her. She would not allow them to stop her.

The shuffle of footsteps behind Nehal disturbed her thoughts.

"Did you come to fetch me, Yusry? I've barely been five minutes." Nehal turned, but her playful smile turned into a scowl when
she faced the man standing before her.

It wasn't Yusry.

It was Attia Marwan, standing so close to Nehal she could feel
his breath.

"What are you—" But before Nehal could finish her sentence,
or react in any way, Attia reached out and thrust something into
Nehal's neck. It was a pinprick, nothing more, but she flinched and
lunged at Attia, only to be held fast by him; his free hand gripped
the nape of her neck, hair and all, and Nehal could fast feel her limbs
growing weaker and her vision blurring, until she felt herself collapse to the ground, and the starlit sky went dark.

36

GIORGINA

"WOULD YOU STOP PACING?" ETEDAL DEMANDED. "YOU'RE making me even more anxious."

Giorgina paused mid-stride, then turned to face Etedal, who was sprawled on the floor, one knee pulled up for her arm to rest on. Next to her, Bahira stood stock-still, arms crossed and expression dour. With a sigh, Giorgina leaned against the nearest wall; she wouldn't pace, but she was too nervous to sit.

The bells of the Alamaxa Citadel had not stopped ringing, and Giorgina struggled with the knowledge that it was all her fault. One misstep on her part, and their country was at war. She almost laughed—here she had spent all her life thinking she was nobody, utterly powerless, and yet now it was at her hand that Alamaxa was under attack, even if nobody but Nico knew it. And after all that, here she sat, imprisoned.

She could hardly believe that in the short space of a year she'd seen the inside of a cell twice. They had only spent a single night here and already they had exhausted all threads of conversation. Bahira had lamented their decision, Etedal had snarled at her to shut up, and Giorgina had tried to make peace between the two of them.

At least that had given her something to do. Now, though, she was in her own head, realizing how far she'd come since the last time she was imprisoned, when she was fretting over what her father would think. Now, Giorgina had only herself to worry about, but wasn't that enough? What was the sentence for disturbing the peace during times of war? Would her trial be a sham just like Malak's? Would she spend years languishing in prison?

But then a thought struck Giorgina:

Could a prison cell *hold* her?

For something strange had been happening to Giorgina ever since she had attacked—she swallowed heavily at the thought—*killed* Naji Ouazzani. Her earthweaving . . . it was different. Before, though it had always been present, it had existed somewhere just under the surface, just outside of Giorgina's conscious reach. It certainly erupted in time with her emotions, but she struggled to get a grasp on it, like there was a barrier separating her from her abilities.

Now, though, she found she could . . . *grasp* it if she so desired. It was as though she had discovered a new joint in her body of which she had been previously unaware, and now calling on weaving was as simple as deciding to bend her knee. She could feel the earth around her, feel the pulsing of it, and though Giorgina had no idea how she might go about it, she thought she might, with enough time and will, be able to dig herself a tunnel. Their cell was just bricks and dirt, after all. Just bricks and dirt.

Just earth.

And it would not just be Giorgina escaping. Malak was here as well. Malak, whose trial had been a joke, who would likely be sent to prison for life for nothing at all.

No. These abilities . . . Giorgina had spent all her life detesting her earthweaving, fearing it, but wasn't it the only power she had at her disposal? Her only real weapon? True, she had killed a man—the thought continued to turn her stomach—but that had been entirely accidental, and only because she had had no way to learn control over her earthweaving.

It was not her fault.

It was *not* her fault.

Giorgina took a deep breath, ignoring Etedal and Bahira, who continued to bicker behind her. Their chatter turned into meaningless noise as Giorgina knelt and placed her palms flat against the ground. There—dirt and mud and brick and *earth*. Giorgina could feel it in her bones, and her earthweaving . . . it was there, a muscle she could flex . . . she closed her eyes, concentrated, *willed*—

And something exploded.

Giorgina's eyes shot open as the reverberations coursed through her. No—radiated *from* her.

Distressed shouts came from the women in the cells on either side, and Etedal shouted, "What the *fuck*?"

Giorgina, who had intended only to create a neatly dug tunnel beneath the bars of the cell, had instead blown a hole through the cell, scattering debris everywhere before her. It was not neat or controlled or anything she had intended.

But it was still an escape route.

Giorgina stood and pulled at the metal bars, which had come clean from the ground. She only had to wriggle one bar slightly to the right to create an opening large enough for the women to crawl through. She turned to Bahira and Etedal.

Bahira looked aghast. "What in the world are you doing? Since when have you been an earthweaver?"

"I've always been an earthweaver," said Giorgina calmly. "And I'm leaving. We can find Malak and we can all get out of here."

"And become fugitives?" Bahira demanded. "Are you out of your mind?"

But Etedal was grinning; Giorgina's revelation seemed to have cheered her. "You're out of your mind if you stay here, Bahira. I'm with our brand-new earthweaver. You think any of us are gonna get a fair shot in here? I'm not rotting in prison. But if you wanna stay, be my guest." Etedal glanced around. "But I don't think you'd want to be here if an army gets in. I doubt invading Zirani solders are gonna be too friendly to female prisoners." Without waiting for Bahira to respond, she turned to Giorgina. "Can you do that trick again?"

Bahira, who had paled at Etedal's words, quietly followed them outside. Giorgina went straight to the cell beside them and told the four prisoners gathered inside to stand back. She knelt and laid her palms flat against the ground once more. She had no idea what she could do differently to trigger a less violent result, so she simply *willed* again, and again the ground exploded. The imprisoned women cheered and clapped as they dug their way out.

"Where to now?" asked one young woman in a dirty orange galabiya.

"Just follow us until we figure it out," said Etedal.

Thankfully, there were only two more occupied cells, as Giorgina was growing exhausted. She had begun to feel somewhat faint with the first explosion she had created, and now she was beginning to sway. By now they were a group of thirteen, and they still needed to find Malak. Giorgina walked down the length of the cellar, and finally, there she was.

Malak stood at the bars of her cell, and when she saw Giorgina she gave her a smile that settled all her nerves.

"I was wondering what all that noise was," said Malak, who did not seem at all surprised to find Giorgina earthweaving. "Do you need me to stand back?"

Giorgina smiled. "Please."

When Malak was out of her cell, Giorgina was relieved to let her take the reins, which Malak seemed all too happy to do.

"We can't go back upstairs," said Malak thoughtfully. "I heard the bells, but we can't be sure the police station has emptied. We could take the chance and fight our way out, I suppose, but I'd really rather not . . . Giorgina, do you think you could do something a little different?"

Giorgina doubted it, but she asked, "What do you mean?"

"The station is slightly elevated," Malak explained. "So we're really only halfway underground. If we walk to the end and you blasted a hole in the corner of the ceiling, theoretically it should open up into the street. What do you think?"

Giorgina nodded uncertainly. She and the others followed Malak to the end of the cell block, which was nothing more than a wall of packed dirt. Giorgina laid her hands against it and felt its thickness.

"Come here." Etedal motioned and knelt, and Giorgina climbed atop her shoulders, so that she was perched high enough to touch the ceiling. Here, the wall felt much thinner than it had below, and weaker, and Giorgina thought, *I can do this.*

She took a deep, deep breath and focused all her will, all her energy, into pushing through this wall. For a moment, she thought perhaps she was too tired—she could feel her weaving nearly slipping away. But Giorgina allowed her desperation to come crawling out, and then she felt the explosion, so powerful it knocked her and Etedal back, where they tumbled to the ground in a heap.

Coughing, Giorgina sat up to cheers: moonlight shone through the large hole in the wall Giorgina had created.

"Go on now," said Malak, motioning to the women behind them. "Hurry."

Using each other as stepladders, the women began to crawl through while Etedal, Malak, Bahira, and Giorgina watched them. When the final woman was through, she reached her hand down.

"Come on now," she said, her large ringlets falling around her face. "I can lift at least two of you up."

Bahira didn't hesitate. With Etedal's help, she was through, followed by Giorgina, Etedal herself, and, finally, Malak.

Outside, the cool breeze was a balm against Giorgina's skin, which had grown warm. Malak laid a hand on her arm.

"That's a lot of weaving for someone with no training." Malak looked around at the other women, who had begun to scatter after shouting their thanks. "You need to rest."

"Where?" said Etedal. "Giorgina's family won't take her, and the pigs know where you and I live."

"Zanuba's," Bahira said somewhat resignedly. "The police don't know anything about me; I gave them a false name."

Etedal clapped her on the back. "How wily. I'm proud of you."

Bahira grimaced. "Anyway, I doubt they'd ever think to look there. It's a start, anyway."

"It's a good idea," said Malak.

Giorgina was fading; she hoped she could endure what would surely be a long walk to Zanuba's. Malak hooked her arm through Giorgina's, supporting her, and Giorgina felt reassured by her steady presence.

Bahira looked up. "It's quiet now."

It was true; the bells had stopped ringing, and Giorgina had hardly noticed. The quiet surely wouldn't last long, though, if Zirana was approaching. Soon enough Alamaxa would be filled with the sounds of war.

But Giorgina was free, or had at least achieved a modicum of freedom, and she had done it herself, with her own will and her own ability. The same ability she had always feared had granted her power and caused others to look at her with the kind of fear that had crushed Giorgina all her life. Her earthweaving was her only weapon, her only protection, and Giorgina was swiftly realizing she relished having such power at her fingertips.

As she gazed up at the starlit sky shining down on Alamaxa, Giorgina wondered if it was finally time to stop fearing what she was capable of.

ACKNOWLEDGMENTS

I'VE ALWAYS ENJOYED READING AUTHOR ACKNOWLEDG-ments, so writing my own feels pleasantly surreal.

Thank you to my agent, DongWon Song, for seeing the potential in a rather rough draft, for coming up with a much better title, for helping me brainstorm new plot threads, and for guiding me through the publishing world. Thank you to my editor, David Pomerico, for supporting this book, and for prompting me to make a very scary structural edit that ultimately paid off. Thank you both for helping me shape the aforementioned rough draft into something I'm proud of.

Major thanks to Mireya Chiriboga, and to the rest of the team at Harper Voyager, for helping to make this book a reality. Thank you to Nadia Saward and everyone at Orbit UK for bringing this book across the pond!

To Nehal Amer, my very first reader, who read snippets of this book when it was still less than fifty pages long. Thank you for your endless enthusiasm and support, for making me laugh, for always sending me Supernatural memes and pictures of cute farm animals, and for sharing in some very complicated feelings about our homeland. I hope you enjoy reading a fantasy book featuring a main character who has your name!

To Ashley Hall, the first reader of my first completed draft, and the first to offer Serious Critique.

To Rachel Hullett, for over a decade of friendship, for introducing me to Vermont, and for always hyping me up.

To Abby Schulman, for reading and loving a very rough draft. I would not be here, at this exact moment, if not for you.

To Harini Kannan, for so, so much. Thank you for your friendship, for your support, for all the laughs, for the endless texting, for being the person I go to with random minutiae, for sharing my excitement over my publishing journey, for shipping my characters, and for so much more.

To my fake cousins, Ameer Mohamed and Shereen Said, thank you and your parents for being my chosen family in this country. You are my oldest friends and siblings in spirit, and I am so glad I grew up with you by my side. Thank you both for always asking questions about my writing even though books aren't really your thing.

To my brother, Mohamed Elsbai, for listening to me babble and puzzle out plot holes, and for doing your best to make me better at marketing (it's a futile effort, but I appreciate it).

To my family in Egypt, for all your excitement and joy over this milestone, and for demanding copies of my book in a language you can't read, just so that you can have it in your home. That means so much.

To Leigh Bardugo, for being so gentle and kind and encouraging when I handed you a truly terrible writing sample at Madcap Writing Retreats. Thank you for teaching me more about three-act structure in two minutes than years of English classes ever did. Your stories are an endless inspiration.

To everyone else who has ever supported me, or provided assistance big or small: thank you, thank you, thank you.

And finally, to my mother, who has always, always believed in me.

ABOUT THE AUTHOR

HADEER ELSBAI IS AN EGYPTIAN AMERICAN WRITER AND librarian. Born in New York City, she grew up being shuffled between Queens and Cairo. Hadeer studied history at Hunter College and later earned her master's degree in library science from Queens College, making her a CUNY alum twice over. Aside from writing, Hadeer enjoys cats, iced drinks, live theater, and studying the nineteenth century.